Family, friends, food, a glass of bubbly and, of course, a good book make me smile. I believe in following your dreams, and my love of writing led me here to HarperCollins publishers. Stunning Northumberland is my home – golden sandy beaches, castles and gorgeous countryside that have inspired my novels.

The Second Chance Supper Club

Caroline Roberts

H Q

ONE PLACE. MANY STORIES

HQ
An imprint of HarperCollins*Publishers* Ltd
1 London Bridge Street
London SE1 9GF

www.harpercollins.co.uk

HarperCollins*Publishers*
Macken House, 39/40 Mayor Street Upper,
Dublin 1, D01 C9W8, Ireland

This edition 2025

2

First published in Great Britain by HQ,
an imprint of HarperCollins*Publishers* Ltd 2025

ISBN: 9780008769680

This book is set in 10.7/15.5 pt. Sabon by Type-it AS, Norway

Printed and bound in the UK using 100% Renewable
Electricity by CPI Group (UK) Ltd

FSC
www.fsc.org

MIX
Paper
FSC™ C007454

For more information visit: www.harpercollins.co.uk/green

For Eva x

'Cooking with love
provides food for the soul'
EMERIL LAGASSE

Chapter 1

Cath sliced a line through the brown tape, the scissors in her hand beginning to tremble. She opened the cardboard lid to reveal a stack of tissue-wrapped photos and frames; mementoes of her not-so-long-ago-life, memories and waves of emotion crashing out with each item. She was still so bloody angry . . .

The third picture she unwrapped – the one she hadn't quite had the heart to send to the tip, though it had *certainly* crossed her mind – stripped another layer off her heart. White lace and promises . . . looking so young and hopeful. Such a damned waste. All that time, all that togetherness, trashed. Thirty effing years in fact.

All she had left was a heap of memories, some happy, some sad. It was all gone. *They* were all gone. Divorce looming dangerously close on the horizon. Though Cath knew, all too well, divorce papers or not, you couldn't unravel the seam on a long-term marriage that easily.

They had separated, moved homes, changed lives. And yes, over time, she'd accepted the inevitability of the divorce, but it was still so unsettling. Rejection and loneliness coming in ripples, like the circles in a lake after a stone is thrown in. Cath couldn't help but feel like she'd lost her anchor after all these rooted years as a wife and mother. She'd bloody well given up her full-time role as deputy head and maths teacher too, which though stressful of late, she'd always loved – oh yeah, it was all part of the 'enjoying an early retirement' master plan the two of them had talked about and dreamed of. Perhaps she'd been the only one dreaming, after all.

Numbers and figures, they were safe, reliable. They always added up. She'd thought she would have it all worked out by now, moving solidly and securely into her fifties. She and Trevor working part time – she'd taken on some freelance maths tuition – and going off on some exciting new adventures. Cath just hadn't imagined the adventures were going to be so damned traumatic . . . and on her own.

It had all kicked off eighteen months ago. Their son, Adam, away in his third year at uni, and she in what was to be her last year of secondary school teaching. She'd thought she and Trev would soon be slipping away on their travels, gathering magical memories of the Mediterranean, sitting side by side by a balmy sea, with glasses of chilled wine and some tasty tapas or mezze. The stresses of years of hands-on parenting, whilst holding down a demanding job, a thing of the past.

They were settled, content, or so she bloody well thought. She'd assumed she and Trevor would see their relationship through to old age like a comfy set of slippers. Okay, they weren't exactly setting the world on fire anymore, but who was when they were in their fifties? And yes, sex was a bit of an occasional (okay, *very* occasional) afterthought. But wasn't that just *normal*? She was okay with normal. But Trevor evidently had other plans – plans that didn't include his partner of thirty years. Those comfy slippers had worn far too thin for him.

She dropped their wedding photo face down on the carpet, unsure what to do with the damn thing. Relationships, *arrgh*. Something old, something new, something borrowed, something blue . . . The only thing left feeling blue was her.

But, she reminded herself, clutching at the positives, it wasn't all a disaster, they did share a wonderful son. But that hurt in itself too. He was off and away now. Finished his final year at Leeds Uni, and was travelling. Talk about empty nest. It was like some eagle had dived in and taken the bloody lot.

Right, Cath, pull up those big girl knickers. This was no good. This was *not* the time to mope, no way José. She sighed, stood up tall for a few seconds, giving her aching knees a stretch. Then she went back to her task, pulling out more trinkets and images, and digging deeper to find a shoebox of letters and mementoes. It had been a super busy day already, both physically and emotionally; these could be stored in the bedroom cupboard for now. A task for some other day.

Just a couple more photos left. She unwrapped the white tissue folds, and found herself holding a black-and-white image of her parents, both now having passed away, bless them. Rock solid they were, right to the end. Not all relationships were doomed to fail, she reminded herself. Her dad had only held out for a few lonely months after Mum died of bowel cancer. The grip of grief, of loss, still feeling raw. And lastly, she found herself clutching a silver-framed photo of her son, who was grinning widely at the camera, sporting floral-patterned boarding shorts and a washed-out T-shirt, in some exotic beachfront location on his latest travels. That one at least made her smile.

Cath got up, on those worryingly creaky knees. (What

the hell? Since when had twenty minutes' kneeling turned her into some kind of geriatric?) As she was currently in the lounge, she put Adam's picture in pride of place on the cottage's weathered-oak mantelpiece, giving it a heartfelt pat. She took a brief sniff to ward off any self-pitying tears.

Brace, brace, brace. Weirdly, the plane crash mantra drummed in her head. The flights of fancy, the travel dreams of her own, all on hold for now. Hah, she felt like she'd been severely delayed at the airport for let-down middle-agers.

The cardboard packing box, now empty, sat there looking back at her, a gaping hole. She wiped a sneaky twinkle of a tear from the corner of her eye. She felt exhausted with it all. *Oh, my.* How everything had changed over these past few months.

Gazing out of the white sash window, trying to shake her thoughts, she re-focused on the here and now. A row of stone cottages sat opposite hers, gardens pretty with spring tulips, and bold pink and yellow primulas. And a little chink of light found its way in through the window and into her mind. She was here in her countryside cottage. Bottom line was, she'd done it. Moved into her 'dream' house, if slightly jaded (hah, it suited her admirably right now), in this pretty rural Northumberland village of Tilldale. Okay, so her head and her heart were still a bit fuzzy with the humungous change, but she *had* done it.

Tilldale village had been central to several family summer holidays for the three of them – she, Trevor and Adam – with walks in the moorland hills, trips to the coast, and supper at The Star Inn, a gorgeous country pub. There had been lots of good times spent here. She also remembered visiting the area

4

years ago, as a teenager herself, with her parents and sister, all squished into a touring caravan. Beach days and BBQs, sun-burnished skin and freckles, teetering on the edge of youth, filled with 99 ice creams and fish and chips, and the odd stolen kiss . . . her first taste of romance. She'd even taken a little drive to the coast yesterday, for a breather from the packing. Though it had felt a little lonely being without her family this time, the salt air was invigorating, reviving.

Northumberland's wildly rugged beauty had drawn her back. Yes, she felt she could make a home here, given time. No doubt some of her friends thought she was crazy going so far away (almost a three-hour drive) from her old life in suburban Leeds, but the thought of having to move out and still live on the doorstep of her old house, well, *that* would have felt far more bizarre to her.

She'd spent weeks scouring the internet and touring a line-up of 'possibles': attractive two- and three-bed detached and semis, both younger and more mature, all with 'kerbside appeal'. It had felt like property speed dating some weekends! After a long drive up the A1, she'd walk in and then within minutes, sometimes seconds, knew that it wasn't going to work out. It was only when she drove down into the lush green valley of Tilldale, entered the calming white-washed walls of Cheviot Cottage, and looked around the cosy sitting room with its log-burning stove, the two small but characterful double bedrooms upstairs with their sloping ceilings – plenty enough room for her and the odd visit from Adam, or perhaps a friend – and the practical but pretty galley kitchen, that she had at last sensed that comforting feeling this was 'meant to be'.

And now the kitchen was exactly where she headed next.

Time to pop the kettle on and celebrate finishing her unpacking finale with, *whey-hey*, a cup of tea and a chocolate hobnob. She unfolded that last empty cardboard box and placed it next to a plastic bread-crate from which she'd unloaded some crockery earlier, and pondered where in fact she might store them. The cottage didn't exactly have a lot of space, after all. Oh well, another job for later. For now, it was time to rest those creaky knees and her overloaded mind.

A few minutes later, with a mug of strong builder's tea to hand, she took in her new kitchen. The cupboards were a light-oak shade, the work surfaces a mottled-grey marble effect; she could live with that, but the walls had faded to an aged off-white. The sash window overlooked a back garden with slightly wilding grass and borders. The sun was trying to streak in through dusty panes – one more job for the list. Hmm, it could do with a lift in here really. Perhaps she might change the wall colour to a cheery shade of yellow? She looked outside to the garden for inspiration. Oh, yes, perhaps some-where between a primrose and a daffodil colour. Let a little light into her life. Why not?

After all, the kitchen had always been one of the most important rooms for her: the heart of the home. She resolved to find a hardware store and buy some paint and brushes, adding this to her ever-growing to-do list.

Gazing out of the window above the sink, with her mug in hand, she then found herself staring at a garden shed. *Her* garden shed. It nestled beside a leafy beech hedge where the grass levelled at the top of the rise. The shed was medium-sized, wooden, and had been painted a pale moss green, quite some time ago by the looks of the cracked and peeling colour.

Hmm, now that might work for storage. Hopefully, it wasn't too damp in there. The packing boxes and crate might come in handy at some point in the future, yet they would be out of sight and out of mind there.

With her head still humming with memories, she pictured the shed at No 3 Limestone Lane, Roundhay, Leeds: Trevor's domain. Tidy rows of tools, neat stacks of seedling trays on the potting bench, the tomato plants by the glass windows trained on wires in their compost grow-bags. She had in fact enjoyed the fruits of that particular labour, as a keen cook, and used them to experiment with various Mediterranean flavours and recipes.

With no time like the present, she grabbed the boxes and headed out of the back door, onto a small paved patio area and then up the stone garden steps. Dishearteningly, the grass was rather unkempt on each side of her, looking more like a dandelion-and-daisy weed meadow. Up close, the shed's green paint was peeling heavily, and the middle pane of glass in one of the two front-opening doors had a zig-zag crack in it. There was a rusty padlock securing the doors together, which on closer inspection was no longer functional, though, luckily for Cath, had seized up in the open position.

Placing the boxes down, Cath removed the padlock, and with a tug, the doors opened outwards with a slight creak. A musty smell hit her, as she took a small step forward, straight into a dangling cobweb, which startled her, tickling then, *eek*, sticking to her face. *Oof, oh shit*. Her fingers floundered as she hurriedly swiped it aside, hoping there were no straggly legged spiders about to land on her. She *hated* spiders . . . and now there was no Trevor or Adam to catch the hairy little blighters for her. She pushed on; she'd started this outhouse expedition, so she'd darn well finish it.

On first inspection, the floor space at least looked relatively dry, though up above, several tendrils of ivy had found their way into the shed, pushing through a tiny gap between the slanting roof and the wooden walls. A few terracotta pots had been left behind on a shelf, along with an old set of hand tools poking out of one of them. Some bamboo canes were leaning dejectedly in a corner.

She'd learned from the estate agent that an elderly gentleman had lived in the cottage before her, having had to give it up just a few months before, after a bad fall and being too frail to stay on his own. He had moved into a residential home in the neighbouring town of Kirkton. It must have been hard for him to leave, she thought, imagining his weathered hands using those tools and tending this garden over the years, nurturing this space. Oh, he'd surely be cross about the state of the wilding grass – *note to self, lawn mower to buy asap*. She'd never really been much of a gardener, except for growing a few potted herbs to cook with – the grass and the shrub borders, well, they had always been Trevor's domain.

Now she was inside, the shed looked as though it was about to fall apart at its rickety wooden seams. Blimey, there was an awful lot to take on here by herself. It wasn't just the old stone cottage to keep up with. She was the owner of a garden, and a shed, too. What the hell was she thinking? Doubts didn't just creep in, they exploded in her mind like popping candy. Was she up to the task? Would she be able to keep up with it all? Crikey, she was going to have to up her game, for sure.

Stepping back out into the gentle glow of the April morning

sun, she spotted an orange-breasted robin cocking his head at her as he bobbed about the border. She looked around at the unruly shrubs in need of a prune, wishing her old dad was still about to give advice on the overgrown plants. Then, she looked down upon her honey-stoned, two-hundred-year-old abode, and thought of this other elderly man, no doubt most reluctant to leave this place, and she made a vow, there and then, that she'd look after this house, *his* old home, as best she could. In fact, she'd give it a brand-new chapter – much like herself.

Chapter 2

She was tucked up in bed. All was dark. The room a little too dark for her liking, to be honest.

Screeek! That piercing screech was way too close.

What the **hell** was that?

Was it a dream? Was she still awake? Cath blinked and stared. There was a glimpse of silver shadow through the gap in the curtains. Yes, it was definitely nighttime. Her heart was pounding so hard, she could hear the blood thrumming in her ears. Awake then . . .

Was it a fox? An owl, maybe? But weren't they meant to go twit-twoo? She rattled her brain for things that made noises in the night. Things other than horror movie stuff. Could someone be lurking outside? Dare she find out what, or who, it was? Lying there, with her imagination on full pelt, she was never going to get back to sleep now. Stepping gingerly out of bed, she walked over the woollen rug onto cool wooden floorboards, and peered through the tiny gap in the curtains.

Looking out into the grey-white light of the street lamp, she saw a patch of silvered tarmac highlighted, along with a shadowy tree, its arms all skeletal. The darkened blocks of the cottages opposite . . . no lights on over there. All was still, or so it seemed.

Screeek. She jumped back. *Oh, shit*. There it was again, even closer. She peeked again. No stealthy-limbed furry fox, no flap of wings, not a sign. She hadn't heard any of these blood-curdling noises in her city suburbs. Maybe the odd echo of a siren, blue flashing lights. There was no sensible Trev here either, to reassure her with a: 'Don't be so bloody silly, woman, get back to bed.'

And no one to snuggle back up to after her 3 a.m. meanderings (oh yes, they'd kicked in good and proper during perimenopause a few years ago, and were still going strong now). Back then, in her spacious suburban semi, she'd slip downstairs for a cup of camomile tea, making a dump-list to get her to-dos off her midnight mind. Then back to a cosy bed, with a warm and steady – if a little grumpy at being disturbed, yet again – husband waiting.

In the half-light, not yet knowing the number of stairs, she reached the lower hallway with a jarring thump. She turned the downstairs lights on and headed for the kitchen, intending to make herself a herbal tea, and sit for a while. There was something slightly desolate about being on your own in the middle of the night. The house was chilly too. The novelty of this newfound freedom was already beginning to wear off.

Kettle on, the scent of camomile and honey, and then its warming fragrant taste. No more shrieks or calls outside in the dark, phew. Just a head full of thoughts. Of life and loss, and everything in between. Of Adam – where in fact was he, right now? Cambodia, that was it . . . Ooh, wasn't that the place where they'd found all those dreadful skulls? Another brick to add to the wall of anxiety she seemed to be building for herself.

Oh, they might actually be in the right time zone for a chat. She spotted her phone, charging on the kitchen side. He might be mid-breakfast, looking out on some idyllic sandy beach or about to trek to some ancient monument . . . or in bed with some lithe young thing, or – oh, God, no – high on drugs. Who bloody well knew? She stalled at picking up the phone, imagining him wondering why on earth his mother was ringing him in the middle of the night, UK time.

Perhaps she'd just send a text. Yes, a short, '**Hey, how are you getting on?**' (Code read: *Are you still alive?*) '**Bet it's amazing there. Miss you. Love Mum x**' from the cheery, happy person she so wanted him to remember. Not this stressed-out, recently dumped singleton. She posted that brief message, adding, '**Have fun, but STAY SAFE. xx**' She couldn't help herself.

And then, with a yawn, it was time to go back to bed, to the double where she still slept on her side (always the right). She was trying hard to embrace this new route her life was taking, but under a duvet for two, she couldn't help but feel alone.

*

Nursing a coffee at 8:30 a.m., Cath decided to sort out her kitchen space despite feeling jaded after her restless night. Keeping busy seemed to be the way forward. And the kitchen had always been so important to Cath.

She'd put everything swiftly into the cupboards when she'd first got there, without really planning how it might work best. She chose to tackle the spice rack first. With so much to unpack on her arrival, she'd merely popped the small cardboard box, filled with those little glass jars of fragrance and aromatic wonder, straight onto a kitchen unit shelf. Now was the time to order it properly . . . herbs, spices, seasonings, oh yes, and colour co-ordinating the lids. That felt satisfying. Instilling order in the kitchen cupboards, at least.

Handling the spices and herbs made her think of all those meals she'd prepared over the years: the family roasts, the dinner parties, after-work suppers, the pizza in a rush, the birthday celebrations for Adam, homemade sausage rolls, the pineapple-and-cheese hedgehog, crisps and sandwiches, cupcakes galore, and of course, the huge event of the annual Christmas dinner. She paused, standing with a jar of dried sage in her hand.

Her well-used recipe books sat there on her 'new' kitchen shelf but . . . Oh. From now on who was there to cook for, other than herself? She found herself feeling all wrong once again, with an ache of loneliness in her gut. Everything seemed so downright hard just now. Even the simplest of everyday things.

Keep going, a little voice inside pushed her on. She remembered the inspiration to paint the walls yellow, which she'd had the day before. The white walls through the house were easy to live with, but on closer inspection the kitchen walls had faded and been marked, especially around the hob area. Okay, so she'd go and find the hardware store in nearby Kirkton, get some bright yellow paint, and put her mark on the place. The kitchen – and bloody hell, yes, her whole damned life – was in need of some va-va-voom.

*

After a slice of toast and a self-talking to, she was ready to hop in the car and get that paint. As she popped her jacket on, Cath heard the ringtone of her mobile phone. Oh, might it be Adam having seen her text, looking to catch up at last?

Pulling out her mobile from her pocket, she saw *Caller ID Helen S.* Ah, her friend from back home. Home? The word jarred in her mind. Wasn't that meant to be here now?

'Helen . . . hi.'

'Hey, how's it going?' Her pal's voice was as chirpy as ever. 'And when can I come up and see this cute cottage of yours?'

Helen was one of those upbeat, super-chatty types, always full of energy. This morning, it served to make Cath feel even more deflated.

'Good . . . yeah, all's fine here. Just finding my feet really.' Cath tried her best to sound positive. 'And, of course, you can come up *soon* . . . but, uhm, maybe I need some time to get sorted out here a bit first,' she stalled. 'It's only been a few days since I moved in, after all.'

It was all too soon. Cath certainly didn't feel up to visitors as yet, and though the two women were close, having been neighbours and friends in the same couples' social group for years, that just made her feel all the more vulnerable. Helen's life was carrying on in safe semi-detached suburbia, just as Cath's should have been. Everything still felt emotionally raw here in her new surroundings, and Cath was worried that Helen might tune in to her unease. Cath still very much needed some time for herself – time to get to grips with this new phase she found herself in.

'Okay, it's just I'm dying to come up and see it all, and you, of course, lovely.'

'I know and thanks – soon, okay? Well then, how are you all doing?' Cath deftly switched the conversation.

'Great. Oh, I had a gorgeous afternoon tea at The Ivy in town with Tracy and Gina yesterday. They send their love, by the way. The boys were off playing golf. My Geoff was full of himself having hammered . . . Trevor.' (There was a second's delay, and Cath was sure she'd been about to say '*your* Trevor'.) 'Mind you, bless him, I have to tell you, he's a bit off the boil right now, Trev, that is. It seems to be going pear-shaped with that Steph woman from work, already. Of course, we all knew that wouldn't last.' Her voice was see-sawing on.

Cath felt a tight knot form in her gut. Steph was the fling. The straw that broke the camel's back, and put the noose around their marriage. Cath really didn't want to hear all the 'ins and outs' of her almost ex-husband's life, especially now that she was one of the 'outs'. Her silence spoke a thousand words.

'Oh, sorry, Cath . . . I'm being thoughtless.'

It was only natural that Helen would tell her things – things she might think Cath would want to know. They had been friends as couples after all, but whilst Cath and Trevor's partnership had sunk, good old Helen and Geoff were still floating along in the stream of married life, the same as ever. She could picture it all; there'd be drinks at the local pub, a cosy dinner for two or maybe four, shopping trips together to Waitrose . . .

'Cath? You still there, lovely?'

'Yeah, yeah.' Her voice sounded absent, however.

Helen evidently realised she'd better change tack. 'So, how's Adam doing? Whereabouts is he now on his travels?'

'He's great. Enjoying his adventures . . . in Cambodia, the

last I heard. Touring some long-lost temples.' The last she'd heard being well over a week ago now, but hey-ho.

'Ah, that sounds interesting. Jonathon's just lined up a job with Pearson's. You'll know them, one of the top accountants in Manchester.'

'Hey, well done, Jonathon.' Cath tried to sound chirpy. 'That's great news. Bet you're all delighted.' She couldn't help feel the stab of parental comparison.

Cath was sure that Adam was nowhere near sorting a job in the real world, post-university and his Zoology degree. It would no doubt all fall into place at some point in the (fairly distant) future, once he'd finished exploring and chilling out on the Asian continent. The fact that his parents were at the very same time throwing their marriage to the wolves probably hadn't helped his feeling in a state of flux, Cath mused. '*Why throw your life away stuck in some boring job*?' had been Adam's motto for quite some time now. *Like teaching,* was surely the subtext.

Indeed. *Why throw your life away stuck in some boring marriage*, had seemed to be Trevor's choix de vie recently.

Whatever had happened to commitment, hard work, trust and compromise? Or was she the only daft fool in that house, who'd been living by those steady rules these past years?

'Cath?'

'Yep, still here.'

Cath then heard the distant ding-dong of a doorbell down the line.

'Oh, well, that's Janice here for coffee. It's the Macmillan fundraising event coming up soon, so we're having a planning session. Scones, afternoon tea, or do we do cakes and coffee? To Tombola or not? We'll miss you there, darling.'

Yes, Cath would have been there doing her bit, enjoying the chit-chat and the cake, glad to be helping a good cause. 'I'll be sure to give a donation online. And I'll miss you lot, too. Enjoy.'

'You could always pop back down for the event? Stay at ours,' Helen ventured.

Three doors down from all that might once have been? 'Ah, maybe . . . but you know, I just need to settle in up here first. It feels a bit too soon . . .'

'Of course, I understand.' Her friend's voice softened. 'Well, look, I really do have to go. We'll catch up again soon. And do let me know when I can visit? I'm ready for a night away and a good old gossip over a glass or two of fizz. Give me a call, soon . . . we'll sort out a date.'

As much as she appreciated Helen's friendship, a meet-up was exactly what Cath was desperate to avoid just now. Cath was sure she'd been, and still was, the target of local gossip, albeit in, hopefully, a non-nasty way – more of a 'There but for the grace of God go I'. Her and Trevor's downfall had been feeding them all sorts of juicy lines and scenarios to fill the social chatter for some time now.

Cath ended the call feeling ruffled. Here she was in her new nest, and though she was trying to take some brave new steps towards flying, well, perhaps flapping her wings at this stage, she felt like her feathers were still being slowly plucked one by one.

Chapter 3

Time for a breath of fresh air. After her wobbly day unpacking yesterday and Helen's phone call just now, she needed to get outside. Remind herself why she'd chosen to move here – how much she loved this rural part of Northumberland. In a quick change of plan – she'd go and fetch the paint for the kitchen this afternoon, instead – Cath popped on her trainers and grabbed her jacket. There was no point feeling sorry for herself when she had a whole new life to lead.

Stepping out of her cottage front door, the fresh air brushed her cheeks, and she could hear the bleating of sheep in the nearby fields. And there, in the low-walled small square of her front garden, she noted the daffodils were just going over, and several clusters of pretty bluebells were starting to bud. A pot of red and yellow tulips, no doubt planted last autumn by the old man who'd lived here, greeted her as she locked up. She wondered if he had lived here on his own for a while. Had he enjoyed his life of independence in the village? Had he been married once? He'd certainly loved his garden by the looks of it, tending the borders with care, planting bulbs. The bold shoots of those tulips giving a spring-like sense of hope, of new beginnings.

She walked along the little main street, with its row of honey-grey stone houses and cottages, turned in by the ancient stone parish church, through the graveyard with its mossy headstones, heading to the fields on the public footpath. Yellow bursts of celandine scattered the grassy floor of the ancient cemetery making it look far from gloomy. Blackbirds and sparrows were busy tweeting away as they gathered twigs and moss. A shady path led her under huge beech trees that were just starting to bud, and then she came out into the cool sunshine of late April. Sheep grazed the field, giving her a nonchalant glance as she passed, their young lambs skipping in giddy groups, as she made her way along the mud track that edged the pasture, following alongside the river. The gentle rush of the River Till murmured its way soothingly through the valley.

Cath spotted a moorhen with three fluffy black chicks paddling in a sheltered spot near the bank. A pair of white cabbage butterflies fluttered past. The steady beat of her steps, the vivid greens and golds of late spring, the soft sounds of nature began to work their magic. Being out in the countryside always calmed her.

She strolled on through two fields, coming out onto the back lane that would eventually lead to the market town of Alnwick one way and back to Tilldale the other. She paused for a while to take in the vista, gazing towards the purple-brown hues of the Cheviot Hills in the far distance. Rolling farmland, and then moorland, that would scarcely have changed over the centuries. Life didn't feel so rushed here. Maybe it was time to slow down, for her to take stock, to just be. To feel the breeze on her face, the warmth of the sun, the scent of . . . ah, manure. She smiled to herself; whilst idyllic, this place was also real, people worked and lived this land. And that was a good thing, it felt grounding.

She came back to the village along the lane; the vroom and then air-thrust from a couple of passing cars, a touring campervan trundling by, followed shortly afterwards by a big noisy tractor. Crikey, she'd backed into the hedgerow for that one. She set off again with a new sense of purpose. Tilldale village was soon within her sights. A cluster of cottages with dark-grey slated roofs, a few cars parked along the main street, and the village pub, a pretty stone building with a small grassy garden in front of it, The Star Inn.

It was nearing midday, and with nothing much planned for lunch, she thought she might as well call in to the village shop. The jingle of an old-fashioned bell marked her entry as she opened the navy-painted door. Wooden shelves lined with all your grocery basics, large wicker baskets of fruit and vegetables, local arts and crafts, cards and newspapers, and the smell of freshly baked and far-too-tempting pastries greeted her. Along with, and behind the counter, the tanned and toned body of a slightly shaggy-haired male, his chest sculpted into a white T-shirt. Not what she'd expected.

She gave a smile, as he said a cheery 'Hello.' Well, things were looking up.

His hair was dark, his eyes a deep brown, set off by olive-toned skin. He looked to be in his forties, definitely a tad younger than her. But it was very nice indeed to be greeted by an attractive man. A man without a pot belly, and years of history together.

'Good morning, is there anything I can help you with?'

There was a slight edge to his tone that suggested foreign climes . . . and perhaps something a little more sensual? Or was that just her imagination? Hah, she'd been out of the dating game for far too long. In fact, she had absolutely no intention of getting back into it. Now was the time to enjoy her newfound freedom and a simple life, away from the trials and tribulations of any relationship.

'Ah . . . well, yes, lunch. Something for lunch.' She sounded all dithery, for goodness sake.

'Of course. In our deli selection, we have freshly made sandwiches, locally baked pies, a feta and spinach quiche. And for sweet treats, I've made some fresh baklava and a honey cake this morning with our beautiful Northumbrian heather honey . . .'

'Wow, that all sounds delicious.' Cath's eyes scanned the gastro goodies. Had she just discovered the village shop from heaven? It must have changed hands since they came here on holiday. Mind you, that was several years ago. She'd have remembered this kind of fab food for sure . . . and the owner, if indeed he was the owner. 'Ah, I'll take a slice of the quiche.' Oh, and she saw that the baklava was drizzled and sticky, with a sprinkling of walnuts too. 'And I'll have to try the baklava – two pieces, please.' One for her . . . and one for her. She felt like she'd been transported to some delightful Mediterranean deli.

'Andreas, we have a lemon drizzle ready now too,' a further male voice floated from the back room.

Andreas. Now that did indeed sound Greek.

'Okay, and there's a lemon drizzle. But it'll not be a patch on my baklava.' The guy behind the counter gave a cheeky wink.

'I can hear you,' the voice fired back with an edge of laughter. Then a friendly face, with close-shaven greying hair and piercing blue eyes, appeared around the door frame. He was taller, slimmer, and much paler than the first chap. 'We're very competitive with our baking. Can't help ourselves.'

Andreas introduced him. 'This is my partner, Dan.' He placed a hand on the other gent's shoulder in a way that looked intimate. 'We co-own the shop here.'

'Ah, lovely to meet you both. I'm Cath.' She smiled, feeling the warmth of their friendly banter, but also feeling an idiot at her previous thoughts of lusting after him. Where was her gaydar when she needed it? Bloody fool. She had been out of the market for far too long.

'So, are you here on holiday?' Andreas asked, as he boxed a generous slice of quiche.

'Actually, no, not this time, though I've holidayed here in the past. I've just moved into the village. A couple of days ago.'

'Oh, so you must be Cheviot Cottage lady. How marvellous. Welcome to the village,' Andreas said with a broad grin. 'Yes, that was Reggie's old place, such a lovely chap.'

'Oh, I do hope he's doing okay?' Cath suddenly felt concerned. Oh, and it was Reggie, so she knew the old man's name now.

'Yes, he's doing fine. All set up in a local care home. He'd had a couple of falls, I think it was getting a bit much for him, the garden and everything, all on his own there.'

'Well, hello, and welcome.' Dan offered a handshake across the counter. 'We've been here in the village for eight years, and we've never looked back.'

'Yep, left the city behind to start this little venture. And still here and loving it.'

'That's good to hear.'

'Well, I hope you're settling in nicely? And anything you need, we're always about, so just shout,' said Dan.

How sweet of them. 'Thanks, I appreciate that.' She sensed the offer was genuine. Did they know that she was here on her own, she wondered. Was she giving off that lone middle-aged woman vibe? Was it that obvious? Or had the village grapevine done its work already, the local estate agent filling everyone in on the status of the new resident?

A phone started to ring out the back. Andreas looked up sharply, a crease forming across his brow. 'Dan, would you take over . . . Nice to meet you . . . uh . . .' With that, he was away.

'Sorry,' Dan began to explain, 'it might be the care home. He's been waiting for a call back. His elderly mother's there too, and she's not been well lately.'

'Oh, I'm sorry to hear that. I do hope everything is fine.'

'Yes, me too. She's such a love. Been quite poorly with a chest infection, bless her.' Dan placed the sticky-sweet pastries into a second smaller box.

Cath then paid, saying her goodbyes with a further thank you. She'd have to find out if Andreas was of Greek heritage some other time. Though they'd only just met, the lads seemed lovely – she felt lifted by their warm welcome – and the shop felt like a little haven. On the short walk back to the cottage, she trailed the aromas of still-warm spiced baklava with her and was very much looking forward to sampling the pastries with a cup of tea.

Chapter 4

Sitting on the back patio in the sunshine, in a cream wicker chair she'd brought with her from the guest bedroom in Roundhay, with the taste of honey, nuts and filo still melting on her tongue, Cath remembered calling in to that same village shop many years ago. It would have been on a holiday with Mum and Dad, no doubt stopping for ice creams with her older sister, Susie. They'd been having summer holidays up in Northumberland for years. She was sure the brown wooden shelving had been the same, and back then they'd had one of those Walls freezers crammed with Cornettos, Twisters, Rockets and Lemonade Sparkles – they were her favourites back then, all lemony zing.

And then her mind moved on . . . to that last holiday, the one before Susie went off to uni. Their parents wanted a trip together for old times' sake, back to their happy Northumberland haunts. Cath was so young, just sixteen, but of course felt all grown up. Her thoughts drifted back. It was the year of her first ever romance, with that lad from Belford village, where they'd stayed in a caravan . . . Matty. Floppy dark hair, gorgeous hazel-brown eyes, she could picture him now. Hah, after all this time.

She'd been allowed to walk into the village with her sister as chaperone. They'd chatted with the local teenagers, sat around the granite steps below the market cross. And for the next few days, they'd meet at the same place, 5 p.m. The two girls eagerly offering to go on an errand to the little supermarket. It was she and Matty who'd clicked in the group. And boy, it had felt so special when he'd put his arm around her.

Mum had even warmed to him when he'd called politely at the caravan one morning, hoping to see Cath. As they were just about to go out, Mum had asked him along too, and they'd all gone down to Bamburgh beach together for a picnic lunch and a game of makeshift cricket (to please Dad) – simple pleasures. Salt and sunshine and sand. And there, hidden in the dunes, her first kiss.

Why was she thinking about all this now? That was . . . crikey, thirty-six years ago. A touch of nostalgia stirred within. Life, love, relationships . . . Her heart gave a weird pulse. She still felt a bit guilty that she'd had to leave that lad Matty in the lurch in the end. It was all too much, too soon. But hey, that was all donkey's years ago, and well in the past.

There had been a couple of boyfriend non-starters after that. A few months of high-school holding hands, cinema trips and such like, until it all fizzled out. And then, there was Trevor. They'd fallen for each other pretty quickly in those early heady days at university, and well, that was it. Over thirty years together . . . and now this. The anger still buzzed within.

Had it been a total waste? She took a slow sip of tea as she pondered her own question. Not really, she had to confess, there had been much that had been good over the years. Their relationship had just veered off course in these past eighteen months. Well, more like a car crash to be honest – dramatically, painfully. But, a small voice inside admitted, maybe it had run its course.

That was so very sad, even if it were true. But life was full of peaks and troughs, and though you couldn't always see over the next hilltop or when the fogs came down, if you just kept going, kept plodding on, somehow, you'd find a way to get there in the end. Wherever there was . . . ? There was always that glimmer of light, that branch of hope. She had to hold on to that.

*

The baklava and tea filled her up, so she didn't really need to stop for lunch. She'd popped the quiche in the fridge for another time, her appetite having gone AWOL lately. Time to go and get that paint, and liven up her kitchen. She got into her Mini and drove towards the hills, along winding roads lined with hawthorn hedges. Within ten minutes, she had reached the small market town of Kirkton, nestled at the base of the Cheviot Hills. The hardware store was at the far end of the high street.

Entering, it was like an Aladdin's cave from the Seventies, with shelves piled high and narrow aisles. Looking about her, probably much of the stock actually dated from then, too. Kitchenware, homewares, pest control, cleaning materials, lightbulbs, DIY supplies, and yes, paint. She was itching to get going now, so didn't bother with tester pots, instead finding herself standing in front of the large tins and homing in on the yellow shades, checking out which matched her mood. Bright and cheery, without being too in your face. There was one called Sunbound that caught her eye. A warm golden-yellow shade, like a daffodil's trumpet. It looked perfect. How much to buy? One can or two? She hadn't a bloody clue.

She went to ask the man behind the till, who looked nothing like gorgeous Andreas by the way; this chap was well into his sixties with greying curly hair, wearing a drab grey overall. She felt rather inept. The last time she'd done any decorating was for Adam's nursery, when she was still pregnant and had gone into full nesting mode. She'd chosen a gorgeous pale lemon shade, she remembered nostalgically. Since then, Trevor had always insisted they paid for painters and decorators.

'Well, those are a five-litre size you've been looking at. It's for a kitchen, you say? What kind of size room are we talking, pet?' The assistant's Northumbrian lilt was warm.

'Ah, it's a cottage, so not too big . . . there are wall units and cupboards in place, so it's not all needing done. Oh, and a small dining area at the far end, galley style,' she floundered. Damn, he was probably wanting a concrete answer, square metres and such like.

He nodded sagely. 'Aye, I think one five-litre'll do yea. Yea can always pop back if you need more. We've plenty in.'

'Thanks, and I'll need the tools to paint with too . . . brushes and everything, please.' She was starting from scratch with all this.

He gathered together a roller, brushes, a plastic tray, some tape for the edges – 'Save your skirts and coving' – and some white spirit cleaning fluid. 'Aye, that'll do.'

'Thank you so much.'

Cath paid, and as she was gathering her goods, the shop-keeper gave a warm wink, adding, 'Good luck, pet.'

'I think I might need it,' she admitted with a wry smile, wondering if she'd bitten off more than she could chew. What if she made a right mess of it? But with finances stretched after the split, there was no way she could afford to get decorators in herself.

As soon as she got back, she was going to have to YouTube 'How to paint walls' to refresh her memory. It was twenty-two years ago when she'd last used a paintbrush, after all.

*

Back at the cottage, with YouTube watched – several clips in fact – stepladder up, and one of her older bedsheets on the floor plus a couple of protective towels on the surfaces, she was primed to make a start. She was going to brushstroke the edges first, and then fill in with the roller. Well, that was the plan. She took a deep breath as she tottered up to the top of the ladder, brush to hand along with her filled paint tray, and went in for the first stroke. The colour was bold, all right. A splash of vivid yellow on white. She'd done it now.

Better keep going then. She was glad of the masking tape, as her hand felt unsteady at first, wobbling over the edges. But as she settled into it, with Radio Two on for company, she began to relax into the task. Well, as relaxed as you could be up a ladder with a tray of paint – when there was no one to catch her if she fell.

Stepping down for a break a half hour later, and stretching out her shoulders and knees which were nagging already, she surveyed her work so far. Crikey, the shade looked darker than the square on the front of the tin. She wasn't sure about it at all. It looked more egg yolk than daffodil. Oh, bugger, had she gone and got the colour wrong in her haste? Would it darken the kitchen rather than lift it?

She made herself a strong coffee, finding sticky golden tints to her hair, and on her jeans. Definitely egg-yolk coloured. But this was no time for doubts, and hey, if worst came to worst, she'd just have to buy another yellow shade – after testing it, naturally – and go again. There wasn't even anyone to ask their opinion. She could take a photo and see what her sister, Susie, might make of it, she supposed. But you know what it was like with phones, it might look different again in a picture.

After her caffeine hit, and diving in to the second baklava, she decided to soldier on, hitting the paint roller this time. Broad strokes filled the space much more quickly now. She lost herself for the next hour, humming away to the sounds of the Sara Cox show. It felt a little like having a friend in the kitchen with her. Perhaps she could send a picture to Sara and team, see what they thought? She bloody well hoped it'd dry a bit better than it looked now. She wanted primroses and daffodil tones to lift her mood, not runny egg yolks.

A 'ping' went off in her pocket. She carefully dismounted the stepladder and pulled out her phone to see a WhatsApp message appear on the screen. Ah, bless, it was Adam.

Hey Mum, how's it going? Vietnam is amazing. ☺

Oh, Vietnam. Cambodia left behind now, she mused, as she read on.

The people here are great, so friendly. In Ho Chi Min now. Been on a scooter tour of the city.

Oh, jeez, her heart blipped at that – images of manic streets filled with vehicles, perhaps even animals to dodge, and her son free-wheeling on some slip of a Vespa. She hoped to goodness he'd worn a helmet, but seeing as he was texting, it was most likely over by now. At least he had made it back in one piece.

And then a photo pinged in of him in a jungle, his head sticking out of some hole in the ground – he'd been at the tunnels used by the Viet Kong back in the Vietnam War. *Incredible place.*

His beard had grown longer and was looking a touch curly. He looked like a man, not so much her little boy. But the cheeky sparkle in his green eyes was still there. He looked happy. Cath sighed and gave a relieved smile. He'd be back in the UK in a couple of months. Plenty of time to look for jobs and find his sensible feet. She was glad he was out in the world having adventures and enjoying his travels. There was time enough for being sensible. She'd been that for the past thirty years, and look where that had got her.

Looks amazing, Adam. Enjoy every experience. x Cath responded.

Then the tease of the three dots as he typed, before: **Hope you're settling in well at the new cottage. Love you. x**

How was she settling in? She still wasn't sure of anything, really. Perhaps she should send him a photo of the river, one she'd taken on her walk that morning. The English countryside in all its fresh springtime glory, silvery light reflecting off the water, and a dapple of cloud in a pale-blue sky. It had looked so scenic. And with that realisation came a moment of gratitude. However hard this big change was, her new home was in a most beautiful place.

She sent the photo and finished with a: **Love you too. Take care xx**, and a sigh.

*

Back to the not so mellow-yellow painting. Sore back, achy arms from stretching her brush and roller here, there and everywhere. Four hours after starting and it was done. Standing back and looking in from the hallway, she still wasn't sure about the bloody colour. And dammit, it appeared slightly streaky in places, but hey, she'd given it her best shot. She'd let it dry before fretting too much.

After having demolished Andreas's gorgeous baklava, and deciding to keep the quiche for supper, she felt ready to crack on with a few admin chores she'd been putting off; she needed to notify the world of her new address for one. She also had a couple of maths tutoring sessions booked for this evening. She'd set up a professional website, and had plenty of contacts in Leeds. There were always GCSE and A Level students from her old school looking for extra tuition. She needed to build up the number of sessions she did, however, perhaps taking on some university students too, as her savings were getting heavily dipped into just now. She was hopeful that word of mouth would work in her favour. Thankfully, it was something she could easily do from home in her cottage, and if it grew as she hoped it might, then it'd keep some much-needed money coming into the coffers. With Trevor's financial support in their 'early retirement plans' down the pan with their marriage, it was all over to her now.

As the light faded, her mood began to change. The evenings

seemed awfully long when you lived alone. She sat at the table for two, in her yolk-yellow kitchen, aching all over, with her slice of very nice village-shop quiche. It was let down, however, by its accompaniment of sorry-looking side salad, consisting of a few limp lettuce leaves and some wrinkly cucumber she'd brought with her on her arrival day and had been lurking in the bottom of the fridge. Though the village store was great for treats and the essentials, she really did need to do a supermarket stock-up.

Blimey, it wasn't only the cupboard shelves that needed taking stock of, she realised, it was her whole life. She felt rootless, shifting uneasily into this new phase, uncertain of herself. Her confidence had taken a real bashing. It wasn't at all like her to feel like this, and it wasn't pleasant.

Casting her eye over this new kitchen space, she spotted her much-loved cookbooks perched on the rustic wooden shelf. She used to love cooking, experimenting with new recipes, trying out foreign flavours. Trevor would tuck in to a newly created dish, or old family favourite, with an appreciative 'Really good, love.' Adam would dive into some spicy Thai curry, it hardly touching the sides. It was honestly like watching a spaniel eat, and she wondered at times how he actually tasted anything. Then he'd look up from his empty plate with his trademark cheeky grin, saying, 'Epic, Mum.' Perhaps, she'd planted the seed for his travelling with her foreign dishes; she liked to think there might have been a little inspiration there.

Funny how back then she'd longed for this kind of freedom. In their family home, stood in the midst of Adam's debris-strewn bedroom, with dirty coffee mugs, cheesy aromas of stray socks and teenage testosterone, and a never-ending pile of laundry, she yearned just to have a few minutes' peace in the melee of motherhood. She'd known Adam would one day spread his wings, but she never imagined steady Trevor would be up and away at the same time, too. Sometimes you had to be careful what you wished for . . .

*

Well, then, if there was no one to look after her, she'd look after herself. In fact, she'd go right up and run a bath in that gorgeous Victorian-style white tub, and fill it with decadent bubbles. She'd use one of her Jo Malone oils, and perhaps pour herself a glass of chilled white wine. Rest her tired limbs and troubled mind for a while. She'd finished her tuition for the evening. Why not?! It was all down to her now.

Yes, you could go on thinking the cup was half-empty, feeling a bit sorry for yourself, or you could damn well start filling that cup up. *Onwards and upwards, Cath Taylor.* Today, a small glass of Chablis, tomorrow perhaps champagne and cocktails. But . . . what she really wanted was someone to share those celebratory drinks with.

Still, she quashed that thought, and managed to feel a little lift in her spirits. It was time to go and try out her new bath. The bubbles awaited.

Chapter 5

Much as she had loved the characterful village stores and meeting Dan and Andreas yesterday, there were several items she needed from a supermarket that she wouldn't find there. She'd been putting off going 'proper' shopping since her arrival – her cupboards and bathroom shelves were very like Mrs Hubbard's.

Cooking for one was going to be a new challenge, and admittedly was not the most exciting prospect. She needed to get some oomph back into her kitchen, check out new recipes and get inspired. She could be super organised and batch cook for herself, filling the freezer with her favourite meals in single portions. But her heart wasn't in it. Finishing the dregs of her morning cuppa, she felt a little weary about it already.

Her life, she suddenly realised, had been so focused around Adam and Trevor, along with her teaching job and her pupils, that she'd lost sight of herself. What did *she* fancy eating, cooking . . . just for her? The question lingered. Sadly, her appetite had lost its way these past troublesome months. Maybe the supermarket shelves would provide a little inspiration.

She got together some shopping bags, and hopped into her Mini to drive once more along the winding country roads back to Kirkton, past rolling hills dotted with sheep – a rather different trip to the usual suburban roads to Waitrose. Arriving at the small supermarket car park – a rather niche space between the shop building and the high stone wall of a churchyard – she did a quick loop and realised it was full. She then spotted someone backing out. Perfect timing.

Another car, a blue Audi, then pulled into the parking area too. Cath stuck on her indicator, giving the newly arrived driver warning that she was about to take that free space. A quick look in her rear-view mirror, and she started reversing. However, the blue hatchback must have kept moving forward. There was a dull thud as the two vehicles collided, luckily at slow speed, but still enough to jar Cath's torso and give her a fright.

What the hell . . . ? Surely the driver had seen her indicating, ready to back in!

Shit, this was all she needed. She pulled on the handbrake, and leapt out of the driver's seat, ready to face the music and assess any damage. She sighed. Even a minor scratch seemed to cost a bloody fortune to fix these days. And after all, it hadn't been her fault.

The other driver, male, medium build, dark hair with salt-and-pepper sides, perhaps in his early fifties, stepped out at the same time. His face was like thunder. 'What the hell?!'

Wasn't that her line in the circumstances? 'Well, I'd say the very same to you . . . didn't you even see me? I was already moving into that space, when you rolled in.' Her tone was heavy with annoyance, her head already beginning to thump. She wasn't great with confrontation at the best of times.

A couple of bystanders had stopped to see what the drama

was about. 'Well, I think we need to exchange insurance details at the least,' she started. That was something Trevor always drummed into her. Not that she'd had many scrapes or car incidents in her thirty-four years of driving.

'Shouldn't we just check if there's any damage to speak of, firstly?' Blue hatchback driver raised his eyes as if she was being a bit dumb, his brooding look and those hazel irises distracting her for a second. Then he flicked his gaze to the area where the two bumpers would have collided, taking a few steps closer to assess any harm done.

Cath followed his lead and moved in, too. There was in fact only the tiniest scratch on the bumper of his vehicle. And amazingly, despite the 'bumph' on impact, her Mini's bumper showed no sign of damage at all. 'Oh' was all she could muster, feeling some relief at least.

'Damn lucky, it looks like we've got off lightly. I'm not worried about calling in the insurance companies with all the hassle that entails, are you?'

'No, I suppose not,' she conceded.

'Though I'd be more careful when reversing next time,' he added, giving her a sharp look.

Pompous ass! She was riled up once more. Typical bloke, assuming it had all been her fault. She was certain she'd double-checked the mirrors and indicated, before she'd made the manoeuvre. 'And you'd better learn to take a little more care with your driving . . . and your manners,' was her parting shot.

She got back into the vehicle, and with hands that were a little shaky, managed to pull into the space she'd already claimed as hers. Mr Grumpy had evidently backed off as he drove farther down the car park to wait for another space to become available.

Once parked, she sat for a few seconds, trying to calm her frazzled nerves. She'd had so much bad luck lately. This made her feel even worse. She couldn't even go food shopping without some bloody drama now. She was left feeling really unsettled. Was it the accident? Was it the thought of having to deal with all this stuff on her own from now on? Or was there something about Mr Grumpy? Weirdly, she was left with this vague feeling that there was something familiar about the guy. Some deja vu experience, perhaps? But she hadn't had any near misses in any other car parks in the past that she remembered.

Cath then rallied herself, she'd better whizz round the shop, pick up what she needed, and get back to the refuge of her cottage. The last thing she wanted was to bump into Mr Grumpy again in a supermarket aisle. Keeping her head down, and with slightly rosy cheeks from all the car park fuss, she accomplished her mission before swiftly leaving the store and exiting the town.

She landed in a heap in her egg-yellow kitchen with a bag of groceries, and a banging head. So much for this new relaxed country life. She'd thought everything was going to be so much simpler, that life would be calmer. What had she been thinking coming all the way up here on her own? Nothing was familiar. There wasn't even anyone to go and have a coffee with, and shrug it off with a laugh.

Chapter 6

After the car park drama, the next couple of days passed uneventfully, thank goodness. Still, the cottage seemed almost too quiet. Life had moved from the top gear of the family/work/suburban-social-life motorway to a slow uphill crawl – even if it was the most scenic of hills that she found herself on. It was as if her emotions, after the rollercoaster of hurt and destruction she'd been on, still needed to slow down to match her new life . . . her new place in the world.

She was beginning to warm to the yolk-yellow walls of the kitchen. After re-positioning her recipe books on the shelves, alongside a pretty floral mug and a scented candle, and popping some pink tulips into a colourful spotted Emma Bridgewater jug, which she placed on the window sill, it finally came together, looking more country kitchen chic.

Cath found herself craving another piece of Andreas's baklava, hmm or perhaps that honey cake. Yes, something sweet, sticky and satisfying to follow her planned supper of cheese omelette and new potatoes. (Her cooking inspirations were still rather on hold.) Okay, so she might end up putting on a few extra pounds if she wasn't careful, but she'd lost weight these past months with the stress of everything. And, she reasoned, she was now walking far more than she used to, making the most of the glorious late spring countryside around her. With any luck, she hoped, one might just cancel the other out.

She'd better get her skates on as it was past 4:30 p.m., and she had a feeling the shop closed at 5 p.m. She was out of the cottage door within minutes, soon arriving at the store where Dan greeted her with a cheery, 'Afternoon, Cath. How are you?'

How lovely that he'd remembered her name. She was about to ask after Andreas's mother, when the doorbell jangled, and in dashed a spritely young woman with a mass of wavy dark-blonde hair, dressed in black jogging bottoms and an orange polo shirt with a logo that read 'The Canny Cleaning Company'.

'Hiya, lads,' the woman called out. She briskly ferreted in the freezer section, pulling out chicken nuggets, French fries and then grabbed a tin of baked beans from the shelf. 'Ah, this'll have to do,' she muttered, in part to herself. 'I've got a twenty-minute turnaround before football training – the kids not me,' she added for the benefit of Cath, as she suddenly spotted another person in the shop. 'I'm all out of ideas, and time . . .'

'Busy day, Nikki?' asked Dan.

'You could say that, it's been bloody manic. And old Mr T had a fall, so as well as cleaning his house, I ended up taking him to A&E in Alnwick for a check over. No major damage done, thank goodness. But, of course, that was an extra hour and a half on my day.'

'Poor old Terry. And he's okay now?' Dan seemed concerned.

'Yeah, just a bit shaken up, bless him. I left him back at home with a cheese and pickle sandwich and a cup of tea. I'll pop back in the morning and check on him again.'

'Well, let him know if there's anything he needs from the shop, we'll happily deliver if he's feeling a bit shaky.'

'Aw, will do.' She whizzed her provisions to the counter, adding, as she glanced at Cath, 'Sorry, pet, is it okay to nip in with these bits first?'

'Of course.' Cath had all the time in the world these days, almost too much time. How life could change.

'I don't know,' Nikki chattered on, 'I used to love cooking the family meals from scratch, but it's all such a rush nowadays and it always seems to fall to me to work out what's for tea. Well, I'm all out of ideas . . .' Poor thing, she sounded stressed.

'Well, I'm sure they'll be fine having this tonight,' said Dan kindly. 'And if there're any complaints tell them to cook their own . . . especially Kev. That's the hubbie,' he added for Cath's benefit.

'Oh, to have someone cook for me for once. That would be such a treat. Kev can just about manage to put a pizza in the oven, and that's it.'

'Well . . . nice to meet you,' said Cath.

'Sorry, you must think I'm rude, but I really do have to go.' She gathered up her things.

'No problem. Bye.'

'Bye. Thanks.' And she was off in a buzz of frenetic energy with the woosh of the closing door.

'Now, that lovely lady is Nikki,' Dan explained. 'Lives in the village, three kids, a lazy husband and has her own cleaning company. Really nice, but always in a spin, dashing off somewhere or other.'

Andreas then popped out from the back storeroom to join them. 'Was that our resident whirlwind, by any chance?'

'It was indeed,' Dan answered.

'Gosh, I remember those days,' joined in Cath. 'Working all hours, juggling the afterschool clubs and running Mum's taxi, doing the washing, ironing, sorting out all the meals. It's never-ending when you've got a young family.' A sudden stab of nostalgia hit her, for her old life, when Adam was younger and she'd felt like the hub of the home. Then she added, with a twinge in her voice, 'And now, well I'd love to have someone to cook for. I've recently found out cooking for one isn't very exciting.'

'Oh, I can imagine. It's the joy of sharing food that makes it worthwhile. We love our cooking,' said Andreas.

'And eating! That's the best part.' Dan grinned.

'Absolutely. And I do like trying out a new recipe,' his partner added.

Cath could imagine Andreas looking very dashing in the kitchen, all Mediterranean chef-style.

'Oh, so do I . . . well, I used to. Actually,' she added wistfully, 'I'd love to have someone to cook for again. To have someone to savour the flavours, to sit around the table and chat with. Someone to look after, I suppose.'

Both lads were looking at her with sad eyes. Cath suddenly felt a bit awkward. The words had just flowed with her thoughts, and it felt like she'd opened up a little too much. She hardly knew these guys after all.

'Indeed, cooking with love provides food for the soul. Food was always the heart of our home,' Andreas agreed. 'My mother is Greek Cypriot, so food is central to our family. There was always something tasty simmering on the hob or baking in the oven.'

'Oh yes, talking of which, I've come back in for some of your baklava, Andreas. I think I have an addiction already.'

'Ah, well, sorry, petal, but we're all out of that today. I took the last few pieces through to Mama in the care home. I'll be making a fresh batch tomorrow, though. If you call back at around ten-thirty in the morning, it should be ready.'

'Perfect, just in time for my morning coffee.'

'And in the meanwhile, can I offer you a slice of my Greek-style honey cake?'

Cath was drawn to the glass-dome-covered cake stand, where a gorgeous honey-drizzled golden sponge sat. 'Ooh, how can I refuse? Looks amazing.'

Andreas served a generous honey-orange-scented slice, ready to box and take away.

Out of nowhere, there was a sudden scamper of paws and a 'woof'. A white fluffy terrier appeared with waggy-tailed enthusiasm at Cath's feet.

'Ah, sorry. The little minx,' Dan exclaimed. 'She's done it again! Escaped out of the doggie gate somehow.'

'She's not meant to be down here in the shop, health and hygiene and all that,' Andreas elaborated.

'Well, seeing as she's already here, meet Shirley . . . our Westie,' added Dan.

'Hello, Shirley.' Cath gave the cute terrier a rub behind her ears. 'Love the name.'

'Right, that's long enough, Shirley. She'll be escaping all the more if she thinks she'll get fussed.' Dan gave a wry smile. 'Come on then, madam. Back upstairs now. Before we have the environmental health agency on our backs.'

'Named after the dance presenter – the very sassy Shirley

Ballas,' Andreas filled Cath in, as the terrier was gathered up by Dan, 'Or "Shirley Ballsie" as Dan sometimes refers to her. The dog that is.' With that, canine Shirley gave the most huffy look as she was despatched back out of the store, and up the stairs. 'A bit of a madam at times, but adorable. She's such a character.'

'Hah, I can tell.' Cath chuckled. She'd always loved dogs, but between her and Trevor's hectic working lives, they'd never been able to get one of their own.

With the kerfuffle over, Cath remembered the phone call Andreas had received last time she was in the shop. 'Oh, how is your mother, Andreas? Feeling better, I hope.'

He gave a small sigh. 'She's so-so, just now. She's had a couple of bad weeks with a chest infection that she can't seem to shake off. I'm just back from visiting her actually, been trying to keep her spirits up with baklava and banter. But she's really not herself. Mama's usually so with it and chirpy . . . even being in her eighties. But she seems shattered, bless, like the stuffing's been knocked out of her.'

'Oh, I'm sorry to hear that. I do hope she feels much better soon.'

'Me too. If she can shake off this damn cough, then she might be able to sleep a bit better.'

'Oh, let's hope so.'

'Can we tempt you with anything else today?' asked Dan as he returned, still drying his just-washed hands.

'Hmm, I was thinking of making an omelette for supper, so I'll take some mushrooms and a red onion to spice up the filling.' It was going to be plain cheese, but hey-ho, she needed to make more effort with this cooking-for-one.

She couldn't help but think about the lads planning and enjoying their meals together, Andreas baking baklava for his ill mother, even Nikki, feeding her brood among the full-on buzz of family life, albeit in a rush. 'Ah, it'd be so nice to cook for someone again . . .' she said, her thoughts spilling into words once more.

'Well, why don't you?' Andreas was matter of fact.

'Umm, well for starters, I don't really know anyone here, yet,' Cath confessed. And with Adam away, and no one due to visit soon . . .

'You know us.' Andreas gave a cheeky wink. 'Sometimes, when we've been cooking for the shop all day, and with the busy life we lead, cooking at night can be a chore. It'd be wonderful to be served a cosy supper.'

'It would indeed.' Dan raised a hopeful smile accompanied by a tweak of an eyebrow.

Had they just invited themselves over? Cath couldn't help but grin. She sensed with the extra worry about Andreas's mum, and a shop to run, life might well be a bit tough for the lads just now. 'Ooh, well I could . . . I suppose.' The lads seemed friendly enough, and everyone knew them here in the village. Why not? Her mind began racing . . . Hmm, having another person might just help the numbers, four was a better number table-wise, and would help keep the conversation flowing. It was out before she knew it. 'What about asking Nikki along too?' Cath ventured. 'Do you think she'd like a supper out? Would her husband look after the children for her? Seemed like she might be in need of a break.'

'Ooh, I bet she'd love it,' said Dan. 'She's good fun too, when she gets the chance to let loose, that is.'

'Oh, yes, remember that time at the Christmas pub quiz?' Both lads grinned. 'A Prosecco or two was enjoyed . . . dancing on the table in The Star she was.'

Cath smiled. 'Okay, well I'll check some dates . . .' she started. What on earth was she saying? What exactly did she have on socially, in the next couple of weeks? And wouldn't it be good to start some new friendships here in the village? 'Actually, lads, you tell me when's good for you in the next week or two. And would you mind putting the suggestion to Nikki, seeing as you know her better than me? I'm pretty flexible on days just now. Evenings are good after seven . . . Oh, other than a Monday, and a Wednesday, that is, as I do some tutoring then. What do you say?'

'That would be lovely. And hey, it sounds like we just launched ourselves on you. We could take a turn too . . . we'd love to have you back here sometime. Wouldn't we, Dan?'

'Of course.'

'Sounds like a plan,' said Cath. 'Oh, it sounds a bit like a supper club,' she added with a bubble of excitement, already picturing the cosy gathering.

'Brilliant, yes. Food with friends. I'm feeling perkier already,' said Andreas, the buoyant mood catching. 'Something to look forward to.'

And with that, the hostess-with-the-mostess-to-be went off with her provisions and a newfound spring in her step.

Hmm, a supper club indeed! Good Lord, had she just gone and made herself a social life?

Chapter 7

What on earth was she going to cook? And how would they all manage to squeeze around her galley kitchen table?

Later that evening, sat with a camomile tea, which wasn't working very well at calming her nerves, Cath's mind was whirling at the thought of entertaining again. There was a sense of excitement, yes, which was also laced with a touch of panic. After all, she hardly knew these people or their culinary expectations. Yes, she was a good home cook, but she wasn't capable of anything particularly fancy. And, in her old life, she'd had a separate dining room for entertaining and plenty of space in her kitchen, meaning no onlookers to observe her as she cooked and served. Here in the cottage, blimey, the far end of the galley kitchen was the dining room.

Oh, bloody hell.

Why was she in such a spin? Was it because it mattered so much that this new life worked out? Did she still need to prove to herself that leaping off into rural Northumberland was in fact right for her? Think positive, she reminded herself, as she got ready to head upstairs for bed, checking the doors were locked and switching off lights as she went.

She mounted the narrow stairs, one step at a time, which suddenly seemed very apt.

One step at a time to build her new life. And well, at least her social life was looking up.

*

'We're on!' exclaimed the lads, as Cath walked into the shop mid-morning the next day, ready to claim her freshly made baklava for coffee time. 'Nikki's up for it. She was delighted to be invited. Thought it was a brilliant idea.'

'Ah, that's great news.'

'And oh . . . yes,' Andreas added, 'I hope you don't mind or think us presumptuous, but there's a gentleman in the village . . . Nice chap, Will.' The lads gave each other a knowing look at this point. 'He was widowed a year or so ago, only in his mid-fifties. They were a lovely couple . . . and well, he's finding life on his own a bit difficult, not that he'd admit it. So, we thought he'd be an ideal candidate for a supper-style gathering, and we've asked him along too. Hope that's okay?'

Uh-oh, there was a definite whiff of matchmaking going on here. Cath felt slightly uneasy, but they were both smiling at her. There was absolutely *no way* she was interested in going anywhere near the dating game after her recently burnt-out relationship. But hey, as long as she made that quite clear to them all from the start, things should be fine. After all, the more the merrier, and this other lonely soul in the village might feel just the same, and be happy with some good food and company. She could settle for that – in a group scenario.

'We've also mooted a date of sixteenth of May, a Thursday,

if that's okay? Gives you a couple of weeks' notice, that way,' added Andreas. 'And sevenish you'd said, yeah?'

'Great!' It was all coming together, and fast. A whizz of panic zipped through her gut. But, despite her misgivings – and her very small dining area back at the cottage – she was determined to be upbeat and give this her best shot. 'That's wonderful, lads. Thanks for organising.'

*

The cookbooks were open in front of her. Hmm, a pinch of Mary Berry, a tablespoon of Hairy Bikers, and a dusting of Nigella Lawson. The weather was getting warmer, an Italian or Mediterranean-style supper theme with a hint of summer to come could work well. But, she mused, she'd definitely avoid going Greek. Her culinary offerings might well fall short on that front.

In the shop earlier, whilst collecting her baklava, she'd discovered more about Andreas's culinary background. Learning that the Greek-style baklava is generally walnut and honey based, such as in his mama's recipe, with the Turks using alternative ingredients such as pistachio and rosewater for their baklava.

Cath was sat at her pine kitchen table, which was squeezed into the far end of the galley, flicking through the foodie pages, with some tea to hand in her favourite white-and-blue polka dot mug. This really was such a small space to fit five people. And she certainly didn't want to end up nestled too close to widower Will, giving out the wrong signals.

Her lounge was pretty much filled with a two-seater sofa

and armchair, no room for a table in there. Outside? She could certainly shift the dining table out to her flagstone patio, and pretty it up with a jug of flowers and a candle or two. But oh, if the weather happened to be dull or wet – this was the far North of England, after all – then, they'd have had it. What exactly had she let herself in for?

She gazed out of the window hoping for some inspiration. Could she fix up some kind of canopy from the back door to give a little shelter? But what if it was windy? Maybe they wouldn't mind the small galley space and a bit of knee jostling after all, if the food was amazing. She'd have to really up her game with the cooking.

A sip of tea or two later, and the same space that had saved the day for her storage boxes when she'd first arrived, looked back at her from the top of the garden. The garden shed. Hmm, it had two glass doors that could open wide. A roof – shelter indeed – and it was a bigger space for sure than her mini dining area in the house? Could this be the answer?

Then she took in its shabby paint-peeling exterior, and remembered the spiderwebs, the indoor ivy trail. But, a voice in her mind struck up, all it needed was a little love and a bit of a facelift. A tweak or two of renovation. It would be so nice to have it as a feature in her garden, not an eyesore. She thought of all those outdoor sheds turned into home bars and family-and-friends dining spaces through the Covid pandemic. She had two weeks. It could definitely work.

She'd need to get her woodwork skills back into force. She had studied wood and metal work at school, back in the day, plus her dad had been a great home DIYer too – they'd often worked on little projects together. With a few repairs to the wood, a new pane of glass to replace the cracked one, and a fresh lick of paint, it might turn into the perfect spring-summer dining area. A garden retreat. The idea had wings. She felt a frisson of excitement. Hmm, she'd put her sensible head to work though, (the maths teacher in her wasn't going anywhere fast) and think on it properly through the day and overnight.

A 'Supper Club Summerhouse' came to mind. She had visions of a pastel-painted exterior, and inside . . . a character-ful wooden table, a mish-mash of vintage chairs, the finishing touches of a couple of bud-vases with flowers cut from the garden borders, and oh yes, some twinkly tealights.

Could she make that a reality? To be honest, she had nothing better to do just now. With tutoring booked in on just a few days per week at present (she was still trying to build her online profile), she had time on her hands. And, after the supper event was finished, it might well end up being a lovely place to sit in herself, out of the breeze on a sunny day with a cuppa, or a glass of wine and a good book. And hey-ho, if it didn't quite work out in time for the sixteenth . . . well, they were back to a knee-jostling supper stuck at the end of the kitchen. Nothing ventured, nothing gained.

*

With a newfound spring in her step, Cath unloaded her DIY goodies. Shed challenge accepted, she'd hit the road and been back to visit the hardware stores in Kirkton. Having examined the state of the shed roof, she'd assessed that two new roof plies and some waterproof sheeting were needed to make that watertight and sound again, plus eek, a whole heap of other materials. The savings were up for another battering by the looks of it.

Two tins of exterior paint in 'soft sage', a clean white silk emulsion for the interior, some plywood strips for essential repairs, roof felt in black, various paintbrushes, a saw and wooden-stand, sander, nails, screws, a jazzy new toolbox and more came out of the back of the Mini. It was like Pandora's box. Unfortunately, she hadn't thought of raiding the toolbox back at Limestone Lane – well, not for more than a couple of screwdrivers and a hammer for putting up her pictures with – which might have saved her several pennies.

Of course, she couldn't afford to go too crazy spending all her hard-earned savings. Her work pension wouldn't kick in for a few years yet, the plan had been for Trevor to support them both in the meanwhile. The sale of her half of the marital house had helped her to purchase Cheviot Cottage, but she now had a small mortgage and the household bills to cover. She needed to get busy building her private tuition, which did pay pretty well. In fact, she might pop up a poster in the village shop. She'd spotted a noticeboard there, and was sure the lads would help her with that. She wasn't struggling as such, but it was down to her to future-proof her finances.

She'd figured the DIY box and new tools would actually save on repair bills in the longer term. The thought of the renovated garden shed also gave her something to dream about, to look forward to. There really hadn't been much of that in her life lately, so she was determined to grasp this new opportunity.

Armed and ready with those practical supplies, she headed through to the back garden to prepare for Stage Two. She needed to get inside that shed, and give it a damn good clear-out and clean. Putting her arachnophobia to one side, and kitted out with rubber gloves and a broom, as well as a large bucket of hot soapy water, with a deep breath and a head full of determination, she dived in. Cobwebs came down, yuck, dust flew, the internal ivy was trimmed and pulled back away from the roof. The packing boxes came out – she might have to find a new home for them in the spare bedroom for now – and the terracotta pots, no doubt left by elderly Reggie, were taken down to the kitchen for a good wash. They could be repurposed and replanted, perhaps with something cheery like a miniature rose or some herbs, ready to be placed back in the shed on a little sage-painted shelf that she could see in her mind's-eye. Then, the scrubbing began in earnest.

Twenty minutes in, and her mobile phone buzzed in her pocket. She frisked it out, with rubber gloves on and bubbles aplenty, only just catching the call.

Her sibling's cheery voice: 'Hey, hi, sis, how are you? And how's life *up north*?' Susie added, in some kind of odd Yorkshire/Geordie twang.

Cath had to smile. 'Hi, Suz. Great to hear from you. And yeah . . . I'm doing well, thanks.' It was wishful thinking, but she was trying to smooth over the cracks.

They'd been messaging each other most days, but it was lovely to have a chance to chat.

'You sure?' Susie knew what a rough time her younger sister had been having lately, and clearly wasn't prepared to be fobbed off.

'O-kay, so it has felt a bit strange, moving up . . . being on my own . . .' She'd had a removals company do the transfer. It hadn't taken long. Her worldly goods and life, loaded on and off a small transit van. She paused, then continued, 'But hey, I'm now a week in, the village is lovely . . . and I'm already starting to get to know a few people.' Cath was determined to sound upbeat.

'Well, that's good. Early days yet, I suppose. It's bound to feel a bit odd. And is there anything you need? Or you'd like? I still haven't gotten around to sending you a new home gift.'

'Aw, thanks, that's kind. And yeah, I'll have a think.' Something for the 'Supper Club' shed came to mind, but she needed to be sure that project was going to actually work out, before she said anything more. It might all come tumbling down yet, literally. And what about her new life here, could that yet come tumbling down too? Had she really done the right thing?

'Well, just let me know. And hey, how are you . . . really? You sound tired, honey.'

'Yeah, I am tired . . . it's weird, I have loads of time on my hands now, and yet I still feel so shattered.'

'You're bound to. Give yourself a break, sis. This is a big life change – everything you've been through, all that emotional trauma, no thanks to shit-face Trevor, as well as the move . . .'

'Do you think I've done the right thing . . . really? Moving here?' The façade was finally beginning to crack.

'Honestly? I think you're brave, but I think you've taken on an awful lot at a time when you're already vulnerable. But I admire you, too. It's always been somewhere you've loved. So, good for you. Maybe, it is just the change you need.'

'Only time will tell, I suppose.'

'True. And hey,' Susie added, 'if you'd like me to come up

and visit soon, I could bring your new home gift in person, just let me know.'

'Aw, thank you.' Cath sensed that was Susie's way of placing a supportive foot in the door, without making her little sis have to admit that perhaps she was a tad lonely. 'That sounds great, and I'd really love for you to come up soon, but . . .' She needed to be honest here. 'I really need to give myself chance to settle in . . . on my own, just for now. It's the only way I'm going to find my feet.'

'Yeah, no worries. And if you change your mind, and you want some company, I'm just a phone call and a couple of hours drive away, okay?' The Peak District, where Susie now lived, was actually a three-and-a-half-hour drive, but Cath knew she was trying to make it sound simple to drop everything and go. She loved her for that, and for all the other things that had made her such a great sister over the years. Yes, they'd had their fair share of sibling bickering as teenagers, and indeed occasionally as adults, but that was just the way their family was. They let off steam with each other, because they felt safe to. This was one of the most rock-solid relationships in her life. Her sister knew her inside out. She'd been the keeper of her secrets, the shoulder to cry on. Closer than any of her friends (and she'd had some good ones) had ever been.

'Okay, thank you. So, how are Beth and Hannah?' They were Cath's nieces, Susie's two girls. Beth had got married last year and was now living in Sheffield (it was the last official engagement she and Trevor had attended together, and unfortunately hadn't been the easiest of days for Cath, despite it being a beautiful wedding). Hannah, who'd definitely inherited the family's mathematics gene, was now in her second year at uni in Bristol, doing a Maths degree.

'They're good, thanks. Beth's getting on great with her new job in the corporate legal team with Westerleys; most of it's online with the odd trip to London now and again. And Hannah seems to be enjoying student life. Making the most of the socialising as well as the studying, I think.'

'Ah yes, she always was the party animal of your two. Bit like her mother, hey.' Cath smiled. Susie was far noisier and more confident than Cath, growing up. 'Well, good on her.' It was great to think the young ones were enjoying life, as long as they were keeping up with their studies too. 'Send them both my love when you next speak.'

'Will do.'

The conversation flowed, with Susie asking about Adam, and then if Cath had heard from Trevor at all, either directly or otherwise.

'Nope, and that's not a bad thing. *It's all about the moving on*, Suz.' Cath sounded braver than she felt at that point.

If she repeated the mantra enough to herself, she hoped that one day soon she'd find it was actually working.

Chapter 8

Lying in a hot bubbly bath, Cath soaked her sore limbs. After speaking with her sister, she'd gone back to working on the shed, and time had run away from her. She now felt physically as well as mentally shattered, after all that sawing, sanding, scrubbing and hammering. The roof was fixed, the waterproofing shed-felt was on, and the inside was clean. She'd made a good start, but she was aching from head to toe. Despite all that, she felt brighter than she had done for weeks, no, months. It was like a little light had been switched back on inside. She felt purposeful, even a spark of hope.

There were hours, possibly days, of work yet to complete before the shed might be useable as a dining area – the task still felt Herculean. Hah, she'd love to be able to call up 'SOS DIY' and get a team in for a 24-hour takeover and transformation – a glimpse of hunky presenter Nick Knowles might be very nice too – but that so wasn't going to happen. The best thing she could do was get an early night, and get ready to go again.

But for now, whilst she lay here in the warm suds, she may as well have another ponder on what to cook. After all, she mustn't get so wrapped up in the renovations that her focus drifted from the main event, which was in fact to cook her newfound friends a tasty supper. Ah, it was going to be wonderful to have people to cook for again. Fingers crossed for fine weather and a summery feel to the 'feast' – she was using that term loosely.

Mediterranean-style food was definitely calling her. Italian, a summery pasta dish, something with prawns? Or perhaps a Spanish-style supper . . . a large pan of paella, or an all-in-one chicken and chorizo bake? Whatever it was, it needed to be fairly easy to cook, ideally prepared mostly in advance, taste delicious and look good. Oh, jeez, she was feeling a bit panicky already.

Trying to calm herself, she closed her eyes and tried to picture the scene, with her shed all finished and a balmy evening. A starter platter of charcuterie meats, local cheeses and olives came to mind, with a glass of chilled rosé wine. Yep, that might work well. She had a couple of olive-wood boards that would look great for that. Oh, yes, she'd bloody well made sure those had been packed, as well as all her best kitchen equipment, crockery, serving dishes and all the herbs and spices. If Trev had hardly bothered to cook for them in the past thirty years, he darned well wasn't going to get half the contents of the kitchen – he probably wouldn't have known what was in there, anyhow! The only things she'd left him were a kettle and toaster (choosing to buy herself a nice new cream-coloured set that she knew would look good in her cottage kitchen), a basic set of crockery and cutlery, and a few essential pans (the ones that used to stick and annoy her). It had felt like a small but meaningful victory in the scheme of things.

Okay, when she got out, she'd go and jot down her menu ideas so they didn't float away by morning, but for now she was going to enjoy her soak, with those fragrant bubbles popping around her, and a vanilla-scented candle glowing on the side. She closed her eyes, and breathed in slowly. Making the most of these small and simple pleasures . . . in a world that she knew could be so big and complicated.

*

Cath had never expected to be starting from scratch again at fifty-two years of age, arriving in a village where she knew no one. She was desperate to find her feet in this new community and make herself some friends. But as the days counted down, she felt anxious about the impending supper event. And yes, whilst the lads in the shop had seemed really chatty, she'd only seen Nikki for what, all of five minutes, and then there was the *merry* – hopefully – *widower*; she had to admit she really didn't know any of them that well. What if they didn't get on together? Or if the gathering felt a bit forced? Roundhay-based dinner parties of latter years had been with well-established friends, people she'd known for years. She was so about to step out of her comfort zone.

With a mere twenty-four hours to go, she was finally getting a grip on the shed renovations, with one last coat of exterior paint needed, before she could move the dining furniture up from the house. Then tomorrow, she could focus on the cooking and the finer details. There she was, paintbrush in hand, four steps up the ladder, when the looming black clouds – clouds she hadn't spotted massing behind her, being so stuck on her task – decided to give it their all. Not a simple shower, oh no, but a biblical downpour which drenched her in seconds, spoiling the batch of paint she'd just poured out into the painting tray. She scrambled down, ducked inside the shed, shutting the glass doors (that she'd now fixed) behind her, and stood there watching rivulets running down the panes . . . Then, soul-destroyingly, a stream began to form, soon pouring down her garden steps – and, oh bugger it, right into her still open back door. And with it, seemingly, all her hopes and dreams . . .

Dammit, the shed would never be ready in time now, and her kitchen – the back-up plan dining zone – looked as though it was filling with bloody water. Why hadn't she thought to close the back door? But it had been such a lovely morning just an hour or so before.

Shitty McShitface. Out she flew, securing the shed doors behind her, bolting down the aforementioned stream of now-slippery steps, and more or less tumbling through the kitchen door, slamming it behind her. Wet through to her T-shirt, jeans and knickers, she stood in a dripping daze. Luckily the kitchen area had wooden floorboards rather than carpet, but already it was soaking.

Mission mop and bucket next, then. After finishing the clear-up exercise, she went for a much needed pee, catching sight of her frazzled-wet banshee state in the bathroom mirror: hair a bedraggled tangle, mascara running into panda eyes. What the hell had happened to her? It wasn't just the rain, she thought drearily, she'd not bothered going to the hairdresser for months now. And, that flash of mascara and lip balm was about all the make-up she managed these days. OMG, she really had let her self-care slip dramatically. Her hair, face and clothes no doubt echoed her recent mood – utterly devastated.

When had all that begun to drift? When had she in fact stopped looking after herself? Oh, probably when Trevor stopped caring what she looked like, far preferring his little fling, who, no doubt, was perfectly coiffed, groomed and made up to the nines. (Cath actually had no idea what *she* looked like. She had never, and would never, want to set eyes on the woman.) But as she registered the sodden mess in the mirror, a big note-to-self flagged up in her mind, to find a local hairdresser, and soon. It was perhaps not possible in time for tomorrow's supper club, and she had so much else to do anyhow, but yes, some hair TLC was absolutely in order.

Feeling pretty miserable at this point, Cath was in need of a pick-me-up. She made a cup of strong coffee, took a long, warming sip, and sat for a while, looking out at the now drying garden. It looked fresher and greener than before with a raindrop-glistening glaze. A blackbird dipped its head, enjoying a drink out of an old saucer that had been left in one of the borders – ah, so that's what it was for. It then warbled a happy springtime tune.

She thought she may as well get a step ahead for her big day tomorrow and organise some of the utensils she'd need for her cooking. Wondering where she'd put away her big pasta pan, she crouched down and delved into the lower kitchen cupboards. It wasn't that long ago she'd unpacked, surely it had to be in there somewhere. Ferreting about in the back of the cupboard, behind her everyday pots and pans, she felt something else there. She leaned in a little further, and pulled out an old-fashioned ceramic mixing bowl. It was white-and-blue-striped and in good condition, other than a tiny chip in the top. There was a wooden spoon left in it too. They looked all ready to mix up a cake. It reminded her of the bowl on the cover of the old Be-Ro recipe book her mother used to have. It must have belonged to the old man whose house it had been. Reggie, that was it. Or perhaps it had been his late wife's and this was her much-used and loved bowl, which he'd kept as a special memory? Well, he wouldn't be needing this now. She decided to wash it up and keep it. It felt like it belonged with the house.

*

After locating her pasta pan on the bottom shelf of the other low-down cupboard, plus a square baking tin for a bread recipe she wanted to try, she made an easy supper for herself of cheese on toast; she'd save her culinary efforts for tomorrow. She then sat and read her latest crime novel for a while in the sitting room. It wasn't long before she felt ready to go to bed. It had been a busy day after all. But just then, a call came in from her sister.

'Hi, lovely.'

'Hey, Suz.'

'Just seeing how you are?'

'Oh.' They'd only spoken yesterday, but perhaps Susie had picked up on the nuance of her tone, and sussed that she was feeling a bit down. Cath's sigh slipped out slowly. 'Yeah, you're on to me. Feeling a bit fed up.'

'What's up, chicken?' Her sister reverted to her childhood term of endearment, spoken as Mum and Dad would have said it, filled with warmth and love. Cath was 'chicken', and Susie 'petal'. Come to think of it, hers wasn't particularly flattering, was it? But that realisation only made her lips crease into a small smile.

'Ah, it's nothing much really,' she started. 'Been a long day, and well, I've had this plan of doing up the garden shed . . . and I've set myself a big task,' she confided. 'And it's rained like billy-o today. The back steps turned into a bloody fountain, and it's gone and flooded my kitchen. And now it's too wet to finish painting the damned shed . . . and well, the dinner party's tomorrow.' It all came out in a blurt.

'*What?* You're having a dinner party? I mean, oh shit, about the flood and stuff . . . but wow, that's great, who's coming?'

Of course, she hadn't told her sister about any of this as yet. 'Ah, just a few from the village. The guys from the shop, a woman with a youngish family who runs a cleaning company . . .' She stalled at mentioning the widower, no need to give her sister that snippet of information to feed on just yet. 'And I don't really know them very well, so I just wanted it to all go off well. You know, make a good start. And now this . . .' She puffed out a heavy sigh.

'Well, that's great that you're making friends already. After all, you've only been there a couple of weeks, Cath. And I'm sure you can dry out the kitchen in time . . .'

And there it was, suddenly back in perspective. Yes, the bigger picture was that she had new friends coming around. Susie was always great at pointing out the positives, whilst not making you feel bad for getting in a flap.

'Oh, and I also happen to look like someone whose been pulled through a hedge backwards,' Cath added, letting it all spill out.

'Oo-kay . . .'

'Need a haircut . . . badly.'

'Well, I did wonder . . .' She could hear a hint of laughter in her sister's tone, not at her but with her. 'That last selfie you sent, you did look a bit . . . rustic, sort of windswept.'

Well, that brought her right back down to earth. 'Hah, the country life, hey. Rustic, you cheeky madam.'

'Just telling it as it is. You've evidently noticed yourself now, anyhow. It's about time you embraced being fabulous in your fifties, Cath, not frumpy.'

'Gee, thanks. Now I'm feeling soo much better about this dinner party. I've failed at fixing the shed up, and I look like a frump too,' she said huffily.

'Soz, I was only trying to cheer you up, chicken.'

Cath took a breath; Susie wasn't telling her anything she hadn't seen for herself. 'I know, it's just, catching sight of the bird's-nest hair was the straw that broke the camel's back. This whole new life. Have I gone and bitten off more than I can chew, Suz? New house, new area, new friends – well, hopefully, if tomorrow goes okay . . .' She tried to put her emotions into words. 'When it all went tits-up, should I at least have stayed where I knew people, where I had some roots? This is a whole new chapter, Susie . . . but I'm worried I'm not up to it. Not that I've got a lot of choice now.' Cath gave a heavy sigh.

'Hey, you've been brave and bold. Listened to your heart, going to a place you love, and good for you. Yes, it's a new chapter, a new beginning, and you know what, it sometimes takes lots of pages to get into a new book, doesn't it. Even when the book's a brilliant one. One page at a time, one day at a time, and then suddenly it all begins to make sense . . .'

'When did you become so wise?' Cath jibed, whilst appreciating her sister's words.

'It comes with age.'

'Hah, well you are older than me.'

And, of course, Susie knew all about new beginnings and getting on with life, with one failed marriage behind her, being left at only twenty-nine with two young children to bring up single-handedly, and what a brilliant job she'd done of that. That was all before meeting Mark, who'd then taken on Beth and Hannah as if they were his own.

'Aw, thanks Suz . . . I'm feeling a bit better already.'

'You're welcome. And hey, call anytime, that's what I'm here for.'

Her sister's words stayed with her well into the night, settling in her mind like drifting blossom. Cath lay awake in bed in the early hours, looking forward to, yet inevitably still anxious about, tomorrow's supper hosting. She was indeed only in the first pages of a whole new story. She had to be patient and give it more time.

Chapter 9

So, this was it! Supper club day had arrived. There was no going back now. She just had to buckle up, enjoy the ride, and do her utmost to make it a success.

The dining shed was almost ready, despite the heavy rains of yesterday, which had stalled Cath's well-laid plans. Thankfully, the roof had held firm overnight without any leaks. She'd checked it first thing this morning. Unable to wait, she'd headed out to the garden in her dressing gown and wellies. An apparition for the elderly couple next door, should they have happened to look over the fence.

She decided to take a chance and give it that final coat of exterior paint early this morning, as the sage colour still looked rather uneven. Fingers crossed for some blustery sunshine to help it dry in time. And then, she'd go ahead and set everything up inside later this afternoon – as well as doing the cooking. Nothing like cutting it fine!

No one on the guest list knew anything about her 'summerhouse' supper venue (oh, that sounded so much posher than garden shed!). She hadn't wanted to risk it not being ready in time, and well, she hoped it would be a lovely surprise for them. The weather forecast was good, thank heavens, after yesterday's downpour, with a fine evening due. So, it was 'wish-me-luck' time for Cath, and all systems go.

A Kirkton stock-up was next on the list: visiting the deli for her charcuterie and cheese, fresh salads and veggies at the greengrocer, and stumbling upon a cute candle shop where she chose a pack of delicate floral-scented white tealights – a small treat. She was soon back again at the cottage ready to put her chef's apron on.

It was now midday, the hours slipping by all too fast, and she was in the kitchen with Radio Two on to keep her company, enjoying the buzz of cooking for a social event again. The old Cath from years back, the one who loved cooking for a crowd, was peeking out from her shell. Space was tight in her galley, with not a great deal of work surface, but she managed. Firstly, to make her focaccia bread. She took Reggie's bowl to hand – it seemed fitting to use it, like a christening of the kitchen, measuring out her ingredients into it, mixing and then kneading the dough on the surface. She then covered the dish, leaving it to prove in the warm kitchen. Wonderfully, she'd also spotted some fresh herbs flourishing in the garden border, one of which was a fragrant rosemary bush. The garden was proving to be a legacy too. She'd snipped some aromatic sprigs from that earlier, ready to pop in the top of the loaf before baking.

Next, she needed to prep her lemon king prawn tagliatelle dish, chopping and lightly frying spring onions and garlic with fresh lemon rind in olive oil and butter. She made a green salad from fresh local leaves, which she popped in the fridge, to add her olive and vinegar dressing later. And then, she halved juicy peaches, laying them neatly in a terracotta baking dish with a sprinkling of brown sugar and a knob of creamy butter. Covering and leaving the dish aside until it was time to bake them later, before serving them warm with a dollop of pistachio cream. This was one of her 'old favourite' recipes, an easy but delightful pudding. Memories of summer evenings with their old friends suddenly flooded in on a wave of wistfulness. Her life had altered so much already. But how would it be with these new friends, she couldn't help but wonder?

With no time to waste, and putting her memories on hold, it was on to the charcuterie and cheese starter platters. She'd prep as much as she could now, slicing small wedges of cheese, fruit and celery, and then lay everything out fresh – hopefully a feast for the eyes – just before arrival time.

A welcome drink of fizz was on the cards too – two nice bottles of Prosecco were chilling in the fridge, with an alternative of Tanqueray Flor de Sevilla gin (again, brought with her from the Leeds house) and tonic. They'd discovered this orange gin on a holiday in Majorca four years ago, just before Adam went off to uni – which was in fact one of their last happy family adventures. A pang of nostalgia stabbed her, ready to put her off track. She swiftly refocused, however. Today was about moving on, she reminded herself, not looking back. And she returned to the drinks menu: a chilled white wine and a rosé were both ready to go with the meal, along with some iced water too. Nothing too flashy, just good wholesome food using local ingredients where she could, plus a cheeky tipple or two. In fact, at this point, she might need a little 'Dutch courage' herself, and she poured herself a small pinot grigio now that she was within sight of the finishing line – chef's prerogative.

She then heaved the dining table up the garden steps, one

side at a time in a hefty game of zig-zag, a tricky task single-handed. She should have waited, or asked for some help really, but then there'd be no dining area set up in time. And if she went to ask Andreas or Dan now, well, she'd be giving the game away. She wanted her supper visitors to walk in, feel relaxed, and see everything set out prettily. With a bit more pushing and shoving, and a hot-sweat in the making, she managed to wedge the table in through the wide-open glass doors, phew.

Next, setting out an assortment of chairs: two directors-style garden ones that she'd brought from home – *check that thought, what was once home* – the two from the cottage's kitchen-dining area, and one new addition in a re-stained white wood which she'd found at a bargain price in a charity shop last week. Mix and match 'shabby chic', which seemed to work fine. She popped the mini vases on the table, which she'd filled with cow parsley picked from the hedgerow (it was prolific in the country lanes, so she hadn't felt bad plucking a small bunch) mixed with bluebells and spring anemones from the garden, and a leafy-green sprig or two cut from a border shrub. The tealights were set out on vintage floral-patterned saucers – a family heirloom passed down from her grandmother – ready to light later, as the day faded to dusk. Hopefully by then, they'd all be settled in well.

She stepped back to take a photo of her garden shed all ready for the off, feeling a warm glow (possibly a hot flush from all that pushing and shoving of furniture!) and a real sense of pride in her achievement. It would certainly be cosy in there, there wasn't heaps of room, admittedly, but it was way better than the cramped kitchen. And it looked so pretty.

Wow, she'd only gone and pulled it off! Welcome to the summerhouse supper club venue.

*

An hour before ETA, Cath headed back up to the shed for a final check. A gentle prod at the woodwork revealed that the sage-green side panels were still a little tacky, oops. She'd just have to make sure she told the gang, so no one was tempted to lean against it. But the doorframes were fine, and inside, the white paintwork that she'd completed a couple of days ago looked fresh and inviting, setting off the table display perfectly. And there was her sage-green shelf (yes!) with Reggie's row of aged terracotta pots, now filled with parsley, sage, rosemary and thyme – their aromatic scents filling the space.

As the minutes ticked by, however, her anxiety mounted. She wanted this to work out so badly . . . this evening, being part of the village, making new friends, a new life. It was like tonight was the first domino in a run for her future, how it fell or faltered really mattered.

*

With twenty minutes to arrival time, she topped up her wine glass, put on some easy listening music, and began to lay out the selection of local cheeses and charcuterie on wooden platters – getting a bit arty-farty with a blob of caramelised chutney here, small clusters of grapes and mini celery sticks there. The pasta sauce was ready on the hob, just needing to be warmed through to then add the prawns and extra lemon zest. A big pan of water was also stood on the hob for the tagliatelle. A tray of rosemary roasted potatoes were ready to bake, as well as the focaccia to serve. So far so good.

Ping. Message from Susie. **Hope it all goes well this evening. You'll smash the supper! You were always the hostess with the moist-est. Enjoy! Xx**

Cath had to re-read the words, moistest, really?! A silly grin was plastered over her face.

The message was swifty followed by: **OMG! That was a typo – hilarious! Hostess with the mostess! 😂😂**.

Cath started giggling uncontrollably . . . and that's exactly when the doorbell went.

Chapter 10

'Helloo! It's only us!'

On the front steps stood Andreas and Dan, bearing huge grins plus a gorgeous bunch of colourful tulips, and a Tupperware box which looked to be filled with goodies. 'Baklava made by moi, and handmade boozy chocolate truffles care of Dan.'

'Ooh, delightful. And the flowers are beautiful, thank you. You boys certainly know how to treat a lady.' Cath smiled broadly. 'Come on in . . .' She led them through the hallway to her kitchen at the rear of the cottage, where a bottle of fizz was ready in an ice bucket. 'Bubbles, or G&T?'

'Bubbles sound good.' Andreas beamed.

'And for me. Thank you, lovely. And how are you? Been a busy day, I'm sure.'

'Good, thanks, all good.' She didn't want to share how flustered the earlier part of her day had been. It was all going to go calmly from now on, she told herself.

'Oh, you've really tidied things up in here. It looks really sweet, homely. Poor old Reggie, bless him, couldn't cope with it all in the end. He's in the home where my mum is now,' Andreas reminded her. 'They've been feeding him up, and he looks far happier, I have to say. They have all sorts of activities on there, too. I think he's enjoying the social scene.'

'He loved this place though,' added Dan. 'Much as he didn't want to leave here at first, he was definitely finding it all too much . . . and having the garden to tend as well. He'll be delighted it's in good hands.'

'Ah, that's nice to hear. I'm glad he's okay.' That was heart-warming news. 'Tell him I'm looking after the old place for him.' She felt like the cottage custodian, and that was a nice feeling.

A home had its own heartbeat, its own rhythms. It was yours for a while, and then in time you passed it on, giving it the chance for new stories, a new life. This new home was her second chance, a place to start her next adventures as a single woman, a little more experienced and wrinkly, admittedly. The pages were yet to be written. She hoped she'd be brave enough to take life by the horns and do this little house, herself, and Reggie, proud.

'And what a lovely evening for your supper.' Dan, dressed smartly in dark jeans and a striped blue shirt, sauntered towards the back door which had been left open to the garden, the early evening rays giving a warm glow to the flagstone tiles and the kitchen's yellow walls. 'Such a pretty garden here.'

'Yes, aren't we lucky with the weather . . . And the garden, well it does need a bit of TLC out there, but I've made a start with it.' Her mind pulled to the shed that she'd worked so hard on, but she didn't want to spoil the surprise by telling them about it yet. 'So, fizz it is then.' Cath popped the cork with a flourish, and began to pour. There was always something exciting about opening a bottle of bubbles. 'Cheers, boys.'

'Cheers. Happy new home. Here's to a gorgeous evening. And thank you so much for having us,' said Andreas.

'Hah, you might change your mind once you've tasted my cooking.' She gave a wry smile.

'I'm sure we won't. It's just wonderful to be looked after,' Dan reassured her. 'Especially after a hectic day in the shop.'

'Absolutely,' Andreas agreed.

'Oh, and how's your mum getting on now, Andreas?'

'Ah, still struggling with that nasty cough, bless her. But the home's been brilliant, and her care's second to none. She's comfortable and as happy as she can be, considering.'

'That's good news. I hope she picks up really soon. And how's sassy Shirley?'

'Fabulous, darling,' he said in a Craig Revel Horwood voice. They all laughed. 'All tucked up with a chew toy, and the music on. She likes a bit of classical.'

Bringg . . . There was guest number three, no doubt.

'Won't be a mo.' She left the lads chatting in the kitchen, and headed for her threshold, feeling a buzz of excited anxiety, as she began to open the door. Who would it reveal this time?

'Hi, sorry if I'm a few minutes late . . . been trying to get the kids settled. A losing battle as it was. Left them up with their dad for popcorn and a movie in the end, even though it's a school night. But they all seemed happy with that option, and it's a one-off after all. Oh, and here's a little something . . .' She offered up a bottle of Prosecco, in a pretty gift bag.

'Ah, thank you.' Cath leaned in to give Nikki a friendly kiss on the cheek, hoping that wouldn't seem over the top. She would have done that with friends at home, after all. Oh, damn, was she still overthinking it all? *Relax*, she told herself.

73

'You are very welcome, and boy, I am sooo ready for this! A whole evening off. Bloody bliss. Thank you so much for asking me.' Nikki seemed chatty and friendly, which put Cath at ease.

The ladies joined Dan and Andreas in the kitchen, with of course, no need for introductions.

'Glass of fizz, Nikki?' Cath pointed to the bottle propped in the ice bucket.

'Don't mind if I do. That sounds amazing. Will set me up nicely. And, I've told the lot of them not to ring me under any circumstances.' She was evidently still thinking about the family she'd left back home. 'In fact, I might just ditch my mobile here.' She popped it up on the kitchen shelf, abandoning it with a grin. 'Perfect.'

Cath took a flute glass, placing a raspberry into it, and poured over sparkling Prosecco for Nikki.

Well then, there was just the merry widower to arrive.

The doorbell chimed.

'Don't worry, I'll go to the door while you're busy,' Nikki announced. 'Don't want to stop you pouring my drink. It's most likely Will, last, but not least.'

Cath was sure she saw a squint of a conspiratorial wink between Nikki and the lads, but perhaps she was just being sensitive. She heard the sound of Nikki unlatching the door, a brief welcome chat between the two guests, followed by footfall through the hallway. And there they stood, Nikki and—

Oh, my God!

It was him! It was only *Shitty McShitface*, Mr Grumpy from the bloody Co-op car park. Oh, jeez. Well, *that* was certainly going to spoil the ambience of the supper group. Of all the people . . . unbelievable. And just her flippin' luck.

She felt herself flush, as her eyes caught his, barely able to conceal the flash of surprise and horror at his arrival. 'Oh, hi,' her voice came out awkwardly.

'Ah . . .' He sounded strained.

So, he had recognised her too.

Unfortunately, the shocked looks didn't pass the others by, either.

'Do you two know each other?' Dan was on it in an instant.

'Ah, well . . . yes, actually. We kind of bumped into each other in the car park . . . in Kirkton,' Cath started, trying to keep it light, but feeling so damned awkward. She hadn't forgotten how sharp the guy had been with her that day.

'Yeah, a bit of a close shave,' Will followed up weakly.

Nikki honed right in. 'Come on then, spill. There's more to this, you're both looking sheepish.'

'So, what's the news?' Andreas was all ears, alert to some drama going on.

Will stepped in, Cath had to admit rather gentlemanly. 'Well, we had a minor scrape, that was all. Car bumpers. No real damage done.'

Cath was thankful that he'd explained it briefly and politely at least. 'Yeah, that's about the sum of it.'

Both managed a slightly uncomfortable smile.

Cath was sure she heard Nikki utter, 'Awkward', under her breath.

'A glass of fizz then, Will?' Cath held the bottle aloft, swiftly moving the conversation and the focus on. After pouring his drink, she made sure her own glass had plenty of fizz. She had a feeling she was going to need it.

*

With all the guests now arrived, and after several minutes chatting and sipping sparkling wine in the kitchen, Cath suggested they head on up the garden to make the most of the evening sun, still keeping quiet about her summerhouse supper club venue. Leading the way up the garden steps, she felt a buzz of anticipation.

Nikki was the first to notice. 'Oh, my, what's this? Is that Reggie's old garden shed? It looks amazing. You've given it a right revamp. Oh, lads, look at this . . . and it's all set up so gorgeously inside.' She peeked in, smiling broadly.

'Crikey, last time I saw this outhouse, it was rotting away,' added Dan.

'Have you done all this?' Andreas's mouth gaped open.

'Yep, all my own work.' Cath felt herself brimming with pride. 'Welcome to your supper venue for this evening.'

'Amazing!' Nikki was gobsmacked.

'Well done you, it looks really great,' added Will, with a flicker of a smile.

The table was set with a white linen cloth, her best cutlery and floral paper napkins. The bud vases were filled with their country-garden flowers, the scent delicate and fragrant, along with the potted herbs up high in a row, and the finishing touch of the tealights helped capture the pretty country-casual theme. And, in the sun's soft glow, her green cut-glass tumblers (brought from the Roundhay semi) and the matching jug filled with iced water and lemon slices, glinted in the light.

'You dark horse. Well, that's it, Daniel, we need to up our game. The shop's outhouse might need an overhaul now.' Andreas chuckled warmly.

'We've got enough on our plates, don't you think, hun?' Dan said to Andreas. Turning to Cath, he added, 'But I must say it looks fabulous, petal.'

'Well, thank you. Now feel free to take your seats and get cosy. Dan, perhaps if you two pop over there. Nikki, Will, you two go opposite.' Cath had decided on this seating plan earlier, putting the lads together at one side of the table with Nikki and Will on the other. That way, she could place herself at one end – declaring that she'd need to hop in and out of the kitchen – deliberately positioning herself next to Nikki rather than Will, to save any potentially difficult moments with the merry widower. And thank Christ for that; he was absolutely not so bloody 'merry' now that he had been revealed as Mr Grumpy!

After a top-up of fizz, and some easy-going small talk, Cath felt it was time to start serving some food. 'I'll just nip back to the house and bring the starter platters up.'

'Can I give you a hand?' offered Mr Grumpy . . . oops, Will, politely.

'Ah, thanks but I'll be fine.' She really didn't want to find herself facing any awkward kitchen conversations at this point. She was still recovering from the shock of seeing 'Mr Grumpy' turn up on her doorstep.

Cath had to admit the platters looked good as she carried them up to the summerhouse. The dishes were greeted with smiles, and a 'Wow, that looks delicious' from Dan, and a 'Scrumptious' from Nikki.

'So, what's everyone been up to this week, so far?' Cath asked, as they dug in to the cheese, chutneys, crackers and charcuterie.

Andreas started, 'Been full on with the shop, had our usual trip down to the suppliers, and then fitted in a few visits to Mama, of course.'

'Oh, and don't forget we had that stocktaking evening too . . . thrilling,' added Dan.

'The giddy life we lead.' Andreas was smiling, as though steady as it was, they were both happy to be doing it.

'Cleaning, cleaning, and more effing cleaning for me – all day at work, then sorting out the mess from my lot at home. Oh, and then throw in a bit of cooking and washing. Tonight is certainly the highlight of my week so far!' Nikki added.

Will said, 'And I've had a good few days at the shop. Kept myself busy.'

'Oh, so you have a shop, too?' Cath was curious.

'Yeah, more of a repair place really . . . bicycles. It's over in Kirkton, just past the garage there.'

'Ah yes, I think I've seen it.'

'The Cycle Man. Very original . . .' He gave a wry smile.

'Does what it says on the tin,' added Dan with a grin. 'He's good, and doesn't charge silly money, I can vouch for it.'

'Yeah, it's quite a new venture for me, but it's going okay.'

He did look the sporty type, Cath mused, lean and healthy looking for a middle-ager. 'Well, that's good,' she responded. 'Not quite my thing, cycling, I have to admit. But I imagine it's great if you're into it. You said your business is quite new? So, what did you do before that?'

'I used to be a fireman until recently, took early retirement and well, my hobby's always been cycling. Lots of locals are into mountain biking and road cycling around here. It's been a passion of mine for years. I used to do repairs for friend's bikes. So...' He looked slightly troubled. 'When I found myself with more free time on my hands, and a small unit came up nearby on a short lease – well, the idea came to mind, thought it was worth a try, and see how I go. So far so good.'

Cath suddenly remembered about his wife having died. Was the 'free time' a lot to do with that as well as retiring? Finding himself on his own, with his world turned upside down. They had that in common, at least. She didn't want to dig any further, nor probe too deeply, and make him feel upset or awkward – anymore than he already was. She merely added, 'Right, well that sounds interesting. Best of luck with the new business.'

The conversation rolled on again, and soon, after a quick whizz to the kitchen to boil the tagliatelle pasta, and add prawns and freshly grated lemon rind to her sauce, the next course was ready. *Phew.* The olive-oil roasted potatoes had crisped up in the baking tray, the addition of rosemary sprigs fragrant and flavoursome. The focaccia had risen well and had a springy-salty rosemary top. A fresh and crispy side salad, with her own oil-and-vinegar dressing, was the final touch. Nikki popped down to help her, and as they set the serving dishes out on the summerhouse table, it all looked and smelt good, she had to admit. The meal recalled Mediterranean summers, commented Dan. Aw, that was just what she'd hoped for. They all tucked in.

With contented tummies all round, a rest with a glass of chilled white wine to hand was very much needed. A large one for Cath, who was so relieved that she had somehow managed to pull the supper off nicely, so far. Foodwise, at least.

Chapter 11

Later, as the dusky sky became tinted with streaks of rose and orange, with the tealights giving off a warm glow, Cath began to feel more relaxed. She had to admit that the supper had gone well, with the savoury food enjoyed, lots of praise and 'Mmms', and virtually clean plates all round. The guests were now chatting away, but of course it made it easier that they all knew each other beforehand. It was Cath who was playing catch up with this social circle as the newbie in this village, but it was going okay. *One step at a time.*

She headed back down the garden to the kitchen to take her dessert of baked peaches out of the oven. She returned to the shed soon afterwards, carrying a tray with bowls and a dish of thick pistachio-swirled cream, along with the hot syrupy-smelling peaches in their terracotta dish.

Oh. The guests had swapped places, with Will now sitting where Nikki had been – next to Cath. She took up her seat again, resigned to having to make conversation with him. Despite their dreadful first meeting, he hadn't seemed too obnoxious this evening, after all. In fact, she had to admit that he seemed a different person to the grumpy guy she'd met in the car park. Perhaps, he was the sort that was oversensitive about his vehicle.

On a Prosecco and foodie high, Nikki was chatting away with Dan and Andreas about her chaotic family life. With their attention diverted, Will discreetly turned to Cath. 'I must apologise if I was a bit sharp with you the other day . . .' His tone was sincere, as he added, 'Let's just say I was a bit "off" that day.'

He didn't seem to want to elaborate, and Cath was happy to leave it at that, accepting the apology graciously. 'No problem. We can all have bad days.'

And hey, she should know, she'd had plenty of those recently.

Cath tuned back in to Nikki then, who was telling of her boys' latest antics involving the washing machine. Hamish, the eldest, had finally decided to do something to help out at home, putting all the reds, whites and blacks in together, with the whole lot coming out as a greyish-pink mess, including Nikki's best white shirt, grrr. But how could she complain about it? They'd never help again!

Cath grinned, knowing that feeling all too well, then turned to Will. 'Do you have any children, Will?'

'Yes, two girls, grown up now.' He gave a warm smile. 'Maddie and Sophie. Mads lives in Newcastle, she's an oncology nurse. Sophie's at uni, down in York.'

'Ah, that's lovely that you have two girls. And nursing, that must be a hard, if rewarding, job.'

'Yeah.' His tone was suddenly clipped.

She felt she was touching on sensitive ground here.

'And you?' he asked. 'Any family?'

'A son, Adam. He's just finished his studies at Leeds uni. He's off away at the moment on some world travels. Latest I heard, he's in Vietnam, having a whale of a time.'

'Well, that sounds cool. And you're new here to the village, I gather. What's made you move up here?'

Cath felt a knot in her stomach. Did she really want to go into the gory details of her marital break-up at a dinner party? Absolutely not. 'Ah, I just needed a fresh start,' Cath replied. 'I knew the area a bit, have always loved it up this way, and thought why not . . . ?' She missed off the part about her cheating husband.

'It is a beautiful place,' Will agreed, nodding gently.

'It is indeed,' Andreas chipped in. 'Never looked back after our move, did we, Dan? It's so peaceful.'

'It's not so peaceful halfway up the street at our bloody house,' Nikki was laughing.

The evening rolled on with more chit-chat, and as they talked around the table, Cath had an odd sense that there was something vaguely familiar about Will. It had hit her in the car park, too. Something about those eyes, a deep brown with touches of hazel-green, and when he actually smiled as he was doing right now, they looked so much nicer than the cool hard stare she'd received that day. In fact, they were almost sparkly.

Ah . . . that was it: Marti Pellow! He looked a bit like Marti Pellow from . . . oh, what was that band now? They were one of her favourites back in the day. The Eighties, it must have been. That was it, Wet Wet Wet. God, she used to fancy him like crazy in her teens.

Her mind suddenly flew back to Susie's text, about being 'the hostess with the moistest'. *Wet, Wet, Wet.* It was all she could do to stop herself from laughing out loud. She pursed her lips and then dipped her head to take a sip of wine, letting a small chuckle slip into her glass.

And as she looked up again, those hazel-brown eyes were smiling back at her, filled with a hint of curious amusement. Something dipped, like a butterfly flutter, in her stomach, something she hadn't felt for a very long time. Surely, she didn't fancy him just because he had nice eyes? *It's Mr Bloody Grumpy from the car park*, she reminded herself, giving herself a stern telling off. She was steering clear of men and relationships forever. No point jumping from the frying pan into the damned fire. It must be the wine. She'd better ease off it, right now.

*

The end of Supper Club rolled around with the midnight hour. It was time for coats on, with 'thank yous' and hugs in the hallway, and kisses on the cheek for the hostess from Dan, Andreas and Nikki. Will hung back rather reticently, which Cath found herself relieved about. Despite her crazy thoughts on how attractive his eyes were, going from him shouting at her in a car park to all kissy-kissy was a step too far for one day.

'It's been a wonderful evening, Cath, thank you so much. I've loved every minute of my night off,' smiled a fizz-filled and grateful Nikki.

'It's been really lovely. Thank you, Cath.' Will was polite, and offered a farewell handshake. *Is this now a truce?* It felt as though they'd drawn a line under the car park incident at least, and thank heavens for that. She needn't be afraid of bumping into him again in Kirkton, which had crossed her mind every time she'd needed to visit the local supermarket.

'Our turn to host next,' called out Andreas, as he crossed

the cottage threshold into the cool starry night air. 'We'll have you all back soon to our little nest above the shop.'

'Definitely,' added Dan. 'Mind you, we're going to have to plan carefully to match up to Cath's fabulous hospitality.'

'Ooh, the challenge is on.' Andreas grinned.

Dan gave a cheeky wink. 'You do know he has one of those nude-Greek-statue aprons. I'm just warning you! We got it in Halkidiki in a tacky gift shop last holiday.'

'It's my favourite item of clothing. Don't spoil my fun,' Andreas countered, his eyes sparkling with amusement.

'Well, don't let me stop you . . .' Nikki cackled. 'And another evening being wined and dined sounds bloody good to me. Just give it a few weeks, so I can get Kev used to the idea of child-sitting again.'

'Of course.'

'That sounds great,' added Will politely. 'Thanks for letting me join in with you all. The food was delicious, and it's been a wonderful change of scene.'

Cath suddenly pictured him alone at home, somewhere up the street. The home that was missing his wife. She felt a pang of empathy.

The supper guests trooped off merrily up the pavement, leaving Cath to her empty house and the last of the clearing up. To be fair, everyone had helped clear the final dishes and glasses down from the shed, but she'd insisted they leave the washing-up. A yawn escaped her lips, and she realised just how tired she was, a heady mix of adrenaline, a full-on day (two weeks, more like), nerves, a drink or two, and the last couple of hours in relax mode, now kicking in. She made an executive decision – the rest of the tidying could wait until morning.

Despite feeling shattered, it took her a while to come back down emotionally. Lying in bed, her mind was running over the events of the day, and pulling out threads of conversation and images from this evening. The caffeine from the last round of nightcap coffees was also playing its part. She felt far too buzzy to sleep.

The supper group were indeed rather lovely. Hah, even grumpy Will had had his positives. Yes, new friendships were being formed, and it was good, exciting. Yet everything was so early on in her new second-chance life that it felt raw somehow. These new relationships seemed fragile, she realised, like the unfolding of brand new buds. Opening up her home – and herself – this evening had left her feeling strangely vulnerable.

Chapter 12

In contrast with the hectic two weeks she'd spent getting ready for the supper club, the next few days were dreadfully quiet. Cath tried to keep herself busy doing the usual household chores, several online tutoring sessions, and pottering in the garden, but sitting there on her own of an evening, a sense of gnawing loneliness crept up on her. Of course, she knew she couldn't keep socialising every day. Everyone was busy and back at work. Even dropping by the shop, hoping for a catch-up, hadn't quite panned out. By chance, she'd managed to hit a particularly busy spell at the village stores with several people queuing at the counter, so Andreas and Dan, whilst superefficient and friendly, had no time to stand and chat.

The supper group's working hours meant she couldn't even ask the lads or Nikki in for a daytime coffee, and well, she didn't want to over encourage Will – not that he had given any vibes he was looking to spend any more time in her company either. Other than a polite thank-you note popped through her letterbox the day after the supper, he seemed to be too busy for her also. Life as a single lady wasn't quite what she'd pictured it might be. No one but herself to cook for, clean for, do laundry for . . . who'd have thought she'd miss that? The flip side of this newfound freedom seemed to be loneliness.

As she was sitting with a cup of strong coffee and this sense of unease, wondering how best to shake off these dark feelings, she got a call. *Oh great, some human contact.*

It was a blast from the near past: Helen from Roundhay once again.

'Helen, hi, how are you?' Cath tried her best to sound chirpy. Out of all her old friends, Helen was probably the one she least wanted to chat with just now.

'Oh, I'm fine thanks, busy, busy. But more to the point, how are you doing? You didn't call back after our last chat, and well, I was starting to get a bit worried. How have you been? How's village life?'

'Yeah, fine, all good.' Unfortunately, Cath's voice resonated a flatness from her recent confusing emotions.

'You sure you're okay? You don't sound quite yourself, I have to say. I know it's been a tough time for you. And then, sailing off to the back of beyond like that. Well, it must be hugely different. We've all been thinking about you.'

Gossiping might be more like it, Cath mused.

'Well, it's certainly very different from life back in Roundhay, I suppose.' She'd swapped the beeping of horns and the hum of traffic for birdsong and tractors. And exchanged the constant round of social invites in the city– afternoon teas, suburban suppers, charity this and that – which at times could almost feel too much, for new buds of friendship (which were naturally growing rather tentatively, just yet). 'But yeah, I've been making a few friends . . . starting to get to know some people in the village.' She didn't get a chance to tell her friend about the supper club and how it had gone, as Helen was straight in with her own dinner party details.

'Oh well, that's good. They'll be nothing like your old friends here though, I bet. We miss you. Gosh, we had the most a-mazing dinner party Friday evening at Trish and Terry's. Spoilt us rotten they did, with champagne and cocktails. Fliss got a bit tipsy and we had a bloody hoot playing Twister. Then, we were out at the theatre last week, with Emma and Tony. A new take on *Macbeth*, it was brilliant. Ah, there's always so much to do in the city, isn't there?'

Why did this sound like Helen was pulling the oh-so-cool city card on her, implying life there just had to be so much better? Her tone sounded superior, or was that Cath just feeling tender? It was the life she'd left behind after all. The life and the city buzz she once loved.

'And have you been out and about much?' Helen continued, undaunted by the limited response. 'I bet it's been fun having a whole new area to explore.'

Blimey, this conversation was beginning to feel like twenty questions. Cath hadn't been that far at all actually, still settling herself into the village and her new home. 'Ah, yeah, been out a bit. I took a drive through to the coast the other day.' The white lie slipped from her lips. The trip to the coast was actually a few weeks ago, when she'd first got here. It had been nice down by the sea, but without someone to say, 'Wow, look at that stunning view', and discuss the merits of either fish and chips or going into a nice cosy pub, it had ended up feeling a bit flat. She'd sat in the dunes with a cone of hot, salty chips in the end, which were rather good, and then taken a stroll along the sands. But it felt far emptier than when she'd been there on family holidays. Memories had flooded in of her and Trevor and Adam, back in happier days, tarnishing things somewhat.

'On your own, I suppose?' Helen cut in, still fishing, hoping to pin Cath down on her new life.

'Well, yes.' Did she expect her to be heading out with a new fling, or on some Saga-style bus tour?

'Oh, Cath,' Helen managed to sound disappointed in her. 'Bless you. With everything that's gone on, I more than expected you to take a step back for a while. That was quite understandable, after all. But well, you can't keep hiding away in your country cottage like a hermit. Now's the time to get back out there, show Trevor what he's missing. Time to crack on with life.'

'Well, I've been trying. It's not been that bad. It's just all new. And building friendships can take a while . . .'

'Cath, darling, I can tell you're not yourself. That's it, I'm coming up. No ifs or buts. It's time you had a bit of company. And of course, I'd love to see your cottage . . .' This was nosiness at its fore.

Oh, Lord, it sounded a done deal. Was her friend eager to report back, give the old group the rundown on her new home, on her? Cath felt a sense of foreboding, but what could she say? She hadn't even had a chance to mention her supper club event, the fact that she was actually establishing a few friends. But her defences were down and some of this conversation rang true, in all honesty. Cath wasn't sure what to say without sounding rude. She'd already put Helen off a couple of weeks ago. 'Ahm, well . . .'

'Next weekend, I'm free. Geoff's got a golf tournament on then, too. It'll be ideal. You'll not have any plans, will you?'

'Ah, umm, noo.' She felt railroaded. It wasn't that she didn't like Helen, they'd been good mates over time and their children had virtually grown up together, but she could be rather bossy, and a bit overpowering.

They ended the call with the usual pleasantries, but as Cath pressed the 'call over' button, she felt a sense of doom. Helen was no doubt online this very minute, booking her train tickets. Oh, bugger, she was coming up to stay in the cottage the following weekend. And well, that was that.

Blimey, after that call and the impending arrival of a full-on Helen, perhaps another trip out, even if it was on her own, might be exactly what she needed, especially now that she was finding herself at a loose end with the supper club event over. A change of scene was a good idea – time to get in the car and head out to one of the stunning Northumbrian beaches that lay just twenty minutes' drive away. Time for some fresh sea air, time to take herself out of this contemplative mood, and go off on a coastal hike.

*

Taking a zig-zag of country lanes, the hawthorn hedges each side bursting with a froth of wedding-white Maytime bloom, a dotting of sheep in the grassy fields and cattle with young calves, she whizzed on by in her Mini. Cath headed to the coast, crossing over the A1, back on to twisty lanes, over the railway crossing, and towards the village of Bamburgh with its impressive castle. The ancient stone fortress, which bordered the sandy beach on its far side, with a picturesque village nestled on its other, stood grand and enchanting before her.

She turned into a lane called The Wynding, following the road to a car park, where she pulled up. Turning her back to the castle and the miles of sandy beach, she headed away from the tourists, taking the coastal path that meandered below the golf course, over rocks, past seaweed-twirled salty pools, striding out over the golden sands that led towards Budle Bay. The rush of waves came foaming in to shore, the cry of gulls filled the air, and above bloomed an expanse of blue-grey sky with a hint-of-pink-edged cloud.

The rhythm of her steps, the cool salt-sea air, with nature all around her, served to lift her spirits. *This* was why she'd escaped the city, and the never-ending hum of traffic, the constant round of 'who had what', be it the latest cars, clothes, makeup . . . her friends had even started comparing their grandchildren's achievements, for goodness' sake. Life wasn't a competition. All of that had felt exhausting at times.

It wasn't what you had, it was who you were . . . and where you were, the here and now; seeing, feeling it, experiencing the magic of the world around you. A gorgeous view, a heart-pumping walk. The warmth of the sun on your face, and the tangle of the wind in your hair. As well as lifting the spirits, it helped to ground you.

Her mind wound back to childhood holidays here in Northumberland all those years ago. The happy times in the no-frills, but always fun, caravan with Mum and Dad. In stark contrast, she remembered nursing her mother through those last few traumatic weeks, firstly at home and then nearer the end in the hospice. Bittersweet emotions swirled within, as a pang of grief unfurled in Cath's chest. That sense of loss was never far away when she thought about her parents.

She strolled on, finding a flattish area to perch on a rocky outcrop, and sat for a while looking out to sea. More memories . . . Cath found herself once again thinking of Matty, her first love and holiday romance. She was sweet sixteen, he was seventeen, both probably quite naïve compared to the youth of today. A lovely lad he was, good-looking with his dark wavy hair. He'd seemed so kind that week too, there was a gentleness about him. Thinking of him now made her smile. They'd spent a day here on the beach at Bamburgh, along with her sister and parents. A picnic and a game of cricket, all very innocent that day. Then, a stroll in the dunes, holding hands. A kiss . . . or three, the heady newness of it all, and a powerful teenage crush that felt very like love. Stolen moments the next day, just the two of them, and then the going home, and all the angst that followed thereafter. Those further memories shot up unbidden.

A splash of waves and a shower of salt spray took her out of her reverie. The tide must be coming back in, but she sat a while longer. She watched a pair of gulls circle above. Her thoughts moving on to The Trevor Years, the early days of love and marriage, and motherhood with Adam. Those blissful, busy, tiring years as a young mother. That all enveloping love. Being a wife, a mother, caring for them all, keeping them close and safe. Working, teaching, all those young adults she tried to coach, doing her utmost to get them to reach their potential. It had always been about others she realised . . . but what about her?

And now, what now? What came next in the life of Catherine Taylor? The pages were yet to be written. The sky above was now a watery grey-blue, and beautiful, despite the threat of the rain clouds that were beginning to swell over the sea. The breeze that whirled around her was brisk and invigorating. She didn't have all the answers, after all, she was learning how to live all over again. But she needed to look up, not down. Forward, not back . . .

Chapter 13

However hard she tried, Cath couldn't stop her old life catching up with her. Inevitably, the weekend of Helen's visit rolled around. At least the impending arrival had given Cath a new focus, filling her time with getting the house and the spare bedroom ready for its first staying visitor. She'd have much preferred to have had Adam back, or her sister Susie staying, who'd be far easier company, but as the Saturday morning approached, she found herself looking forward to seeing her old friend once more. There was a lot of catching up to do.

Helen landed in her sporty BMW, having decided to drive. She arrived with a flurry of air kisses, a waft of heady floral perfume, and a clatter of high heels. Perched on the threshold, she gave her friend a thorough lookover that resulted in a slight frown – oops, Cath remembered that she still hadn't got to a hairdresser as yet.

'Hello, there. Well, you've certainly settled into the country look well.'

Cath's smile turned into a part-grimace at the backhanded compliment. 'Well, come on in. Welcome to my new home.'

After touring the cottage, which didn't exactly take long – Helen declaring it was 'sweet and compact'– she handed over a thoughtful gift of a cream pottery jug which was actually very pretty and would suit the kitchen. Cath then helped her in with her luggage, and got her settled in the 'quaint' spare room. She let her friend know that they'd be sharing bathroom facilities; no en suites here. She saw Helen's eyebrows twitch at that.

After a lunch of poached salmon, watercress and new potatoes, served with a glass of chilled white wine, the two friends were now sat in the garden, enjoying some afternoon sunshine and a cup of Earl Grey, catching up on old times. The initial conversation and trip down memory lane weren't anywhere near as bad as Cath had feared. It touched briefly on some Trevor moments, but mostly those that involved the whole gang. There were eight of them in their regular posse; being four couples who'd got on particularly well. They'd had some fun times over the years; dinner parties, New Year's Eve nights, and when the children were younger, fireworks parties with soup and hot dogs in one of their back gardens, with the torch-and-taper-bearing dads ready to light the rockets somewhere down the far end of the lawn.

So far, they'd managed to steer clear of any in-depth infor-mation on Trevor, and that was fine by Cath, who was enjoying catching up on their grown-up children's latest activities, at uni, home and worldwide. Those same little kids who'd dashed around the gardens with their sparklers. Where had all the years gone . . . ?

The low hum of a tractor working in some nearby fields filled the air, but it wasn't too distracting; Cath was becoming used to the sounds of the countryside already. There was bird-song and the buzz of bees, too. Her garden was looking rather lovely now, with its bluebells fading and various shrubs and roses coming into bloom. The borders were full of surprises this first spring and summer of living here – thanks to Reggie and his keen gardening over the years. She had no idea what was going to pop up next. However, a new, and not so fresh, surprise was about to hit them. It was when the ladies decided the yardarm had stretched enough to pour a second glass of wine, that the offensive smell hit their nostrils.

'Bloody hell, what on earth is that stench?' Helen screwed up her face.

The hum of the tractor was closer, and so was the aroma. *Pig muck*! It had to be.

'Oh God, that is bad!' Cath felt slightly nauseous. 'I think the farmer is fertilising.'

Strong and pungent 'aroma de pig poo' hit them, and it was going nowhere fast. Ideal as a fertiliser, no doubt, but not great to sip a glass of white wine alongside.

'Sorry, Cath, but that is foul. I don't think I can stand it. Can we go inside?' Helen was up on her feet and heading for the back door as fast as she could, muttering, 'We certainly don't get any of this in Roundhay!'

Cath had a rather stronger constitution, but still, she had to agree that the smell wasn't pleasant. A day or two at the most and she knew it would pass, but for now, no more sitting in the garden, and no supper soiree for the two of them in the summerhouse either. She had considered that as a nice way to spend the evening. But having Helen here, and witnessing her already prickly approach to country life, Cath now felt glad that her converted shed would remain private, and remain as her little haven – her supper club secret.

*

Later, after quaffing far too much wine, the lid began to blow off Helen's filter, and tales of Trevor became the focus of the conversation. So here it was, the moment Cath had feared: a tiddly Helen with unrequested stories of Trevor's recent romantic antics now coming thick and fast.

She started on the new girlfriend Steph, Cath's replacement: 'Oh yes, we've met her a few times for the odd meal out . . . oh, and drinks at ours one night. Fairly attractive, just a bit younger than us, blonde, tall, an accountant.' Well, that figured, it was obviously someone he worked with. Someone who hadn't 'wasted' their maths degree on teaching – as Trevor had so often liked to remind Cath after her more stressful days in the classroom.

Then, the tales moved on to the recent waning of the romance, and then (another glass of pinot down) the lovers' tiff. *'Lovers'*, oh good lord – just picturing Trevor, with his midriff overhang, flouncing about with his bit of stuff, made her feel downright queasy. Helen continued, oblivious, telling Cath that the couple had had 'words' apparently. Trev had confessed when he was round at their place last week, that the new woman had said he was a bit . . . (*'boring'*, *'of a fuckwit'* – Cath wanted to interject) . . . *'clingy'* at times. 'So, it's not looking quite so rosy, right now. In fact, I think he might be regretting his rash move.'

Was that meant to cheer her up? Get her rushing back into her errant husband's arms? Cath found herself increasingly irritable. 'Well then, let him stew in his own mess. He certainly let me know I was surplus to requirements at the time, didn't he?' she said sourly. 'So, there's no point him running back with his tail between his legs, now it's all going tits up with the new floozie.' Cath also had had rather too much of the vino by now.

Emotions were running high, and the conversation was running away with them. 'Please, Helen, for god's sake stop going on, will you? I really *don't* want to hear any more about bloody Trevor.'

Helen was sensitive enough to look chastened. 'Sorry, Cath. I wasn't thinking. I imagined you'd want to know the latest . . . but I can see I was wrong.'

'Ah, it's not you I'm annoyed with.' Cath's tone softened. 'It's *him*. And the car crash he's made of our marriage. I thought we were good, solid. That we'd see in our old age together. But hey-ho, that wasn't to be, was it?'

'Yeah, I thought you were good together too,' Helen agreed. 'Kind of steady. Reliable. It's shaken us all up seeing what's happened. The group really doesn't feel the same.'

'Yes, I'm sure . . .' There was a pause and then Cath confessed, 'It still hurts you know. Far too much at times.'

'Of course it will. It's such early days. And I'm sorry again, for raking everything up . . .' Her friend pulled an exaggeratedly forlorn face.

'Ah, it's okay. It's Trev I need to punch, not you.' Cath gave a wry smile. She didn't need to be falling out with her old mates.

'Still friends?'

Cath nodded, quietly confirming, 'Yeah, still friends.'

'Thanks,' Helen sighed. 'And blimey, you really don't know what's around the corner in life, do you?'

'Nope.'

'Probably as well.'

'Probably.'

And they gave their wine glasses a dull clunk.

The past felt stirred and shaken.

Chapter 14

The next morning, thankfully, started more relaxed, with coffee and croissants and lighter chat, after a bit of a lie-in – and a couple of much needed paracetamols. Cath really wasn't used to drinking that much nowadays.

But then things began to shift . . .

'Oh, damn, I forgot to pack any antihistamine,' Helen announced, gesturing towards the window, the countryside around them. 'My eyes are all itchy, and I bet it's all that grass out there.'

Cath had noticed her friend's red eyes this morning, but had put it down to excessive alcohol, which after finding the empty wine bottles on the side this morning, could well be partly the cause.

'Oh, I really need some tablets. There's a shop in the village, isn't there?'

'Yes, worth a try.'

They popped on trainers, Helen's a spanking new white pair, and had a little wander to the village stores, in the fresh – or perhaps not quite so fresh – pig-muck-tainted air. The country walk Cath had imagined they might take this morning might not now go down too well. What with hay fever, white shoes, and muck-spreading smells aplenty, Cath tried to think of a Plan B.

The tinkle of the store bell, and the smiling faces of Andreas and Dan behind the counter greeted them.

'Good morning, ladies.'

'Hi, guys, this is my friend from Leeds, Helen.'

'Hello, lovely. A friend of Cath's is a friend of ours,' said Andreas with a grin.

'Welcome to our little shop, Helen. And how can we help you?' followed up Dan.

Helen briefly scanned the shelves, without success. 'Okay, so my eyes are starting to pour here, and I'm beginning to feel nasal. Where are your antihistamine tablets?'

'Sorry, my lovely, that's something we don't stock. Tried them in the past and they didn't really sell, so we had to withdraw them,' Dan explained.

Helen's eyebrows shot up angrily. 'Oh, for goodness' sake. I thought that'd be a standard.' Her tone was sharp. Cath felt a bit embarrassed.

'You'll be sure to find some over in Kirkton. There's a pharmacy there.' Andreas was trying to be helpful.

'Humph. And how far is that?'

'Oh, not far. Five miles.'

'Five miles?' Helen didn't disguise her huff. 'Cath, you'll have to take me . . . I can't cope with this all day. What with my hay fever kicking off and the stench from the fields. It really is the back of beyond here.' She rolled her eyes.

'I'm sorry. We're just a small concern, our stock is limited,' Dan tried to explain further.

Helen's response was to 'tut' heavily.

How rude. Cath, Andreas and Dan shared a look, with Cath mouthing a 'sorry' behind her old friend's head. Feeling rather awkward, and trying her best to divert Helen's grumpy attention on to something more positive, Cath moved towards the cake display – looking for a little pick-me-up treat to go with their morning coffee. After Helen's ill-mannered outburst, she also wanted to give the lads some custom.

'Cake?' Cath said in a forced cheery tone. 'These lads do the best bakes in the area by far. The moistest of sponges, Greek-style baklava, you name it.'

'Hmm, well. Won't do my thighs any good . . . but yes, why not,' Helen conceded. 'I am on holiday after all.'

Her attention was then duly diverted by the gorgeous-looking cakes (Helen had always been a big fan of an afternoon tea, Cath remembered), she and Cath each choosing a slice. As Dan carefully wrapped them, Cath enquired how the lads were getting on, and they chatted briefly about village life. Helen remained quiet, which was unusual. Cath hoped she'd bloody well cheer up soon; they had the whole day and night to fill before her return journey tomorrow.

*

The cakes – a slice of Dan's white chocolate with raspberry, and one of St Clements – went down well with their coffee back at the cottage kitchen, and the mood between the ladies lifted a bit. Cath suggested a tour of the countryside in the Mini, with a pitstop at the pharmacy at Kirkton, before heading up into the hills for some scenic views. She thought they might then cut back in a big loop via the coast.

Helen seemed to have calmed down a bit after the Kirkton stop. She sat in the passenger seat, her antihistamines now taken and a bottle of water to hand, and the conversation rolled on easily, thank heavens, much like the rolling hills around them.

They were up a narrow lane when a guy on a quad motioned them to wait, as he backed out from a muddy field entrance.

'Hold on there, lass.'

He made a few hearty whistles, and then 'baah-ing' noises could be heard which got louder, as a herd of sheep scurried and trampled their way out of the gate and up the lane ahead of them. Tens, then, it must have been hundreds, scattering giddily, some backtracking until the quad revved at them to turn them around. So many sheep with their biggish lambs, pooing merrily as they went. More and more . . . Cath was actually entranced. It was no problem really, even though they must have waited well over five minutes already. The farmer had a job to do after all.

'For Christ's sake, when are the bloody things going to stop?' Helen was pulling a face. 'Ah, look, they're shitting everywhere . . . your car's going to be in a right state. Shall we just turn around? There can't be a lot up this way, anyhow? Haven't seen a shop or a tea room in ages.'

There was in fact the most beautiful view at the top of this valley, where you could stop and see the tops of the bracken-covered Cheviot Hills one way, and turn to look over the undulating countryside towards the inkiness of the North Sea the other, but Cath didn't feel like explaining that. Helen just wouldn't get it, she could tell. So that was it, they made a U-turn and headed back.

Returning to Tilldale, Cath hoped her plan of Sunday lunch out might prove more successful. On walking into The Star Inn in the village, Helen couldn't help herself, noting rather loudly that the décor was 'a bit dated'. Yes, the bar was made of dark wood in a traditional style. And when the middle-aged sandy-bearded landlord, dressed in his well-worn country tweeds, came across to serve them with a 'Good aft'noon, ladies' and introducing himself as Bill, she saw Helen smother a chuckle at his thick Northumbrian accent. Then she muttered, not in the least subtly, 'Blimey, he looks like something out of *Last of the Summer Wine.*'

Bloody hell, Cath wanted to be accepted as part of this village, not be seen to be sniggering at the locals. The tension she had been feeling went up a notch. It was like everything Helen said or did was intended to put a nail into her new life, every comment feeling like a little dig at her. She was trying to stay patient, but she wasn't quite sure what was going on. After all, the two of them used to get on okay back in Roundhay. It was like her old life was clashing with the new.

They chose a table in the bay window, and ordered the Sunday roast and a couple of glasses of Merlot.

'Well, that was an eventful morning . . .' Cath was thinking of the sheep and the stressful village shop visit, saying the words rather tongue in cheek.

'Well, nothing much has happened really, has it? We trooped off into the middle of nowhere and got stuck behind a herd of sheep.'

'Well, if you look at it that way . . .' Cath suddenly felt extremely tired. How many more hours of this were left? She took a sneaky glance at her watch: 1:15 p.m. Still another evening at home to fill – too many hours by far. She sipped her wine and gazed out of the window at the cottages opposite, unable to feign interest in conversation any longer.

The food came fifteen minutes later, and was delicious. A tasty roast beef dinner that hit the spot, with crispy Yorkshire puddings and veggies aplenty, served by a friendly waitress.

'So, this must be the only place you've got to eat out then? It's all right, I suppose. Food's okay, but the décor, well, it's so back in time. I feel like I've re-entered my childhood in the Yorkshire Dales.' Helen was harking back to that again.

'It's a traditional country pub, Helen, there's no need for it to look like a city bistro. The staff are great, and the food's more than okay, it's bloody lovely,' Cath pointed out, before tucking into a crispy roast potato dripping in gorgeous gravy. She found herself sticking up for her little village and its pub.

The pair then ate in silence for a while, the air crackling with tension between them.

*

Later, back at the cottage, things came to a head.

'Well, you are a bit reclusive, here. The village is so remote.' Helen was off again.

'That's exactly what I wanted, Helen. It's how I like it. It's beautiful here . . . and it's quiet.' She needed that quiet life, that time away from stress and work and feckless husbands.

'Oh, I'm sure the novelty will wear off soon enough . . .'

'*Why*? Why should it? I chose this, I wanted a change. I was sick of life down in Leeds. There's not only one way to live, Helen.'

Helen looked a bit shocked. 'Well, I'll be telling the gang all about my stay. I'm meeting up with the girls on Tuesday, actually. Coffee at Hugo's in town.'

Oh yes, the latest 'ladies who lunch' venue. Cath had heard about it; it was just about to open when she'd left. That get-together must have been planned in advance, Cath mused grouchily, Helen's opportunity to give a full report on Cath and her new surroundings.

'Oh yes, go ahead. Feel free to run me and my little rural life down,' Cath hissed.

'What? Of course, I won't be . . .'

'Well, that's all you've been bloody well doing since you got here.'

'I haven't.' She sounded so indignant, which was laughable.

'You bloody well have . . . first the country smells, then the lads not having antihistamine, as though that was the crime of the century. The farmers around here aren't allowed to move their sheep according to you . . . and the country pub is too old-fashioned. Well, that's exactly what it's meant to be.' Cath was sick of her going on.

Helen just glared at her.

Cath bit back once more. 'Well, I don't suppose you'll be wanting to stay here again then. And you know what, that's fine by me.'

This sent Helen into even more of a tizz, announcing, 'Well, I may as well go home now, if you feel like that!'

Cath took stock, having said her bit, and merely looked at her friend calmly, 'You can't.'

'What do you mean? Are you going to hold me here against my will?'

Cath couldn't help but chuckle at Helen's indignation.

'What?'

'Helen, you've already had two glasses of Merlot and a Prosecco . . .'

'Oh.' She let the facts sink in – driving right now was not an option. 'S-sugar.'

There was an awkward silence for a few heavy moments.

'Come on, I'll make us a coffee.' Cath felt calmer. She'd said her piece, sticking up for her village and new, if still slightly tentative, friends, but she wasn't going to stew on it. And, she had a feeling there was more to this than Helen was letting on.

She gave her friend a bit of space to visit the upstairs bathroom while preparing a cafetière of coffee. Helen came down looking a little chastened.

'I-I'm sorry . . . for flying off the handle with you. You're just trying your best to settle in here, aren't you?'

'Yeah,' Cath responded. 'Look, Helen, is everything okay with you? It's just ever since you got here, you just seem so . . . prickly.'

'I'm fine . . .'

The two women looked at each other.

'Ah, well, I don't know. It just feels all wrong. You being here. Our group's all in pieces, back home . . . and everything's the same old . . . but then it's not, not anymore. You've gone . . . and the kids are grown up and gone . . .' Helen looked deflated.

'Empty nest syndrome hitting you, too?' Cath asked empathetically.

'God, yes. Nothing's the same anymore, is it? And then there's the getting old . . . the wrinkles. And I can't even laugh without peeing a bit these days.'

They both started chuckling then.

'Don't bloody start me off.'

But that just made them laugh louder.

'I actually don't think I could cope with country life, though.' She paused, as if thinking. 'But you know what, good on you for giving it a try. For going out there, after everything you've had to contend with, and shaking things up.'

'Thanks.'

At last, they'd been able to be honest. She hadn't wanted Helen to leave here in a huff. The change had hit her old friendship group too. It was inevitable really. The bomb had ricocheted far further than Cath had first imagined.

Since leaving Roundhay, and in those few weeks of moving on and beginning to find her feet in a quieter rural world, distance and time had made her see her old friends and relationships differently too. She'd heard enough about Trevor and his antics last night, plus the social gatherings in suburbia, to make her head spin. Helen would be setting off in the morning. And yes, whilst she'd keep in touch with the old gang, she found she didn't need that social group in the same way anymore. It belonged to a different life, a different Cath.

Her old life, or more so, some of the people in it, didn't seem to fit all that well with this new one. But it didn't mean she had to cut them off totally, either. In time she might reconnect. But for now, there was no rush for that.

And she realised that that was okay. Changes were afoot, and she was open to that. No point wallowing in the past. Something old, something new . . .

Chapter 15

Helen had taken flight the next morning, back to her suburban nest. Cath was relieved that they had at least smoothed out some of the weekend's furrows between them, and they had left things on a polite footing for the future, both coming to an understanding that they were in very different places right now.

Back at the shop later that morning, Dan and Andreas were full of apologies.

'Morning, Cath.'

'Hi, lads.'

'Oh, I'm so sorry we couldn't help your friend with her medication yesterday.' Dan looked concerned.

'Ah, don't worry, Dan, it's no problem. You've probably done me a bit of a favour, actually. I have a feeling my friend Helen won't be rushing back to the country life, or my cottage, any time very soon.' She gave a knowing grin. 'And you know what . . . I think I've realised that's not such a bad thing. We get on fine to be fair, but she's a bit of a blast from the past. And obviously very much a townie.'

'Yeah, she did seem rather, how can I put it, *full-on*.'

'Demanding,' added Andreas.

'Hah, don't I know it.' Even though they'd accepted their

differences, and had their heart-to-heart last night, Cath began to wonder what tales of village life and 'country Cath' Helen would now be going back with. What gossipy news was being passed back to Trevor and the old crew? And then she realised that she didn't particularly care, which was a very satisfactory revelation indeed.

'Well, sounds like it's been a stressful visit for you. Andreas, this is a sure sign that Cath is in need of some suppertime solace . . . a further supper soiree in fact.'

'Oh, yes, agreed. You made us so welcome the other evening. We had a truly wonderful time. And Dan's right, we *must* arrange another supper club soon. We'll host this time. It'll give us a chance to pamper you.'

'Sounds perfect. Just let me know when . . .' Cath found herself smiling, delighted that their supper group was going to continue.

'Same old gang?' asked Andreas. 'Shall we ask Nikki and Will again? It seemed to work well, didn't it?'

Cath was nodding. They had all got on fine. And she had no real reason not to invite Will. Just because they'd had the car park bump, and the fact he looked a bit like the lead singer in Wet Wet Wet, which had set her slightly off kilter. And, how did you start to explain that?!

'Well, we'll not get away with not asking Nikki,' added Dan, smiling. 'She's desperate to get out and about again. She was asking about a supper re-run just yesterday when she called in, in fact.'

Cath browsed the shelves as they chatted, choosing some fresh fruit and veg, and a crusty baguette, along with a chunk of local Doddington Dairy cheese, to make some cheese and chutney sandwiches for lunch. At the counter, Andreas was already planning. 'So, how does a week's time sound? Dan, get the diary and we'll check dates with you now, Cath.'

'Okay. Well, yes, great.' Cath really didn't need to check hers; other than a dentist's appointment and her tutoring, she didn't really have anything else to work around. Christ, she *was* close to being a recluse. Perhaps Helen did have a point . . . not that she'd have admitted that to her.

'Now then, give us a couple of days that suit you best, and we can moot them to the rest of the gang.'

*

Messages had been sent, and a supper soiree 'chez Andreas and Dan' was arranged for early June, just a week away. Andreas was to be lead chef, apparently, and was buzzing about planning his recipes and tempting tipples. It was going to be 'a night to remember' with a Greek Cypriot theme, so Dan enlightened Cath in the shop a couple of days later. And, except for her mixed feelings about Will, which she'd have to learn to live with or risk spoiling the new friendship group, Cath couldn't wait.

*

There was a bicycle perched outside the village shop, later that week, as Cath was about to head in. Out came Will, *oh*, in full Lycra, with a takeaway coffee to hand. She couldn't help but notice his toned muscles through the clingy material, especially those in the upper thigh area – well-defined cyclist's muscles.

She swiftly lifted her gaze. 'Oh . . . hi.' Her throat felt dry all of a sudden.

'Hey, Cath. Nice to see you. How are things?'

'Good . . . yep . . . fine.' It was odd that Mr Grumpy was now Mr Chatty . . . and jeez, Mr Lycra. She didn't know quite where to look.

'I hear we're on for another supper evening. The lads have just been filling me in on all the details. Sounds like we're going to get spoilt.'

'Yeah.'

'Mind you, you did an amazing job at yours that evening, too.'

'Yes . . . thanks.' *Cat got your tongue*, echoed within her mind. One of her gran's old sayings. But she was finding it very difficult to concentrate and make conversation. 'So, you're off cycling,' she managed.

'Yep, heading for the hills today. Give these muscles a good workout.'

'Right . . . ah, good.'

'Have you ever cycled?'

'No, not really, probably not since I was a teenager, anyhow.'

'You'll have to give it a try some time.'

'Yeah, maybe.' Did he mean cycling with him? Or just a generalised comment? The fact that she didn't have a bike might be a bit of an issue, she mused, but she didn't bother going into that.

'Right, well I'm looking forward to the next supper night.' He smiled.

'Yeah, me too.'

'Catch you soon.' He downed his coffee and popped the

cardboard cup in the bin. Then off he whizzed, leaving her rather aflutter.

She gave herself a few seconds to settle, before going on in for her small shopping list of fresh bread, eggs and veggies.

Dan greeted her as she entered the shop, with a 'Morning' and some brief chit-chat.

'And where's Andreas this morning?' Cath asked after picking up a gorgeous-smelling crusty fresh sourdough.

'Up in the flat . . . I can't keep him out of the kitchen just now. He's been baking and prepping for Thursday night already. You'd think he was in the final of *MasterChef*, or something.' He gave a wry smile.

There was a creak of footsteps on the wooden stairs, and a call of, 'Daniel, I can hear you . . . stop spinning tales.' Andreas then appeared, in his naked-Greek-statue apron, with a 'Morning, Cath.'

She couldn't help but chuckle.

Andreas looked down at his torso area with a smile, realising what he was still wearing. 'Oh, it helps get me in the mood.'

'I'm still not sure what for . . .' Dan quipped cheekily.

Andreas just shook his head with a grin. 'Greek food and culture. Anyhow, it's all in the planning. I like to be a step ahead. Mezzes don't make themselves you know . . .' He gave Cath a wink.

'I'm so looking forward to it, it sounds wonderful.' Cath felt lifted by their cheery banter.

'We're very much looking forward to having you all,' said Dan. 'It's been a while since we entertained. I've missed it.'

'Life's been super busy, and somehow you don't get around

to organising things. But we always used to love having people around. Foodie evenings are such fun,' added Andreas.

That was how Cath had always felt about hosting, too. Looking after people, be it friends or family. The pleasure at watching them enjoy the food you'd made, listening to the chatter around the table, getting people together. Making new friendships too. And though (especially after seeing him Lycra-clad) she was a little unsettled at the thought of spending time with Will again, she was sure this next supper event was going to be a lovely get-together and a good night. Andreas and Dan were certainly going all out to make it so, by the sounds of it.

*

The day of the second supper event came around, and Cath found herself humming in the kitchen whilst making her morning coffee. She was planning on doing a bit of gardening, having made an excursion to the local garden centre yesterday. She'd bought compost, busy lizzie flowers and some herb plants, ready to fill some pots that were left on her patio: including a curly parsley, some mint, a thyme plant, plus a fragrant lavender, hoping to attract the bees. Once the herbs had settled and were hopefully flourishing, they'd be ideal to cook with, adding to the prolific sage and rosemary bushes that Reggie had left behind too.

Her mobile sprang to life, and there was Dan on the phone. 'Oh, Cath, I'm so sorry we're to going to have to cancel, my love.' He sounded totally deflated.

'Oh, is everything all right?'

'No, not really, petal. It's Andreas's mother, Maria, she's had a nasty turn. They've had to take her into hospital down in Newcastle. We're off right now to see how she's doing. I can't see us getting back for several hours. And well . . .'

'Oh goodness. Of course, and no worries about the supper at all. Another time. Send Andreas my love . . . and if there's anything I can do . . . ?'

'Thank you. I've managed to get hold of Will, but Nikki's not answering, if you can perhaps check she's got our message a little later on. Don't want her turning up and no one's there.'

'Yes, of course. If you can forward me her number, I'll try again for you. You get away . . . and take care both. Oh crikey, I hope Maria is okay.'

'Thanks.'

The poor things. Cath ended the call, remembering well the difficult time spent nursing her mother through the final stages of her bowel cancer, alongside the help of the hospice care. The worry, and yet trying to hide that gnawing stress as she'd held her mum's aged hand, trying so hard to give a little light and cheer to those final days. Reminiscing about precious shared family memories; a time to laugh a little, to smile, and then privately a time to cry.

*

A short while later, the doorbell went, and there was Andreas on the step. 'We're on our way, but you may as well have this. It's all prepared, ready to pop in the oven. Twenty minutes. It's the starter. Seemed a shame to waste it.' Bless him, he looked pale and drawn, not himself at all.

'Ah, thank you. But you shouldn't be worrying about that now. Get yourselves away.'

'We are. We're off . . . right now.'

'Aw, take care.' Cath managed a brief one-armed hug, holding the dish in the other hand. 'Now go.'

Andreas turned and nipped back to the car, where Dan was waiting in the driving seat, the engine still running. They both gave a little wave as they left, moving off with a rev of acceleration.

She watched them go, feeling a lump rise in her throat. Daft man, thinking of her and the supper group in the midst of his crisis, when he could have just popped the starter in the fridge. But it was a lovely gesture. She peered under the silver foil lid to find what looked like a feta bake that had been drizzled with some gorgeous-smelling oils and . . . she sniffed again, the sweet aroma of honey. Strands of fragrant rosemary were there too. With tears in her eyes, she wondered if it was a dish that Maria might have once cooked for Andreas and her family.

Chapter 16

'Hi, Nikki. Have you heard from Dan and Andreas?'

'Ah no, I've been out, doing my cleaning jobs and then it was straight into Hamish's football practice. My feet have hardly touched the ground. Jeez, am I looking forward to tonight.'

'Well, that's just it. There isn't going to be a tonight.'

'Oh . . . ?'

'It's Maria, Andreas's mum. She's been rushed into hospital, bless her. The lads have followed her down.'

'Oh, I see. Poor Maria, oh, and the boys will be so worried.'

'Yeah.'

'Ah, what a shame all round. Of course, I'm gutted for them. I really hope she'll be okay. But boy, was I ready for an evening off. I've got Kev all lined up looking after the kids and everything. He's quite happy for a change, too, as there's some big footie match on the telly, and he's letting Hamish stay up with him, once the other two have gone to bed.'

Cath was at a loose end herself. Hmm, and she did have the wonderful Greek feta bake all ready to go . . .

'Well, I suppose I could do something here . . .' The idea was forming as she said the words. Just an easy supper. The feta dish, and then some kind of simple-to-make main. She must have something she could concoct from the contents of her fridge and freezer. A girlie night in, just her and Nikki, perhaps? But then she thought of Will, all on his own up the street, missing out on his supper night too. It didn't seem fair. 'You don't happen to have Will's number, do you? I mean, it'll just be something casual . . .'

She didn't give herself time to think about whether it was a good idea to have 'Marti Pellow' around, even after the way he'd looked in that Lycra. She just dived in, made the call, and that was that. Will said he'd 'love to come along', Nikki was delighted, and supper at Cath's Round Two was on.

*

After launching in with her last-minute invite, Cath had only a couple of hours to get organised. Not particularly wanting to get in the car for a trip to the shops – the village stores of course being closed – she rummaged in the freezer to see what foodie inspirations she might find. A pack of minced beef, one chicken breast, some pitta breads. There were plenty of veggies in the pantry, including potatoes, and a bag of salad leaves in the fridge. Dried herbs and spices, lots of those to hand in the cupboard, and a clove of fresh garlic. She had Reggie's rosemary plant in the garden, too.

She suddenly felt like she was on that programme *Ready, Steady, Cook*, having been given several ingredients and left to her own devices to create a masterpiece in an hour. It was all adding up to . . . ta-dah . . . koftas. Spiced minced beef koftas with salad and grilled veggies all in a pitta wrap. Wow, she'd even impressed herself. She could prepare the koftas this afternoon and griddle them later once the guests were here, served with a Mediterranean-style veggie oven bake on the side. Hmm, the only other thing she might need was a dip. Ah hah, there was her fresh mint recently planted, she could take a few sprigs off that, and she had natural yoghurt in the fridge that she liked to have with honey for breakfast. That was supper sorted, then!

Checking her phone app, she saw that the weather forecast was a bit mixed. Once again, they were due sunshine and showers, and the temperature was relatively cool for June. Would the shed work this time? It was indeed pretty up there and a unique space. She'd worked so hard on revamping it, too. Okay, a plan was forming: early evening drinks at the summerhouse, unless it was pouring it down as the duo arrived, and then she'd see how things went. With it just being the three of them, her kitchen-diner would work fine to eat in, too. She took another look at the gathering clouds and decided to prepare both areas, just in case. She really hoped Andreas and Dan were getting on okay at the hospital, and sent a brief message wishing them and Maria well. Saying she was thinking of them, and again, offering to help where she could.

In the midst of setting up the garden shed for drinks and nibbles, the phone in her pocket started vibrating.

'Hiya, Mum.'

Ah, wow. 'Hey, Adam. How are you, my love?' Seeing her son again, even if it was via a WhatsApp video call from the other side of the world, never failed to make her heart swell.

'Great, yeah, all cool here. I'm in Thailand, well, on the island of Koh Samui actually – really chilled vibe. Loving it.'

'Oh, it sounds lovely. Beautiful beaches, I bet?'

'Yeah, golden sands and warm blue sea. Island life is pretty cool. Hey, you'll never guess what we saw on the golf course yesterday. A massive lizard, I mean like mammoth. Some kind of minotaur – nah, not minotaur, though that thing was pretty scary too, a monitor lizard. Shit, you wouldn't wanna upset him. He was as big as a croc. Epic. I'll send you a pic.'

'Sounds frightening.'

'He looked it, but I think they're pretty chilled as long as you don't go too near.'

'Amazing.' She was glad her son was making the most of his travels. Life was full of adventures, new places, people, cultures. Perhaps she ought to get her own travelling shoes back on soon.

'Mu-um.' Adam's tone became more serious. 'Is Dad okay? It's just . . . he was on the phone last night, and well, he didn't sound right. Bit low, I think.'

So, the rose-tinted glasses were getting steamed up, were they? It all added up with what Helen had been telling her.

'Well, we don't exactly have many cosy chats these days, Adam. The only conversations we've had lately are about financial or legal matters.'

'Ah, yeah. I suppose . . .'

'But from what I gather from Helen – you know, our old friends from down the road. She stayed over last weekend – from what I heard, I don't think things are going so well with the new woman.'

'Yeah, Steph. That makes sense then . . .'

Cath took a breath. He knew her evidently. Had they all been out for a cosy meal at some point? A getting-to-know-you-drink before he'd headed off on his travels? Even though Adam was an adult himself, and she might have guessed that'd happen, the thought of the three of them palling up made her feel awfully raw.

'He made his bed . . .' *With his bloody floozie*, Cath didn't add, trying hard not to draw her son into her negative emotions. He shouldn't have to feel he needed to take sides.

'Yep, I know how much he hurt you, Mum.'

'Well, it's all water under the bridge . . .' She was reverting to clichés, but Cath really didn't want the conversation to turn dour, not when he was calling her from the other side of the world. 'So where to next? Are you staying in Asia?' She switched the subject.

'Maybe another week or two tops . . . want to see Hong Kong. And then, I have to confess the funds are running low, so it'll soon be time to book a flight back to the UK.' His voice dipped as though he was reluctant to return, to leave the adventures behind. The world of work and a sensible life loomed for him on an English horizon.

'Oh well, it'll be wonderful to see you again.'

'Yeah, you too, Mum. Right, better go, Carl's just got me a beer, and in this heat, it'll be warm before I know it.'

'Hah, get your priorities right, son.' Cath laughed. 'No worries, you enjoy it. Look forward to seeing you soon.'

'You too. Love you, Mum.'

'Love you. Cheers. Oh, and send me some pics. Including that minotaur.'

He gave a thumbs up along with a big grin, scanning his phone camera across the bay to show her the scene of the palm-thatched-roof bar and a sun-glinting azure sea. A little piece of paradise. Then, he disappeared from the screen. Thousands of miles away, and yet always held close in her heart.

Chapter 17

It was now only a half hour to go until 7 p.m. and the arrival of her guests. And oh, what about a drink for their arrival? In light of Dan and Andreas's bad news, she certainly didn't want it to feel like a party, more a supportive gathering. Perhaps a good old G&T would be nice to start – she still had a third of a bottle in her cabinet, left from the last supper club.

She had also popped a bottle of sauvignon in the fridge earlier. Luckily, she kept a little stash of 'emergency' wine in her rack. A glass or two had helped get her through some lonely evenings over the past few months. It was heartwarming that she now had friends to share those bottles with, she mused, with a small smile.

Hi-ball glasses were placed on the kitchen side, lemon slices cut, and ice in the freezer. In the garden, the shed doors were opened, mix-and-match chairs at the ready, and the table set out with two green-glass tealight holders and a pretty patterned bowl filled with crisps. Cath found herself hovering, waiting for the doorbell to ring. Who would be first, she wondered. And an image popped to mind . . . *ah, for goodness' sake, stop thinking about those tightly toned muscles.*

It wasn't long before her question was answered. She

responded to the doorbell's chime to find Will standing there, thankfully in jeans and a shirt, with a small bunch of yellow and pink carnations, a bottle of red, and a smile. Oh, and those gentle hazel-brown eyes fixed right on her, beneath the salt-and-pepper-edged dark hair. 'Thanks so much for organising this last minute.'

'You're very welcome. And thank you, these are lovely.' She took the colourful bouquet.

'Have you heard anything from the lads? About Andreas's mother?'

'Yes, I had a brief message back, saying that she was having some tests and that she was stable.'

'Oh, well that's reasonable news at least. Such a worry.'

'Yeah, it is. Oh, and come on in . . . sorry, we're still stood on the step.'

He followed her through to the little kitchen. Just the two of them for now. He was wearing smart dark-denim jeans and a navy-and-white paisley patterned shirt. It suited him. Cath found herself feeling awfully warm, and she busied herself with finding a vase to pop the flowers in. What was the matter with her?

'A G&T, or would you rather a glass of wine?' she offered.

'A gin would be lovely, thanks.'

She clinked some ice cubes into two of the glasses. But, before she had a chance to pour it, the doorbell was off again – phew, saved by the bell. 'Oh, that must be Nikki. Won't be a mo.'

'Shall I do the honours?' Will gestured towards the gin bottle.

'That'd be great, thanks.'

'I'd better make it three.' Even with her back turned she could tell from his tone that he was smiling. 'Nikki's bound to want one.'

'Helloo!' There she was, a blast of brightness in a vivid yellow polka-dot top and denim three-quarter jeans. 'Boy, am I ready for this. Full on at work, craziness at home as per usual, but I'm away, a three-hour window just to be me. Thank you so much for stepping in, Cath.'

'It's fine, no problem at all.'

'Sorry, I didn't have time to make anything, but I picked up a box of chocolate truffles on my way back from Alnwick – good old M&S.'

'Perfect, they'll be wonderful after the meal with a nice coffee.'

'Gin's ready.' There was Will with three tall glasses that were filled and lightly fizzing.

'Thank you. Cheers, my lovelies.' Nikki took one.

'Cheers.'

'Chin-chin.' Cath smiled. 'And here's to Andreas's mum getting better very soon.'

'Absolutely. Get well soon, Maria.' Will lifted his glass.

'She's such a lovely lady,' Nikki said. 'I met her in the village a while back. The boys had her out to lunch at The Star. Bit of a character, she was. She was enjoying bossing Andreas about, as I remember. He was trying to stop her having an extra glass of wine, something to do with her meds, and she was having none of it.'

'Hah, I like the sound of her. Fingers crossed that all is well.'

'Yeah, absolutely.'

'Ooh, are we up in the shed? I loved it there last time,' asked

Nikki, glancing up the garden, as the trio stood chatting in the kitchen.

'If you'd like to be, yeah. I've set it up for us, just in case.'

'Ah, yes, please. It was so gorgeous. I still can't believe how you've transformed it. Plus, up there, you get a view across the hills, as well as your lovely garden.'

'And the evening sun's on it for now, too,' added Will, gazing out of the back door. 'May as well make the most of it.'

There was in fact quite a lot of grey cloud bubbling up as well as that golden glimpse of sunshine, but Cath was more than happy to head up there. With a bowl of nibbles to hand, she led the way.

'So, how's everyone's week been so far?' Cath started the conversational ball rolling as they took up their seats near the open summerhouse doors. 'Sounds like you've had a busy one, Nikki.'

'Don't I always . . . What's gone on this week? There's always some caper. Oh, yes, Mrs Douglas's cat got stuck up a tree in her garden. The old dear was all stressed about it. So, there's me wobbling on stepladders trying to get the little bugger down – for forty bloody minutes, no less. Not a chance, he just kept going further up. Then, when I gave up, ready to crack on with the cleaning I was meant to be doing, he climbed down himself. I'm sure he was smirking at me as he waltzed back into the house, tail and head held high.'

Cath and Will were chuckling. Nikki's life always seemed to be full of drama, and she had a great way of telling a tale.

'Mine was a bit quieter than that,' added Will. 'Steady away at the cycle shop. Did a coastal run, then went out on the bikes, fifty miles with a mate. And yesterday, I went off for a bit of a hike in the hills. It was stunning up there.'

Blimey, he really was a bit of an action man. *Don't think of the Lycra* . . .

'Yeah, I love the walking around here, too,' added Cath. 'The countryside is so beautiful.'

'Hah, no need for all that huffing and puffing. I do enough of all that at work. It's lovely just sitting here.' Nikki stretched her legs out, lifting her face to the evening sun. 'Your cottage is so peaceful.'

'Yes, it's really beginning to feel like home.' And it was, Cath realised with a glow.

'That's good. Oh, by the way, you two, would you mind if I invited my niece along if we had another supper night . . . if I did it at mine?'

'Of course not. The more the merrier,' said Cath.

'She's a bit younger than us lot, only seventeen, and she adores cooking. Told me she wants to be a chef one day. A pastry chef actually. She loves watching all the cookery programmes. *Bake Off* and *MasterChef* are her favourites. In fact, I'm hoping she might come up with some patisserie style puds for us all. There's a method in my madness.' Nikki winked.

'Sounds great,' added Will. 'She's just a little younger than my daughters. A great age, the whole world's ahead of them.'

'Yes, all those dreams and good times ahead,' added Cath rather nostalgically, unable to stop herself thinking, *before it all goes wrong.*

'It's a confusing time too, mind. So many choices and pressures,' expanded Nikki.

'Yes, you're right, it can be.' Cath used to love chatting with her pupils at school, guiding them where appropriate. So many paths to choose, and so easy, seemingly, to get it wrong, but every child, every person was different. You just had to try to make the best decisions you could, once you'd taken everything into consideration. Better to take a chance than miss out on an opportunity in life. Even the failing was a lesson in itself, that's what she told her students – you could always learn and take something forward from that.

'That's the thing. Her parents – my brother Jason and his wife – well, they aren't too keen on her going down the catering route. She's a bright girl, and I think they're pushing hard for her to take up a traditional university place, something like a Geography or an English degree – those are her other A Level subjects. I've heard they're at loggerheads, just now. I think she might need a bit of moral support.'

'We can certainly provide that,' added Will.

'And I've had lots of experience with youngsters in my teaching role. Our supper group might be a nice space for her to try out her cooking skills, and also to take a bit of time out. That's important too. A Levels can be a really stressful time.'

'Aw, thanks, guys, that sounds brilliant.'

They sat for a while longer, enjoying the evening sunshine and sipping refreshing gin, continuing to chat about their prospective weeks so far.

'Right, well, I just need to nip back to the house to get the starter ready.' Cath was getting up on her feet. 'Lovely Andreas dropped in the most amazing feta dish that he'd prepared for us. It just takes a short while in the oven, so I won't be long. Another gin, guys? Or are you ready for a glass of wine? I can bring up a bottle of white if you like and then one of you can do the honours.'

'Wine sounds good.' Nikki was settled in to her chair with a tired but relaxed smile.

'Yep, and I'll come down and fetch it. No need to be dashing around for us. We can help,' offered Will thoughtfully, those meltingly dark eyes fixed on hers.

'Ah, thank you.'

He followed her down the slightly rickety paved steps. 'It's great of you to step in this evening, Cath. But I hope we've not put too much on you.'

'Honestly, it's fine. It's nice to have company . . . and well, I was really looking forward to this evening, getting together again. Shame for the lads, and the circumstances of course, but we'll have to do something special for them another time.'

'Yeah, we will. Andreas and Dan are such fun . . . and they're so kind, too. Honestly, they try and look after everyone in the village, where they can. That little shop is more than just a store, it's a kind of community hub.' He took a slow breath and looked a bit wistful.

'Oh yes, I've got that impression already.'

'I'd love to be able to thank them by hosting a meal. I just wish my cooking skills were up to scratch. I'm not sure if I can match any of this . . .' He gestured at the food already prepped and on the side. 'Hah, we might have to go to the pub when it's my turn. Probably be the safest option . . .'

Cath looked up. He really did seem a nice guy, despite her early misgivings. 'And if so, I'm sure that would be lovely, too. But cooking wise, it's all about keeping it simple and using good ingredients, nothing too fancy. But hey, if you'd like any lessons . . .' The words were out before she'd even had time to think about it, oops. An image rose of her and Will all cosy in her galley kitchen cooking together. And why did that suddenly make her blush? It wasn't as though there was anything at all between them. She was still in her no-go relationship-free zone. Far too problematic.

'Ah, well, one day I might just have to take you up on that.' Will's smile was warm, yet there was a flicker of lingering sadness in his eyes.

And that touched her heart, too. The poor guy must have had a hell of a lot to deal with losing his wife. The cooking offer, well, it was just a friend helping out a friend after all, Cath told herself. But why was she feeling a bit flustered?

*

After opening the bottle of chilled white wine, and passing it to Will to take back up to the summerhouse, Cath popped a sourdough baguette to warm in the oven beside the feta bake.

That's when the doorbell went. Oh, had the lads managed to get away early? Perhaps visiting hours were over or something? Hopefully, it might mean that Maria was suddenly better and had been let out quickly.

Cath nipped to the door to find out . . . and there, stood facing her, was not at all who she'd imagined.

Chapter 18

'What on earth are you doing here?' Cath's mouth gaped open. It was the last person she expected to find on her doorstep.

'Just thought I'd drop by.' He sounded so damned casual.

'Trevor, you live two and a half hours away.' *What the hell?!*

Out of the blue, and right in the middle of her supper do, her bloody ex had decided to turn up! It was seven-thirty at night. What was going on?

'Uhm, well, I'm busy. I've got friends around. You haven't even called . . . to let me know you were coming or anything.' She was flabbergasted.

'Yes, sorry. It was all a bit last minute. Impulsive . . .'

Since when had Trevor been impulsive? Well, certainly not with her, anyhow. But here he was.

'Well, I suppose you'd better come in . . . for a minute.' What the heck was she meant to do with him now? She found herself feeling irritable. All those times, early on, when she'd desperately wanted him to turn up to say he was sorry, that he'd got it all wrong. But not now . . . not when she had a supper party on the go, and certainly not when her world was just starting to turn around.

He trailed after her to the kitchen like a spectre, looking

a bit dishevelled and downtrodden. His normally trimmed dark hair – he'd somehow managed to avoid many greys as yet – lay lank and slightly straggly. 'Ooh, something smells good,' he perked up.

It did indeed; the feta, honey and rosemary aromas were drifting from the oven. Oh yes, the arrogant git would be inviting himself for dinner next. Well, *that* was so not going to happen. He couldn't just turn up like this.

'Like I said, I'm busy,' Cath repeated, 'I've got friends here for supper.'

'Oh, I was hoping we could chat. Have a bit of a catch-up.'

'Oh, finally . . . when it suits you. You decide to turn up out of the bloody blue, and want a nice cosy chat. Well, now is not convenient.'

'I'm sorry, Cath, really I am . . . I just felt I had to come, to see you, explain a few things.'

She turned down the oven with a simmering sigh. She'd give him a few minutes and that was it; he'd evidently driven a long distance. But there was no way she was letting him get too comfy here. If he really wanted to talk things over, it could wait until tomorrow.

And it felt wrong, him stood in her cottage kitchen. This was her little haven. *Her* new start.

But he was waiting, in beige chinos and a work shirt she recognised, having ironed it dozens of times, sort of hang-dog style. 'Just a few minutes?'

All of their past and her present stood clashing in that kitchen. He didn't deserve any of her bloody time after the way he'd behaved, how he'd let her down. But, a little voice in her head reminded her, he was the father of her son, after all.

That they'd need to keep in touch for Adam's sake at least, to be polite and discuss ongoing matters relating to him.

Oh, bugger it, she'd let him have a few minutes, and that was it. And then she'd 'about turn' him and shove him back out of her kitchen and her cottage. Hopefully, before Nikki and Will realised that he was even here.

'Okay, five minutes and that's it. So, why are you here, Trev?' Her tone was short.

'There are some things we need to run over. And well, I thought it might be easier in person. It's been too long, Cath. I hoped we could stay friends, at least.'

'Well, it was you who started this whole fucking chain of events.' Her voice was terse. She didn't usually use the 'f' word but she couldn't help herself. There was so much more that she could say, but Cath really didn't want to dredge this all up. 'I can't do this right now, Trevor. I have company. I'm in the middle of cooking dinner. And, you should have bloody well let me know you were going to turn up . . . at least have had the decency to ask if it was okay? What the hell were you thinking? Did you imagine I was sat here on my own pining for you?'

'No, of course not.'

She could feel her cheeks flushing, anger brewing within. She was not going to let him take the piss out of her again. Not now. Not ever. She was going to get the upper hand here and set things straight from the start. 'And where are you meant to be staying tonight? It certainly isn't going to be here. There's a good pub and a couple of B&Bs in the village.' She needed to make things crystal clear. He'd made his bed, and he absolutely wasn't going to be able to come back to lie in hers, not even the one in the spare room.

'Yeah, of course, I'll sort something out accommodation-wise. No worries. But crikey, that does smell good whatever's in the oven. I am really hungry, it's been a long drive, and I didn't have time for anything earlier.'

Wow, the audacity of the man. If it hadn't been Andreas's gorgeous food in the oven, she'd love to have got it out and tipped it right over her soon-to-be ex-husband's head.

The air in the kitchen felt like it could crackle with static.

'Oh hi.' Will appeared, stepping into the back door from the garden. He took in the surprise extra guest. 'Ah, just thought I'd pop down and see if you needed a hand with anything. As you seemed to be taking a while.'

'Well, yes, I have an unexpected visitor.'

'Oh, joining us for supper?' Will asked innocently.

'Ah . . . well.' No, was on the tip of her tongue, but she didn't get a chance to get it out.

Before she knew it, Will added politely, 'I'm sure there'll be plenty to go around.'

She flashed her eyes at Will in warning, but it was too late. Trevor was on to it. 'Well, if it's all right with Cath? Yeah, I'd love to . . .'

Grrrrr! Cath sighed aloud, dammit, it would seem rude to say no now. Mr Grumpy Will was being so nice!

There were a few seconds of uncomfortable silence, with both men looking at her, then she conceded with an 'O-kay, you can have some supper, but that's it.' She glared at Trevor as she added, 'And you'd better get on to the pub right away and sort out your accommodation, or else you'll be sleeping in the car.'

Will realised his error, mouthing a 'sorry' as he pulled an apologetic face from behind Trevor's head.

'Will, meet Trevor, my *ex*,' she emphasised the word with a slight hiss, 'husband.'

'Right, I see. Well, hi.' He sounded rather awkward.

Jeez, this was going to be some night.

'I'll just nip back up to Nikki, then,' Will said, ready to make a swift exit from the emotionally laden kitchen. 'Anything you need me to take up?'

Cath took out the warmed bread, added a knife and butter to the board, and passed it to him with a 'Thanks. I'll be there shortly with the starter. Help yourselves to the wine in the meantime.'

Wine, she needed more wine. She took a glug from hers, which was on the side.

'Will do.' Will gave an empathetic smile, evidently sorry to have landed her in it.

She busied herself for a few moments getting the feta bake out of the oven, with her back to her ex, her husband of thirty years, trying extremely hard to get her thoughts and emotions in order.

Trevor was here in Tilldale.

She set the baking dish down on the trivet, then said, 'Look, if you want to talk . . . properly . . . I'd rather tomorrow morning, certainly not now in front of my guests. Why don't you come for a coffee at say ten?'

'Right-o, thanks. I appreciate that. And hey, thanks for saying I could stay for supper.'

She smothered a sigh. Whatever was up with him, he seemed rather subdued. In some ways, Cath felt she'd really rather not know. He'd set them on this new path, changed everything between them. Kicked down and then rewrote the story of their imagined future together. She felt reluctant to get involved again. She'd only just come down off that heart-tearing emotional rollercoaster. And she'd only just begun to find her feet here in Tilldale.

*

They made their way up the garden. The summer evening still warm for now, the soft light playing on the carpet of grass, shrubs bursting into flower, with clusters of whites and pinks in the borders. A flutter of sparrows twittering as they darted in and out of the beech hedge.

'Pretty, here,' Trevor uttered, looking around him.

It is, and it's all mine, she thought without answering.

No doubt, Will had filled Nikki in by now, but as Cath entered the shed, she introduced her surprise guest. 'Nikki, this is Trevor . . . my ex-husband.' They weren't quite divorced as yet, but it was imminent. 'He's surprised me by turning up out of the blue.' Cath's taut face said it all.

Nikki's eyebrows raised a little. Cath sensed her sympathy as well as her surprise. 'Hi, Trevor.'

'Hello.' He seemed unsure what else to say.

'Glass of wine, Trevor?' Cath ventured, rather reluctantly. But she was resigned to her fate; he was already here now, wasn't he, infiltrating her new 'gang'. They couldn't really sit there sipping wine and offer him a mere glass of water, though a part of her would very much have liked to . . . with a little arsenic chaser.

The group sat talking pleasantly enough about village life, and the many differences between this rural location and suburban Leeds, Trevor's journey up, general chit-chat really, keeping things light and polite, but the relaxed atmosphere had died for poor old Cath.

Andreas's honey and fig feta bake was dished out. Although it was delicious, Cath couldn't help feel it lodging in her throat.

A while later, the conversation turned to hobbies, and that's when Will and Trevor began to get competitive.

'So, what do you enjoy doing with your time off, Will?' Trevor asked.

'Well, obviously cycling.' He'd just told him about his cycle repair business. 'I put in a few fifty milers on the weekends, generally.'

'Ah, great.' Trevor was nodding at this point, Cath knowing full well that cycling had never been his forte. The golf course, other than work, was his go-to place where he exhibited his sporting prowess.

'And then I enjoy the odd hike,' Will went on. 'The Cheviot Hills are great here for that. And sometimes, I'll head up to the Highlands or over to Cumbria. Scafell Pike is a good climb, love that one. Stunning scenery.'

'Ah, yes, I've done that one. Damn good hike, I remember,' Trevor chipped in, puffing out his chest a little.

Cath looked up, not knowing whether to laugh or expose the truth. Trevor had only ever rambled, and generally to a pub pit-stop at that. Suddenly, he's scaling Scafell Pike in the Lake District. She was certain they'd only got to the lower slopes of that mountain on their holiday several years ago now. She gave a knowing smile. There was Will talking about his cycling and hiking, and Trevor was suddenly going into one-upmanship.

'Yeah, I'd love to do some climbing in the Alps next year,

actually,' Trevor added, as though he was Roundhay's answer to Bear Grylls.

'Really?' Cath couldn't help herself, pursing her lips, with her eyebrows raised in disbelief.

'Yeah.' Trevor remained serious.

Hah, perhaps the new bit of fluff was a gym instructor or into serious hiking or something. He'd have his work cut out there then, as he'd never been particularly sporty. But she had a feeling this was all bluff. Did he see Will as some kind of a threat? This was quite amusing.

In response, Will told him about the amazing treks he'd done up the Matterhorn and Mont Blanc, recommending certain Alpine routes, adding whether you needed crampons or not at certain times of the year. Interestingly, Trevor went rather quiet at that point.

*

Cath had excused herself from the group to return to the cottage kitchen and put the final touches to the koftas. She was enjoying a few minutes out, when Trevor snuck up behind her, with empty glass to hand. 'Just coming for a top-up. Bottle's empty.' He then began ferreting in the fridge, looking far too comfortable for her liking. She was regretting her decision to let him to stay for some food.

'Hey, Cath,' he said, as he pulled out a new bottle of Sauvignon, 'this . . . tonight.' There was a hint of concern in Trevor's voice. 'Well, it isn't some kind of singles club, is it?' He'd evidently established that Nikki and Will weren't an item.

'No, Trevor, it's a supper club. But well...' She couldn't resist winding him up a bit. 'We do usually have the lads Andreas and Dan here too, but they couldn't make it tonight.' She didn't enlighten him any further, and she certainly wasn't going to tell him that they were a couple. Hah, let him stew in his own thoughts.

'Oh.'

'Yeah, we get on really well, all of us.'

Life didn't stop when you left me. I have a new home, and a social life of my own. I'm doing okay. That was what she wanted him to take from that. He didn't need to know about the recent wobbles, the ongoing hurt, and the loneliness.

'Right, well, main course is ready.' She took the koftas out from the grill. 'You can take these up for me. And after that, you'll be you fed and watered, and I really would appreciate some time to spend with my friends.' She spelled out a reminder that he wasn't to get too comfy. 'And if you haven't already booked, you'll have to get going and see if the pub has any rooms left.'

'Yep, noted.'

He had to have some other agenda, she mused warily, her guard firmly up. But whatever it was, she'd rather leave it until tomorrow to find out.

*

At last, with the main course over, Trevor left. He gave Cath a clumsy hug on the doorstep, after thanking her for the lovely meal. Cath felt a weight lift watching him go. She'd been so damned tense through the whole meal, she hadn't particularly enjoyed her food. How did cheating Trevor still manage to do that to her?

After closing the door with a sigh, she headed back to her friends and poured herself another glass of wine. 'Well, that was awkward. Sorry, folks, I had absolutely no idea he was going to turn up like that.'

'And hey, I'm sorry, I hadn't thought to find out who he was before putting my foot in it about supper.' Will looked abashed.

'It's okay. We were always going to have to face each other at some point, I suppose. And it made it easier in some ways having you two by my side.'

'No worries,' Nikki replied. 'He seemed all right to be fair, except for being a dick about mountaineering – even I know he hasn't got a clue about climbing in the Alps.' The three of them laughed at that. 'But obviously we don't know the full history . . .' Nikki added cautiously, knowing full well that relationships and exes were tricky business.

'Wolf in sheep's clothing. Been married for thirty years, and then he did the dirty on me eighteen months ago,' Cath began to explain. 'It's been a long and messy journey. But hey, I'll keep that little gem of a story for another time . . .' She tried to keep her tone light, though the hurt still squished her inside.

'Hey, I'm sorry to hear that.' Will sounded caring without being nosy. 'I hope you're feeling okay. And I'm sorry if I made it more awkward. That couldn't have been at all easy this evening.'

'Ah, I'm all right. Feeling better now he's away.' She meant for tonight, and also her life.

'Right, well I'm going down to the kitchen to nab those chocolates.' Nikki stood up purposefully. 'This situation needs something sweet.'

Cath smiled. 'Actually, it is getting a little chilly up here, and the sky looks a bit ominous.' Inky-grey clouds were massing above them. 'Shall we head back down to the cottage?'

'Sounds a good idea, before we get a rain shower,' agreed Will.

Settled in the lounge fifteen minutes later, with mugs of freshly ground coffee and delightful chocolate truffles, they chatted some more. It wasn't long before Nikki managed to nod off. She must have been exhausted, bless her. Aside from this evening, she never seemed to stop. Her head had bobbed to one side, and a light snore escaped from her lips.

'I think she's out for the count,' commented Will, with a kind smile on his face.

'I know. Her life sounds so full on, it's no wonder. Three kids, her cleaning business . . . It's exhausting just listening to everything she has to cram into one day.'

'Yeah, it's like that with young families, when you're full-on working, isn't it. And then, all of a sudden, it's all gone.' Will's brow creased and his eyes looked a little melancholy. 'Suddenly they're all grown up, and you wonder where the time went . . .' He sounded nostalgic.

'True.' Cath felt for him, knowing that his wife had died not so long ago. And then she thought of her own little family unit. Her, Trevor, Adam . . . The good times, and there were good times over the years, especially those early years of marriage and motherhood. Yes, and there were the times when she was bloody worn out, and it had still felt right, worth it. They were a team. A unit. Now Adam was off and away, and Trevor had done his disappearing act, too. How things had changed.

'Well, I'm just glad it's not Trevor making himself comfy

there on the sofa,' Cath added wryly, 'I was beginning to wonder if I'd actually be able to get rid of him this evening.'

'Ah, I see. So, has he headed back to Leeds now?' Will quirked a dark eyebrow.

'No such luck, staying over at the pub, as far as I know . . . We've a lot to talk about, apparently. He's coming back tomorrow morning for coffee.'

'Oh, ri-ight.'

Was that her imagination, or was there a trace of disappointment in his tone?

Chapter 19

The wolf in sheep's clothing was back on her threshold looking, well . . . rather sheepish.

'Morning, Trevor. Well then, you'd better come on in.'

Her husband had become the enemy, the betrayer. But now, after all that had happened between them, he looked rather lost. But, she steeled herself, after these past eighteen months, they were still very much on different sides.

He followed her through to the kitchen where she clicked the kettle on. Her finger on the trigger – hmm, was it coffee or another bout of marital war they'd be making?

Small talk was safer to start, she figured. 'So, how was the pub . . . or the B&B, or wherever it was you ended up last night?'

'Ah, fine. It was the pub, got the last room. Mattress was a bit thin, didn't sleep that great. But breakfast was good.'

She hadn't slept that well either, with everything buzzing through her mind after his unexpected arrival. But the more she'd thought about things, the more she'd come to the conclusion that there really was no going back. 'Glad it was okay,' she managed. 'Coffee all right for you?' *Polite, polite, and you'll be all right*. The words sang in her head. She had no idea where they had come from.

'Yep . . . please.'

She pulled the cafetière down from the cupboard, and began spooning out roasted coffee. The aromatic smell took her back. She used to do this every morning for the two of them as they got ready for work. Kick-start with a strong coffee, juice, toast and butter, getting Adam's PE kit ready or whatever necessary item of the day it was, geeing the lad on – their son was always on slow mode in the mornings – packed lunches at the ready, coats, keys, and finally off to work to a day of deputy headship at the secondary school. A life they once lived. A life no longer shared.

She popped biscuits onto a plate, plain digestives. He wasn't getting any of her chocolate ones. And moved the cafetière and cups to the small kitchen table. She was using her bistro patio set in here now. After lugging the wooden kitchen table up to the shed, that was precisely where it was staying.

Trevor took up a seat. Hers, she moved a little further apart, subconsciously emphasising the distance between them, before sitting down.

'Nice in here,' he commented. 'Cosy, a bit different than our old place, mind.'

The kitchen at the Roundhay house was big, with an island, breakfast bar, two ovens, loads of cupboard space and a plethora of work surfaces. It had also felt rather lonely these past couple of years, with Adam away at uni, and Trevor often out at golf, or 'working late'. She wondered now how much of that was the truth, when he'd turned up late and tired for yet another overcooked dinner.

'It might be smaller here, yes, but it suits me.'

'It's charming, yeah,' he conceded. He took a large gulp

of his coffee. His shoulders slumped dejectedly, before he let out a long slow sigh and looked up at her with hang-dog eyes. 'Cath, love, I've made a huge mistake . . . I'm so, so sorry for wrecking everything.'

So, this was the face-to-face apology she'd waited so long for. It was far too little too late.

His eyes were trained on hers. 'Is there any way back at all?'

'What?' She was so incredulous, she nearly choked on her coffee. 'You want a way back in? *For us*? Are you serious?'

He was nodding, looking rather pathetic, she thought. 'Trevor, you've shacked up with some other woman. We've sold the bloody house and half the stuff in it. And God, don't you even realise, it's *so* much more than that? A quick shag I might have coped with, that's not to say it wouldn't have bloody well hurt . . . but we were planning for our retirement together, our amazing second chapter once Adam had left home. All those dreams, the travels, the adventures . . . they all went up in smoke too. I left my teaching post, my *deputyship*, for all that. I had to walk away from my students. And you let me do it...' She paused, suddenly feeling knackered. Her final words were quieter, filled with sorrow. 'It's the future I thought we were going to have that you took away. You wrecked all that. And then you left me wondering if the past was all a lie too . . .'

'I'm so sorry, Cath. It wasn't . . . it wasn't a lie . . . we'd had a good marriage, before . . . I didn't ever stop loving you, not really.'

There was a difficult silence, both lost in their thoughts. The ticking of the wall clock too loud. Like time was slipping away for them.

It was Cath who resumed the conversation. 'You've hurt me so much, Trevor. This . . . it's all just words . . . words that are far too late, too meaningless. You don't do all that to someone you love. And you can't just turn up like this, and think we can turn back time . . . go back to how things were. Just because it's fizzled out with your new woman. Well, that's what I assume has happened. It doesn't work like that. It doesn't fucking work like that, at all.'

Trevor looked up. 'I know . . . and I'm truly sorry. I can see how much pain and disruption I've caused you . . . and Adam. If I could change things, I would.'

'There's no way back.' Of that, Cath was certain. 'There's no magic wand, Trev.' What she'd hoped for, what she'd wanted for the last few months was to rewind time, to make the affair never happen, to be able to trust again . . . but that could never be, she realised that now.

'Look, I don't expect you to forgive me just like that. I certainly don't deserve it. But, maybe in time?' He looked utterly deflated. 'What we had was good . . . before . . .' Nostalgia, regret, remorse; his voice was soft, yet the tone so heavy – filled with his own burden.

Cath could see he was in earnest, but she'd been hurt too much and for too long. Her tone was matter of fact. 'A long time before, Trevor . . .' She couldn't deny that their early years of marriage, of having Adam and seeing him grow up, they'd been happy years. 'We did have some good years, way back . . . but things have changed, so very much. And since I've been away, living here on my own, I can see that maybe what you did – going off like that – it was a sign . . . of how things had altered for us, over time. Maybe the glue had already become unstuck even before you went off . . .' She let the words hover there, her own understanding of the situation growing as she spoke them. 'Adam's grown up and away now. Life's changing all the time. And sometimes you either grow together or apart . . . and for us, well, it was apart. We were too busy just getting on with life to notice what was happening.'

'Oh . . .' was all Trevor could manage. He took another gulp of coffee.

Cath paused to take a sip too. She'd said far more than she'd intended. It was emotionally draining, but it was needed. They should, in fact, probably have had this conversation months ago. But back then, it was hard to talk, to even see rationally, not when you were damn well hurting so much.

Trevor made an attempt at an explanation, which sounded more like an excuse. 'You were working all hours, Cath, always giving your all to those kids at school. Marking, most evenings, the weekends . . . then the planning. It wasn't just me who'd drifted away . . .'

'Teaching was my job, and I loved it, well, most of the time. I wanted to give those kids everything I could, what Adam had. Give them a chance in life, push them that bit more. Most of them would never get that kind of support at home . . . that's why I did it. But I was prepared to stop it all, give up the job I loved and step back . . . for us. That's why I left . . . but what was it all for? You were already bloody well seeing someone else. You'd already gone. There was no us left.'

'Oh, bugger, it's too late, isn't it. I've pushed you too far.' There were tears in his eyes.

Cath was nodding gently. 'Look, it doesn't mean we have

to be enemies. Adam will always be our son, and hey, we did a good job raising him. We need to be civil, to be a team supporting him, even if he is almost a fully grown man. This doesn't have to mean we don't talk. We don't have to be bitter and resentful going forward.'

'Okay . . . yeah, of course. One day at a time, hey.' He sounded accepting but also hopeful. 'I need to earn my forgiveness, I understand that. And yes, we absolutely need to support Adam. He's finding it hard, too . . . us breaking up.'

'I know. It's been tough all round.' Cath nodded, suddenly feeling shattered. She waited in silence for a second or two, the conversation. letting their words sink in, before resuming. 'So, how's the old Roundhay gang? What have you all been up to lately?' She shifted the conversation on to safer pastures, telling him a little about Helen's recent visit too.

After all, there was no point going around in circles talking about their relationship, when actually it very much felt to Cath like they were at the end of the road.

*

Watching Trevor go, she gave a small wave from her doorstep, experiencing all kinds of mixed emotions.

Her husband – ex – hopped into his car. It was still the family saloon of old; she'd half expected him to have swapped that too for some sleeker, faster model. He nodded to her in his rear-view mirror as he held up a hand in farewell, and gave a parting toot on the horn. A small salute to everything they'd once had, and all they had been through. Despite it all, there was a huge lump in her throat . . . and a strange pang of longing for what might have been. Underneath all the layers of hurt and sorrow, was there still a little love left?

The past and present were at a crossroads, she told herself as she closed the cottage door. The future, the road ahead. She had, what, perhaps thirty years ahead of her hopefully, if she had a good innings and made it into her eighties. So, what was she going to do with that precious time? Bloody hell, how did you decide the best way to go? Sometimes as Cath well knew, the path wasn't always clear, but you just had to keep on going, one foot forward, one day at a time . . . and always listen to your heart.

Chapter 20

Cath had cooked a double portion of supper for herself last night, partly to take her mind off the rollercoaster of emotions of the last twenty-four hours since Trevor's surprise arrival, and also intending to take a dish of home-cooked lasagne around to Andreas and Dan this morning. She'd heard from Nikki that they were back from the hospital, but no doubt they were having a difficult time.

En route to the village stores and about to cross the road, Cath spotted a bicycle heading her way. She waited a few moments on the kerbside. The cyclist came to a halt before her, looking up with a friendly, 'Hi.' She recognised those deep hazel-brown eyes . . . Will.

'Oh, hi.' She felt the warmth of a blush creep over her face.

'Hey, how's it going? Uhm, were you okay, after the meal . . . with Trevor? I've been thinking about you, about how you must be feeling . . .' He sounded rather awkward, stumbling a little over his words. He looked a little flushed, too.

But hey, she told herself, he'd probably just completed some thirty-mile stretch or something. 'Ah, I'm all right . . . thanks. It all went fine, meeting up, in the end, if a bit awkward, as you might imagine. All that past history. But yeah, the next morning, we managed to sort a few things out between us. We've left things in a good place.' Cath didn't want to go into any more detail, or 'air her laundry' here on Tilldale's main street.

'Ah okay . . . Well, that's good.' He sounded thoughtful, then paused, before adding, 'It was a lovely evening at yours. Thanks again.'

'You're welcome. I'm just off to see the lads, actually. Going to find out how Maria's doing, and I'm taking them a little food parcel.'

'That's kind.' He smiled warmly. 'Send them my best wishes, too.'

'Will do. So, where are you off to then?' She nodded towards the bicycle. 'Or are you on your way back?' Hmm, he was back in his Lycra and looking pretty good, she couldn't help but note. His chest was broad and toned, and he slimmed at the waist, unlike Trevor's portly middle-aged spread. He looked naturally healthy and fit.

Oh, was she in fact staring at him? Oops.

'Ah, I'm just heading out, a few miles along the coast to Bamburgh and Seahouses, and then I'll loop back in via a country route, up over the hills, and take the Claverham road home. Be back by early afternoon.'

'Wow, I think that'd take me all day . . . and the rest,' she grinned, 'well, enjoy.'

'I'm sure I will do. Catch up again soon, yeah?' It sounded like a question. Something he was keen to happen. 'And if you ever fancy a bike ride . . . ?'

She felt a little surge inside. *Don't jump from the frying pan into the fire* suddenly came to mind, like a warning shot. Cath just nodded in reply, then decided to be honest. 'Actually,

I don't own a bike any more . . . haven't ridden for years.' Ah, no, she went even redder then. Why had she started telling him this? Even though it was true on all counts, she didn't want to give him ideas.

'No worries, we have bikes for hire at the shop. And hey, I can loan one for free, if you'd like to see how you get on . . . ?'

'Maybe . . . might be fun.' What was she doing? This was encouraging him, when she had no intention of doing anything like that. Why did she find it so hard to say no to things?

'Great. Well, see you around then.' Will pushed off on his pedals with a gorgeous parting smile, and was soon away.

He was just being friendly, of course, she told herself. And okay, so if she felt a little buzz around Will, then that was fine. At least it proved she still had some libido left, thank Christ. It had been hiding away for far too long. And anyway, it wasn't as if she needed or wanted to do anything about it, did she?

*

The shop lights were on and it appeared to be open as usual, which was hopefully a good sign. Last night, she'd had a text message from Nikki saying the lads were back, which was when she'd decided to cook some extra supper. As she stepped inside, it was good to see Dan there behind the counter.

'Morning.'

'Hello, lovely. So sorry about letting you all down for supper the other night.'

'Oh, that's no problem at all, Dan. No need to worry about us. We were just concerned for you and Andreas. And how's Maria getting on?'

'Well, she's meant to be coming out today, back to her care home, so that's good. But it's knocked the stuffing out of her, bless. I think it's going to take some getting over. She's had that chest infection, which seemed to be clearing up, but is obviously a bit weak still as she keeps getting giddy and falling. She's back on antibiotics, and they've done some tests, but they haven't seemed to quite get to the bottom of it. Andreas is there again at the hospital ready to drive her back, once she gets discharged . . . hopefully this morning, all being well. Be good to get them both home. It's been an up and down few days.'

'Ah, I thought it might have been. I've been thinking about you all. So, I've brought you over a little something to help out. A homemade lasagne. Hope you both like that.' She lifted out the foil-covered baking dish from her shopping bag.

'Aw, that's amazing, and so sweet of you, thank you.'

'Oh, and it's freshly made too, so it'll freeze if you've already got food in, or you don't fancy it.'

'We love it. Lasagne is one of Andreas's absolute favourites, so it'll certainly be enjoyed. I was just wondering what on earth we might eat for tea. My cooking mojo has disappeared completely these past few days.'

'No wonder. You've had a lot on your minds. And you know, if I can help at all… If, say, you need to free up a couple of hours for visiting, well, I'm more than happy to mind the shop. It'd give me something to do, to be frank. I have to admit, I've been feeling at a bit of a loose end since I've given up full-time work.'

'Okay, well, if you mean it, perhaps for a few hours . . . I'll have a chat with Andreas. It's been so full on lately. We've hardly had a chance to catch our breath. And with Maria having been so poorly, and still frail, I feel very much like a terrier chasing its tail. Thanks, we might well take you up on that.'

'Oh, and I can dog walk too.' Cath smiled. It'd give her morning walk a bit of focus having a cute Westie in tow.

'Ah, thanks for the offer. She can be a bit of a madam, but she's great fun. Thank you, lovely, you're a gem. Supper service, shop minding and dog walking . . . wow. We'll definitely keep you posted.'

'I'm still building my tutoring business, but that's more in the evenings and on a Saturday morning, so I can work around that.' After a lifetime of running around at everyone else's beck and call, having time on her hands was a new and unusual place to be in.

Cath picked up a wholemeal loaf, a wedge of local blue cheese, some milk, grapes and a couple of apples. There was no baklava to tempt her today, with Andreas still doing his shift at the hospital. She wished Dan and Andreas all the best, also remembering to send Will's regards on to them too. Hah, as well as running the shop for a few hours, she might well end up on a cycling trip in the near future.

'Thanks, petal.' Dan brought her back to the here and now.

'You're welcome. And I mean it . . . happy to help.'

She hoped they'd take her up on her offer. She'd love to be more involved in the village, it'd be a chance to meet more people from the local community and to feel useful again. Fingers crossed they'd say yes. Her life here was going well, but it was a quiet life, too quiet at times . . . and yes, though the roots were forming and friendships were budding, it still needed a little working on.

Chapter 21

The following day, Cath was sat with a cup of coffee watching the rain drizzle down the window panes, wondering what to do next. A wet (no doubt muddy) walk or tackle the ironing pile? When had her life become so bloody boring? She had two hours to fill before an online session on differentiation with an A Level student, and even that wasn't filling her with much enthusiasm today.

Ping. A notification. She picked up her phone, happy for the diversion. WhatsApp Group Supper Club popped up. Just seeing that made her smile. Nikki had evidently created the new group, and oh, look, using an image of them all sat in the summerhouse shed from Cath's first gathering as the profile picture.

Nikki: **Right guys, the next supper club is at mine! Can either do 20th or 27th June. x**

A further *ping*. Nikki again: **Have by some miracle got my Kev lined up to take them all overnight to his mum's. Woo hoo! Any takers?! X**

As Cath was typing up her answer, another *ping*. Nikki: **Now don't get too excited about the cooking side of things, but will try my best.**

Cath responded straight away; a grin plastered over her face: **I'm in! Either date is fine. x**

Brilliant. It may not be gourmet but I promise we'll have some fun. ☺

Aw, this little foodie friendship group was firmly establishing itself, with the others seemingly wanting it to continue as much as she did. Within a couple of hours, Will had answered with a 'That sounds lovely, thanks.' And Dan had come back on behalf of himself and Andreas with a big 'YES! for the 20th...' And a thumbs-up, followed by several food and drink emojis and a smiley face. Cath felt delighted that she, with a little help from Andreas and Dan of course, had started this off.

The date was set: Thursday 20th June, 7 p.m. at Nikki's house, No 10 Tilldale's Main Street.

Life was looking up again, despite the rains. There wasn't too long to wait either, as Supper Club Part 3 was all set for less than two weeks' time.

Another message then pinged, directly to her, from Will.

Oh . . . It must be something to do with the supper event, she mused. Yet still, as she opened it, her pulse was beating a little faster.

Hi, Cath. Hope you're fine? Do you fancy that bike ride? Weather looks better for Wednesday. Nothing too strenuous, I promise.

That was only two days' time. Her pulse rate went up a further notch.

Did she fancy that bike ride? Did she, in fact, fancy the cyclist? Should she go? Would that give him the wrong impression? Was it just a friendly gesture? You couldn't count a bike ride as some kind of date, surely? Could you . . . ?

Cath's confident persona kicked in. *Look, you've been*

sat here lonely and bored . . . *it might be just as friends, it might be more, but it's just a bloody bike ride. It'll get you out of the house, and it might even be fun. Go for it!* Hah, weirdly she could now hear the voice of her big sister encouraging her.

And, go for it she did: **Okay, yes, thanks.** (No kiss, that was a step too far!)

Great! I'll fetch you a bike over from the shop. We can set off from the village. 11 a.m. sound okay?

Perfect.

What had she done?

*

What on earth had she let herself in for? The last time she'd got on a bike she was a teenager, cycling through the Derbyshire Dales with her friend, Tracey. Even then, in their prime, they'd had to get off and walk up the hills. The best bit was stopping for sweets and milkshakes, she remembered, the sugar hit much needed after all that hard-earned exercise. And then, the next day, the sore bottom and stiff legs . . . her mother joking about her looking like John Wayne just off his horse, and sister Susie in fits of laughter.

A stiff-legged cowboy with a sore bottom was not the impression she was hoping to give new friend Will, at all. But she'd gone and bloody well said yes, hadn't she? (This was all Susie's fault, her sister's voice taking over her head and prompting her.) Well, here she was, walking up Tilldale's Main Street towards his house, No 18, where they were to meet for a countryside cycle ride. She'd warned him to be gentle with her, but she feared, as a cycling expert, his idea of gentle might be very different from hers.

He met her outside his front door, with a broad smile – hmm, looking rather handsome – and his and hers bicycles at the ready. She'd cobbled together an outfit of some old gym gear; she didn't possess any cycling seat-padded leggings, but was now wishing she'd gone ahead and bought some. She'd decided to see how she got on today, before wasting money on any cycling gear. But right now, after remembering her youthful experience, she wished she had. She had a bottle of water, and her sunglasses at the ready, and had already put some sun lotion on.

Will had sorted a helmet for her to borrow from the shop, and a bike. A second-hand road model apparently – was he hoping for a sale, thereafter? She still wasn't quite sure of his – or her – motivations.

'Ready to roll?' He grinned, lifting her bike from its leaning position against the wall, and moving it towards her.

'Ah, I think so. Where are we going? And more to the point, how far?' She was feeling a sense of trepidation as she gripped the handles, ready to mount.

'Just a twenty miler. Ten firstly, and then a stop halfway.'

Twenty miles. That sounded a long way to a beginner. 'O-kay.'

'Yeah, thought we might stop for a half pint at The Black Bull in Lowick.'

'Right-io.' She'd need a drink by then, for sure.

'You can pop your water bottle there.' He pointed to a clip holder on the bar of the bike.

'O-kay.' She found fear was freezing her tongue.

'Great weather for it today. We're lucky,' Will continued.

'Yep.' *Let's just get on with it.*

Will then mounted, and they were off, heading down the village street and towards the shop. Cath made a wobbly start, filing in behind Will. She hoped to goodness the supper club lads weren't about to witness her looking like a toddler. Hah, perhaps stabilisers might be a good idea at this point.

Once they were out of the village, a huge tractor pulled in behind them and then began to pass. Cath felt a blast of air and found herself wobbling again. She stopped, and waited at the roadside. She didn't fancy getting too near – or under – those massive tyres. Her heart was racing. She set off again, and Will had slowed to let her catch up.

'All right?'

'Yeah, thought it was better to stop.'

'No worries. That's always a wise move on these lanes if there's anything you're unsure of. You're just getting the hang of it again, after all.' Will sounded patient, which was reassuring.

The road stayed quiet for a while, and she coped with the backdraft from a passing car or two. The stunning vista began opening out before them: fields filled with bold yellow rapeseed, and grassy meadows dotted with cattle and sheep. Gradually, other than the slight burn of her thigh muscles, she began to relax into it. And hey, downhill was fun, exhilarating in fact. There was birdsong, and sunshine, and Will pedalling away in front of her. Watching his sleek muscles work, his tight buttocks on the seat ahead, well that was not a bad view at all.

After pausing at some crossroads for a quick swig of water and a check that she was doing fine, they soon turned on to the road for Lowick. The small village was getting nearer, and the prospect of a cooling glass of lager pushed them on. They parked up the bikes, and feeling slightly sore on the rear end, but still generally okay, Cath found a wooden picnic bench to rest on in the pub's garden, whilst Will went in to get the drinks.

Once he'd returned with the best-ever chilled lager, they sat, enjoying the countryside pub and the chance to chat. Will seemed easy-going and was good to talk to, mentioning his previous job as a fireman and telling her about the time they had to rescue a horse stuck in deep mud up on the fells. They got the poor thing out in the end, with several ropes and pulleys. Amazingly, after being checked over by the local vet, and having a good wash-down, it was declared fine. It was so lovely chatting away like this, having company . . . his company.

That then opened up the conversation enough for her to speak about her role as a teacher. 'Yeah, I've been teaching in secondary schools, all the while. And I was also a deputy head more recently.'

'Good for you. Must have been quite demanding, especially with that age group. And Maths,' he pulled a slight grimace, 'it's not exactly everyone's favourite subject, is it?'

'It has been demanding, yeah, but you know, I've really loved it over the years. And Maths is fine. Mind you, I'll let you in on a secret here, you absolutely never ever let a sum add up to sixty-nine, or you've lost the damn lot of them. Honestly, it'd descend into chaos, the whole bloody class. That's all the lads are thinking about most of the time, anyhow, at that age . . . sex. Yep, up and down the country, you will never find a sum or equation in a classroom that equals sixty-nine.' She shook her head, whilst still smiling.

'Life as a teacher, hey, who'd have thought . . .' Will raised his eyebrows, looking distinctly sexy.

A sudden vision of having sex with Will, flashed up in her mind. Uh-oh, the whole 'sixty-nine' thing. Why mention that?! And . . . she certainly hadn't done that for years and years.

Cath found herself feeling hot, flustered and blushing. Of all the stories from her time at school, why did she have to go and tell him that one?

Will gave a small cough, quickly finished his beer, and stood up. 'Right, time to get going again. Before we stiffen up.'

The words weren't lost on her but she didn't dare grin.

'Yes, absolutely.' A good get-out clause, at least, despite its double entendre, and thank God for that. 'Think I'll just nip to the ladies,' she added, making her escape. In the bathroom, she cooled her face down with splashes of cold water; it wasn't just the fresh air and sunshine that were making her glow.

They set off again, and the trip back started well. Cath was just getting into her pedalling stride, the miles rolling pleasantly by, the countryside looking gorgeous with the rolling hills in a patchwork of earthy colours, when disaster struck. She hit a pothole. The country lanes were worse for wear after a hard winter, and Cath hadn't spotted the ragged hole missing big chunks of tarmac. *Bumph*, she was off in a flash, and was flung into the verge. Landing with a thud and tumble on mud, grass, her head ended up in a scratchy thicket of brambles. *Shit*.

Will stopped immediately, hopping off his bike to get to her. 'You okay, Cath? Are you hurt?'

She groaned, already feeling as if she'd been kicked by a horse, but then, slowly moving, tentatively trying out her arms and legs. It seemed nothing was broken, at least.

'I don't think so,' she managed. 'Well, only my pride.' She tried to give a smile, but her eyes felt all watery.

'Bloody potholes. I'll be reporting that one to the council. You could have been badly injured. You sure you're okay?'

Cath was trying to drag herself up to her feet, but felt a little giddy. 'I think so. Just a bit of a shock.' She pulled a bramble away from her face, spotting a smear of blood on her hand. Of all the ditches to fall into, she had to find a thorny one.

'Here, let me help you.' Will was calm, but compassionate. She felt a strong arm lifting her torso, supporting her around her back and under her armpit. 'You took a bit of a fall there.'

'Hmm.' She just nodded, trying to get the wind back in her sails. He was being so kind, but she felt such a bloody idiot. Why didn't she see the damned hole, and avoid it?

Scratched and inelegant, images of her landing in that hedge, tangled in brambles, kept filling her mind on her now wobbly way back. Her confidence had vanished. She must look a right bloody state – pulled through a hedge backwards was about it. This was so not the impression she wanted to leave Will with. Hah, this was even a step up from John Wayne. Mortified.

Will took it steady thereafter, slowing the pace, and looking over his shoulder every now and again to ask if she still felt okay. Back at her cottage, he offered to accompany her inside, and check over her wounds. But all she wanted was some quiet time, on her own, with no fuss.

'Thanks, but I'll be fine now.'

'All right, if you're sure you're okay? I'll walk your bike back up the village then.'

'Sorry, it's probably all dented now.'

'Hey, it's no problem. The main thing is you're okay.'

Those gorgeous dark eyes were on hers, and she felt such a clumsy idiot.

'Yes, I'll be fine, thank you.'

They both had a feeling she wouldn't be asking to use the bicycle again. That was the start and end of it.

'Bye, then.'

'Bye, thanks . . .' her voice drifted weakly.

*

In the cottage kitchen soon afterwards, with some antiseptic cream to rub into her grazes and a now banging head, she cursed herself. This was so damn typical of her. It had been a good day really . . . up until then. Will seemed a real nice guy. The friendly chat between them, the relaxed drink at the pub, the stunning countryside. Why did she have to spoil things, starting off with the 'sixty-nine' story – mortifying in retrospect – and then the grand finale of falling off her bike and being such a clumsy oaf? She sighed, she was being harsh on herself she knew, but embarrassment was biting at her.

Perhaps her thoughts, however brief, of having some kind of special friendship, were pie in the sky. She was running ahead of herself. Those giddy emotions were unsettling, best keep them in check. And the chance of another bike ride together after that, well that was zero.

Chapter 22

Later, in the bath, resting her aching and rather battered body, she noticed the purple-green bruise that was blooming on her left thigh where she'd taken the biggest impact. It looked rather like a potato that had tarnished in the sun, coming out of the earth too soon. With a strange pang, she felt that's what had happened to her too, it was all happening too fast, this friendship, she'd been coming out of her shell far too soon. She should never have agreed to it, it had just made things worse. These weird feelings of longing (uh-oh) when she was with him, the subsequent embarrassment, and uneasiness. Despite her efforts to steer clear of any new romantic relationships, she still found it difficult to say no . . . and that's how life got messed up. She needed to retreat from Will, just a little, and look to the group gatherings to bolster her. The supper club, with safety in numbers, could be her refuge.

She was heading downstairs in her comfy pyjamas to catch up on a little easy-watching TV, when she heard the ping of a message coming in. This one was from Trevor…

Hi Cath, Hope you are fine. Lovely to catch up the other day. Thanks so much for seeing me and for the meal which was great – as always.

Sorry that I hadn't thought to let you know I was coming up. It was amiss of me, but I was just so desperate to clear the air between us.

She read it through twice. Hah, he was missing her cooking most likely. Perhaps this Steph might be a whizz in bed but not in the kitchen, lol. Then there were three dots pulsing on her screen showing that he was writing some more. They looked like little heartbeats. Cath waited, feeling in no rush to reply.

His next words: **Thanks again, and I do miss you. Xx**

She didn't quite know how to feel, and left it a good half hour before responding, making herself a cuppa and watching an episode of *MasterChef* in the meanwhile. Trevor didn't deserve to get her time and attention back that easily. But her feelings were still conflicted, with so much history, so much past love and new hurt between them. She wanted time to think how best to respond. Friendly, but not too personal, seemed the best option. She needed to learn how to get the balance right, how to be as an ex. There should be a guide book.

Finally, she came up with a simple: **You're welcome. And it was good to clear some things between us.**

To kiss or not to kiss?

NOT!!! *He's still been a bastard to you* – a sassy new kick-ass voice in her head shouted at her. *Do not be too nice, too soon.*

*

She must have nodded off. The *News at Ten* had just started, and her ringtone woke her. Her phone tucked beside her on the sofa.

'Ah, hel-lo?' She sounded a bit dopey.

'Hi, hey, it's me, Will. Sorry, I know it's a bit late, but I just wanted to check you were all right? That was quite some knock you took.'

'Ah, yeah, I'm okay . . . Well, a bit sore, and bruised. But I've had a nice bath, feel a bit better after that.'

'And your head's okay? No headaches, dizziness? No feeling sick?'

'No, nothing like that.'

'Ah, that's good.' Bless, he'd evidently been worrying about her. There was a beat or two of silence, then he added, 'I'm sorry it had to end up like that, the bike ride . . . such a shame. It had been a nice day. Well, I enjoyed it.'

It had been good, up until that damned crash. But Cath was determined not to get too chummy, not allow herself to get sucked back in. 'Yeah,' was all she permitted herself to say.

'Well, I'll let you go. Get yourself a good night's sleep. And hey, I'm really glad you're okay.'

'Thanks. Night, Will.'

'Night.'

She closed the call. Her emotions were doing a whirly-gig; first Trevor getting in touch, and then Will, who was just being kind, she reminded herself. No doubt it was all part of his training with the fire brigade and as a serious cyclist, checking up after someone has been injured. But did it also mean he cared . . . ? Argh, stop it, woman, there was no point even thinking about it.

*

Cath felt like some company the next morning. With still a week to go to the next supper club, she felt rather strange and at a loose end. Seeing Trevor in person again and his message last night had fired up all kinds of emotions, and so had her bike ride with Will – though that one she'd keep to herself. She also realised she was missing her old friendship group – that camaraderie, having someone to chat things over with. She had Nikki's number. Hmm, she had a feeling she'd be easy to talk with and someone on her side, so she fired over a quick text:

Don't suppose you fancy going for a walk with me some time? Could be followed by a coffee or a quick drink in the pub. x ☺

A reply soon came back:

Hah, what kind of a walk are we talking? Be warned I'm no hiker. x

Followed by: **Am pretty full on with work most days, but might be able get away for a short walk after school-pick up time – if I have a bit of notice to organise the boys.**

And then: **Can deffo fit in a Prosecco at the pub, sometime though! x**

Cath sent back: **Not too far. Short walk in the hills perhaps. Be nice to have some company. And yes, be good to have a quick drink afterwards. x**

Nikki: **You okay, hun? How did things go with Trevor after that supper night? X**

A text was no place to open her heart nor let down her guard. Cath's answer was brief: **Okay. Let's chat some more when we see each other. x**

An hour or so later, and Nikki had got herself sorted. They settled on the next day, when Nikki's Hamish had rugby training and Angus was already going back to a mate's house for tea. There had only been her youngest Scott left to sort, and Granny had jumped in to pick him up from school. That would give them an hour for a walk, plus time for a quick drink afterwards.

Perfect, Cath had replied, delighted that Nikki was open to meeting her outside of the supper club. She was already looking forward to it. Cath felt that this was the friendship she should be nurturing. A far safer friendship zone.

Chapter 23

Cath pulled up outside Nikki's house, her walking boots at the ready in the rear footwell.

She waited a short while, and just as she was wondering whether to get out and knock the door, Nikki appeared in jeans and trainers, pulling on a lightweight rain jacket, with a hang-dog look.

'Hey, I can't believe I said I'd be up for this . . . after a full day's work an' all,' Nikki was muttering, as she opened the car door. But she also had a smile for Cath, too.

'Afternoon, Nikki,' Cath was full of cheer.

'I'm no walker,' Nikki continued as she got in. 'I do enough exercise all day. I'm only doing this for you, you know. So . . . where are we heading?'

'Homildon Hill. It's not too far away. I know you're pushed for time.'

'Ah, I knew it. A bloody hill . . . up in the moors too, that one. You've got me going off hiking, haven't you? I've only got trainers, mind. Don't possess hiking boots . . . on purpose.' Nikki had seemingly reverted to stroppy teenager mode.

Cath had to laugh. 'That'll not get you out of it.' She

grinned, as she pulled the Mini into gear and they set off. 'You'll be fine up there in trainers. It's been pretty dry lately.'

'Hah, I could be at home with my feet up and a nice cuppa. I've got no boys in the house, and Kev's still out on a job.' She was shaking her head, but her smile gave away that she wasn't overly bothered. Nikki loved a bit of drama and was enjoying her theatrical moan.

After a ten-minute drive, they were pulling up into the car parking area above Kirkton in the Cheviot Hills.

Cath then swapped her shoes, lacing up the hiking boots with a flourish. 'Ready?'

'As ready as I ever will be . . . I suppose.' Nikki was still pulling a face.

And they were off. Walking and talking as they went. It was a dry, fresh afternoon. The walk started gently along a mud track, then up through a small pine-tree wood.

Nikki reckoned she was 'puffed out' by the top of that. Hah, they were still near the start. They reached a wooden gate which opened out onto rugged, beautiful moorland. Bracken adorned the slopes, bold and tall with its lacy summer fronds of rich green, and in between there were patches of sheep-grazed, short stubby grass. A hoot from a pheasant echoed through the valley. The path wound on . . . and up.

Pausing for a moment, to look at the view and catch her breath, Nikki asked, 'So what was going on that day, with Trevor, your ex, turning up?'

Cath slowed too, taking in the rise and falls of the hills around them, the landscape softening as it rolled towards the coast. The indigo-blue of the North Sea away on the horizon.

She took a breath, then said, 'Yeah, Trev turning up like

that, that hit me right out of the blue. I had no idea . . . he'd not phoned or anything. It was all a bit weird. We're meant to be split, over, done and dusted – except for dealing with our son – and suddenly there he was talking about missing me.'

'So, what went on between you? Before . . . ?' Nikki prompted gently.

'It's been awful to be honest, Nikki. These past couple of years have been such a dark, tough place. Things began to feel all wrong at home . . . and then, finding out about his girlfriend, it all began to make sense, in the most dreadful way.'

'Oh, I'm so sorry, Cath. I knew you must have had a hard time, whatever had happened before you moved up here. But that sounds pretty damned heartless.'

'It was . . . It was like he'd just tossed me, and all of our life up to then, aside, just like that. Like none of it had even mattered.'

'Bloody hell.' Nikki rested a hand gently on Cath's shoulder, as they stood together, the cooling summer breeze swirling around them.

'Come on, we've still a way to the top,' Cath chivvied them on.

The hill was getting steeper now, and they slowed their pace. Cath could feel her thighs burn.

'Jeez,' Nikki puffed away beside her.

The path became rocky. They had to watch their step.

'And then him coming back like that . . .' Cath continued as they neared the brow, feeling there was more to say. 'Walking into my new home, my new life . . . It made me angry and there was all that hurt still there. It just shook me up a bit.' She paused, then added, 'And I don't really like to admit it, but it's been confusing. It's like, seeing him again and talking, he reminded me of everything we did have before, before the huge bloody mess . . . that it had mattered, and it does still matter to him. I'm no mug. I'll not be daft about it. But why do I still feel something? It's so weird. Just thinking that, I feel like I'm letting myself down . . .'

'Oh, Cath, hun. You can't just switch off your feelings. You were together for so long . . . what was it, twenty-odd years . . .?'

'Thirty.'

'Thirty . . . crikey. Well, I'm sure there's been good times and affection. You must have loved each other once, as well as all the hurt and pain. You don't suddenly forget everything you once had. I don't know what the hell I'd do if Kev went off like that . . . murder him first and foremost, if he'd been playing around. But I'd miss him, us. You just get used to being together, don't you? I think I'd even miss the damn bickering.'

Cath was nodding, glad she'd opened up. That she had someone beside her to chat with, discuss these difficult feelings. 'And then Trev's been messaging since his visit, all apologetic and caring. I don't know what to make of it, really. It's just stirring everything up again.'

'Bet he's regretting his decision to leave now the initial lust-filled passion has passed. He'll be missing his home comforts. And I know how good your cooking is, too. *I* wouldn't have left you.'

Cath had to smile at that. 'Yeah, most likely . . . but you can't just turn back time, not after all this. He's burned his bridges.' She sounded more resolute than she felt, but a lump had lodged in her throat. Why was she still feeling so sad about it all? It was like, now it really was over, they'd realised what they once had. The moving on had hit a rut in the road.

'It's tricky, isn't it . . . relationships. I mean I love Kev to bits, mostly, but sometimes he drives me mad too. A lot of the time, actually. Sometimes you wonder, what if . . . ? What if I'd married that lad I used to go with, back in the day . . . or maybe found someone new?' Nikki paused, stopping for a few seconds. Catching up, from a few paces behind, to stand by Cath's side, she added, 'This hill . . . is mean. What are you doing to me?' She was panting, trying to catch her breath. 'But then you think . . . is the grass really greener? Yep, you might get a slightly better-looking version, but then they might end up having all sorts of weird traits, and you've just swapped one lot of problems for another... It's never going to be perfect, is it? And of course, me and Kev, we have the boys to think of. Why would we go wrecking it all for them?'

Cath felt a dart of emotion hearing that. Had she gone and wrecked things for Adam even though he was an adult? Cath still felt that mum-guilt. But it was Trevor who'd changed everything, she reminded herself. He was the one who'd let them both down, after all. Confusion and hurt bled through her thoughts. 'Yeah. Nothing's ever simple in life.'

Nikki carried on moaning about the hike. 'Have we still not reached the bloody top?' But Cath could tell she was actually kind of enjoying it. It was nice to talk, the two of them, as they kept pace. Nikki opened up a little more too. 'My lot, I just wish they'd sometimes stop and think what it's like for me. Running around after them all the time. Dirty socks and jocks, sweaty PE kits. Where's the romance and the fun in that?!'

Cath let out a chuckle.

Nikki changed tack, disconcertingly so, and started fishing about how Cath felt about Will. 'So, what do you think of our resident widower, then? Bit of a dish, isn't he? Now seeing him, that's when I do wish I was single . . .'

After their eventful bike ride just two days ago, this was far too close for comfort. Cath felt herself flush, and it wasn't just the uphill climb.

What did she think, indeed? He certainly made her heart beat faster, and they had been getting on well. Chatting with him at the last supper evening and on the bike ride was pleasant. In fact, it felt like she'd known him for a while, not just mere weeks. He was easy company, and yeah, she had to admit it . . . damned good-looking, which was nice. There was no more to it than that, though. And there was never going to be. 'Yeah, he's a nice guy,' she answered simply.

'You fancy him a bit, don't you?' Nikki probed. 'You'd be daft not to. Go on, tell me.' Nikki egged her on. 'Look, a bit of gossip is the only thing keeping me going up this hill, right now. You owe me . . .' She was grinning cheekily. 'I won't tell anyone, if you do. Your secret is safe with me, honest.'

Cath merely gave a knowing smile, saying, 'Look, I've had my fill, and more, of heartache. It's way too soon for me to get involved with anyone else. So, there's nothing going to be happening on that front, sorry to disappoint you.'

'Hah, so you do fancy him though. I knew it.' Nikki looked delighted with herself; somehow, she'd managed to wheedle a bit of a confession out of her new friend.

'Okay, yes, so he is quite pleasant on the eye . . .' That was all Cath was going to concede.

'Hah.' Nikki grinned.

At last, they reached the summit. They stood taking in the panoramic view (and for Nikki extra gasps of air); the purple-brown shades of the Cheviot Hills rising behind them, a delphinium-blue sky dotted with puffy summer clouds above, a buzzard soaring over them, and the slight chill in the air, now that they were higher.

Cath had enjoyed the hike, finding the walking invigorating and the chat somehow freeing, letting her troubled thoughts have a voice at least. Nikki even admitted as they stood there, that it had been 'nice' to get out and do something different, as long as Cath didn't get any ideas that they'd be doing this particular activity again any time soon.

'Well, what goes up must come down,' announced Cath with a smile, gesturing to the hillside track that wound down before them.

'Thank Christ for that,' said Nikki, adding, 'And, all roads home lead to the pub.'

'Hah, of course.' Cath had a feeling the way back down was going to be far, far quicker.

*

Back at The Star in the village, they each had a glass of well-deserved wine, sat at a corner table by the sun-streamed window. The conversation had by now turned to easier topics, with the main point of discussion being the next supper event. Nikki was still in 'thinking-cap mode', apparently. She wanted to make it a fun night for everyone, and she and Lily were soon to have a planning session.

Back home at her cottage, after saying their goodbyes at

the pub, Cath reflected that it had been a lovely couple of hours. She was left with a warm and heartening feeling that this particular friendship with Nikki could well blossom over time.

Chapter 24

Going for a 70s theme for my supper club night! Please dress accordingly. X 😊

The next day, being just five days before the supper event, this group message came through.

Followed by: **Of course this is not in any way a tactical ploy to distract you all from the quality of my cooking.**

Oh, and my niece Lily is coming too! x

Sounds great. Looking forward to it, sent back Cath. Her brain already buzzing about meeting up with the gang again – including Will – and also what she might wear. Now was the time to garner her inner boho-chic, Seventies style, apparently. Hah, she'd never been a very flamboyant dresser, her clothes being practical in the main, the smart if sensible maths teacher, in or out of school.

Ooh, love a bit of dressing up, answered Andreas. A thumbs-up symbol appeared from Dan, and an 'OK' with a smiley face from Will. Everyone would soon be raiding their wardrobes, browsing online or perhaps nipping to the local charity shop in Kirkton. The men of the group likely hunting down some nice brown flares and large-collared shirts to team with tank tops. Cath remembered a floppy Seventies-style felt hat she'd

176

once had, but hardly worn. Did she bring it with her? It might be somewhere in the wardrobe. Hmm, perhaps a colourful hippie-style dress might work with that, which she certainly didn't have. Indeed, a trip to the charity shop was now calling.

Despite fancy dress not being particularly her thing, she found herself warming to the idea and the challenge. It was in fact lovely to be doing something totally different with a new group of friends.

However, half an hour later, stood in her underwear in the charity shop changing room – well, more of a curtain pulled over one corner of the store, with a wooden stool and a long mirror – she had a bit of a shock. Oh, God, there in the mirror's reflection, her undies set looked almost more saggy and grey than herself, but not quite. What the hell had happened to her? To her body and her hair . . . these past few months, perhaps years?

She'd never got around to booking that hairdresser's appointment that she'd promised herself, either. She looked again, filling with gloom. Everything had sunk and lost its colour. And well, she hadn't invested in any new bras and pants in an age – no one had been looking, after all. That trip to the local hairdresser was the next thing to get organised. Bloody hell, hopefully they might squeeze her in before supper club next week. Perhaps some highlights, or some colour might bring her salt-and-pepper, wavy, okay frizzy, long bob back to a semblance of its former brunette glory. An online order for some M&S undies could be sorted.

And her body, well the walking wasn't enough, evidently. A body boot camp? Jeez, that might finish her off, but she'd ask around, there must be some kind of exercise class in the area.

She used to like doing a bit of yoga back in the day. Crikey, that must have been when Adam was little, trying to recoup her post-birth tummy. So that was, yep, over twenty years ago. No wonder it had all gone southwards in the subsequent years.

Feeling down in the dumps, she could almost see how Trevor might have lost his interest too. But then, she told herself off. It really wasn't her fault. He was no Tom Cruise. And he hadn't been to a gym in years, either.

Well then, no one else was seeing her like this, no way. Sex, in her current condition, was an absolute no-go. Why the hell did Will slip into her mind then? She'd have to be trussed up in a Victorian nightie or something. Full cover, except for essential access. She made herself giggle.

'Are you okay in there? Need any help?' The assistant's voice came through the curtain.

Body double. Face lift. Magician of a hairdresser, came to mind.

'I'm fine, thanks. Just need to try on a couple more things,' was what she actually said.

'Just shout if you need anything.'

'Okay, thanks.'

Right, back to the issue in hand. No use standing mourning her lost figure. A boho Seventies-style dress, that needed to look acceptable, was required for the impending supper club do at Nikki's. She did at least have a reasonable bust left, she noted, as long as it was firmly lifted in a brassiere. The first gown was a green paisley print, which looked okay but made her feel like she needed to burst into some Irish dancing. The second was a white cheesecloth with lace. Nope, far too bridal, and virginal. She looked much too old for it. The third, and last, was a floral number with flared long sleeves (a good covering for the bingo wings – bonus) and though it was just above knee level, her legs were still fairly slim (about the only darned things that were!). She figured they could be allowed on show, with a pair of tights as cover, and perhaps long boots.

'Any good?' The assistant was hovering outside the curtain again.

'Yeah, I think this one might do.' She dared to reveal the outfit.

'Ooh yes, it looks good on you.' The sixty-something lady was smiling. 'I remember wearing something like that back in the day. Wish I still had legs like yours for it now, though.'

'Do you think I can get away with it? I'm no spring chicken, after all.' Cath was a little hesitant.

'Of course. Flaunt it while you can, dear.'

She had to smile at that. 'Boots?' she ventured. 'Do you have any long ones, that might go with this? Size six. It's for a Seventies party.'

'Ah, now I'm with you. Just give me a mo. I think I might just have the perfect pair.' She bustled off, apparently enjoying her mission.

Cath loitered in the changing area.

'Here.' A couple of minutes later the curtain shifted, revealing a pair of white lace-up boots that looked like something the girls from Abba might have worn. The platforms on them were extremely high. Cath could feel the blisters forming just looking at them.

'Ooh, sorry, but I need to actually walk and spend a whole evening in them,' Cath explained. 'They fit the Seventies part well, though. Do you have anything else?'

'Damn, I thought I'd finally found a home for them. But never fear . . . give me a mo, and I'll check again.' The lady set off once more. There then followed some rummaging noises from the shop floor.

The curtain shifted. 'Here you go, brown leather, knee high . . . What do you think?'

'Now *they* look perfect. Let's hope for a good fit.' Cath smiled. They were a really lovely tan leather boot. They'd look fine with the dress. And, even after the supper event, they'd go well with many an outfit over the autumn and winter months.

They did, in fact, slip on like a glove. She did a quick sway in front of the mirror. The dress swished about her. The boots were stylish, making the legs less revealing too. 'The job's a good 'un. Thanks so much for your help.' Cath grinned.

By some miracle, the woman reflecting back at her in the mirror already looked so much better than the half-naked saggy one she'd spotted a few moments before. She paid a bargain price for the two items, happy to be helping out the local hospice charity too, and left feeling a positive surge. Boho chic might be the way to go, thought the new-style Cath.

And to the hairdressers next! There was one at the end of the high street. No time like the present. Pausing outside the door, she suddenly felt embarrassed that she hadn't set foot inside a salon for . . . well, a very long time. And her locks would certainly be showing it. She took a deep breath and opened the door to a blast of warm air and fragrant hairspray.

'Good morning,' a lady with a classy blonde bob greeted her from behind the counter.

'Hi, umm, I'm new to the area. Looking to get a cut and

colour done. It's been a while . . .' She grimaced apologetically. 'Do you happen to have any spare appointments?'

'Actually, it's unusual, but I've just had a cancellation for Monday morning, 10 a.m. How does that suit?'

'Sounds like it's my lucky day. I'll take it, thank you.' The trip to the local town was proving to be positive.

The hairdresser gave her a swift and sweeping glance above shoulder level. 'Are we talking restyle or just a trim? And colour-wise, any thoughts?' She was trying to be polite, but Cath knew she must be thinking *this is some kind of a bird's nest I'm dealing with.*

'Better be a restyle . . .' Cath conceded. 'And I used to be a brunette, but I'm not sure quite what to do with it colour-wise now.'

'No problem. We can do a quick patch test now if you'd like, and then why not take one of these hair magazines, and also have a look online at any styles you think you might like, and we can chat about that and the colours that might work with your skin tone on Monday. Sound okay?' She came across as practical but friendly. Cath had already warmed to her.

'Sounds great. Thank you.'

Crikey, the supper event had somehow turned itself into a makeover.

Well, it was about bloody time, a voice in Cath's head shouted out.

Chapter 25

All dressed up with somewhere to go, Cath walked up the village street carrying a wicker basket filled with six mini-bottles of Babycham (which she'd been delighted to find online) and a hand-tied posy of pink roses from her garden for Nikki. She felt a little warm in her tall leather boots on this balmy summer's evening, with her knee-length green-and-red floral dress swishing about her, but looked very much the Seventies part.

She was pretty happy with her new look, but also a little nervous about arriving in this alternative guise. Was it too much? Mutton dressed as lamb, perhaps? The knees were out, plus a fair amount of decolletage in this hippie dress, and her hair, well . . . Louise, at the hairdresser's, had performed miracles indeed.

'Wow, well who do we have here?' Nikki, in full Abba-style white-and-blue-trimmed kimono plus long blonde wig, stood open-mouthed. And, on her feet, the charity shop white lace-up boots! They'd found their perfect home. 'Goodness, Cath, you look amazing.'

'Hah, well I could say the same about you. A real Dancing Queen. Brilliant. And those boots – Kirkton Charity Shop by any chance? They look fantastic on you.'

'Yes! Come on through. The lads are here, and Lily.'

'Oh my! Cath, is that you? You look fabulous, darling. And the hair, is that real?' Dan leaned across to stroke her lovely locks. 'Has to be, it's far too good to be a wig . . . I love it.' He was dressed in orange corduroy flares teamed with a black silk shirt, open-necked beneath a hilariously dreadful patterned tank top. Andreas, who stood beside him, had gone full 'Magnum Pi' Tom Selleck style, his naturally dark hair in a bouffant, and a bushy fake moustache in place, above flared denim trousers and a Hawaiian-style red floral shirt. It made Cath chuckle seeing the pair of them.

Cath's hair had indeed gone from hanging in a shaggy greying mop to a wavy shoulder-length bob that was now a glossy mid-brown shade. It might need a bit of root work doing now and again to keep it in order, but she felt so much more like her old self that it'd be more than worth it. The colourist at the salon had advised that full brunette might be a step too far, but a mid-brown with some lighter tones through it would be 'a gorgeous and more natural-looking alternative'.

'Drinks anyone? I've made a jug of Blue Lagoon cocktail. Or there's a G&T alternative,' offered Nikki.

'Oh, go on, I'll give the cocktail a try,' answered Cath.

'It's lethal, I warn you,' Dan said, with a grin.

'This is our second. Rocket fuel,' added Andreas.

'Don't be so soft,' tutted Nikki.

'Oh, and here's a little contribution to the evening, and some flowers for the chef.' Cath offered over her basket of goodies.

Nikki pulled out one of the mini bottles. 'Hah, Babycham, that's brilliant. Used to love that stuff. I'd be allowed one at Christmastime. Made me right tiddly back in the day.'

'Needs a whole bottle of Prosecco nowadays, Auntie Niks,' Lily chipped in, as she came through from the kitchen with a bowl of Hula Hoops in one hand and one of prawn-flavoured Skips in the other. She was striking with her dark hair edgily cropped into a short style, her red lipstick bold, dressed in boot-cut jeans with a flowing white broderie anglaise hippy-style top.

'This is Lily, folks. My niece.'

'Hi, everyone.' She had a broad smile, which came right from her kohl-lined green eyes. 'Snacks? Do help yourself.' She popped the bowls down onto the wooden coffee table.

'Sorry, I warned you I was no chef,' added Nikki. 'Though, I have actually made the next two courses myself.'

'Well, they fit the Seventies theme. And who doesn't love a Hula Hoop,' said Dan, helping himself.

Nikki's front room was neat and tidy, painted a soft grey, with a traditional open fireplace and oak-wood mantelpiece. There were pictures of her family dotted around. The two sofas were a cosy dark-blue velour and a little on the large side for the room. A big TV stood in one corner with an X-Box and controllers tucked beside it. It was a family room, and Cath had the feeling that it was never normally this orderly, for sure.

The doorbell then went. Nikki soon coming back with an apologetic Will on her heels. 'Sorry, I know I'm cutting it fine, everyone. Been a busy day at the shop. Then I had to get my costume sorted. It's been thrown together a bit last minute. Fancy dress is not my forte. I made a quick trip to Belford to raid my parents' wardrobe.'

Ah, so Will had family in Belford. The village was around five miles away, midway between Tilldale and the coast. Cath's mind flitted to **her** childhood caravan holidays there in the past. And then settled on that last holiday as a teenager. Oh . . . Cath felt herself flush, complex emotions surging forward that had been kept down for so many years. Swiftly pulling herself back to the present, she took a large sip of her Blue Lagoon.

'Hah, can't believe my old dad has kept this shirt for all these years,' Will chortled. He was sporting a very loud swirly-patterned orange-and-brown polyester shirt which had huge Seventies-style collars. Somehow, he still managed to look quite dashing in it. 'You guys all look great, too.' He gestured around the room.

His toffee-hazel eyes settled on Cath. She smiled, but felt kind of odd.

'So, how did you decide on a Seventies party then, Nikki?' asked Dan. 'After all, you're a mere whippersnapper compared to us lot. Some of us might actually remember the Seventies, but I bet you weren't even born then.'

'True, '87 is my year of birth. I'm still holding on to my thirties . . . just. Child bride and all that.' She smiled. 'I dunno, there's something super-nostalgic about the Seventies . . . sort of iconic. The clothes are something else. And the food, well my mam must have still been cooking all that stuff when I was a kid, 'cos when I looked it up, there it all was: prawn cocktails, Spam fritters and steak suppers . . . oh, I'm giving the menu away.'

'Hah, yes, Spam, and those cans of corned beef. My mum used to make a really good corned beef hash, actually,' added Dan.

'It was corned beef pie in our house, with a nice shortcrust pastry,' added Cath. 'Oh, and do you remember those metal cans were bloody lethal . . . the ones with the sideways turna-round ring pulls. Many a cut finger from those.'

'God, yes, you needed danger money to open them.'

'And the desserts of the day . . . Well, you'll have to wait for the pudding course for all to be revealed.' Nikki gave a knowing wink.

'Can't wait. This is going to be such a fun night.' Andreas sounded cheery. It was nice to see him in the moment and smiling again, after all the stress he'd been having with his mother's ill health.

'Oh, and remember those Spangles sweets, and Opal fruits, yes – what are they called now?' reminisced Will.

'Starburst,' advised Lily.

'Ah, yes, that's it.'

'And oh, the giddy days when Snickers used to be Marathons,' added Dan.

'And when Mars bars used to be big,' said Andreas. 'Is it just me or has everything shrunk?'

Dan gave a cheeky laugh before responding, 'Everything has shrunk, my love.'

Will nearly spat out his gin and tonic at that (having not been tempted by the lurid-coloured Blue Lagoon). The group were chuckling en masse.

Stood chatting away in Nikki's lounge, they began to settle into the soiree.

'Nibbles then. Prawn Cocktail Skips anyone, or perhaps a cheesy Quaver?' offered Dan. 'Hey, I love that Nikki's taken this Seventies thing to every level.'

*

186

'So, it's time for the culinary delights, folks. Brace yourselves,' Nikki announced a short while later. 'Come on through.'

She led the gathering through to the dining room, where the table had been set simply with a white linen cloth, cutlery and sparkling-clean wine glasses as well as water tumblers. In the centre was a white church candle, a jug of iced water, and a small posy of sweet peas in a cut-glass jar. The dining room dresser was adorned with more pictures of the kids at various ages; some of the lads sporting football trophies, a holiday snap of them all in Tenerife. And there was a wedding photo of Nikki and Kevin stood outside Tilldale's village church, both looking extremely young.

Nikki caught Cath's gaze. 'Yep, that's us pair on our wedding day. And look at Kev with a full head of hair – his brown locks have receded these past few years, he's now sporting a buzz cut.'

They were frames filled with love, and tales of a busy family life.

'Lads, I've got you two at the far side. Lily, you're that end, Will and Cath over here, and I'll take the other table end for easy access to the kitchen.'

Nikki might not be saying a thing but the cheeky look in her eye told Cath that the table seating was by design. Cath took a breath and settled herself beside Will. The table wasn't the biggest, so they found themselves sitting quite snugly side by side. If she moved an inch her thigh would in fact be brushing his, she realised, feeling the heat rise through her at the mere thought. She swiftly poured herself a glass of water, taking a cooling glug.

'Oh, I may as well serve the Babycham at this point,' said

Nikki. 'Lily, before you sit down, petal, could you help get the Prosecco flutes? Top right-hand cupboard, above the kettle. Thanks.'

Soon, everyone had one of Cath's individual bottles before them, and they all unscrewed the tops at virtually the same time, with a hearty 'Cheers.'

'It's a shame I haven't got the proper little glasses.'

'Ah yes, those circular low-sided ones with the little deer on.' Cath remembered them well.

'Coupes,' Andreas elaborated.

'Ooh, delish. Seems a lot sweeter now, mind,' added Nikki as she took her first taste. 'But it's still lovely.'

'That's because you've doused yourself in Prosecco these past few years.' Andreas winked.

After a few more sips, Nikki disappeared to the kitchen. When she came back, she was carrying a tray of glasses filled with layers of crispy green and creamy pink. 'And the first course is . . . ta-dah, my bloody Mary prawn cocktail.'

'Oh, that sounds positively delightful, Niks,' said Cath.

The glasses were loaded with crisp iceberg lettuce, a rich cocktail-style sauce and king prawns. A half-moon slice of lemon had been placed over the rim.

'These look gorgeous, Nikki. Thank you,' Andreas said.

'Oh, this has certainly got some oomph,' said Dan, after his first spoonful.

'Delicious. Spicy, with a kick of vodka, yes?' Will grinned.

It certainly tasted great to Cath. The prawns were juicy and the sauce had a chilli-vodka kick. 'Love it,' she added. 'What a great idea, to twist up a prawn cocktail.'

'Well, there wasn't really much cooking involved, I have

to confess. A bit of mayo, tommy puree, spices, lemon, and a splash of vodka that I found at the back of the cupboard.'

'Don't put yourself down,' said Dan. 'Good food doesn't have to be complicated, just tasty. And if you don't happen to be slogging all day in the kitchen, all the better. As you get to enjoy the occasion too.'

'Ah, thanks, guys. Though I am a bit nervous about the main,' Nikki confessed. 'I've set myself a task, I'm cooking steak for everyone. Hope you like them medium, 'cos I don't think there's any way I can do them all different.'

'Oh, that sounds wonderful. But I hope you didn't feel you had to go to all that expense and trouble for us,' Will said thoughtfully.

Indeed, Cath thought, supper club had been about getting together over good food, but it shouldn't mean it had to cost a fortune. Her own funds were limited just now, and Cath really didn't want to put pressure on anyone in the group financially or otherwise, nor make them feel uncomfortable. 'Absolutely,' she agreed. 'There's no need to spend a fortune.'

'Nah, it's fine. I got a good tip on Monday, did an oven clean as an extra,' Nikki explained. 'And well, I know how to cook a steak for me and Kev, as it's his favourite. So, I figured it was best to stick with what I know. Just need to have two pans on the go at once. Also, it just happens to be a Seventies classic, and Lily's made a "Diane" sauce for them. And the chips are in the air fryer as we speak.' The hostess was up and ready to go again.

'Let us know if we can help?' offered Andreas.

'Thanks, but I have Lils as my sous chef. She's been doing a grand job.'

With Dan and Andreas deep in conversation about some technical issue with the post office that had cropped up at the shop, Will leaned in to ask Cath how she was feeling after the bike accident, and then what she'd been 'up to' lately. How did he make that question sound sexy? His breath was warm on her cheek, and his long, manly fingers were clasped gently around his wine glass. She felt her pulse rise, her nerve endings tingling. His eyes caught hers, those dark pools hiding depths of emotions, his inevitable grief still lingering there as well as the flickers of humour and light. Why did those eyes seem familiar, when they'd surely never met until she moved into the village? And why, dammit, was she feeling so very odd, like a bloody teenager with a crush?

Man up, Cath. Don't overthink it. He's just a friend, a new friend . . . who happens to be rather attractive . . . and looks like Marti Pellow. Gulp. Hmm, it was that melting kind of look across the eyes that she seemed to recognize for sure. Those 'Angel Eyes' really were setting her on fire.

And as they finished their starter, he asked, 'So Cath, how did you come to choose our little village of Tilldale as your new home?'

'Well, we'd been to the area often as kids. My mum and dad used to bring us up to Belford . . . to the caravan park there.'

'Ah, right.' Will took a sip of wine. Suddenly shifting in his seat, he leaned back, away from her.

'Then later,' Cath continued, 'as I loved the area so much, I came back with my own family. It's so beautiful here, the coast, the countryside. We booked a cottage a few times in the summer holidays. That's when I rediscovered Tilldale. We ate in the village pub.'

'Hah, always a good watering hole.' Will managed a tight smile, then went quiet, looking pensive. The conversation between them came to a halt, and thankfully, the main course of steaks arrived, Lily and Nikki bringing the plates in.

'Sirloin steaks à la Diane. Bloody hell, I hope I've cooked them all right. I've been worrying about this bit all day.'

'I'm sure they'll be delicious,' reassured Will.

Everyone tucked in, and despite Nikki's concerns, they were cooked well – still a little pink in the middle – served with chips, broccoli, and Lily's piquant garlic-mushroom Diane sauce. The tummies around the table were soon full and happy.

'You've done us proud, Nikki. And Lily. Thank you,' said Cath.

'Compliments to the chef.' Will raised his wine glass, now filled with a smooth Merlot. 'Or chefs should I say. That Diane sauce is delicious, Lily.'

'Bravissimo!' Andreas gave a salute. 'Or, *Yperocho!* should I say. Wonderful.'

*

Watching the group chat together, Cath had been thinking about how hard it had felt starting over again in a new place, yet already she was making friends. Dan and Andreas must have done the same, moving here several years ago, but their situation would have been very different.

'Do you mind if I ask you something, guys?' Cath ventured,

looking to the lads as she spoke, and feeling far more comfortable with the group.

'Absolutely, fire away . . .' said Andreas.

'There's not much can faze us.' Dan smiled.

'Well, coming here, starting again . . . it's not easy for anyone.' Cath was thinking of her own bumps along the road, as she tried to settle into rural life. 'But for you as a gay couple . . . how did you find moving to this small village? Did you struggle at all? I mean it's such a tight-knit community here.'

'Ah, well, it was fine in the main.' Andreas was nodding, thinking back. 'And we *were* the only gays in the village,' he added with a grin.

'Uhm, there can always be hints of prejudice . . . wherever you are,' Dan said more honestly. 'But we never faced anything major, nothing at all threatening.'

'Ugh, some people can be so small-minded,' chipped in Lily, frustrated on their behalf.

'Of course, but I think some of the early comments we heard came from curiosity . . .' Andreas continued, 'and some preconceptions, which in time they realised we just didn't fit.'

Dan said, 'We didn't come in all bells and whistles. We just opened the shop and got on with it.'

'And that was great,' Will spoke up. 'You gave that old shop a new lease of life.'

'I think at first, many thought we were business partners,' Dan explained. 'But then, living together above the shop, and socialising together, some began to put two and two together . . . and well, you know what Tilldale can be like, the news soon began to spread.'

'A few eyebrows were definitely raised,' Andreas agreed, raising his own emphatically. 'But you know what, people had got to know us and on the whole they were absolutely fine. They still wanted their bread, milk and paper supplies . . . and my cake and baklava. We'd reeled them in by then.' He winked.

'Do you remember old Kenneth asking if we were one of those "queer" couples? He blurted it out right in the middle of the shop, that day,' Dan elaborated.

'I do indeed. And Veronica, who happened to be in at the time – she's a rather, how shall I say it, hmm, domineering type . . . in charge of the village hall committee – well, she shot him down in flames. "I think you'll find that's a derogatory term, Kenneth. You absolutely cannot use that any more . . ." She'd pulled herself up to her full five-feet-two and was plumped up like a peacock.'

The visual made Cath smile.

'It had helped that we'd just given a generous donation to the village hall fund,' added Andreas.

'Oh, the committee would be more than happy to take your money off you, whatever they might be saying behind closed doors,' Nikki added wryly.

'Back to Kenneth, well, he'd flushed bright red by then. "Ee, I'm sorry, lads. I was just asking,"' Dan continued.

'Actually, Kenneth, "queer" is one of the words we're fine with,' Andreas recounted. 'Veronica, you're right in one way. It used to be offensive, but we and the LGBT community use it with pride now . . . And it's fine you asking questions, that's how you find out the truth. Yes, we are a gay couple.'

"Gay, blimey . . . that used to mean happy back in my day," Kenneth had said,' Andreas continued.

'Well, let's just say we are very happy,' Dan retold the finale. 'And that was it. The old chap was more interested in getting his milk and newspaper then.'

'Naturally, Veronica was off swiftly spreading the news that yes, we were a gay couple. And once the news was out, no one seemed to bother much about it anymore. We were just the lads, or the boys.'

'People around here are pretty straightforward in the main,' Nikki added. 'If they like you, they like you, and if not, that's nothing to do with the colour of your skin or whether you're gay or otherwise, it's down to who you are and how you treat people. Like everyone, we just need a little respect.'

'Well said, Niks.' Will nodded in agreement, having lived in the area for a long time.

'Now that reminds me of a song . . . you know, the Erasure one. "A Little Respect".' And with that, Andreas started trilling away.

*

As if they could fit in any more . . . soon afterwards came the puds! Yet somehow, they managed.

A Viennetta – brilliant! – was served on a white porcelain platter by hostess Nikki, with a fanfare of pretend pipes from Lily, along with an Arctic Roll (which had been hunted down and sourced from Asda, apparently). The group couldn't help but laugh as these retro desserts arrived. With everyone bar Lily remembering these ice-cream puddings fondly, they had to admit they still tasted good.

The follow-up surprise, and the real pièce de résistance was

Lily's creation – a divine Black Forest gateau: all chocolate sponge, whipped cream and plump black cherries soaked in Kirsch. And wow, could that girl bake. It looked like something Mary Berry might have made, neat and professional, and at the first bite it was evident that the sponge was light and airy too, and oh so chocolatey.

'Wow, Lily, this is incredible,' Cath purred.

'Hey, girl, you should be on that *Bake Off* programme. What a talent!' Andreas grinned.

'It's sooo good. I can hardly speak,' Nikki murmured. 'I knew you liked baking . . . but this, wowser.'

'Heaven, I'm in heaven,' Dan began singing.

The grin Lily gave brightened not only her face but the whole room. 'Aw, thanks, guys. I adore cooking . . . baking especially. I did follow a recipe for this one, but I also like experimenting with flavours. In fact,' she began to reveal her aspirations, 'I'd really love to work with food . . . maybe even become a chef one day. That's my dream. Once I've learned the skills and worked my way up, of course.' Her face lit up as she spoke of her ambitions. 'Got to get the A Levels smashed out first, though. And well . . . going the chef way, it might not quite be as easy as that . . .' She bit down on her lip, then sighed, as her face dropped. She went quiet, looking unsure of herself.

'Well, I think I'd mentioned that Lily's parents – my brother and his wife,' Nikki stepped in to explain, 'want her to go the "sensible" route. To go off to uni and study something traditional. You're a clever girl, after all . . . aren't you, petal?' Her aunt gave her a supportive wink.

'But what I'd really love to do is to go to catering college, learn the trade,' admitted Lily. 'And it'd be amazing if I could get an apprenticeship with a good chef. And, if it were a pastry chef, well, that'd be the dream.'

'There's a bit of a battle going on at home just now,' Nikki continued. 'It's time to choose unis and courses . . . and, I can see both sides to be fair . . . but if you have a talent in something that you love, how wonderful to try and make a career out of it.'

'Lily, I've been teaching students of your age group for years,' started Cath. She had heard so many youngsters' dreams in her career, and this one sounded positive and achievable. The young woman seemed as though she was prepared to put the work in, too. 'I'd look at all the options if I were you, find out as much as you can about the catering courses you're interested in, *and* look into your parents' preferences. Then narrow it down, and go and visit the unis and colleges you like the best. Talk to people, be brave, be interested. Find out more about any local chefs you admire too, offer to help out, perhaps see if you can do some work experience for them.'

'Yeah, that sounds good.'

'Be honest with your parents about your dreams, but be prepared to listen to them, too.' The mother in Cath was coming to the fore. 'Then you might be able to make a good decision all together.'

'Sounds like good advice to me,' encouraged Dan.

'And if you need anyone to try out your baking, or recipes, in the meanwhile, you know where to come,' Andreas added with a touch of warm humour that lifted the mood.

'And if you ever want any more help or advice, Lily, feel free to ask. I've had pupils go off and do all kinds of incredible things. There are so many opportunities these days. Do your research, and then go for it.' As she spoke the words, Cath realised she should be taking her own advice. After the move, which was a huge step admittedly, it had felt like she'd holed herself up too much. Her self-confidence had been knocked so badly by all that had happened. Was it time to dream big once more? To keep trying new things, to find her wings.

Chapter 26

The end of the evening came around all too soon. It was great that Dan and Andreas had made it for the supper, despite the difficult time they were having personally. Cath had asked about Maria earlier, learning that she had settled back into the care home, but was still quite frail. They had all made the most of this fun and relaxed evening. Nikki admitting that her cooking still needed a little help from her friends, but the Seventies idea had been a huge hit.

As Dan and Andreas were about to leave, Andreas swept Nikki up in a warm embrace. 'What a wonderful night. And thanks so much for putting a smile back on our faces. You've done fabulously with the Seventies theme.' The lads turned to the gathering in the hallway then. 'Thank you, everyone, thank you so much. It's been a really tough couple of weeks for us.' Dan was nodding with an emotional tear glistening in his eye at this point. 'And, this group, this gorgeous supper club . . . well, it's been like a great big hug, getting together again with you lot.'

'Ah, you're very welcome, lads. And it's all thanks to you two and Cath. It's you who brought us all together, after all.'

'Aw.' Cath felt a lump in her throat.

The two lads then set off down the street, Tom Selleck with his flared-corduroy-hero partner, arm in arm and slightly wobbly on their feet, after the Blue Lagoons, Babycham and several top-ups of Merlot.

'Oh, it's been nice to see them enjoy themselves.' Nikki closed the door after them.

'Yeah, bless them. They've had such a rotten time lately,' agreed Cath.

'Now, then, can I walk you two ladies home?' offered Will, addressing Lily and Cath.

'Oh, thank you.' Lily smiled.

'Ah . . . yes, that'd be good, thanks.' Cath sounded slightly hesitant.

It wasn't far, and it was nice that Will was looking out for them both. But as Cath lived at the far end of the village, it was likely, she realised, that she and Will would be alone for some of the walk. The pit in Cath's stomach did a little stupid flip. *Get a grip*, she told herself.

She spotted Nikki giving her an eyebrow raise at that point, with what looked to be a smug smile. Why had she ever confessed on their hike that she agreed he was good-looking? And surely, Nikki hadn't got wind of Cath's teenage-style dizzy emotions that were going on this evening. Bloody hell, she'd never hear the last of it. The lid needed to be kept on this crazy little crush, and firmly closed. She silently vowed not to say anything else at all about Will to Niks, however many Proseccos down they might be.

*

The air was cool and calm as the trio strolled down the village street in the velvet-dark of a midnight summer sky. Will was in the middle of them, with a gentle arm supporting the ladies each side. Cath's high leather boots gave an echoey clonk at each step. A smattering of stars twinkled above them, the occasional street lamp lighting their way, as they chatted about what a fun evening it had been.

It had been a late night and a great night. The supper club group gelling even more, with the delightful Lily fitting in like a breath of youthful fresh air.

First drop-off – as anticipated – was Lily, at a converted barn, which was set back slightly from the main street. She found her key, thanking the pair of them for seeing her home. The young girl gave Cath a warm hug, saying she was grateful for her advice earlier that evening.

'Any time,' Cath replied. She'd enjoyed being able to chat things through with Lily. The cloak of teacher and at times 'life coach' to her students had slipped back on easily, and it felt good. Even with the unavoidable stresses in her last years of teaching, with the role constantly changing, the core of it had always been to try and help, to open minds and inspire. Learning wasn't just facts and figures, and maths wasn't just equations, life skills were part and parcel of that, too. It felt good to be able to help someone again.

'Night, Lily, and no need to rush those big decisions,' added Will sagely. He had two grown-up daughters too, of course. 'And hey, remember that sometimes there's no real right or wrong way. It's just about finding the best fit for your life, and giving it your best shot.'

Cath gave him a heartfelt look. His words were so right.

'Thanks, Will.' Lily paused, adding, 'You know, I thought it might be a bit boring tonight, what with you lot all being, like, my parents' ages.' She gave a cheeky smile. 'But it's actually been pretty cool.'

'Hah, I think we'll take that as a compliment.' Will grinned, as Cath shook her head whilst laughing.

'Good night, Lily.'

'Night, you two.'

They watched her safely in, waiting to hear the lock click securely on the door behind her. Then they set off once more, Will's hand gently resting in the small of Cath's back, two pairs of feet walking in time to a rhythm that echoed down the little main street of the village.

'She's a great girl, isn't she,' said Will.

'Yeah, so vibrant and enthusiastic. And I do think she has every chance of succeeding in a catering career. Her baking was wonderful. And with an attitude like hers, she'll go a long way.'

'Yep, and I can understand her parents' concerns, too. We were all sent the sensible route, back in the day. Well, I certainly was . . . I wasn't really that academic. So, the fire brigade it was for me. A good steady job.'

'And I did the uni thing. Got a good degree, and then became a teacher.' Cath half-sighed, thinking . . . *And got married, had a son, brought him up. And then, it all went horribly wrong.*

'Too sensible?' Will questioned.

'Umm, I don't think so. Well, not career-wise anyhow. I always loved teaching, still do. Keeping my hand in with the online tutoring just now,' she explained. 'I always felt I made a difference, well most of the time. And yeah, it was great chatting with Lily tonight.'

'Yeah. You two seemed to get on well.'

'Oh, what it is to be young. You have the whole world ahead of you, and yet it feels so very confusing too.'

'Not much different now, really,' mused Will wryly. 'Just as confusing . . . with a bit less time.'

'Hah, you're so right. Didn't we learn anything?'

She was exquisitely aware of his arm held gently against her back. Cath glanced across at him in the half-light. He must have gone through so much, having to cope with losing his wife. And for her, there was her mess of a marriage. Did it ever get any easier? Did you ever know what life was about? Or which way you were meant to go?

He caught her gaze, slowing his steps, then suddenly switching tack. 'Hey, you know you said you used to come up this way on holiday, back in the day . . . ?'

'Yeah, yeah. We used to hire a caravan over at the site at Belford. Of course, you must have known that place, if you lived there.'

'Ca-th.' Will's voice softened, sounding serious. He stopped walking, and looked right at her in the silver shadows of the street light. 'Back then . . .' There was a second's silence, and a flash of angst crossed his face. But when he spoke again, all he said was 'Hah, all that stuff from the Seventies tonight . . . I've just remembered, didn't Twix bars used to be called Raiders?'

'Oh . . . yeah.' Cath felt like that was a bluff, that it wasn't what he had been about to say at all. 'Yeah, I think they were.'

She wanted to ask if he was all right? What was he remembering? Something to do with his wife? His childhood? But she didn't really know him that well, and she didn't want to spoil what had been a lovely night so far, by prying too much.

'Yep, it was a fun night, wasn't it? Despite her fears, Nikki did us all proud.' Will slipped the conversation back to safer ground.

Now they were back at Cath's cottage. Stood on the doorstep, just a foot or so apart, Cath once again felt unable to stop that teenage-style rush of emotions. What was wrong with her tonight? Her defences felt dashed.

Will gave a careful smile, which she returned. The night air between them feeling strangely charged.

'Ah, well . . . thanks for walking me home, Will.'

DO NOT ASK HIM IN FOR COFFEE. GO INSIDE, RIGHT NOW, CATH TAYLOR, rang in her head like an alarm bell.

The gap between them closed as Will took a slow step forward. OH SHIT . . . might he be about to . . . did she want that? What would his lips taste like, feel like, against hers? She hadn't kissed anyone in an age, not even her husband in those past couple of years.

Panicking a little at the prospect, her fingertips fumbled for her house keys. They dropped to the ground with a metallic clang. Flustered, she crouched down, rummaging about on the dimly lit front step. The moment broken, no chance to find out now. He'd taken a step back. Oh well, it was all for the best.

She said a polite goodnight and went in through the door. But inside, stood with her back against the wall of the hallway, catching her breath, she wondered if in fact that was what she really did feel? That it was for the best. Or had a special moment just slipped through her fingers?

*

Upstairs in her bed, tucked under the white cotton covers, the realisation hit her. Dammit, she did want to find out what his kiss felt like. *Ah, dear God, I like him, I really like him.*

Well, that was no good, that was no good at all. And some things were indeed best kept under wraps. After the stress and hurt of the past few years, the last thing she needed was to dabble in a new relationship.

Friends, that was the best way to stay. No need to change things, to find out how it might go horribly wrong, risking messing up the supper group in the process.

And hey, she reminded herself, after recently seeing her middle-aged body in the cold light of a changing room mirror, the fear of revealing any of it was enough to stall any lustful inclinations she might have and stop them dead in their tracks.

It was time to sleep, to stop this silliness.

*

Yet, she was still mulling it over in the morning, with the aid of a strong cup of coffee. Will – to be or not to be?

Nope, I'm NOT going there. It's NOT going to happen. It's just a stupid crush.

Who knew you could still feel like this in your fifties? But the crux of it all, was that there was absolutely no point jumping from the frying pan into the bloody fire.

She absolutely did not want to risk the wonderful ambience of the supper group by messing things up with some romantic notion that might all too soon go horribly wrong.

They just had to stay friends, and that was that.

Chapter 27

'Hey, Mum, I'm coming back!'

'Ah, that's lovely news, Adam. When?'

'Set off tomorrow. Flight lands Tuesday, Edinburgh. It's an early one as the last leg's overnight. You don't fancy a trip to the airport, do you?'

Hah, that was typical, but also rather lovely. 'Well, yeah, of course. It'll be wonderful to see you again. Be great to catch up on all your news and adventures.'

'And the washing . . .' he chortled.

She might have known that was coming her way. But after months apart, it was probably the least she could do. She felt a buzz of excitement at seeing her son again. At being able to hold him in her arms. However old your children were, there was nothing quite like being able to give them a hug.

'And can I stay with you for a bit, yeah? 'Til I get sorted with some digs? Maybe for a week or two. Dad didn't seem too keen on having me at the flat, to be honest. Says things aren't quite settled with Steph, right now.'

Jeez, had he gone back to her already, after all that faff turning up in Tilldale like a lost soul? Or was her ex trying to sort out his own place to rent? Whatever was going on, it seemed he might well have reverted to Turncoat Trevor mode.

'Yeah, I'm basically homeless with you two selling up.' Adam's tone was light, but the fact was that their family home was gone, sold.

A dart of guilt hit Cath once again, but she reminded herself, it wasn't her misdemeanours that had started the whole crashing down of the Roundhay house of cards. She suddenly felt irritable, feeling the shine was being tarnished on Adam's impending arrival, but she held back from dissing her ex-husband to their son. 'Well, even if our old house has gone, we'll both always be your parents and have a home for you.'

But undoubtedly, the new family dynamics were going to take a bit of getting used to for them all.

*

After an early alarm call, and a quick shower, she was on her way up the A1, heading north towards Scotland. Just twenty-five minutes from Tilldale, and she was over the border and on a stretch of single carriageway past Berwick-upon-Tweed, where the cliffs shelved sharply and rather stunningly down to the pewter-grey North Sea.

Next, a series of dual carriageways led her up the coastal route, then up over hills and down again, passing rounda-bouts off Dunbar, Haddington, soon to hit the traffic of the Edinburgh City By-Pass. It was still only just past 5 a.m. – she'd given herself plenty of time – and yet there was already quite a flux of vehicles and lorries. She felt slightly anxious as she didn't know the roads here that well, even though she'd always been okay negotiating the Leeds city traffic. The roads in Tilldale were quieter by far. In the past few weeks, she'd gotten used to the odd tractor, farm truck, a tourist vehicle or two and the slower pace of the country roads.

Cath hoped her satnav would be kind to her. It was the first time she'd ever been to Edinburgh Airport, and she'd researched the on-airport car park best to pick up from. Oh, there it was, the slip road she needed to take. A quick indication, manoeuvre, and off she went. Another busy road, following signs for the airport. Her heart beat a little faster, with the tension of finding the right car park. She felt a flutter of excitement at the thought of seeing her son again. It had been many weeks after all. She'd given him wings and let him fly, but it felt good that she'd be getting him back to her nest – even if it was her new nest – once again.

She'd whizzed about yesterday, making up the spare room with fresh linen, moving out her laptop and work gear from there, and cooking his favourite Thai chicken curry – oh, might he actually be sick of curry after all that Asian travel? Maybe, it should have been a cottage pie or something more English, she began to fear. Perhaps she could do something like that for tomorrow. She'd ask what he most fancied, later.

There it was, Short Stay 2, so far so good. Oops, tight little gap at the concrete post for the barrier entrance, thank heavens she was in a Mini. A multi-storey maze affronted her, and finally a space, phew. She pulled up in good time and in one piece. She sat for a few relieved seconds, and then sent a message.

Text: **Here in Short Stay 2. Will come and find you in Arrivals! x**

She chuckled to herself thinking she should have made one of those little signs with his name on, like a taxi pickup.

But he should recognise his own mother, even with her new, slightly more glamorous haircut and colour. She gave it a few minutes before heading in.

In the terminal building, she watched a flurry of people coming and going, wondering what their stories were, and where they were all travelling to and from. Holidays, family trips, work schedules, the airline staff, weddings, funerals, meeting new members of the family, friends, and lovers. It felt like a microcosm of life.

Adam's flight had already landed, she saw. He was here, back on UK soil. She'd seen the little square image of him on the phone on video calls, but what would he look like in the flesh after all those weeks away? A swish of metal and glass sliding doors, and another batch of travellers appeared, with wheelie suitcases and rucksacks galore.

A bearded man with shoulder-length dark wavy hair approached, looking a bit like that PE teacher guy, Joe Wicks. He was heading straight for her with a grin.

'Hi, Ma . . .'

Oh my . . . she nearly hadn't recognised him. Deeply tanned, and with his new beard, he looked to be in his thirties. Her boy had changed. He'd very much turned into a man. She felt a lump in her throat.

He dropped his huge canvas travel bag. And there he was in her arms, so much bigger than her, than even she'd remembered, and slightly sweaty from two days of travel. Adam was home . . . and safe . . . her body relaxed, revelling in that steady flow of deep maternal connection.

'Hello, son. Lovely to see you.'

'You too, Mum. How've you been?'

'Fine, fine. Settling in at my cottage.'

And they were off, chatting about his travels, the places he'd seen, people he'd met, all those new experiences and adventures, all the way back along the by-pass and down the A1. The massive bag and her son very much filling the space in her vehicle . . . and her heart.

*

The first evening together after such a long time was lovely. They sat in the kitchen, chatting as they ate. The chicken curry seemed to be going down well, anyhow.

'Hey, you'd have loved some of the Thai and Vietnamese food I've had. Amazing. All those hot and spicy flavours. And so cheap, lunch with a beer for like £2. Beachside or roadside, in great little wooden huts.'

'Ooh, wonderful. So, what was your favourite dish of the trip?'

'Had the most amazing Thai prawn curry served in half a scooped-out pineapple. The prawns were huge . . . and the sauce, hot and zingy, red Thai style, but so much more flavour than those pastes and mixes at home.'

'And what did you miss?'

'Foodwise, or people, do you mean?'

'Food, I meant.'

'Ah, definitely roast dinner and Yorkshire puddings . . . oh, and your homemade leek-topped cottage pie. Nothing like that in the whole of Asia.'

Cath had to smile. Well, that was tomorrow's menu sorted.

'And you, of course . . . and Dad.' He went a bit quiet then.

'But it's all a bit different now, isn't it. I'm like okay with that, with you splitting . . . overall, you know. But it just takes a bit of getting used to. You both being in different places . . . living different lives.'

She placed a gentle hand on his shoulder. 'It's taken me a bit of getting used to, as well, son. But . . . I'm getting there.'

'Well, that's good. So, how's life in Tilldale? Seems pretty quiet around here? What do you get up to?'

'Well, I've been making a few friends, and we've formed a kind of informal supper club. It's good fun, and they're nice people. Two of the lads run the village shop, in fact.'

'That sounds cool. I've been a bit worried about you,' he admitted, his eyes searching hers. 'All that shit going on with Dad.'

'Well, it happened. And I suppose we all have to deal with it.'

'Doesn't mean it's easy, though. I'm still bloody cross with him. Typical middle-aged crisis. The silly twat.'

'Adam, don't talk about your father like that.' Why the hell was she sticking up for him? Instinct probably, and hanging on to the last shreds of decency, to keep the family from folding altogether. 'It wasn't all bad . . . only the last couple of years. We had some lovely times when you were younger.' She tried hard to keep her comments positive.

There was so much to talk about, and yes, so much had changed for them both, yet she just wanted them to enjoy their first evening together, to chat and eat, and savour each other's company. There'd be time enough to talk more deeply over the coming days.

She hadn't played any music other than the radio for a while, and suggested putting on her Bluetooth speaker, letting Adam choose a 'chilled' mix he liked. He'd always been into his music. Over a cup of proper English tea served with cold milk, he'd said it didn't sound cool but confessed that he'd missed it, they sat chatting some more. She was enjoying listening to the tales of his recent adventures, but as he began to relax, his words began to slow as bone-tiredness took over him.

*

Adam had crashed soon after dinner, jet lag hitting home. And after their talk of family life, memories were whirling in her mind, as she lay in bed later.

Just a few years ago, they'd been a steady married couple: Cath, the maths teacher, and Trevor, the company accountant. And now, separate houses, separate lives. Adam now evidently feeling at a loss in the no-man's land in between them. That made her feel so very sad.

Having Adam back, their son, had stirred up a wasp's nest of memories and feelings. All those ups and downs of her life, all the way from those early uni days with Trevor, the excitement of discovering a new love . . . to the bitter recent end, and the hurt. And here she was on this new track. In her new home.

Second chances – that's how she had to think of it. Keep thinking positively. She had new friends. And like Lily, she could still look forward to lots of new opportunities. *She was fine.* It was all going to work out in the end. In fact, she had felt the roots already forming here, it was beginning to work out already.

But all the change that had been launched upon her, it sometimes felt overwhelming. How life had altered in the past two years. It was no wonder Adam had wanted to go off travelling and get away from it all. Just because your children were adults, it didn't mean the changes didn't affect them too – of course, they did. But they couldn't have stuck together, after all that pain, for the mere sake of it. They'd have just ended up feeling like a patchwork family, with all the seams running loose.

It might have been easy-ish to take Trevor back, when he'd arrived at her cottage the other day, to try again, perhaps even go back to the old life they both knew. But, somewhere deep inside she knew that wouldn't have worked either, not in the long run. They had both changed too much. It was staring them in the face.

But they could try and be friends. They needed to be, for their son's sake. Having Adam here brought that home, all the more. She'd try her best to move forward positively, for Adam and herself. After all, Trevor's appalling behaviour had given her the chance to look at and live life in a totally new way. As well as a gutful of hurt and loss, it was in fact a brand new chapter and a fresh chance at happiness that her ex had given her.

*

A few days later, and after sorting out mounds of sweaty, dirty and occasionally mouldy washing, Cath was now on to the mountainous ironing pile.

Her mobile rang.

'Hey, Cath, how's it going?' Susie was on the line. 'I was thinking of coming up to see you, if that's okay. I've got a few days off next week . . . and well, I'd love to catch up with you at last, see your new place.'

'Ah, Suz, that would have been brilliant. I'd love to see you, but . . . well, there's no room here at the cottage just now. Adam's back . . . and,' she lowered her voice, 'his stuff is everywhere. There's only the two bedrooms.' The new dynamic of having a youth in the house was giving her a reality check. It was feeling cramped already.

'Oh, I see.' Her sister sounded disappointed.

'I suppose you could stay at the pub, or there's a B&B in the village. It's just I don't really know Adam's plans, as yet.' In fact, in just a couple of days, he was looking rather too comfy, being happily fed and watered. There most likely were no plans. There was no job lined up as yet, nor indeed any talk of interviews, or research being done. 'Sorry, sis, but you know what it's like, the lounge has been taken over, as well as the spare bedroom.'

With his body draped on the sofa, and music blaring at all hours, despite her reminding him to use his earphones – oh yes, it'd suddenly blast out in the middle of a teaching session – her cottage didn't feel her own any more. The house wasn't big enough for the both of them, but Cath couldn't voice that. How could she even think it? That was downright mean. After all, she, no, they'd taken away his real home – his own bloody parents. It was just frustration zipping through her veins.

'Bet it's nice to have him back though, after all that time.'

'Ah, it is. It is, of course.' It was good to have his company again. She'd missed him, she really had, but he seemed to have reverted to teenage Adam very swiftly.

'Shall we just leave it a bit, then?' Susie suggested, bringing Cath back to her reason for calling. 'I'd much rather stay with you there, and see the cottage properly. It's no problem, I can look to take a few days off again, pretty much whenever.' The image of the 'sofa-loafer', plus having the experience of teenage kids of her own, had evidently been enough to put her sister off. 'It's just, I was hoping for a bit of chill time, that's all, and some girlie chat.'

'Ah, okay, well let's give it a couple of weeks, and I'll keep you posted.' Cath paused. 'Everything okay there?' *Did her sister need to talk something over? Was there something on her mind?* Was the 'girlie chat' just a catch-up, or something more important?

'Yeah, yeah. Nothing that can't wait.'

'You sure?'

'Yep, no worries, and we'll catch up properly soon, sis.'

Cath felt a little uneasy, but her sister obviously didn't want to expand just now, so she led the conversation to easier territory, asking about her girls, then, telling her about her new hairdo, and the latest antics at the fun-filled Seventies supper club.

'Ah, that sounds such fun. And it's great that you're settling in well.' Susie sounded so pleased for her.

And it was great. She really was beginning to find her feet in this new rural life. But a dart of fear hit home. What if Adam wanted to settle here too? Might he want to stay on with her long term? What would her new life be like with a messy, noisy twenty-two-year-old son in tow? But equally, how could she say no to that? He was her son, and had no real home of his own. She didn't voice those concerns to Susie. Even in her own mind, they sounded wrong, selfish. She was his mother. She loved him. He was just being a normal lad, after all.

'Well, I'd better go,' said Susie. 'Got yoga class tonight,

and Mark will be home soon on a quick turnaround before a five-a-side footie match he's refereeing.'

'No worries. Say "hi" to Mark from me. And enjoy your yoga.'

'Will do. An hour of stretchy peace. Bliss. You take care. Give my love to Adam. Love you. Bye.'

'Bye. Bye. Bye . . .' Cath sounded distant, thoughts of a future twenty-two-year-old lodger son sinking in.

And there he was. Adam appeared, sauntering into the kitchen like a just-waking bear in the search for honey.

'Hey, what's for tea, Mum?'

Cath couldn't help the irritation rising within. Jeez, he'd been lying about on his arse all day, whilst she'd sorted his washing, cleaned the bathroom – his towel left in a heap on the floor! And she'd cooked and prepared all the meals since he'd arrived back.

'Whatever you're making . . . ?' She threw back at him, to test his reaction. She had in fact planned some cheesy jacket potatoes and a salad.

He looked a bit confused; this wasn't what normally happened at home. 'Ah, right.' Then he went quiet.

Cath let the silence sink in for a bit. Mum did not mean 'mug'. And yes, whilst it had been lovely to spoil him those first few days, if he was planning on sticking around for a while, he'd need to help out sometimes at least. New rules would soon be coming into play.

Chapter 28

Adam was up by 9 a.m., relatively early for him, and as the milk and bread were about to run out (supplies weren't lasting long with his youthful bottomless pit of a tummy in the house), he'd offered to nip to the shop.

Cath relished a few quiet moments, sat peacefully in the kitchen, nursing a cup of coffee. No noise but the twitter of birdsong from the garden. Hmm, perhaps she could put her son to good use cutting the grass later. He was soon back, sauntering in with the provisions. 'Hey, Mum, just met this really cool guy in the village . . . runs a bike shop. Had a bit of a chat. He said he knows you. Might get Dad to courier up my road bike, says he'll service it and everything. Reasonable prices too.'

Ah, so he'd evidently bumped into Will. Cath felt slightly flustered.

'Yeah, it'd be cool to do a bit of cycling around here,' he continued. 'There's the hills to challenge me, and the coast is pretty stunning. It'd be epic.'

'Yeah, that's Will. He's a nice guy.' Her cheeks were flushing. She turned away slightly, putting the milk in the fridge and standing with its door still open for a second or two to help cool her. 'He's one of the supper club gang I'd mentioned.'

'Ah, that's good. Even better, might get mates rates. Put a word in for me, yeah . . . ?' He winked.

Oh, sugar... if the bike was coming up, then Adam really was settling in for the long haul. But what had happened to starting work, finding a job? There wasn't an awful lot in the way of employment up here. The money was going to dry up pretty soon, unless Trevor was still subbing him – guilt money perhaps.

'Right, well, yes, I can do. Adam, have you started looking for some kind of work as yet?' Cath prompted.

'Yeah, been checking some things out online.'

'Applied for anything?'

'Waiting for the right thing to come up . . .' He really didn't sound in any hurry to enter the job market.

'Which might be . . . ?' Her words dangled unanswered, as Adam got lost seemingly looking at a message on his phone.

'Sorry, Ma, something I need to answer.'

And Cath had the distinct feeling that it wasn't a job email. There really wouldn't be many employment prospects for him here in rural Northumberland. Oh . . . might he decide to work from home here, too? She'd be pushed out of her tutorial space in the spare room for good. She might have to relocate to the supper shed perhaps? That's if the Wi-Fi would even work up there?

Her lovely new world felt intruded upon . . . in a big smelly trainer kind of a way. It was an odd helter-skelter of emotions being a mother. All the different stages, and ages, and now trying to mesh together two very different lives – middle-aged mother with newly adult son. Just because you loved them, it didn't make it any easier.

At least, she wasn't feeling lonely anymore, she mused wryly. Hah, fat chance of that!

Be careful what you wish for.

*

'Hey, how's it going with Adam there? How are you both? Seems strange my little family all away.' Turncoat Trevor was on the line.

You made your bed . . .

'Yep, we're fine. Adam seems well.' *A little too well and too comfy, in fact.*

'Did the bike get there okay?'

'Yeah, fine. He's got it all kitted up, and he's been off out, making the most of it.'

It had given her a little space of her own, at least. A window of a couple of hours. Some peace and quiet to get on with her maths tutorials, much needed financially, and also some Cath-time. She was really appreciating that again. 'He's out on the bike now, off to Kirk Yetholm in the Borders, apparently. Cycling first, then a hill hike.'

'Ah, good. So, you're on your own then . . . ?'

'Ye-ah.' Something was coming. She knew Trevor so well, the nuance of his tone.

'Cath, the other week, look, I know I didn't get it right when I turned up like that . . . at your cottage. But God, I'm missing you. And I know it's a long shot after everything I've done, and please don't answer in a rush . . .' He was building to something. 'Thinking about you . . . and with Adam back now . . . and all our lives. Well, can you just think on it?'

'What?' *Spit it out, Trevor.*

'Please, could we try again?'

Bloody hell. What world was he living in? How could she forget everything that had gone on?

'It'd be different,' he carried on. 'I know I'd have to make things different for you. I can change. I've learnt my lesson. Been a bloody idiot, to be frank. We could get a new place, a fresh start. Somewhere Adam could stay, too. There's bound to be more job opportunities down this way . . .' That part did ring true at least.

But her new life. Her fresh start. 'But I'm happy here, Trevor. I love this village . . . Northumberland.'

'I know, and I really liked it there, too. There's no need to get rid of the cottage.' Her ears pricked at that. 'I've been looking at the finances. If we bought a nice, sensibly priced house back this way, keep our Leeds base, we could have your cottage as a second home. We could visit whenever we liked. Make the most of this semi-retirement stage. Have a trip on a cruise to the Med like you wanted, too. We can afford it . . .'

Wow, she hadn't expected that. He had been planning. It was all that she had once wanted, there on a plate. But . . . the plate still felt rather like it had been smashed, and the pieces clumsily stuck back together. Did she want that for her life?

'Trevor . . .'

'Don't, please don't answer, not yet. Not in haste. Give yourself a few days to think about it, at least. Talk to Adam . . . It's about all of us.' He knew her weak spot. Her family back together.

'Okay, I'll think about it.'

'Thank you.'

So much for a few minutes' peace. Wow, her head was aching already.

*

With her mind in a spin, Cath glanced out at the back garden. Uh-oh, the weeds were enjoying the fine weather as well as the plants, and were unfortunately beginning to run riot in the borders. What would old Reggie think of that? Her pledge to keep the garden tidy already having been overrun by a twenty-two-year-old turning up on her, and her husband's confusing relationship U-turn. Well, that was it, she'd go get her garden fork and sort out the pesky weeds. That, at least, was something she could control.

And, yes, her lodger son could start doing his bit to earn his keep by cutting the grass. She'd let him have a short break after getting back from today's cycle ride, but the second-hand petrol push mower she'd recently invested in, would be ready and waiting for him. After all, that's the least he could do, now it looked as though he was intending on staying around. Oh, yes, the 'new rules' were coming in to play.

With her old trainers on, and large garden fork to hand, she started on the bed around Reggie's sage and rosemary plants. Turning over the rich, brown earth and pulling out rogue grass and strands of 'sticky willy' (she wasn't sure of its real name but that's always what her dad had called it) from the border. Other plants were appearing now, pushing up from their earthen beds, with leaves unfurling bold and green, some coming into bloom. Tall heads of purple and yellow lupins, bursts of white and pale-pink delicate flowers looking like confetti on a couple of the shrubs. A brown and grey chaffinch perched on a nearby bush watching her, cocking its head as though curious. Who was this in the garden here now?

Above her, a dart of white with navy-black wings, as a pair of house martins whizzed by. Or might it in fact have been the first of the summer swallows? Cath used to like watching the birds on her childhood holidays, her father telling her all the names.

Tidying the borders helped calm her, her mind now busy on the task in hand. The sounds – a bee buzzing, the chitter of sparrows – and the floral and grassy earthen scents of nature all around her. The sun warm on her back, and her legs – which were bare below long denim shorts – feeling the balmy breeze on her skin. The garden was beginning to look better already. And it felt good trying to keep her pledge to Reggie – even though he hadn't ever known it.

*

An impromptu invite dropped into her messages the following day:

Forecast's looking good for the weekend. Who's up for a Supper Club picnic? 12 noon Sunday at Bamburgh Beach. Love Andreas and Dan xx

Ah yes! The timing was brilliant, just what she needed to take her mind off things, and the chance to chillax again with her friends was most welcome.

Cath was straight back with: **Yes, please! Count me in. And**

let me know if I can bring anything? Happy to help with some picnic goodies xx

*

And she knew there was another call to respond to, another decision to finalise. And this one certainly wouldn't be as easy.

Trevor's offer still needed to be answered, and tonight was the night Cath had decided to phone him back. It was Thursday, she'd had a couple of days to think since her ex-husband's call, and had been going over all the scenarios. The 'What Ifs', the 'Might Have Beens' and the 'What Nexts' had been constantly shifting in her mind. It hadn't been easy. She needed to get this right, for all their sakes.

She had spoken with Adam last night, telling him of his dad's latest proposals, and mother and son had had a good chat together. After all, Adam had seen more than most, back then, about what had really been going on at home. She'd wanted to give him the chance to voice his thoughts. Despite the teenage-style house mess on his recent arrival, she could tell that her son had actually grown up a lot these past couple of years. The time away on his travels might have helped him to see the bigger picture, too.

His own hurts were evident, however, as he admitted, 'It's been hard for me too, Mum. It was tough being away, wondering what the hell was going on back home . . . and then when Dad told me the house had bloody well sold, and there was no home any more...' Adam had sounded kind of lost then.

It was upsetting for Cath to see him so down, that rawness revealed. It was the whole family that had been ripped apart . . . not just her and Trevor. She'd never felt it was that simple, but hearing it from Adam himself, and that he hadn't felt able to share this before, made her feel so terribly sad.

Once that confession was out, however, they'd opened up some more, and he'd looked on the whole situation with a big pinch of reality. Though the outcome would affect him majorly either way, in the end, Adam agreed that the only decision to be made was hers. He wanted his mum to be happy.

Now, she needed that honest talk with her husband. After getting through that – with a large glass of something to hand – and finally settling on her plans for the future, it would be great to have something sociable with her village friends to look forward to this weekend.

Time to make that call. Adam was in the house, so she took her phone plus a large gin and tonic up to the summerhouse shed. The chance to go back . . . be a family, was still in her mind. Her decision would affect them all. It wasn't one to take lightly, but she knew in her heart it was the right one.

This seemed the perfect spot to break the news. The place she'd spent so long doing up. It symbolised her new start, and had nurtured new friendships. All this was far too precious to let go. But would Trevor be staying here with her for holidays from now on, or was it hers and hers alone?

The dialling tone; ringing once, twice . . . big sip of gin . . . three times, and then it was picked up.

'Hello, there. Hi, Cath.' Trev sounded chirpy.

'Hi . . .' Her voice came out higher than normal. This was harder than she'd imagined. She knew what it felt like to have all your hopes and dreams trashed, after all. And this was yet another reason why the answer was so clear.

'Good to hear from you. You okay?'

'Yes . . . thank you. Trevor, I've had a chance to think.' She had to get this over with. Now was not the time for chit-chat and pleasantries. 'Trev, I'd love to have been able to make things right, to go back to how we once were . . . but that's just a pipe dream. It won't ever be the same. For me, at least, it won't ever feel right. You've changed, and so have I. I like my new life and my new home. I'm ready for a fresh start, *on my own*.' She let the words sink in. There was silence down the line. 'I'm sorry if hearing that hurts but . . .' She stopped herself from saying more. *Don't rub it in . . . don't say you did that to me and far more.* Revenge wasn't always so sweet, though it was damn tempting. 'But, hey . . .' her voice softened, 'Trev, this is where we stop hurting each other from now on. This is where we move on.'

'Oh . . . ri-ight.'

She could tell he was struggling to speak, and she wasn't sure what else to say either. A few seconds of uneasy silence widened the gap between them.

'It was worth a try, I suppose,' he said after a while, trying to sound matter-of-fact but his tone was anything but. 'Better than to regret never having asked at all.' He took a slow breath. 'And Cath, whatever happens from here on, I will always be here for you and Adam. It's what you've always deserved.'

Whoa. This was harder than she'd expected. 'Thank you.' And despite knowing she'd done exactly the right thing, Cath still felt the weight of mixed emotions, a gutful of relief at having been honest, laced with guilt and nostalgia, but no regrets . . . not now.

'Keep in touch, yeah?' Trevor continued bravely.

'Of course. You too.'

'Bye.' The word sounded small, sad.

'Bye, Trevor.'

And despite her strength and her sound decision, she couldn't help having a good cry as she turned off the phone. Grappling for a tissue in her pocket, she'd wait a few minutes before heading back down to the house.

She sat, gathering her emotions, as she looked out over her garden, where Adam had actually taken the time to stripe the grass, and she saw the bold summer flowers were bursting into bloom.

*

'Have you told him? That you're not going back?'

He'd guessed right. Adam was there in the kitchen waiting, with a big mug of tea made for her, as she got back in from the garden shed ten minutes later.

Cath nodded, unsure as to how her voice would come out. She popped her empty gin glass down on the side.

'Well, that's good.' He passed her the mug.

'Thanks.' Feeling suddenly exhausted, she took up a seat at the dining table, Adam following suit.

'I've been worried about you . . . and Dad,' he confessed. 'Wondering what next for you both.'

'Oh, Adam . . .' She placed her hand over his. 'I'm so sorry, about everything.'

She tightened her grip on the mug, soon she'd find the right words to explain her decision, but for now it was important to let her son speak.

'When I was away, I really thought that it'd be the best thing . . . you two getting back together. This fling of Dad's to just fizzle out, and us all to get back to normal . . . like it was. But since coming here . . . seeing you here, making friends, finding a new life . . . I can see you're happy, Mum. Happier than I've seen you in such a long time.'

'Oh . . .' She hadn't expected that from him. Tears misted her eyes.

'Dad'll be feeling pretty shite, I bet, after all the crap he's caused. But that's no reason to fall in with it all.' Adam paused to look at her. 'I'm glad you've told him that you're not going back. Well done, Mum. Well done for sticking up for yourself.'

'Oh, Adam . . . but what about you? What's next for you?' They were both a bit teary-eyed by now.

'I'll be okay. I've got my whole life ahead of me . . . plenty of new adventures to crack on with.'

'But do you think this could be your home, your new base?' Even with the mess, and the noise, she'd give this to him, her heart and her home, to make her son feel safe and secure once more. That was how it should be.

'It's cool for now, cheers, Mum. But hey, I've no real plans yet. Gonna see where life takes me, I suppose.' He gave a small smile.

'And you're sure you're okay? You will talk to me, Adam, if there's ever anything . . .' She hated to think he'd been keeping everything inside until last night, feeling he had to hide his feelings to protect her, too.

But then she suddenly realised, maybe that just meant he was growing up, that he was taking responsibility.

'Let's just say we'll look out for each other, hey,' said Adam wisely.

'Yeah . . . and Dad too.' Cath found she couldn't hold on to the hate any longer.

'Yep, and Dad too.'

Old team, new programme.

Chapter 29

Just as she thought Adam might well be staying with her for a good while, he announced that he was heading off back down to Leeds 'for a bit'. After all that had recently happened, the decisions made, Cath wondered if he had been talking with his dad. Perhaps they'd had an open father-son chat, and that was a good thing. Apparently, he'd already booked a train ticket, one way, for the next day, Saturday. It was all sorted.

'Yep, Dad's given me the okay to stay with him. Apparently, he's in some new rented flat.' So, they had been in touch. At least all three of them were communicating at last.

'I'm not quite sure how I feel about living with him in his poky new place, though – I Google mapped it,' he gave a wry grin. 'But hey, I haven't got many options, right now. And,' he added, raising his eyebrows, 'who the hell knows what's going on with Steph, lately? Anyhow, I've been doing a bit of thinking myself, and I've realised there's more chance getting a job Leeds way, and it'll be easier to get to interviews around the country from there, too.'

'Yes, of course.' Cath gave a supportive smile. Something must have sunk in at last, workwise, and he'd evidently realised he'd lounged about for long enough.

'And, I'm missing my mates . . . the buzz of city life. It's been cool here, thanks for letting me stay. Hope you're not too disappointed or anything?'

It would, in all honesty, be sad to see him go again, especially after their recent heart-to-heart, but the thought that her 'old' new life might be back, gave Cath a lift. There was in fact a mini happy dance going on inside, which Cath felt a bit guilty about. She'd so appreciate her quiet cottage haven this time round, too. Peace, space . . . her own place.

'No, that's fine, son. You go, see your mates again, make your life. It makes sense to go back to Leeds. Go for it . . . And best of luck with the job hunting. I do love it here, but it is a bit like the back of beyond for you young ones, I understand that.'

'And you'll be okay now, Mum?' His eyes were caring, thoughtful.

'Yeah, yeah, 'course I will. We can chat on the phone. And hey, you can visit whenever you like. I'd like you to think of this as your home, too.' And she meant it. Having him come to stay again, even with the mess and noise that came with him, would be a joy.

Another seismic shift was coming. Her life felt like it was happening in waves just now. Rolling on, and then on again, each time taking her somewhere new, altering things.

*

He was at her threshold, his canvas travel bag to hand. And the big emotional lump in her throat was back once more.

The farewell drive to Alnmouth station for the CrossCountry train to Leeds – where Trevor would be picking him up – started fairly quietly, both lost in their own thoughts. Then with ten minutes to spare they began chatting, easy-going banter, realising that time was short. Parking up. The wait on the platform. His heartfelt thank you for looking after him. The ding-dong voice of the arrival announcement. The train gliding in along the tracks, pulling to a halt. Time to move on.

'Come back any time, love.' And she really did mean it.

'Will do. Love you, Mum.' And he took her in a big bear hug.

'Aw, love you, too.' The platform had emptied, the guard ready with her whistle and baton. 'Go, get on, or it'll be going without you.' Her chest felt tight at his leaving.

He boarded. Swallowed by the train. Then she spotted him waving at a window. She stood watching him go, waving back, the carriage disappearing into the distance. Time for Adam's new chapter. *Take care, my love*.

Having her son with her always warmed her, it was the permanent living status that had been the concern of late. Her small cottage hadn't quite been big enough for the both of them, but her heart always was.

Chapter 30

The sun was shining – yippee! – as Will pulled the car into the parking area behind the sand dunes. It was Sunday, and he'd offered to take Cath, Nikki and Lily along to the beach, to save them all separately driving the twenty minutes to the coast. He was a steady driver, experienced, and Cath had felt in safe hands in the front passenger seat cruising along the winding country lanes. Andreas, Dan and terrier Shirley were making their way in their own vehicle – which was apparently 'loaded to the gills' with food, drink and beach entertainment (whatever that meant?!).

Oh, crikey, she'd hoped a dip in the sea was not on the cards. As a precaution, no swimwear had been packed in her bag of beach goodies. The most she was prepared to reveal, or get cold or wet, was her ankles. This was the North Sea not the Mediterranean, after all.

By the time they arrived, the car was smelling delicious with Cath's still-warm homemade sausage rolls (baked using fragrant sage from Reggie's bush) and Lily's freshly baked croissants on board. Though the lads had said they were happy to provide the whole picnic for everyone, the others wanted to help out too, bringing various snacks and drinks between them. A 'Blooming-Marvellous Bamburgh Beach Picnic' was the theme for today, with a non-alcoholic drinks menu in support of the drivers and a clear head.

As they stepped out, the air was a little fresh, with a salty sea breeze. The view was amazing with Bamburgh Castle standing grand and historic, guarding the sweeping golden-sand bay. Nikki pulled a tartan picnic rug out of the boot, along with a cool bag filled with non-alcoholic punch, two bottles of 'No-secco' and some crisps and nibbles. Cath had her non-alcoholic gin ready for cocktails by the sea. Lily had made a big flask of hot coffee to go with her croissants to start them off – mindful of the cool winds of the Northumberland coast – to be followed later with cream-filled chocolate profit-eroles, her latest bake. Will, apologising for his lack of cooking skills, had brought two large punnets of juicy strawberries and raspberries – to go with said profiteroles – and a carry pack of 0 per cent lagers, which was very acceptable too, the girls had agreed.

The four of them, piled up with picnic fare, trailed their way down to the beach along a narrow track through the marram grass. Seeing them snake their way in front of her towards the sands made Cath smile; they looked kind of like a family. Lily could be her daughter, Nikki her sister, and Will . . . ooh, she stopped in her tracks, both physically and mentally.

She needed to stop this train of thought right here. But her mind kept on going . . . *What if* someone like Will had been her husband, *what if* she and Trevor had never happened? Would she have got to the same impasse with someone else, the same mid-life crossroads, her husband having a fuck-you-after-thirty-years-fling, a relationship breakdown, and a crushing sense of failure? Or, might she have had a son and perhaps a daughter too with someone else, who knew . . .

Okay, stop it, stop it right now. Her sensible head took over. She certainly didn't need to be thinking about any of that. Those crazy little echoes of questions wriggling back from the past. She had her wonderful son, Adam, even if he was noisy and messy – but that was pretty much the norm for his age. And she had been happy with Trevor, for many years at least. The past was what it was. It was the future she needed to focus on. The here and the now.

And right now, with the sun warm on her back, the beach and some picnic fun with her friends were calling her. She caught up with the others on the sands, as they glanced about looking to find Andreas and Dan. It didn't take long.

'There they are!' Lily pointed to their left, at a sheltered spot tucked next to the dunes just before the rock pools started. The pair of them were standing out in their brightly coloured clothes.

'Over here,' Dan shouted, delighted to see the rest of the gang, the lads' sense of fun and joie de vivre so apparent. Shirley was excited and barking, spotting the group approach. The terrier then started digging, pushing up a shower of sand on the just-laid picnic rug.

'For goodness' sake, Shirley. You can stop that right now, madam, or you'll be kept on your lead.'

The dog gave a haughty look but packed it in, hedging her bets on having a good time free roaming with lots of stray snacks from the group.

'Well, we wouldn't have missed seeing you two,' Nikki giggled, as they arrived at the picnic spot. 'Dan, you look like a stripy stick of pink rock, and Andreas, your T-shirt pretty much matches the bright blue-and-white windbreak.'

'Hey, cheeky. We've dressed for the occasion, haven't we, Dan?'

'We have indeed, even Shirley is sporting her spotted neckerchief. Coastal chic, this is. Very à la mode, isn't it, petal?' Dan looked to Cath, with a wink, for approval.

'I love it!' she agreed.

*

They were soon tucking in to freshly squeezed orange juice and delicious Greek-style honey cake – care of Andreas – and flakily melting mini croissants and pains au chocolat, served with little cups of strong coffee, thanks to Lily.

'Brunch on the beach,' announced Will. 'This is great, thank you. I feel my offerings are a little under par,' he apologised.

'Hey, we are all at different stages of our culinary careers,' said Andreas. 'Everyone is welcome, old hands, aspiring chefs or beginners. And don't worry, we'll bring you on in time, it's all in the grand Supper Club plan.'

'It is?' Will looked up anxiously.

Cath had no idea what Andreas was referring to. There was no plan.

'Well, it's been Cath, then Nikki, and it's our turn now. Other than Lily doing a *Bake Off* special, which could be delightful, I think that means it's your turn next.'

'Oh . . .' Will had paled.

'Never fear, we can help,' added Dan.

'Or, there's always good old M&S or a takeaway.' Will was clutching at straws.

'Give him a break, lads,' Nikki interjected. 'We can help, of course we can. And no one needs to feel pressured here. Fish and chips from the van at Kirkton will do me fine . . . with a glass of Prosecco. Perfect.'

'Fish, chips and fizz sounds pretty good to me, too,' added Cath with a smile.

'Phew.' Will visibly relaxed.

'We can't let him off the hook that easily,' said Andreas, still grinning. 'Hook . . . fish and chips . . .'

The group groaned in unison.

'Talking of fizz, anyone for a No-secco at this point?' offered Nikki.

'Or, I've got some elderflower no-gin cocktails, I can make up too,' offered Cath. It was actually nice to have an alcohol-free occasion. With all the stress of these past months, she wondered if she'd been using the wine a little too much as a crutch, lately.

'Ooh, spoilt for choice.'

'Elderflower for me.'

'And I'll try a No-secco.'

The group relaxed with their fizz in the sunshine, chatting away and enjoying the day. A short stroll along the sands towards the imposingly stunning stone castle preceded lunch, which was a fab foray of picnic treats. Dan and Andreas did themselves proud with smoked salmon or local ham sandwiches, Greek-style feta and spinach parcels, olives, nuts and nibbles, including freshly baked cheese straws, and for later, there was still plenty of Andreas's honey cake. The savoury snacks, accompanied by Cath's delicious herby sage-and-onion sausage rolls, went down a treat. And the grand finale was Will's strawberries and raspberries served with Lily's scrumptiously light and creamy chocolate-topped profiteroles. Tummies were contentedly full. Even Shirley's, who'd had ham sandwich crusts and a sausage roll or two tossed her way. Her behaviour was now impeccable, except for the odd bark aimed at any canine interloper who dared get near her picnic-munching human pack.

After all that food, the group had to have a brief lie-down behind the windbreak. Cath lay enjoying the sun and the feel of the gentle wind on her face. Will lay just a hand-stretch away. Hmmm. *I feel it in my fingers . . .* began strumming away in her mind. Giving her a secret inner smile.

All too soon, however, there was a call to action.

'Right, enough of the lazing about. It's rounders time,' announced Dan.

'Really?' Nikki's mouth dropped open. 'I dash around all the bloody time. This is bliss. I could lie here all afternoon.'

'Well, I'm up for a game.' Lily was up on her feet, with a smattering of sand hitting those still prone. A groan or two came in response.

'Okay, me too.' Sporty Will jumped up and was ready to play.

'Can I be umpire?' Nikki asked, apparently in a bid to maintain her current position.

'We don't need an umpire. We need a team. Three on each side, I'll toss a coin,' Andreas announced.

So that was it, Cath scrambled to her feet too, and a pitch was marked out with a stick-line in the sand and a couple of pullovers as base-stumps. A bat and tennis ball appeared out of one of Dan's bags. Teams were allocated – Cath, Will and Dan versus Andreas, Nikki and Lily – and the game commenced, with Cath in as first batsman. She was relieved to at least hit the ball with a satisfying *thwack*, and dashed to first base with a grin.

It was all a bit of fun in the sun. But it got more competitive when each team (Dan's Devils versus Andreas's Angels) had won one game, and they went for a third to decide the overall winner. The bowling by Dan upped the ante, with the ball now moving at the speed of light – well, bruise-worthy, put it that way. At one point, Shirley stole the ball and made off with it, which Will declared an unfair advantage. And they couldn't help but laugh as Nikki ended up in a heap in the sand trying to get to third base, before the airborne ball hit the fleece-top marker.

It was then that Andreas's mobile rang. His smile dropped immediately as he answered.

Cath couldn't help but overhear. 'Oh, oh, I see . . . How is she? Where are they sending her?'

It didn't sound good.

'Is it your mum?' Dan asked, concerned.

Andreas nodded seriously as he listened for a few seconds more. 'Okay, thank you for letting me know. I'll get there as soon as I can.'

The group were quiet as he closed the call. 'I'm sorry, we've got to go. Right now. It's Mama . . .'

'What's happened, love?' Dan spoke gently.

'She's had a fall . . .' Andreas bit his lip, and gave a sad shake of his head. 'That was the care home. She's not so good. They think she might have broken her arm . . . and it's all been a big shock for her, of course.'

'Oh, Andreas. Bless her,' said Cath.

'Poor Maria,' Nikki said.

'Where are they taking her? Have they got an ambulance?' Dan asked.

'Yes, she's on her way to A&E at Cramlington, right now. We need to go.'

'Of course.' His partner was already gathering up their essentials.

'It's okay, we'll sort out everything here.' Cath stepped in.

'Yes, that's no problem,' Lily said.

'Is there anything you need us to do? Anything we can help with?' Will offered, empathy filling his voice.

'Shall I take Shirley home with me? In case you're a while at the hospital?' Cath suggested. 'It's no problem.'

'Oh, would you really . . . ? I don't know how long we might be. That would be such a help.' Andreas was grateful.

'So, there's a key under the big stone by the back step. Dog food's in the kitchen cupboard,' Dan swiftly explained.

'Great. I'll sort it.'

'Go on then . . . get yourselves away. Do what you need,' Nikki encouraged.

'And let us know if there's anything else we can do to help later,' Will added.

'Thank you so much,' said Dan.

And off they set, looking a little dazed. Concern for Andreas's elderly mother clouding his previously happy face. Blimey, you never knew what was next on the horizon. One minute enjoying a sunny fun-filled day, the other in a hospital dash.

'Shall we pack up now, too?' Cath suggested. It somehow seemed wrong to stay there, eating and sunbathing, the magic of the day having been broken by the sad news.

'Yes, that sounds a good idea,' Will agreed.

'It's been a lovely day though up to now,' Lily said.

'Yeah, it really has.'

'Fingers crossed she'll be okay,' Nikki said.

'Yeah, bless her. What a worry for the lads,' added Will.

'Come on then, Shirley. Let's get this show back on the road to Tilldale.'

They gathered up bags and Tupperware boxes, bottles and cans, the rounders set, folded rugs back into squares, and pulled out the windbreaks, rolling them tight. Will's car was going to be loaded to the gills.

Shirley looked up at them packing up and gave a small whine, as though she understood something was up with her owners now gone. 'Here, you can carry the ball back.' Cath offered the terrier the green tennis ball, which the dog took and held proudly in her mouth.

Loaded like sherpas, and rather sweaty by the time they reached Will's hatchback in the car park, they opened the doors wide with a blast of stuffy heat, and then began to pile it high. Shirley sat in the front footwell for the way back, curling up in a slightly damp, sandy, and warm white-grey ball at Cath's sandalled feet. Cath patted her head now and again comfortingly, as much for her as the dog. She couldn't help but worry for the elderly lady and the lads.

It was such a shame for them all. It had been so very close to being the perfect day there on the beach, filled with friendship and summer-picnic fun. Why did things always have to go wrong? Cath mused with a touch of melancholy.

But that was just life, another voice in her head piped up, *you never know when the peaks and troughs are going to fall*. Which was probably as well. But it was your friends who buoyed you back up. They needed to be there ready to support Andreas and Dan in their time of trouble. And they would be.

Chapter 31

'Well, Shirley, it's just me and you for now. Shall we take a little walk and fetch your things?'

After being dropped off, Cath had quickly sorted out her beach garb. She decided to go across to the lads' flat next, to find the dog's bed, her food, and perhaps a toy or two to keep her entertained.

The duo let themselves in, and headed up the wooden staircase to the apartment above the shop. Shirley began skipping up the steps and barking animatedly, no doubt eager to see her owners there. Sadly, the terrier was going to be disappointed. It felt a bit strange letting herself into someone's home. Cath tried not to snoop too much, just taking in the décor en route to finding the pet essentials. The stairs opened out onto a landing area, passing a small cosy lounge with an olive-green velvet sofa and a green-and-navy William Morris–style patterned armchair. She moved on to find a white-painted kitchen-diner, where she hoped the pet things might be. It was all extremely neat and tidy.

Cath, being organised, had brought a couple of sturdy bags with her. In the kitchen, she discovered the terrier's bed – a snug grey-towelling affair. In the cupboard above that, she took out six little pouches of pet food and a pack of dog treats. Shirley looked at her hopefully, then rather confused, as her doggie items got stashed away into the bags.

'Sorry, Shirley. But we're heading back to mine. We'll get you set up there. Your dads won't be too long, I'm sure.' She was talking to a terrier, but hey-ho. She'd always liked dogs, and well, needs must. She was hoping a calm tone would reassure the pooch.

As Cath turned to leave the flat, the dog dug her paws in, locking her legs in protest. She was going nowhere.

'Come on. It's not my fault. We don't have a lot of choice in the matter.' Cath tugged gently on the lead and waited. Shirley glared at her and gave an indignant bark.

One more tug, and a 'Good girl' with the promise of a biscuit and the dog reluctantly started a slow move in Cath's direction. 'That's it, well done.' And they were off, making a slow trot back down the stairs. Cath carefully replacing the door key in its hidey-hole, and heading back over the road and along the lane to her cottage.

She was soon setting up the dog-bed in her kitchen. 'So, this is your home for this evening . . .' Cath gave Shirley a chew, hoping the treat and the new location would feel homely at least. 'We'll do your supper in a while.' It was still only four o'clock after all. The dog's ears pricked right up then and she gave a little yap. Did she understand all that? 'Oh, and I'll get some water for you.'

Darn, she'd forgotten to pick up the dog's water or food bowls, so quickly found a cereal bowl in the cupboard and filled it from the cold tap. After sniffing at the water, Shirley headed for the back door and proceeded to scratch, giving another bark.

'Ah, okay.' Hmm, it could well be toilet time. Cath would

have to brace herself for the inevitable poo pick. Luckily, her back garden was pretty secure, so she could let Madam Shirley have a little wander out there whenever she needed. She watched her meander onto the grass, do a little swirl and settle to her business. Cath gave her some privacy, her eyes now drawn to the summerhouse shed at the top of the bank. She'd spent so long getting that ready for the very first supper club back in May. That first big step, having people around to her new home. How far the group had come in just a few weeks. Andreas and Dan, Nikki, Lily, Will . . . these people really were her friends. She so enjoyed their company, and right now she wanted to do her best to support them too.

*

After her supper, there was a phone call from the lads with an update. Maria was stable, but with the hospital being almost an hour away, they were going to stay down there to be on hand overnight. Dan explained that initially she'd been given some meds for the pain and then had her arm placed in a support, after X-rays showed that she'd broken her wrist. She was comfortable, and had now been given a bed on the ward. She was due to have an operation first thing in the morning.

'Oh, bless, I hope it all goes well for her. And you, how are you both doing?'

'Not bad. It's all a worry for sure, but we're bearing up,' Dan said. 'Andreas is concerned about her having a general anaesthetic, but there really is no other option.'

'Well, all take care. I'll be thinking of you. And let me know if I can do anything.'

'Thanks, lovely. Oh, and how's Shirley coping? Okay? She's not being a madam for you, is she?'

'Shirley's fine. Well, she was bit put out at first naturally, was reluctant to leave your place when I went for her things, but she's coming around nicely. She's sat with me here on the settee now.'

'Oh, she'll love that. She likes watching *Coronation Street*, by the way.'

'You're kidding.'

'No, she loves the start, especially. Always barks at the cat.'

'Hah.' Even in such difficult times, Dan could make her chuckle, bless him.

'Well, you take care. Send my best wishes to Maria. And if there's anything else you need me to do, just shout. I could open up the shop, give you a hand there, whatever . . . Just ask. And oh, give Andreas a big hug from me.'

'I will do. Thank you, my lovely.'

'You're very welcome.'

Cath put down the phone, and gave Shirley a gentle rub. Poor Andreas, it was such a worry as your parents got older. With time marching on, making them frailer each year, each month . . .

Memories of her own mother filled her mind, and her final difficult days at the hospice. Holding her frail hand, trying to be brave for her, when the little girl inside was desperate to cry, to cling on, to beg for a bit more time. But all you could do was your best. There was no stopping the tide of time, and finally the inevitability of death. And at the end, it was all about love . . . about being there with them, and trying to let your loved ones go as peacefully as possible. To be able to say, 'It's okay, Mum, I'm here. It's all right', when your whole world feels like it's starting to crumble and quake around you. Cath wiped a tear from her eye. Blimey, that was over four years ago, and yet it still felt as raw as if it was yesterday.

She sniffed loudly. 'Oh, Shirley. I'm sure they'll be fine,' she muttered, giving the dog a little pat for good measure. The terrier snuggled in a little closer, both providing comfort to the other.

'Well, then, I suppose I'd better find out what time *Coro*'s on.'

Chapter 32

It was rather lovely having a dog to walk, Cath decided. Having a happy, furry and inquisitive companion trotting along by your side in the country lanes and across the fields. She enjoyed their morning stroll the next day, even finding herself chatting to Shirley at one point. Well, no one was around to hear her, so what did it matter. The little dog's ears pricked up as though she knew exactly what was being said.

The hedgerows were lined with a profusion of tall white-headed cow parsley, which was softly swaying in the breeze. It reminded Cath of the gypsophila she'd had alongside white roses and eucalyptus in her wedding bouquet. And for the first time in a long time, that memory, one linked to Trevor and their old life, didn't hurt so much. There were also beautiful wild roses, all pink-and-white petals mixed in with the hawthorn hedge, their delicate scent drifting on the breeze, and lower down in the verge was a scattering of pink campions among the lush grass. Shirley sniffed as she went, stopping here and there to investigate some interesting aroma, neither of them in any real rush as they strolled.

They crossed the stone bridge and entered the pasture fields down by the river. A pair of mallard ducks passed them, paddling downstream, and then a large grey heron swooped over them, its wingspan impressive, like some strange prehistoric bird. Shirley looked up too, curious. The pair of them wandered on, with Shirley on a loose lead, soaking in the sounds, sights and scents, until the dark-grey slate rooves of the village came back into sight, with its cluster of stone dwellings. Home.

Back at the cottage, Cath spotted that Shirley's white fur was now a muddy shade of brown, all up her legs and under her tummy. She'd better have her looking spick and span for the boys' return, so Cath decided a quick wash with a bucket of warm water was in order.

This didn't go down too well! Out on the back patio, with bucket and sponge (kept for the car) to hand, Cath tried to keep a wriggling Shirley still with one hand, whilst trying to reach her muddy parts with the wet sponge with the other. The terrier was not at all keen on this. After much shifting and barking, Cath finally tied her to the patio table, and made a couple of big foamy splashes from the bucket for good measure.

'Gotcha.'

The terrier gave a growly woof of indignation.

It was then time to towel her dry. Cath was armed and ready, bath towel in hand, as she untied the leash from the table leg, but before she had chance to scoop the little dog up, Shirley did the inevitable wet dog shake-and-spray. Cath was on the receiving end of the shower, now standing there dripping herself. She couldn't help but give a wry smile. 'Hah, touché, little lady. Thanks for that.'

As the damp duo had headed back into the house, there was a knock at the door. Cath was surprised to find Will there, with his dark eyes and warm smile fixed on her. It gave her a pleasant fuzzy feeling seeing him.

'Hi, just wondered if you've heard any news from the lads? Or if there's anything I can do to help out at all?'

'Hah, I needed you about five minutes ago when I decided to give Shirley a bucket bath. It was trickier than I'd imagined. I may have ended up even wetter than her.'

'Oops, you do look a bit drippy.' He couldn't hold back his grin, those brown-green eyes glinting with humour.

'Cheers . . .' she answered ironically. 'Do you want to come in? Have you got time for a coffee?' It seemed rude to keep him hanging there on the doorstep.

He followed her through to the kitchen, where she popped the kettle on, and relayed what she'd heard from Andreas last night. She added that she didn't want to pester them at such a difficult time, but was hoping to get a further update soon. Thoughts of the old lady having her operation, and all the implications that might go with that, had been very much on Cath's mind this morning. But the country walk had helped to calm her.

'Let's hope she gets through it all okay. My mum's eighty-five, and I do worry about her,' admitted Will. 'She's pretty good just now, still in her own home with Dad. They rattle on fine, and thankfully they've got each other, but I can see her and Dad getting frailer each year. It's not easy, is it.'

'No, it isn't . . . my parents have both passed.' Cath paused, glad that it was the happier vision of them both in their middle-aged heydays that suddenly filled her mind.

'Sorry to hear that, Cath.'

'Yes, Mum just a few years ago, and Dad soon after,' she

added. 'I feel for the lads. It's a tough time.' Cath poured hot water into the cafetière. The aroma of coffee suddenly rich in the air.

It felt good to have Will there with her, to have someone to talk things over with.

'Yes, it will be. Oh, and I've still got the lads' gear in my car too, from yesterday. Well, except for the spare food which is now stored in my fridge. I was wondering what I should do with it all?'

'Ah, I'd hang on to it for now. Hmm, I wouldn't want to leave piles of stuff for them to sort out on top of everything.' She pictured their tidy zone above the shop, no need to mess it up, and she and Will would have no idea where it all should be stored. 'Foodwise . . . if you've enough space, hold on to it for a day or so in your fridge. We can then pop it back over there, ready for when they get back. Once we get any news, that is. They might appreciate some food to hand.'

'Sounds a good idea. I'll do that, thanks.'

'Shall we sit outside?' Cath suggested. It was another sunny day. Rural Northumberland was enjoying a lovely settled spell, which was fairly unusual – it was more common to get four seasons in one day. So, you really needed to make the most of the sunshine when it was here.

They sat on the lower patio where Cath had put out her little bistro-style coffee table and chairs set. With a damp Shirley nestled at Will's feet – hah, the little dog was obviously still holding a grudge against Cath for the bucket bath – they chatted over coffee.

It was now past 11 a.m. 'Wonder if Maria's had her op yet?'

'Let's hope it all goes well for her.'

'Yeah, and that she gets out of hospital and back to her care home soon.'

Will took a slow sip of his drink, then nodded thoughtfully. 'Hospitals, yeah. Well, I've seen enough of them in the past few years . . . the hospice too.' He looked away then, focusing on a tiny ant on the ground for a few seconds.

'With your wife?' Cath asked softly, with kindness in her tone. As Will had brought the topic up, she felt it was okay to ask a little more.

'Yes, Jane . . . ah, she was lovely. The centre of our home really.' He looked ahead and gave a soft sigh.

'Oh, I'm so sorry, Will. I'd heard you'd been widowed. That must have been really tough . . . still is, I'm sure.'

'She was a primary school teacher. The kids all loved her,' he shared.

Oh, so his wife was a teacher, too. She must have been a kind soul, Cath mused, someone who wanted to give back, encouraging all that growth and learning, especially in those crucial formative years at primary school.

'She was one of those caring, friendly people that everyone warmed to . . .' Will continued. There were a few difficult seconds before he began again, his voice now thick with emotion. 'She got cancer . . . pancreatic . . . about two-and-a-half years ago now. Took her really quickly.'

'Oh, Will . . .' Cath stretched a hand towards his, a brush-stroke of tenderness, and then sat quietly, respectfully giving him the space he needed.

'We didn't have chance to do all the things we wanted. All those hopes and dreams we had went with her. And the girls . . . they miss her so much . . . me too.' His eyes had misted.

Jeez, life was tough. Should she give him a hug at this point? She really wanted to reach out to him, do something to show she cared, but she wasn't sure how that might go down. There was a bristliness about him, a protective shield there. Despite feeling drawn to hold him, Cath also sensed that now wasn't the right time to invade the private space of his grief.

She dropped her hand, adding, 'That must be so very hard for you all.'

Bloody hell, losing his partner in that way must have been brutal for Will. She could feel the rawness of his loss. 'Oh, Will.'

Coffee nearly finished, the conversation moved back to the easier ground of the cycling shop, and her latest and rather unusual online tutorial that she'd had to cut short as the A Level student was slurring his words, having evidently been drinking. Though he was trying hard to pretend that he hadn't, he finally confessed that it had been a mate's birthday and they'd been out for a few beers at lunchtime. She'd told him to go and get a large glass of water and a couple of paracetamols, and they'd revisit his lesson the next day.

At least that made Will smile again. 'The youth of today, hey.' He then gave her a pensive look, that she didn't quite understand.

Gosh, it was so long ago when she'd been a young teenager, when she had all the world ahead of her. All the pages still to be written.

'Right, well, I suppose I'd better be making tracks . . .' Will got up to go.

From their heartfelt conversation before, Cath was left

251

with the sense that they'd opened the shutters a fraction between them.

'Thanks for listening earlier,' Will added, as he headed back inside on his way to the front door.

'You're welcome. Any time . . . And I'll keep you posted if I hear any more from the lads.'

'Thanks.'

They looked at each other for a second, then shared a small clumsy hug in the hallway. And she felt so confused. Buzzing with emotions that she struggled to name or place – could it be longing, loneliness, sympathy, attraction . . . *all of it*?

However her feelings were growing for Will, they needed to be kept in check. He was evidently grieving, and in a vulnerable place, too.

'Once bitten, twice shy' rang in her head as she closed the door. And well, Trevor had certainly taken a big chunk out of her.

*

'Okay, little lady? Am I forgiven?' Cath said to Shirley, an hour or so later, stroking the terrier's silky white head. They were back on the sofa together, all dry now and cosy. She was about to put the late lunchtime news on, when her mobile rang.

'Ooh, it's your dad.' She pressed to take the call. 'Hi, Dan. How are you getting on?'

'Hi, lovely. Good news, the op has gone well. Maria's back out of sedation and settled, so I'm going to head back up. I'll go back to fetch Andreas later, as he wants to stay with her. We're not sure when she'll be allowed out yet, depends on how things go today.'

'Ah, thank goodness. Well, that is good news. I'll keep Shirley with me for now then, and you just say when you're ready for me to bring her over, okay? And anything else, ask away.'

'Thank you, lovely.'

'No problem. See you later.'

*

As soon as Cath heard Dan was coming back, as promised, she gave Will a call. They arranged to meet at the flat, ready to re-fill the lads' fridge with the food saved from the beach. Gosh, the fun and games they'd had seemed like a world away, not a mere twenty-four hours. Cath added a few extra items including a cottage pie (which she had whipped up last night, just in case), some salad leaves fresh from her raised beds in the garden, and sunflower-and-honey seeded bread rolls which she'd baked and batch frozen. She left a little handwritten note for the boys on the kitchen side. Yes, she'd realised that there might well be the basics downstairs in the shop, but the two lads might just want to collapse with some ready-made supper to hand.

'Aw, that's really kind of you,' commented Will, spotting the extra food she'd made.

'Ah, the boys have been great since I first landed here in the village. So warm and welcoming. It's the least I can do for them.'

'Yeah, they are good lads. They really do look out for the

village folk. And it's not just for their own gain.' He sighed, and looked tired suddenly.

Their gaze snagged. She wondered if they'd helped him too, when his world fell apart, with the onset of Jane's illness. Again, there was that feeling that she should reach over, touch his arm, or shoulder perhaps. Show him that she cared, too. But something held her back.

'Right, well, that's it all delivered. Job done.' Will turned, ready to go.

'Yeah, and I'd better get back to Shirley. Thanks.'

'Uhm . . . there's a village pub quiz coming up. For the local hospice,' Will ventured. 'Maybe you'd like to come along? We might even raise a team, if the lads feel up to it, that is. Next Thursday, here at The Star Inn.'

'That sounds good, thanks. I'd like that.' She felt a buzz at the thought of spending the evening with Will. Another chance to get to know each other a little bit more.

*

Dan was back at their flat fifty minutes later, and had phoned Cath, all emotional, after finding the food supplies left in the fridge for them. He explained that he needed an hour or so to get sorted, and the shop re-opened. So, in the meanwhile she took Shirley for a little walk around the village. Several locals, including the elderly couple next door, John and Mary, had stopped her on seeing the familiar Westie, asking about the lads and Maria's welfare, having heard the news on the village grapevine.

There was a real sense of community in this village, and

of coming together. She had a feeling more offers of help and goodies might well be arriving at the shop soon. Dan and Andreas's past kindnesses across the community being remembered and acknowledged.

As she dropped Shirley off later, Cath repeated her offer to help out in the shop for a couple of hours, if that might ever help.

'I'll just get everything straight here today, lovely . . . but we might well take you up on that sometime,' said Dan. 'And thanks so much for looking after our little diva. I hope she's been good for you?'

Shirley barked on cue, as if to say *yes, of course I have*, which made them both smile.

'She's been perfect. I've enjoyed having her. Been good company, to be honest.'

Dan rubbed the little dog behind the ears, then declared, 'Right, up we go, missy. I'll pop you away. No loitering on the shop floor for you.' And up he went, taking the little dog and her things with him. 'I'll be straight back . . .'

'No worries.' Cath waited, browsing the shelves and the local crafts until Dan returned.

They then said their goodbyes, Cath aware that Dan would have plenty to be getting on with.

'Thank you so much again, my lovely.'

'It's no problem at all. See you soon. And send my love to Andreas and Maria.'

'Will do. Bye.'

*

Cath missed her little canine pal very much that night, and the following day, vowing to 'borrow' Shirley more often. The cottage seemed so much emptier without the occasional yap, bark and snuggle, as the terrier had followed her around the house. It seemed all too quiet, once more, serving to remind her how solitary her new life could sometimes feel.

Chapter 33

The winning team were announced as Norfolk and Chance. Liz, the very sensible village carpet bowls team leader, and tonight's quiz host, pronounced the prize-winners, totally unawares as to why the gathering were chuckling so much as she announced their victory. She continued stoically among the giggling chatter, saying that a close second were the new team Will and Cath's Quirky Quizzers. They shared an air punch and grinned. They'd soon discovered that she was good on literature and history, both on geography, and Will on the sport and music questions. They complemented each other well. A runner-up prize of a bottle of homemade sloe gin, kindly donated by a member of the local WI, was wending its way towards them.

'You have it . . .' Will offered, with a gentle smile.

'Sure?'

'Absolutely.'

'Well, we could share a tipple or two with the supper clubbers, sometime,' Cath suggested, 'when Dan and Andreas are back in action, of course.' The lads had passed on this evening, still feeling shattered after recent events, and Nikki was holed up tackling a pile of paperwork. 'How does that sound?'

'The ideal solution.'

'Cheers.' Will clinked his pint against her wine glass.

The two of them had had a couple of drinks whilst quiz-zing, but not too much. Cath aware that she needed to keep a clear head in his company. They were still coming out of such difficult situations, relationship-wise, after all. It was a fun night, they'd got on well, and had enjoyed the buzzy atmosphere of their village pub on a busy Thursday. And okay, yes, she'd enjoyed being in the company of an attractive and interesting man.

In the end, they stayed long after the quiz, chatting and laughing over a glass of red for her, and a further pint of ale for Will. Still talking over some of the music questions, and discovering their shared love of Fifties and Sixties music – the Drifters, Marvin Gaye, among many.

In fact, the pair of them hadn't realised quite how late it was, until the bar began emptying and the staff were clearing up around them. Indeed, landlord Bill, dressed in his trademark tweeds, with a sheen of sweat upon his brow from such a hectic night, made his way over to them. 'Time to drink up, bonny folks.' He gave a rosy-cheeked smile. 'And hey, it's good to see you out, Will.'

It was time to head home. They gathered their jackets, and as they made their way out to the village street it was already getting dark, even though they were in the long late nights of the summer. Pinpricks of stars were twinkling into life above them.

'I'll see you back,' Will offered in a gentlemanly way, his eyes softly focused on her.

'Oh, it's not far . . . there's no need.' But she realised, even as she said the words, that she'd very much like him to. It had been such a gorgeous evening. Warning shots were suddenly going off in her head, however.

'It's okay. I'd like to.' He smiled.

And she didn't argue this time.

They reached her cottage, and hovered at the threshold, both giving a shy grin. Oh, was this going to be the moment for a goodnight kiss, at last? Where they finally broke through the barriers that kept them on the brink of friendship only? Her whole body felt finely tuned to his, just centimetres away. She was excited and scared to death, all at once. Her sensible head scolding, *And don't you even think of inviting him in.*

His dark-hazel eyes caught hers. He seemed to be waiting . . . for her to say something? Perhaps to make that first tentative move?

Don't go there! the voice in her mind clammered, *he might read more into it.* And in truth, though a kiss might be lovely, she wasn't ready for anything more than that and perhaps a late-night coffee and a chat. Life had been complicated and painful enough of late. Her battered soul shouldn't . . . and couldn't . . . take on any more emotional twists and turns.

And yet, she found herself asking, 'Uhm, would you like to come in? Just for a coffee?' She didn't want him to go just yet. She'd loved chatting with him this evening. Laughing at some of the off-beat quiz questions, whispering between themselves as they mooted possible answers – they'd had to lean in deliciously close, of course. His scent, of aftershave and something more, musky . . . of him, well that was rather gorgeous too. And yes, goddammit, he was a handsome man, who was also fun and seemed kind.

And oh, the way he was looking at her right now was melting her and setting her on fire all at once. Her senses were on overload. Her face flushed as she turned, fumbling to unlock the door, as she awaited his answer, feeling very much like a giddy teenager.

'Yeah . . . thanks. Uhm, I won't keep you long, though,' Will said. It was as if he was setting the boundaries, making it clear that there were no expectations to stay.

And that was okay, she realised – the small sense of relief tinged with a frisson of disappointment. Reality then stepped in; Christ, what if he had thought she had meant more than that? Her armpits were definitely fuzzy, and she wasn't quite sure when she'd last shaved her legs. Bloody hell, before anything might ever go to the next level, there would need to be weeks of buffing and bodily preparations. And why, oh the hell why, was she even thinking about that?

In the kitchen, she busied herself, making coffee using the ground decaf she had. Her mind was buzzy enough as it was. It didn't need stirring up any further. She knew she'd have trouble getting to sleep later, as it was.

She took a slow breath, told herself to settle down, and found two mugs. On their way back, the evening air had been calm and balmy. She opened the back door, to let in the lightest of breezes and get some air to her flustered skin, and she noticed her little shed up on the bank. The place where Supper Club had begun, where she and Will had first sat beside each other. She'd bought some solar lights, when she'd been to pick up a few plants from the garden centre the other week, that now guided the way up the steps. It was such a glorious evening, filled with the promise of stillness and starlight. It might be lovely to sit up there, to linger, on what would be one of the last late evenings of July, overlooking the dusky-mauve shadows of the moorland hills.

She poured hot milk onto the rich coffee and stirred. 'Shall we take these up to the shed?' Hah, it made a change from the possible, *Shall we take these up to bed?!*

'Yeah. Why not make the most of these summer nights, hey.'

There were a couple of fleecy blankets up there, should they feel a bit chilly, left from other evenings when she'd sat in the twilight listening to the birds' evensong with a mug of herbal tea, lighted candles and a good book on her back-lit Kindle.

Cath carried their mugs out and up the back garden steps, pausing at the top to ask Will if he'd open the summerhouse doors. She set the drinks down on the old kitchen table that had stayed there since the very first supper club. There was no way she was going to lug that all the way back down again! She'd feared neither she nor the table might make it down those steps in one piece. She lit a couple of tealights in their green glass jars, that glimmered to life, and then pulled forward two chairs to fill the entrance space by the open doors.

Her cottage garden, here at the top of the bank, looked out over the neighbouring slate roofs, and across to the moorland hills. It was no wonder Reggie had positioned his potting shed up here. From the doorway, and also the window above where his bench had been, the rural scene was gorgeous day or night. Even with gathering rain clouds the view was dramatic up here, at times moody and magnificent; you could watch a storm brewing, darkening menacingly over the hilltops, and be ready to bolt down to the house just in time. Cath was seeing nature in a new light here in the countryside of North

Northumberland. She was beginning to learn its lessons and its warnings, see its seasonal flux and to feel its nurturing.

Tonight was calm and kind to them, adding a summer glow to the embers they hadn't quite realised were beginning to re-kindle in their hearts. There was no moon apparent, so as they sipped their warming coffee the stars were becoming clearer, gently sparkling with a magical glow, as the inky dark descended.

'See there.' Will leaned closer, pointing his finger up to the night sky, showing her where to look. 'That's the Swan, Cygnus. A constellation. And the bright star there . . . that's its beak, and the wings . . . here, they span the Milky Way.'

She stared, refocusing on the stellar show above them, and then she found it, discovering its swan-like form in the sky. 'How amazing. And there, is that its tail?' Down below was a further bright star. Millions of miles away, no doubt.

'Yeah. You've got it.' He was smiling, the tealight giving enough of a glow to show the shadows of his face, the crow's feet crinkling gently around his eyes, the lift of his lips. 'It's stunning, isn't it. All those stars . . . all that space,' he continued.

'Mesmerising.'

'And there, just below it, do you see there's a smaller, dimmer arch of light. That's Delphinus the Dolphin.'

'Ah, I think I can just make it out, yeah. How do you know all this stuff?'

'Hah, I loved it all when I was a kid. Got a bit nerdy, in fact. Must have been about ten. Had all these light-up stars and planets in my bedroom. A mini telescope, my parents gave me . . . and there're all kinds of brilliant apps nowadays, too . . . show you exactly what's above you in the sky.' He paused as if thinking. 'But an app doesn't beat the beauty of just looking up on a clear dark night.'

'I'm sure. It's incredible. We never saw anything like this in Leeds, never this many stars . . . everywhere. There must have been too many street lights and houses.'

'Yep, good old light pollution.'

The two of them had leaned in disconcertingly close. Will's breath a wisp of condensation beside her, like a whisper of cloud, or a promise, on the night air. She could smell his fragrant woody aftershave and their joint coffee aromas. And she could feel his warmth, though they weren't actually quite touching. The air about them felt electric, even though there was no hint of a storm . . . not externally anyhow.

They then heard a rustle coming from the hedgerow, and a snuffling sound that moved towards them. There, nearing their feet, a hedgehog, all prickly and purposeful. They sat in silence, watching, not wanting to startle it. Both of them were enchanted by the curious creature. Cath knew for sure that Trevor would have been moaning at this point about it being a flea-ridden beast. But she and Will merely smiled and watched in shared amusement.

And she slipped her hand into his. A quiet, tender gesture, filled with affection . . . oh, and a touch of longing. Will shifted to look at her, his face somehow a question. Was he taken aback? She could feel the tension in his fingertips . . . and then, they relaxed. And after a few still seconds, he gently rubbed his thumb over the back of her hand. The connection between them was physical in the smallest of ways, but managing to fill her whole body with a fluid warmth – a feeling loaded with promise and hope . . . and perhaps a little love.

And there was an understanding that there was no rush. She recognised that they both needed time to come back from the dark places they had been. But this magical unfurling of feelings between them was real. It had started.

But as swiftly as the moment had been there, it was gone. Will seemed to startle himself back to his senses, pulling his hand away.

'Cath . . . uh . . . I think I'd better go.' He was standing up, getting ready to leave. It was like a switch had been flicked.

'Ah . . . okay.' Cath stood too, slightly taken aback by the sudden change in him. She was still part-wrapped in her fleecy cover.

'It's been a lovely night . . . yep, the quiz was great fun.' He deftly switched the focus from the two of them and their starlit moment to the quiz earlier in the evening.

'Yeah.' Cath felt at a loss how to react to his abrupt reaction. From cosy to cool in a matter of seconds. She dropped her blanket onto the seat, and followed his swift steps down to the house and towards the front door, where the earlier promise of his kiss suddenly seemed daft, delusional. And yet her body still felt the warmth of his hand in hers. 'We'll have to do it again sometime . . .' she ventured.

'Thanks for the coffee,' was all he replied.

'You're welcome. And hey, thanks for walking me back.'

'Night, then.' He sounded awkward.

'Night, Will. Oh, and thank you for the stargazing lesson,' she added, trying to claw back some of their earlier closeness.

'No worries.' And he turned to go, without so much as a wave or a glance back.

Cath was left in limbo. What was that all about? She hadn't imagined their connection. Their evening could have surely ended in a tender kiss as easily as this swift exit. And, how the hell did a touch that felt to her like the start of something, end up with Will in a mad dash to leave? Damn it, the can of emotional worms she'd been so determined to keep shut was already starting to prise open.

Chapter 34

Damned stupid middle-aged woman, she should have known better than to let daft romantic feelings go to her head. Last night had been wonderful, a little sprinkle of star-like magic, but it was just a moment in time. Romance wasn't meant for middle-agers like them . . . especially not ones who'd been battered and bruised by married life. Best to steer clear of the next phase of confusion and hurt which was bound to happen, and to keep that evening as a lovely memory. With that in mind, Cath was determined to busy herself today, getting on with her new life, and drive this latest, though lovely, incident aside.

She arrived at the village stores, to the now familiar welcome of the jingly doorbell.

'Morning, Cath. And how are you today?' asked Dan chirpily.

'Good, thanks. You?'

'Fine thank you, petal.'

'And Maria? How's she getting on?'

'Back from hospital and making steady progress,' he replied.

'Ah, that's good.' Cath opened the glass door to the fridge compartment to reach for a carton of milk.

'Oh yes, she's perked up a lot,' Andreas added, as he appeared from the back room with a knowing smile. 'Back to her old ways . . . trying to organise my life.' He shook his head as he raised his dark eyebrows.

With a fresh loaf, some tomatoes on the vine, milk and ground coffee to hand, Cath approached the counter where the lads now stood together with a slightly serious look on their faces.

'Shall we ask her?' Dan prompted.

'Oh, ask me what?' Cath was curious.

'It's a bit of a biggie,' Andreas chipped in.

'Try me.'

'Umm, well, would you consider minding the shop for a weekend? In two weeks' time? It'd be the full day on Saturday, and then, a half day on Sunday.'

'I could! What's up?' She actually felt quite excited by the prospect. This was her chance. It'd be nice to get involved locally. She'd hoped for a couple of hours trial in the shop at first, with help to hand, rather than flying solo, but hey-ho, in for a penny, in for a pound.

'Well, it's a bit of a story. Mama's insisting I attend my cousin's wedding,' Andreas explained. 'Family representative and all that. But well, it's down in London. And after her fall and everything, I have to admit I'm really not sure about leaving her and going so far. Eleni – that's my cousin, the bride to be – says she understands if we can't make it. But Mama is going on and on about it, as though I'm letting the whole family down if I don't go.'

'Well, you did say she's doing okay now, back at the home? Nice and stable,' Cath countered.

'Ye-es, but you just don't know what might happen next . . .' Andreas faltered.

Dan chipped in here. 'They'll be there with her all the time, Andreas. She's in good hands.'

'True,' supported Cath gently. She'd only heard good things about the nursing home in Kirkton.

'It'd be an overnighter for us on the Saturday,' Dan explained. 'And then we'd be back on the train and home by late Sunday afternoon.'

'Doesn't sound too onerous to me. I'd probably enjoy it to be honest.' Cath smiled warmly. 'Yes, I'd love to be able to help.'

'Oh, and then there'd be Shirley to look after, too,' Dan added. 'Or we could try the kennels, if need be. But she wasn't too happy in there last time, to be honest. Was in a huff with us for days.'

'It's a bit of an ask, we know. We'd pay you for working here, of course.'

'Oh yes, we'd insist on that.'

'It sounds fine to me, honestly. And having Shirley, that's no problem. She's a joy. Just give me those dates, and I'll double-check when I get back in. I'm sure I can shift some of my tutorials on that weekend, if need be. And hey, me and Shirley are sofa pals now.'

'Are you absolutely certain? It is a lot to take on.'

'Just give me a lesson on the till before you go . . . and anything else I'll need to know here. But yeah, I'd love to help out. Honestly.'

'Oh, well we're sorted then. London here we come . . . off to our Big Greek Wedding. I'll get online in a mo to book the train tickets.' Dan sounded excited.

'Oh, that's great, Cath. And Mama will be delighted. Though I still don't really feel comfortable about leaving her.' Andreas had been visiting twice a day, every day, since she'd got back from the hospital.

'Would you like me to call in, and visit her whilst you're away?'

'Oh, my goodness, we can't give you any more to do.'

'Well, I'd have some time on the Sunday afternoon, anyhow. Why not? If you let the care home know in advance, and explain to Maria who I am. I'd love to meet her. From all you've told me, she sounds quite a character.'

'Oh, she is that. If you think Shirley's a character, well . . . Mother's a step ahead. And yes, she'd enjoy your company, for sure.'

'Well, that's it then. Shop, Shirley and a visit to Maria . . . sorted.'

'Ah, thank you, petal. We'll make it up to you sometime soon. Perhaps a gourmet supper evening, all bells and whistles.'

'Well, your beach picnic was pretty fab as it was, lads.'

'You ain't seen nothing yet.'

'Well, don't put any more pressure on yourselves, just now. Let me check these dates, which I'm pretty sure will be fine, and then you go and have a great time at your family wedding.'

'You're a godsend, lovely.'

Cath picked up her items and left the stores with a smile, but also a small chink of anxiety about what she had just taken on. Eek, she'd never run a shop in her life, what was she letting herself in for? But surely, if she could control thirty plus hormone-laden teens in a classroom it should be a doddle. And she was more than happy to help the lads out. They deserved a bit of a lift in their hour of need. The two of them had certainly helped lift her spirits since she had arrived as a lonesome newbie to the village.

Could she manage running a shop? Well, there was only one way to find out, and that was to hit the ground running.

Chapter 35

The two weeks until the wedding flew by, and here she was on the Saturday morning stood behind the counter of the village shop, five minutes before opening time, ready to fly solo – gulp. She'd had a quick lesson on the till and card machine with Dan yesterday, and well, she again reminded herself, she'd handled a classroom full of teenagers, how hard could it be?!

After working a couple of hours, Cath realised the flow of customers was all or nothing. There were peak times – the early morning papers, croissants and milk run, followed by the coffee and pie/cake/chocolate bar stop for the local workmen and farmers, and then mid-morning the oldies in for their regular provisions and a chat too, of course – which was lovely. And oh, if you dared to nip out the back to put the kettle on for yourself at what you thought was a lull, well, that would guarantee a fresh barrage of visitors. She'd not managed to get further than an inch down her mug of tea each time before it had gone cold.

She had to admit she was enjoying it, though, the buzz of being back in a workplace, of dealing with customers face to face. She was meeting more people from the village this morning than she had in the whole four months of living here. An elderly gentleman, dressed smartly but with a well-worn appearance, in faded-grey twill trousers and a green checked flannel shirt, then came in. 'Oh, and where are the lads this morning?'

'Good morning,' Cath greeted him, explaining, 'Oh, they're at a family wedding down in London.'

'How grand . . . and who are yea, then?' the chap asked rather forthrightly.

'I'm Cath. Just here helping out today. I've recently moved here . . . into Cheviot Cottage.'

'Ah, so you're the lassie in Reggie's old place. Right you are. Nice to meet yea.' He doffed his tweed cap. 'My name's Kenneth, lived here in Tilldale all my life.' He offered his aged hand to shake over the counter.

Cath shook it, warmly. 'Lovely to meet you, too.'

'So, are yea settling in al-reet?'

'Yes, thanks. It's a lovely village. And Dan and Andreas have made me feel very welcome.'

'Aye, they're nice enough laddies. Andreas usually makes me a mug of tea, actually . . .' The words were pointed and hung between them like a question.

'Oh, well, if you give me a minute. It's quiet, so I suppose I could pop the kettle on.' She wondered if the lads charged him anything, or if it was all part of the service.

'That'd be grand, lass. Milk, two sugars.' He nodded and then settled himself down on the seat that was placed near the till, making himself comfortable. And of course, the second she headed out to the back room where the kettle, mugs, and tea and coffee jars were, the jingly bell went, announcing another customer. She managed to flick the kettle's switch to on and dashed back out.

Two more customers were served. Kenneth seemed to know them both well and sat happily introducing Cath – the new shop helper and owner of Reggie's old house – to them. The first was Geoff, a boiler-suited plumber (*might be a handy contact*, she thought) from the Old Barn at Claverham, and the second was Sheila, a friendly middle-aged lady, from 'the lane' – which lane she never had a chance to find out. The kettle had to be re-boiled, and she just had time to make and pass Kenneth his mug of tea, when in came a couple of workmen asking for takeaway coffees and steak pies.

The rest of the morning had flown by and the elderly chap was still in situ on his chair, his cup long-drained. 'Umm, were you actually wanting anything . . . from the shop, Kenneth?' Cath prompted.

'Oh, yes . . . that's it, pet, I needed milk and butter, a can of soup . . . might go for tomato today, and one of those nice creamy yoghurts for my pudding. Is there a strawberry one there, in the fridge?'

Cath fetched his items for him, and popped them into a bag. She decided the mug of tea would be free, feeling that was what Andreas and Dan might well do. And if not, then it could be her treat. She'd pop an extra couple of pounds in the till, just in case.

The old man sat a little longer, even after settling his shopping bill. Ten minutes later, he finally got up to his feet. Popping his cap back on, he said, 'Grand cup of tea that, lass. Thanks, and very nice to meet yea.'

'It's been lovely to meet you too, Kenneth.'

Cath had a feeling that was his social time for the day, his chance to have some company. It made her appreciate what the lads did for everyone here in the village, keeping the rural stores going, and making them a warm and welcoming place. It was so much more than just a shop; it was a community hub.

She shut the stores for a half-hour lunch break as instructed, whizzed Shirley around the block, had a quick ham sandwich and a cup of tea (a full one, yippee!) back at home, and was soon back on for the next shift.

The afternoon was more eventful. A steady stream of customers, a lack of knowledge of the whereabouts of some items, plus the odd price label being missing meant things were slightly more stressful, but Cath was managing okay until four separate customers appeared at once. The third of those being a middle-aged woman with a sour face who gave her such a scowl when Cath confirmed that all the loaves of sourdough (*such a well-named item*, she suddenly thought) had now gone. Cath felt like saying that she should have called in this morning if she was that bothered – but kept that little gem to herself, not wanting to spoil the lads' ongoing trade. Everyone else she had served, whether or not they needed to wait, was pleasant and chatty, and didn't mind the short queue, understanding that she was still finding her feet and learning to master the till and card machine.

And that was where things really went wrong. She managed to press an extra zero on the charge machine, so instead of £10.90 she had actually charged a poor old lady (thank goodness it wasn't sour puss) £109.00. She realised too late, and the transaction had gone through – oops. Cath was in a bit of a fluster, unsure how to put it right, and after trying several menu keys, was at a loss. She apologised profusely, offering to make a note of the error and get the lads to correct it for her on their return. She hoped to goodness that she hadn't just caused the poor lady to be overdrawn.

Just then the doorbell jingled, and in came Will. 'Hey, how's it going? Thought I'd look in for some milk, and see how you're getting on.' He'd known about her covering the shop.

'Hi, well, it's been busy this aft and, yeah, pretty good . . . but I've a bit of a problem with the card machine.'

The elderly lady was still there, hovering to the side of the counter, packing the last of her things into her shopping bag.

'The transaction amount went through wrong for this lady,' she explained, feeling embarrassed at her error.

'Oh, hello, Irene. All okay?'

'Well, it would be, pet, but my pension's just disappeared for the week,' she answered wryly.

'I'm so sorry,' Cath repeated, feeling herself flush.

'Don't worry, let's see if we can put it right.' Will turned to Cath. 'Can I take a look? Yep, good stuff, I use the same kind of card machine at the cycle shop. So, what have you charged? And what should it have been?'

Cath showed the shop's transaction receipt, and explained her error.

'Okay, I think the easiest way here is to do a full refund, and then re-charge the right amount. Are you okay with that, Irene?'

'Of course, if it means I get my money back.'

'You will. Can I have the same card you used, please?' He efficiently scrolled through the menu options finding the button for the refund, that had totally escaped Cath, and made the corrections, handing Irene her refund receipt and the new one at the right price. 'There you go, all sorted. That's your refund of £109 and here's your payment of £10.90.'

'Well, that's a relief. Thank you so much, young man.'

Will gave a quirky smile at that.

'You're welcome,' he replied.

'Thank you . . .' Cath looked to Will with relief. 'And thanks for your patience,' she said to Irene.

'No worries, pet. We can all make a mistake. It's nice you're here helping out.'

Aw, that made her feel a lot better, and at least she didn't now have to upset the applecart with the lads, having to explain her error, giving them more to do on their return.

After the lady had gathered up her things and left the stores, Will added with a grin, 'Haven't been called a young man for a very long time.'

'Hah, I wouldn't get too excited.' Cath chuckled. 'I think she has to be at least eighty.'

'The cheek,' he said, pretending to be offended, but they were both laughing.

He looked rather lovely when he laughed, Cath thought. And of late, he seemed happier altogether than when she had first met him. She wondered, and hoped, if it might have something to do with their growing friendship.

He seemed more relaxed with her today, here in the shop. Perhaps it was just a bit too much too soon, that evening back at hers under the stars. She'd felt it too, that night. But instead of dashing away, she so wished he'd been brave and run into her arms.

*

Strolling out along the village street in the early evening sunshine, Cath heard the light scrunch of tyres, as Will rolled up beside her on his bicycle.

'Good evening.'

'Hi.' This was a pleasant surprise. Her smile was warm.

Shirley wagged her tail excitedly beside her.

'Doggie duties now?' Will leaned over, to give the terrier a rub.

'Yes, indeed. Been all go today at the shop. But it's been okay. Tiring, just from concentrating and trying to remember it all. But it's been good to be able to help the lads.'

'Yeah, they're great guys. Wonder how the Greek wedding's going.'

'Oh, I had a couple of pictures through before,' said Cath, fetching her phone from her jeans pocket. 'Looks like they're having a great time. Here's one of the bride . . . doesn't she look gorgeous, and so like Andreas. You can tell they're family, all olive-skinned, and those dark eyes and hair. And look, here's another of the lads at the reception, looking very dashing in all their finery.'

'Ah, yeah, very smart. Great photos. I'm glad they're having a good time.' He paused, to take a breath. 'So, ah, what time do you finish at the shop tomorrow?'

'Oh, umm, eleven-thirty. It's just a half day. Why?'

'Ahm, I was just wondering if we might go for a walk . . . in the afternoon? With Shirley too, of course.' He nodded at the dog.

What was this . . . some kind of date? Or just Will offering to help out? She warned herself not to read too much into it, but her heart was doing a little fluttery hammer in her chest.

Then, she remembered her plans. 'Oh, sorry, but I've a tutorial booked and then I've promised Andreas I'd go and visit Maria. I said I'd look in on her while they're away.'

He dipped his eyes, seeming a little disappointed, whilst saying, 'Oh, that's kind. She'll enjoy a visit and some company.'

'But ah, maybe later on,' Cath quickly added, not wanting to miss this chance, and thinking she'd need to walk Shirley after she got back, anyhow. 'How about after four?'

'Ah no, sorry.' He looked regretful. 'I'm committed to a bike ride at four-thirty with a mate.'

Damn, it seemed fate had other plans. Cath felt suddenly deflated, but tried to hide it with a casual, 'Oh, well, maybe some other time.' Despite her easy words, Cath really didn't want to lose this opportunity. She liked the idea of a walk, of getting to know Will even more . . . some time for just the two of them.

'Yeah, okay, another time.' Those melting hazel eyes were looking at her. He gave a small cough. 'Right, well, catch you soon.'

He re-mounted his bike and was off. Cath stayed fixed on the spot for a few seconds, not quite sure what to make of the conversation they'd just had. Was it just a friendly gesture, rather than a getting-to-know-you-more kind of thing? Was Will not particularly worried if it happened or not? After all, he hadn't gone on to suggest another day, had he?

She gave an inner groan. She was overthinking things as per usual, and being a daft eejit. But, she resolved, the next time she saw him in the village, she might just take the plunge and remind him. There was no harm in that, surely? And if it was just a walk as friends then that was fine, she'd avoid any unnecessary complications. Despite her giddy heart, the thought of any romantic relationship was way too risky. It was far too soon, of course . . .

Chapter 36

It was Sunday, and after a less eventful morning in the shop – in fact, she'd rather enjoyed it, feeling much more confident in the role – Cath was heading over to Kirkton to meet Maria in the care home.

She had made a batch of shortbread last night, despite feeling shattered after her busy day. It had actually been a nice way to de-stress, the rolling of the dough, cutting it out, the kitchen filling with aromas of toasted buttery baking. And, she now had a generous tub of biscuits for Maria to share with her fellow residents and the staff.

The home was in an old vicarage, a Victorian stone-built property with large lawns and gardens with pretty shrub borders. It was on the edge of the town, nestled in the valley beside open fields. Cath parked up, and entered a porch area, pressing a buzzer to announce herself to the lady in the reception. As the door released and she walked in, the house had a welcoming and homely feel to it. The entrance hall was light and airy. There were fresh white and yellow chrysanthemums in a vase on a mahogany circular table, and the wallpaper was a cheery floral. A smell of cabbagey-cottage pie, no doubt the residents' lunch, lingered. The lady who'd answered the buzzer came out to say hello, and let Cath know that Maria was up and in the day room. She offered to take her through, realising that she was a first-time visitor.

'I hear the lads are at a wedding?'

'Yes, that's right. Family down in London.'

'Ooh, lovely. And do let them know Maria's been fine. We have already messaged them, but I know Andreas was particularly concerned about leaving her.'

'Ah, that's good news, and I will do.'

'Well, here we are, and that's Maria, just over there by the window.'

If Cath hadn't been shown, she reckoned she would have soon worked it out. Despite her thick grey hair and wrinkled skin, which was far paler than her son's, she had a look of Andreas across those dark eyes, still with a twinkle, as she looked up. She also had her arm in a cast and sling.

'Hello, Maria, it's Cath. I've brought you some biscuits. Shortbread, I've made them myself. And there's plenty there, if you want to share.' Cath set the tin down on the coffee table beside her.

'Why, that's lovely of you, spoiling me. Those other two, yesterday, came here with all sorts. We had some with our tea. Beautiful it was . . . a big sponge cake, and chocolatey little squares.'

'Oh, chocolate brownies, I bet.' It sounded like Lily had been baking too. 'That was Nikki and her niece who came to visit you.' They'd said they'd call in too, Cath remembered, so that Maria would have company on both days.

'Very nice of them. Nikki . . . that was it. And Lily. Pretty girl. Lovely to see the young ones coming in. Get fed up with all these oldies at times.'

Cath had to smile. Maria was talking as though she was a 'young one' herself.

'So, how are you feeling after your fall? How's your wrist doing?'

'Not so bad, not so bad. Silly old boot, aren't I, falling over like that.'

'Of course you're not. These things are easily done,' said Cath. 'Oh, and I've heard from Andreas. I can show you a couple of photos of the wedding on my phone.'

'Ah, that'd be marvellous. I'd love to see that . . . And our Eleni, I bet she makes a beautiful bride.'

'She does indeed.' Cath firstly showed Maria the image of her great-niece in all her wedding finery.

'*Omorfi*. Beautiful!'

It was lovely to see the elderly lady's face light up.

'Do you have a mobile phone, Maria? Then I can send them over for you to keep.'

'Well, I do, it's back in my room. But I don't know how to work the darned thing . . . or remember my number, come to that. Andreas is always showing me how to do things on it, and then telling me off when I forget.'

'Don't worry. The mobiles can seem complicated if you're not used to them. I'll ask one of the team here for your number before I go, and I'll send them on anyhow. They can find them on your phone, and show you them when you want, that way.'

'Thank you.'

Cath then scrolled on to the image of Andreas and Dan. Maria looked like she might burst with pride. 'Oh, so handsome the pair of them.'

One of the carers came over, and asked both Cath and

Maria if they'd like a cup of tea from the trolley, before serving the hot fragrant liquid in little green cups and saucers, and placing them on the coffee table before them.

'Thank you. Oh, can I help you?' Cath offered, realising it might be tricky for Maria to drink with her broken wrist.

'If you can just put it there, to this side of me, then I'll be fine, thank you. I've worked out how to do rather a lot with my left hand. Needs must.' Maria, though frail physically, seemed bright as a button. Cath was very much warming to her.

'Okay, there you go.'

'So, how do you know my boy, Andreas?'

Cath explained how she'd recently moved into the village, and how kind Andreas and Dan had been to her. She mentioned the Supper Club and how their friendship had grown.

'Ah, Andreas has told me about you . . . so you are the lady who cooks like an angel, with the fuckwit of a husband.'

Well, Cath hadn't expected that, she nearly spat out her tea. But yeah, the cap fitted.

'I suppose I must be.' She smiled, shaking her head with mirth.

'Better try one of these shortbread, if you're the canny cook. Don't let them all see, mind.' She glanced around the day room furtively. 'Like a flock of crows this lot when there's food about. Ena over there, she'd eat six biscuits on the trot, easily . . . and Arthur . . .' She pointed to a tall, skinny man who was dressed fairly smartly, but on closer inspection was wearing faded black suit trousers and a white shirt marked with . . . gravy stains, perhaps? He'd evidently nodded off, his head slumped to one side, bless him. 'Yes, with Arthur, the whole tin'd be gone. Hollow legs that one.'

They chatted easily over tea and biscuits, Cath asking what Andreas had been like as a child.

'Hah, full of himself. But joyous, always a sunny child.'

'Sounds like he hasn't changed much,' Cath agreed.

Cath then talked about finding her feet in the village, and how lovely it had been to start meeting up as the supper group. They had a bit of a giggle over Nikki's Seventies night.

Maria reminisced about coming over to London in the mid-Sixties, and life as a young married woman in a new and exciting, yet sometimes overwhelming city, with her handsome Greek-Cypriot husband, Theo. She told how his brother had already made the move, and had helped find Theo an office job within the London-based Greek shipping industry. Andreas and his older sister, Alexandra, came along soon afterwards. Their little Greek-Cypriot community, many of whom still lived in the Palmers Green area of North London, sounded supportive and fun. That's where the wedding was this weekend.

This lovely old lady had a sparkle about her, and had certainly taken life by the horns back then, soaking up life in the capital, and creating a new home for her and her young family.

All too soon, it was time to go, as it was apparent that preparations were being made for supper time, with chairs being shifted in the adjoining dining room and staff busying themselves.

'Well, I'd better get away now, Maria. Shirley will be waiting for her supper and a walk.'

'Ah, you have the little dog. She's a character, that one. Keeps the boys on their toes, good on her. Well, you get yourself away. And thank you so much for taking the time to visit an old girl.'

'It's been a pleasure.' Cath was standing up and popping her jacket back on, realising that she really had enjoyed Maria's company. And it felt good to be doing something kind. She quickly added, 'Maria, would it be all right to visit you again sometime? Would you like that?'

'Of course, I would, *Kopela mou*. It's brightened up my day.'

'*Ko-pela moo?*' Cath queried.

'It means *"My Girl"*. The old lady was smiling warmly, the deep creases etched around her eyes showing her age, her long life. Maria reached out her good hand towards Cath, who gave it an affectionate, gentle squeeze.

'Ah lovely. Well, that's settled then. I'll see you again soon, Maria. Take care.'

With that, Cath was on her way, with a very warm glow inside.

Chapter 37

Cath was kneeling at the border's edge, trowel in hand, digging out some bindweed that had dared to take root among the fragrant purple lavender. She knew better than to leave that invasive plant to take over. It was a sunshine-and-showers kind of day and she was making the most of a dry hour to attack the weeds. She daren't let Reggie's legacy of flowers and shrubs go to ruin. In fact, she'd even bought new seeds, and after weeding the raised bed, last week, had started a small vegetable and herb garden – all the better for her supper recipes. Tiny sprigs of life had already started, the warm and at times wet weather bringing them on. Soon enough there'd be a row of carrot tops, beetroots and lollo rosso lettuce, along with the parsley, sage, thyme and oregano plants that were settling in nicely at one end.

In her jeans pocket, Cath's mobile burst into life. It took her a second or two to work out the vibration from her hip area.

'Hi, sis. You okay?'

'Yeah, fine. Been busy, but good.' Cath brushed some mud from her knees and settled herself down in a garden chair, holding the phone in the crook of her neck for a few seconds as she peeled off her muddy gardening gloves.

'Great. And how's it been with Adam back down in Leeds?'

'Ah, it was lovely seeing him again, but I have to admit that it's a bit of a relief to have the cottage back to myself. It's just . . . we were so on top of each other here. I do hope he didn't feel pushed out, though.' Mother and son had been messaging and chatting, but she had this nagging feeling that Adam was struggling with life. Coming back from his adventures, looking for a bright career, a new focus, and failing in that – other than finding some bar work to tide himself over with – had evidently left him feeling flat. His youthful get-go spark had dimmed. And she hoped she hadn't added to that feeling, stressing him out about sharing the small space of the cottage.

'Ah, he'll be fine. Be having fun back in Leeds. Can't have been much going on for him there in your little village . . .'

'Not for a twenty-something, no, I suppose not.' Cath felt a bit better, her sister's comment helped her put things back in perspective, so she parked her guilt. 'Sounds as though he's getting fed up living with Trev. And, of course, the girlfriend's back on the scene. How did I guess that might happen? Adam's now talking about getting himself moved in with an old uni friend . . . they've found a cheap flat to rent in Kirkstall.'

'Well, it can't be easy living with your dad and his new bit of fluff. It'll give Adam a bit of independence, too. Sounds a good idea. Anyhow, that leaves the spare room free again, I imagine?' hinted Susie.

'Well, yeah.'

'Fab. Because guess what, I have a free weekend next week . . .'

'Are you inviting yourself?' Cath grinned.

'Hah, yeah, absolutely.'

'O-kay. That'd be lovely. Yeah, let's go for it.' There was nothing stopping Cath from having her, no prior engagements other than tuition which she'd squeeze in fine, and already she found herself looking forward to it.

'Brilliant . . . I'll get my little suitcase at the ready.'

Cath could hear the smile in her sister's voice. And, this was one guest she really would enjoy having to stay.

*

Cath was whizzing around, puffing up cushions and generally whipping her cottage into shape. The duster and the hoover had been out, the upstairs windows opened wide whilst she worked, and the spare bed made up with fresh white linen. She wanted her cottage to look its best for Susie's arrival. It wasn't that her sister was particularly fussy or anything, more that she wanted both herself and her new place to appear homely and welcoming; neat, tidy and sorted, in fact.

Susie was due in around half an hour – she'd phoned en route as she was nearing the market town of Alnwick. The sisters spoke every week as well as messaging, but hadn't seen each other in person for a few months now. With Susie living down in Derbyshire, having a full-time job as a personal assistant in a manufacturing company, and a busy family and social life, getting together wasn't always easy. Cath was looking forward to a relaxed girlie couple of days with time to chill, chat and have a damned good catch-up.

A toot of a car horn announced Susie's arrival. Cath dashed out to greet her. There she was, stepping out onto the pavement dressed in orange-linen palazzo pants and a stylish black V-neck top, glossy-brown hair pulled back by a pair of shades. 'Helloo.' She gave a broad grin.

'You've made it! Hello. How was the journey?'

'Not too bad. Ah, it's so lovely to see you.' They fell into a warm sibling hug.

'Come on in. Welcome to my humble abode.' Cath ushered her through the hall and into the kitchen. 'Ready for a cuppa?'

'I am indeed. It was a long slog, and I only stopped the once. Aw, it looks gorgeous in here.' Susie looked around her at Cath's cosy kitchen. 'Love the old stone wall there, full of character. And the yellow shade where the shelves are, that's perfect.'

'Thank you.' And it had, in the end, all gelled together. The mix of old and new. The cottage's original stone walls, Cath's splash of yolky colour, the mixing bowl found in the cupboard, now sat on the shelf alongside memories and the odd photo salvaged from their old Leeds family life.

'And how are you doing?' Susie asked.

'Yeah, pretty good. Things are looking up. I'm really starting to feel at home here.'

'That's great. And, I have to say, you look much better than when I saw you last.'

'Ah, thanks . . . I think.'

'Sorry, I meant, well, you were so tired, and you had that . . .' She paused, trying to find the right word. 'Sadness about you. It's been such a shit time, hasn't it.'

'Yeah, it's taken some getting my head around. The hurt, that feeling of devastation and then all the changes . . . Anyway,' Cath rallied, 'I do feel like I'm moving on. And I love this place, my cottage . . . and it's all my own. Well, now Adam's stuff is all away again . . .' She gave a wry smile.

Cath got her best porcelain mugs and her little teapot for two out. She'd baked a lemon, lime and thyme drizzle cake for Susie's arrival, which she now sliced releasing zingy scents of citrus.

'Ooh, I am being spoilt.'

'Absolutely. It's not often I get the chance to.'

'So, you're still enjoying your cooking, then?'

'Yep, and it's helped me make some new friends.'

'Hah, you've been bribing the locals with cake? I suppose there are worse ways to make friends.'

'Supper actually. And yeah, meeting new people, making friends over food and wine, it's been good.'

'Oh, yes, you were telling me . . . some kind of village supper club. Good for you. Anyone interesting there?' Susie raised an eyebrow.

Cath knew exactly what she meant and felt the heat of a blush. 'Now, you know I'm not in the market for any new relationships. Crikey, I've only just got out of the frying pan, I'm not jumping into the bloody fire.'

'Hmm, shame,' was all Susie uttered.

'And yeah, there are some really nice people,' Cath continued. 'I've told you about the lads from the shop, and then there's Nikki, she runs her own cleaning company, she's good fun. Her niece has just joined us too, who seems to be a bit of a baking whizz, full of ambition to make a career in catering.' There was a slight pause, and then she added, 'And then, there's a guy called Will.'

Susie's eyebrow quirked higher.

'Runs a bicycle repair shop. Nice bloke. But hey, there's nothing in it . . .' Not yet. Cath left it at that. If she told her sister he was a widower and looked like Marti Pellow, and that she actually fancied him, well that would be it. Full interrogation, and a kick up the arse for her hanging back on someone dishy.

Cath grabbed their cups, and they took up the two seats at the kitchen table. Over Earl Grey and luscious lemon cake they carried on catching up with each other's lives.

*

An hour later, feeling much more relaxed, and still settled in the kitchen, Susie asked, 'So, what are we doing this evening, sis? Drinks here, perhaps? Oh, and I've brought a bottle of champagne with me to christen your new home. I'll go get it, and fetch my other stuff in from the car. And then, can I treat you to supper at the pub?' Susie was her usual bubbly and generous self.

'Well, I had made a quiche to warm up at some point, but I suppose we can always have that for lunch tomorrow. Dinner at the pub does sound good.'

'It does indeed. I'll give The Star Inn a quick call – I've already looked it up, menu looks great – and I'll get us booked in. In the meantime, can you find some glasses for the fizz?' Susie was so positive about the village already, the difference between her sister and Helen's visit was markedly different, and that made Cath relax all the more.

Within minutes they were booked, a table for two in the bar area, and after chilling the champagne in the freezer for a short while before popping the cork, they were soon ready to unwind with flutes to hand. The little bubbles making delightful ripples through the pale-gold liquid.

Cath took a look outside the back door. 'Hmm, it's slightly breezy out there just now.' The earlier rain clouds had passed, but it was still on the cool side. 'But are you happy to take these up to the garden shed? We can find a bit of shelter there, and you can see my summerhouse renovations. I'm really quite pleased with it.'

'Yeah, 'course, I'd love to see it.'

They wandered out into the garden, where tall Spode-blue-and-white delphiniums, delicate cream roses, and lacy-pink peonies were now in bloom, sheltered in a sunny spot by the fence – more of Reggie's green-fingered legacies – and headed on up the steps.

Cath opened the glass doors of her summerhouse to reveal its white and sage-green interior with its eclectic chairs and shabby-chic furniture. Earlier, she'd even popped a posy jar of home-grown sweet peas on the table, just in case. She felt a buzz of pride as she showed the little shed off.

'All my own work. It was more than a bit run down when I first got here.'

'You dark horse, you. Wow, it's amazing. I love what you've done,' Susie commented, eyes wide as she took a step inside. 'So, have you turned into some DIY goddess or something, now Trev's off the scene?' Her sister beamed at her.

'Not quite, but I have given it my best shot. And hey, if I can do a few jobs myself, well, it saves spending a fortune on some handyman.'

'Hmm, depends on who the handyman might be?' Susie quirked an eyebrow with a cheeky grin.

And why did Will leap to mind then? He fixed bicycles, not houses or sheds, and certainly not broken hearts, Cath reminded herself sternly.

The girls settled down in the summerhouse, fizz in hand, looking out over next door's slate roof tiles towards the country hills. The barley fields, lower down in the valley, gleaming in the just breaking sun, with ripening ripples of green and gold. The two sisters were ready to catch up on all the goss and family chit-chat from the past few months.

Chapter 38

After a chilled and chatty afternoon, Cath and Susie were browsing the menu at The Star, sat at a table near the characterful old-stone open hearth. Being the summer months, it was unused, but a stack of logs nestled ready in the grate.

'Ooh, nice menu. Anything you'd recommend?' asked Susie.

'I've tried the Sunday roast, which was delicious, though I suppose that'll not be on today. The fish and chips looked great as they were coming by a minute ago'.

'Yummy, though the chicken and wild mushroom risotto has caught my eye. Oh, and there's a ribeye steak and peppercorn sauce . . . Decisions, decisions.'

With a glass of chilled white wine to hand, adding to the fizz from before, Cath was feeling slightly merry. She was enjoying the buzz and chatter of the country pub, that now her local, with its characterful flagstone floors and muted green walls, and was savouring the treat of coming out for supper. The pair of them had hardly stopped talking since Susie's arrival several hours ago, except for when her sister had taken her things up to her cottage bedroom, which she thought was 'adorable'.

After Adam had left, Cath had discovered some second-hand

limed-oak furniture – a dressing table and small wardrobe – in a curious, pre-loved furniture depot in the original old railway station building at Kirkton. Instantly, she knew they would suit the quirky slanting roof and wooden beams of the spare room. She offered a lower price, and after a little haggling, had secured a good deal. They were well worth parting with some of her diminishing savings for, she figured. The double bed, which had come with her from the spare room back in Leeds, was now draped with an oh-so-soft white linen duvet cover, and she'd scattered some grey-and-white damask-patterned cushions (a bargain from the high street charity shop) too. Dusky-pink roses, picked fresh from the garden, were sat in a bud vase on the little bedside table. It was so lovely to be able to put her own touch on things at the cottage.

She'd been excited about her sister's visit. And here was Susie, now sitting opposite her. Older than Cath, she was into her mid-fifties and always looked amazing, her clothes colourful and stylish, and her glossy brunette hair glamorous. Thank heavens she'd finally got her own hair done recently, Cath mused. But Susie, well, her style wasn't overly coiffed or groomed, just sassy and Susie-style.

'Okay, so how do you do it?' Cath asked.

'Do what?'

'Still look so glamorous at fifty-four, and be so bloody bubbly and positive about life?'

'Well, I haven't been through what you have for a start . . . being let down so atrociously by your dick of a husband.' Susie wasn't known to mince her words. She and Trevor had always had this distance between them. Susie had never

295

really taken to him, though she was always polite. He'd finally proven her right.

'True.' Cath took a big sip of wine, pausing to gather her thoughts. There was something about being with her sister that made her open up. 'You know, sometimes I felt more-or-less invisible, those last couple of years with Trev . . . hitting mid-life, sticking to my steady known path, teaching, home . . . doing what everyone expected of me, I suppose . . . And then, I think I let myself slip into being pretty much invisible too.' She thought of the baggy cover-it-all clothes, the unkempt greying hair. The awful vision in the charity shop mirror. 'No wonder Trevor stopped noticing me.'

'Oh, Cath. Don't start shifting the blame back to you. Trev's the one who let you down . . . he's the one who allowed you to feel like that.'

'I suppose. But you didn't let mid-life get to you, you still do all sorts of exciting stuff, and manage to look brilliant.'

'Well, HRT is a wonderful thing, and,' Susie added, 'I made a conscious decision to keep putting myself out there. There's no way I'm going to slip quietly into middle age. I like wearing bright colours, they make me feel good . . . And I want to keep trying new things – be it clothes, restaurants, hobbies.' Susie took a sip of wine. 'Hah, went for my first park run the other day . . . absolutely knackered me. Hannah was home from uni. She whizzed around the track like it was a breeze . . . and there's me just about on my knees by the end. It felt weirdly good though. Once I'd showered and had a massive cup of coffee afterwards, that is.'

'Hah, don't think I'd be up for a run. But I'm walking now, a few miles at a go, it's doing me good. It's great around here for that. Loads of local footpaths, and the countryside is so scenic.' She really was enjoying her daily walks near the village. Finding new routes, and discovering public footpaths she hadn't spotted before. And hmm, she was still looking forward to that stroll with Will.

Cath looked up and spotted a familiar face at the bar. Her stomach did a little flip. Or, perhaps, she might just have to try cycling again, she thought with a secret smile. It was Will, dressed in full cycling Lycra, with a mate. They'd just ordered a couple of pints and were stood chatting with landlord Bill.

The waitress came over and took the ladies' order. Cath sticking with the fish and chips, and Susie choosing steak frites. The wine was slipping down well, as they continued to catch up on each other's busy lives. Cath's eyes were unwittingly drawn to check, now and again, the place at the bar where Will was still standing. Hmm, his muscles looked damn good under the tight cycling shorts and fitted top. His dark hair slightly damp with bike-riding sweat. He hadn't spotted her as yet, so she could let her gaze linger momentarily.

'So, Hannah has done really well in her second-year exams,' Susie repeated, raising her voice a little. 'Did you catch that, Cath? You seem a bit distracted.' Her sister's eyes swept to the bar area.

Cath diverted her gaze. 'Ah, yes, yeah, that's great news.'

And the sisterly chat flowed again.

Their meals soon arrived, drawing her attention back to their table. Cath managed to enjoy her crispy-battered fish and chip supper, despite her stomach doing all kinds of weird things. Every now and then, her eyes were drawn sneakily back to a certain person stood at the bar.

Around fifteen minutes later, Will had to pass their table on his way to the gents, and it was then he spotted Cath. He paused, and gave a broad smile. 'Oh, hi.'

'Ah, hello, Will . . . been off cycling?' *Nothing like stating the obvious*, she cursed herself for sounding so wet. 'Oh, this is my sister. She's staying with me for the weekend.'

'Hi, nice to meet you.' Susie was all smiles too, whilst managing to give Cath a sideways look that said, *This is Will . . . and you didn't tell me*. They could read each other so well. 'I'm Susie,' she introduced herself.

Will gave a nod. Then, in an instant his smile dropped. 'Right . . . well, hope you've had a nice meal. Uhm, got to dash.'

Cath noticed he looked kind of pale. Was he feeling a bit off, perhaps?

With that, he headed to the gents, and on his return, he kept his eyes firmly fixed on the bar area. He and his friend drank up soon afterwards, and Cath spotted them gathering their things ready to exit. She looked over to wave or mouth a goodbye, but he didn't so much as glance her way. Oh. A nip of disappointment hit her in the gut.

She'd thought they'd got closer after that recent heart-to-heart talking about his wife, and about Trevor . . . about life. The stargazing session still lingered on her mind. Oh, and they were meant to be off on their walk together soon. He could at least have said bye. Hah, men, would she ever get used to them, and their odd bloody ways?

*

Back home, in the cottage's cosy lounge, the sisters were nestled together on the sofa, with a cup of tea.

'So, are you happy here?' Susie sounded earnest, like she was digging for the truth. She'd been worrying about her little sister for months now. Cath had been good at hiding her feelings at times, over the years.

'Yeah, I am. It's still early days, of course . . . but yes, it feels like a good move. I really like the village, and the people. And I love being in the countryside. All that space and fresh air.'

'It does look very pretty around here.'

'Yeah, do you remember coming up this way when we were kids? It was so different from home, from those never-ending Sheffield suburbs.' They'd lived in Sheffield as a family, growing up with their parents, before Cath had left for uni, and then moved to Leeds with Trevor. 'It's hardly changed up here . . . still kind of old-fashioned, but in a good way.' Cath's thoughts drifted back to those family holidays, especially that last eventful time . . .

'Oh God, remember that awful time you went through, after that last caravan holiday up here.' Susie was on the same wavelength, evidently. 'Yes, the panic of that pregnancy scare . . . you were only sixteen.'

Cath had finally confided in her sister, after four weeks back home and still no period, being terrified to tell their parents. The holiday romance, and that 'first time' with the lad from Belford. Susie had been the one who'd told her not to panic, given her a big hug, wiped away her anxious tears, and gone to buy a pregnancy test for her. The two women had held that secret between them for all these years. To this day, Cath had never spoken about it with anyone else.

'He seemed a nice enough lad to be fair . . .' Susie continued. 'Matty, yes, that was it . . . but Christ, you were so bloody young.'

'Yeah.' Cath had flushed pink, the memory vivid, emotions still strong about it even now. 'He was a really nice lad, but we hardly knew each other, not really . . . a typical holiday romance.' She tried to make light of it, though that first flush of young love had meant the world to her back then, in those giddy days of youth and inexperience. 'Bloody hell, it would have changed everything, having a baby so young.' She took a large gulp of tea. 'I don't think I could have gone through with an abortion, either. But then, I was about to start my A Levels, and I was fixed on training to be a teacher. That's all I'd wanted to do for years.'

'Yeah, I remember, Little Miss Maths Teacher . . . and hey, you went on and did it.'

'But back then, I was terrified . . . suddenly all my dreams seemed to be in the balance,' she sighed, as the memories came rushing in. 'I was so bloody naïve.'

'Yep, you think you're all grown up, think you can handle those early relationships, but you're still a child really. God, I worry about my girls, even now. It's such a vulnerable age, that near-adulthood.'

'Yeah.' She thought about Adam, too. Struggling to get a decent job, the world an ever-changing place, everything so fast with the constant scroll and hit of social media. There was so much more information, entertainment, but to her it felt like overload. 'Hopefully, the girls are a lot more clued up than we ever were,' Cath continued, thinking back to her youth once more. 'Access to healthcare, better education, availability of the pill, it's kind of the norm. We hardly spoke about it back then. And we trusted the lads to buy the condoms . . . and know how to use them.' She still remembered how it was all a bit of a fumble, way back when.

'But hey, it all worked out in the end, didn't it.'

'There by the grace of God . . . a false alarm . . . bloody hell. Mum and Dad would have had a heart attack about it, wouldn't they? And hey, thanks for being a great big sis . . . you've always had my back, haven't you?' She leaned in to give Susie an affectionate hug, getting a waft of her floral Jo Malone Peony perfume, her sister's favourite scent.

'Hey, I'm sure you'd have done the same for me. Anyway, let's stop harking back to the bad old days. That's bloody years ago. And you've been through a hell of a lot more since then. What's done is done. We need to be having some fun, now. The good times are coming.' Susie chinked her mug against Cath's. 'To your wonderful new cottage home and your new life. It's your turn to shine again, sis.'

'Aw, thanks, Suz.'

And Cath realised that she did feel stronger, here in Tilldale, ready to spread those wings, to take flight once more and find that big blast of sunshine.

'Don't you think it's exciting, now you're all settled in? Now the worst of the Trevor shite is over. You can start again. A clean slate, new page. New beginnings . . . and a sensationally sassy Second Chapter.'

'Yeah, I like that idea.' She raised her tea mug. 'Cheers to my Second Chapter! With plenty of sass.'

Chapter 39

The weekend had disappeared in a flash, with Susie heading back to the Peak District on Sunday evening. After the flush of animated sibling chatter and company these past two days, the quiet of the cottage and the sleepy street outside was a contrast. Cath felt a little emptier, a little lonelier. A solo life was now hers, and she was still trying to adapt to that. She wondered if Reggie had felt this too, over the years. Once his wife had passed away, it was more than likely. She sighed, feeling that allegiance with him.

Well, then, she knew where she could find a bit of company and some chit-chat, plus the bonus of some freshly baked goodies to cheer up her morning coffee time: the village stores. Time to crack on, and remind herself of the happier things in life.

It was fresh with a light breeze as she stepped outside, with the sun trying to peep around some scudding cotton-wool-balls of cumulus clouds. The sound of birdsong lifted her spirits as chaffinches and sparrows darted among the garden shrubs, and dipped artfully in and out of next door's hawthorn hedge. The short run of honey-stone cottages led her to the village green, and on over the crossroads to the shop. Aromas of . . . hmm, croissants and something savoury, cheesy perhaps, delighted her nostrils, getting stronger as the shop door opened, to reveal . . . Oh.

There was Will coming out of the village shop. Her heart missed a beat, but she managed to give a friendly wave. 'Hey, there.'

She hadn't seen him since his swift departure from the pub, a few days ago, when she'd been with Susie. Now was her chance to try and suss out whether Will's quick exit was somehow related to her in any way, if there was still some impasse between them, or if she was just making daft assumptions. 'Hi, how are you doing?' Her voice came out chirpy, but she felt on edge.

'Ah . . .' Will's brow furrowed above his dark eyes. 'Yep, I'm okay. You?'

'Good. Yeah, I had a lovely time with my sister up.'

'Yeah . . . great.' His lips then pursed into a tight line.

Ooh, there was a definite edge there. This wasn't how she'd hoped things might go. 'So...' she persevered, taking the plunge, it was now or never. 'Uhm, do you fancy that walk you mentioned, sometime? It's so lovely along by the river on a nice morning like this.'

'Ah, look, things are pretty busy at the bike shop right now . . . I really need to dash and get over there. Perhaps some other time.' He was already making a move to leg it away, off up the street.

Cath was left standing there, even more confused than when she'd started. Well, that felt very much like a brush-off, if there ever was one. She was left mouthing the word 'bye' and feeling downright rejected. He definitely seemed miffed with her, but why? They'd been getting on so well since the beach picnic, teaming up to help out the lads. The stars had seemed to be aligning literally for them, and more than that . . . a real connection had been building. And, she had to confess, despite trying to protect her bruised heart, the more she had grown to know him the more she found herself falling for him.

*

Cath left it for a few days, but couldn't help feeling that something was wrong. Had Will perhaps felt he'd opened up too much about his wife? Shared too much about their life together, about those last difficult months, and now felt uncomfortable? Were those tender moments watching the stars just too much too soon? Or had she inadvertently said something amiss, without realising it?

Well then, sitting moping about and wondering wasn't getting her anywhere. She hated a bad atmosphere. In all these years, one thing she had learned was to try and face things head on, however difficult things might seem. Even with these crazy romantic emotions she'd been flooded with recently, and her head beginning to fill with half-baked dreams, the bottom line was that her friendship with Will was something that she didn't want to lose.

*

Cath took a deep breath, a step forward, and then knocked on the grey-painted door of the smart semi-detached village house. A potted bay tree neatly adorned each side of the step.

She had never been inside Will's home before, having only met outside for the bike ride those few weeks ago.

This new frostiness between them didn't sit easy with her, and it seemed to have started that evening in the pub with her sister. Well, if she'd done something wrong or upset him, then he needed to tell her why. Outside the shop yesterday, it seemed like he could hardly look in her direction, and those brief words on the village street were cool. But how could she possibly have offended him? Perhaps she was totally overanalysing the situation, and he'd be fine with her today. Stood there, ready to face the music, she tried to lift her mood, she'd go on in with a positive attitude.

She'd figured an offer of baked goodies might make her unexpected arrival more welcome. The flapjacks in the tin in her hand were still warm from the oven. Ideal fuel for an active cyclist, she'd thought. She knocked again, took a slow breath, and held the gift aloft with hope.

Eek, the sound of footsteps approaching made her tense up again.

The turn of a key, the door opening . . .

He was there, handsome as ever, dressed in denim jeans and a casual blue T-shirt. His chin lightly stubbled. Hazel eyes catching hers. 'Oh . . . it's you.' He looked surprised, and not in a particularly good way.

'Hi, Will.' She braved a smile. 'Umm, I've been baking. There are some extra flapjacks I made, which I thought you might like.' Cath tried to sound as normal as possible. As if she'd just had this thought, not that she'd been lying in bed last night wondering what she'd done wrong, since receiving that rebuff in the street.

'Ah, r-right.' The words came out staccato, as he stood blocking the doorway. There was an awkward pause, then he reached out a hand to take the tin that was offered.

Cath hovered on his threshold, feeling distinctly uneasy.

There were a few further tricky seconds where they both waited, then he added stiffly, 'Well, thanks . . . umm, I suppose you ought to come in.'

'Thank you.' She stepped inside, firing up her inner resolve.

Cath cleared her throat, and launched in. 'Will, have I done something to upset you? I don't know what, or how . . . Have I said something without realising it?'

He paled as he uncharacteristically chewed a hang nail on his thumb, his brow furrowing further. 'You'd better come through.'

The house was tidy. The hallway was a little bare: plain grey carpet, white walls, pairs of gents' trainers lined up neatly in a low wooden stand. It was pleasant enough, but the atmosphere felt cool, as if its soul was missing. Then, as they entered the kitchen, she spotted some photos mounted on the wall, a collage of family pics. One in particular caught Cath's attention . . . a close-up of an attractive red-haired lady, with sun-kissed lightly freckled skin, smiling happily, in a floaty yellow-and-white floral dress that sang of summer, of happier days. Cath guessed it must be Jane. Will saw her eyes drawn to the image. He looked saddened, but didn't say a word about the photo.

Was this it? The key to his distance? Was he still hurting too much to move on?

'Umm, can I get you a drink . . . some water, juice?' It sounded like the last thing he wanted to do, seeming awfully put out.

So, this wasn't going to be some cosy coffee and chat over flapjacks, then. 'Ah, water, that would be good, thanks.'

He poured a glass from the fridge dispenser, and handed it to her coolly yet politely. 'Here.'

What was going on?

'Okay, whatever it is . . . please tell me? This is feeling so awkward, and I don't know why.' Cath was sick of emotional games, of secrets, of being let down, she'd had her fill with Trevor – though she knew she and Will didn't really have a 'relationship' to break as yet. But it was hurting already . . . and a friendship, if that's what it was destined to be from here on, that shouldn't feel like this either.

Will took up a seat at the kitchen table, and then drew in a slow breath, before saying, 'Do you really not know me? Hasn't it twigged yet?'

'Sorry? I'm not sure what you mean . . . ?' Cath's brow creased.

'Belford . . . the holiday park . . . It was me.'

What?! His eyes were holding hers. Those eyes that she'd always felt she knew.

'Will Matthewson,' he continued.

She felt a shiver, part excitement, part shock running through her. And the penny dropped, the realisation . . . *Matthewson* . . . 'Matty?'

He nodded, his face tense but still a mask. 'Yep, there was another lad called Will in our group at school,' he explained, 'so I got called Matty.'

'You're Matty. *The* Matty?' She wasn't sure if she was saying this aloud or to herself. 'My Matty. Oh, my goodness.' A strange ache of nostalgia centred within her. She wanted to grab him, the boy she'd fallen for all those years ago, to hold him in her arms . . . but she kept her hands, and her arms pinned by her sides, feeling the tension buzz through them. She knew that gesture would be completely wrong after all this time.

'I had begun to wonder,' he cut in. 'Not straight away, but a few weeks ago . . . you mentioned about holidays, coming up here when you were younger. But then loads of people do, I put it down to coincidence . . . It was so random that Cathy might actually be you, so unlikely. And I really wasn't sure, so how could I say anything? It was years ago . . .'

It was well over thirty years ago. Yet, here were the memories flooding in once more. Glimpses of sunny sandy days, that first flush of love, that first time, and it suddenly seemed like yesterday. Matty was Will. Will was Matty. Her brain was trying to catch up.

'But then, meeting your sister, Susie, in the pub. Well, that had to be Susan . . . and Cath, you were "Cathy".'

And yes, somewhere on a tree bark in the nearby village of Belford, there'd still be an etching, perhaps faded over time, carved into a beech wood trunk: *Matty 4 Cathy*.

Way back then, everyone used to call her Cathy at home, at school . . . it was at uni where it had shifted to Cath. She preferred it shortened at that time; feeling that it made her sound more grown up.

'Oh, my God, yes,' she whispered, feeling her stomach swirl. The reality of the situation was sinking in. Here was Matty, right in front of her, all these years on. Will was Matty.

She felt herself flush. That gorgeous young man who'd made her heart sing . . . her very first love. In those few magical days, they'd gone from holiday friends to tentative first-time lovers. And yet, despite their early letters filled with promise, she'd never seen him or spoken to him face to face again, never told him why. It was so long ago . . . but oh, it must have hurt him back then, been so damned confusing.

'Yeah, it was me . . .' He raised a small smile, suddenly looking at her differently, tenderly, like he couldn't help himself.

Glancing up, she checked those eyes, held his gaze for a few steady seconds . . . yes, those eyes. The same deep, dark pools as Matty's. There had been something there from the start. When they'd met again. She'd felt it, but hadn't recognised it.

Cath felt a lump form in her throat. She wanted so much to lift her hand, to brush her fingertips down over his cheek, to feel how the skin there had changed, but she daren't. The gesture was far too intimate. Trying to take all this in was mind-boggling. She really didn't know at all where they might stand now. Those memories still piling in, of lazy summer days and longing. 'It was such a wonderful week. I remember it all,' Cath confessed, with a small smile curling on her lips.

'Me too, even after all these years.' Will paused, gazing at her once more. 'But Cath, after that first letter, why did I never hear from you again?' He looked troubled. 'You said you'd write back . . .'

His words felt like a small punch, reminding herself of her youthful inaction. She knew all too well after her first letter which reflected the happy giddiness of his, filled with the first flush of love, she had never again responded.

She remembered how this tangle of new and beautiful

emotions had suddenly mixed with bewilderment, with fear and panic. How could she have told him in a letter? Or in a phone call from her family home to his . . . no way. It was in the days before mobile phones were common, when the suburbs of Sheffield, her family home, seemed a million miles away from Northumberland.

And had it even been real? After that fateful, beautiful dizzy evening . . . Then, back home, the angst-ridden wait, when she'd realised that she was over two weeks late with her period.

At first, she couldn't write back, felt crippled waiting to see what might happen. How could she tell him anything? And then . . . when it wasn't real anymore. The sudden heavy period, the clots and pain . . . the negative test. How did you explain all that in a letter, a phone call, to a boy – no, a young man – who you'd really only known for a week? It was easier to let it be. To leave his next letter unanswered. Her parents would have been livid with her had she been pregnant. Her dreams of going to uni, being a teacher, all in the balance. It was a lesson, she'd told herself. She'd been too free, too easy . . . even if she had really liked him. In fact, fallen head over heels. But that experience had scared her so much, she thought it was best to let it be.

'I'm sorry, it was complicated.' The knot of emotions, both past and present, tightened in her throat.

'Look, I know it was a long time ago, and hey, my life has moved on so much since then, but back then, it really did hurt me,' Will explained. 'It was probably daft, but I'd hoped we'd keep in touch, might even see each other again . . . I kept writing . . . I got one letter back, and then nothing. Not even a "Sorry, it's too far, it'll never work", or a bit of news on how you were. I even began to wonder if maybe you'd gotten ill, or had some terrible accident.' He paused, the hurt still there in his eyes. 'Then I figured, maybe it hadn't meant so much to you, after all. It took me ages to trust someone again . . .'

'Oh . . .' Cath felt dreadful. 'I did think a lot of you . . . and I was sorry . . . am sorry . . . about the way things turned out.'

How did she begin to go over what had happened after all this time? And what could it change telling him? She'd cut him off back then, and that was it. It sounded cold and unfeeling now that she was older, with more experience of life, but then, yes, as a frightened sixteen-year-old she'd got scared and ducked out. Will . . . Matty . . . was right to be annoyed with her.

But where did that leave their friendship now? In bloody tatters, most likely.

Cath sat across from Will, in the house he'd shared with his wife, his family, feeling terrible. It was such a long time ago, they were really just kids, but yet she'd done it, she'd been that person. It looked pretty heartless on the face of it. 'I'm sorry . . .' she repeated. She took a big swig of her water. Then before she had time to think, she reached an apologetic hand across the tabletop to cover his, felt its warmth. There was still something there, she was sure of it. That moment in her garden under the stars seemed even more significant now. A tentative new flame, rekindling an old lost love.

Will withdrew his hand sharply. 'I think you'd better leave.' His tone was curt.

'Ah . . . yes, of course.' He probably needed some space. Her brain was trying to process it all. She might be older and wiser, yes. But bloody hell, she was feeling utterly confused and a bit overwhelmed by this revelation.

Cath understood that he'd had enough hurt lately. He'd had to face far more grief and pain with his wife's illness and death. She didn't want to make some big song and dance about what had happened with her all those years ago . . . and if he was feeling miffed with her, then so be it. As she headed for the door, passing the family pictures, the images of togetherness, deep in her heart, she felt glad for Matty that he'd found love. That he'd had a good relationship over many years, until tragedy had struck them, of course. But right then, it was oh, so hard to put any of that into words.

As she approached the front door, she paused. She couldn't just leave things this way. 'I'm so sorry I hurt you back then, Ma . . . Will. It's . . . well, things didn't work out the way I'd hoped . . . and I got it wrong.' It was the best she could do, after all this time. 'Well, I'd better go.'

Will merely nodded; his face looked ashen. 'I think that's for the best.'

'Take care,' she said softly, as she stepped over the threshold. The summer light was far too bright in her eyes. A knot of emotion lodged tightly in her throat.

'And you,' he managed to reply. His words seemed to have an odd finality to them.

Sorrow and regret – laced with some beautiful youthful memories – weighed heavily within her, making her steps drag on her walk back to the cottage. The brightness of the August sky was in stark contrast to the dull dark ache that had formed inside of her. Her new life here in Tilldale, her cottage, her gorgeous new friends, and all its bright hopes suddenly seemed to be out of kilter.

Where on earth did this leave her friendship with Will, and those fledgling hopes that there might be something more between them? And dammit, where the hell did it leave the future of the Supper Club?

Chapter 40

She'd kept it all these years. She wasn't quite sure why, but every time she'd thought to throw it away on some tidying mission, something inside had stopped her. It had almost got put aside in this latest move, but coming back up here to Northumberland, it still felt relevant, nostalgic. And to be honest, it had lifted her, at a time when she'd felt unloved and unappreciated.

After the revelation from Will, Cath had felt strangely hollowed out for the rest of the day. She lay low back at the cottage, trying to get her head around all that she had learnt – how could this Will be that Matty? And it had brought it all back, her shortcomings as a teenager. But that was how you learnt . . . those life experiences, the times you went wrong. Those nagging feelings of regret helped you make better decisions the next time, hopefully. With all this spinning around in her mind, she tried to busy herself with chores, tackling the ironing pile, cleaning the bathroom, grounding herself with some weeding in the garden. Finally, feeling totally shattered at around 9 p.m. she gave in, made herself a cup of mint tea, and decided to have an early night . . . but then, she felt restless again. There was something she needed to do. So, there she was, on her hands and knees, rummaging in the back of her wardrobe.

She was glad she hadn't got rid of it in the move to the cottage. She still wasn't quite sure what had drawn her to keep it. Maybe the words of young love had buoyed her up, when she'd re-discovered them, at a time when she was at her lowest, back there in Roundhay with her marriage in tatters and her packing boxes waiting to be filled.

Ah, there it was; a shoe box filled with bits and bobs and memories. She pulled it out and carefully removed the lid. Firstly, a picture of Adam as a baby . . . oh, and then his first tooth stored in a ring box, a finger painting from his nursery. She smiled. And below, several more mementoes. Then, in an old photo sleeve, a Kodak picture Susie had taken of her and Matty on the beach at Bamburgh way back when – his arm around her, big grin, dark floppy hair and those melting-toffee eyes . . . that she'd started to fall for all over again – along with an envelope, yellowed with age.

She settled down on the floor. The postmark on the envelope was dated 5 June 1988, a few days after they'd returned home from their late-May half-term holiday. Cath took a slow breath as she opened out the once white paper now tinged with age to a pale sepia:

Dear Cathy,

Hope you are fine, beautiful girl. I'm missing you already and you only left yesterday!
What an amazing week this has been. I can't believe I met you and we had such a great time.

I can't stop thinking about you. Getting to know you . . . and more, wow. I think I'm head over heels already.

Been a bit of a boring day here – now you've gone. A rainy morning, so I did a bit of revision (yawn) and then had a ride out on my BMX bike. Mum cooked us all a roast beef dinner which was nice.

Back to college tomorrow. Just a few more weeks and I'm done. I think I told you I'm looking to go into the police or perhaps train up to be a fireman, so I'm finding out all I can about that at the moment, and working hard for my exams. Though I'm not super clever uni material like you!

Hope you had a good journey back.

Say hello to Susan and your mum and dad from me.

*Can't wait to hear from you! **And** see you – and hold you in my arms again – sometime soon, I hope.*

I could always jump on a train down to Sheffield in the summer holidays. Just say the word!

Thinking of you. Love you loads!
Your, Matty xxx

Oh my. Cath felt a stab of guilt, of missed opportunities and what-might-have-beens. No wonder Will had been so put out. That teenage lad had opened up his heart to her, laying all his feelings on the line. His youthful words so loving and hopeful. Memories of that week, chatting away about their hopes and dreams, holding hands on the sands, their first kiss, and then sneaking off that last night for a precious stolen hour at his house, his parents out for the evening.

With a small sigh, Cath neatly folded the letter and placed it on her bedside table. The past and present incredibly, and somewhat perturbingly, crashing together. Wow, what a day it had been. She could still hardly believe it.

There had been further letters, two more, she remembered – full of Matty's hopes and giddy dreams that she had no doubt shattered. That heart-stopping pregnancy scare, followed by the realities of needing to buckle down, being in the midst of her GCSEs that summer, before the big two-year push for her A Levels . . . Her commitment to her teaching ambitions and university plans, moving her forward. But she'd never forgotten that dashing young lad, her Matty.

She crawled into bed, resting against her pillows in the soft glow of the bedside lamp of her cottage bedroom, she remembered reading and re-reading these letters all those years ago in the Sheffield bedroom of her childhood, with her posters of Spandau Ballet and Wet Wet Wet on the walls. Her fingertips had trembled, her teenage heart full but oh-so scared at the same time, wondering what the hell should she do. Her period still hadn't come, and she felt all kinds of wrong, and queasy. Deciding that she needed some advice, she'd resolved to speak with Susie. Her sister was older, she'd know what to do. Cathy needed to find out if she was pregnant. And then, she'd have to decide what next. There was no way she could write back to Matty until then.

All this back in June 1988 – whoa, thirty-six years ago, in fact. No wonder she and Will hadn't recognised each other when she'd first arrived here in the village. Even as they got to know each other. It was so long ago, and they had both changed so much.

Was it fate that they'd met again now? Despite all his recent frostiness, did it mean something to them both still? But they couldn't pretend they were sixteen and seventeen any more. And a hell of a lot of life had been lived since then. Where did they go from here?

Nowhere much, going by Will's curt reaction at his house.

Well then, there was no use pining after something that never came to be. And, certainly no use stirring everything up in the here and now like a hornet's nest. Youthful Cathy had disappointed him then; she didn't want to do that again now. If they had a chance of at least remaining friends, and seeing each other occasionally as part of the supper group, then they needed to find a bit of common ground and forgiveness.

Before what was to be a restless night, Cath got up and put the lovelorn letter back in the shoe box, deciding to absolutely put a lid also on her more recent romantic feelings for Will.

Chapter 41

Despite her best intentions, leaving Will at a distance didn't seem to be helping her much. How strange that after all these years, she and Matty had got to meet, to become friends again.

Cath was desperately trying to get on with her 'new normal' life – cooking, walks in the countryside, her online tutorials, reading, popping to the village shop for updates on the lads and Maria, who was thankfully doing better. But doubts were beginning to niggle about the way she'd walked out of Will's house that morning, even though that was what he had asked her to do, without fully explaining the situation all those years ago. She was worried about how things might be for the two of them from now on. There was an empty place in her heart, and she had an earworm telling her that she missed his friendship, him.

*

As she was mulling their fate, which felt like getting lost in a maze, a call came from Nikki. A most welcome diversion.

'Hi, Cath, do you fancy calling round for a coffee? Umm, after four-thirty would be good. That's when Lily's about too.

We can have a nice chat and catch up . . . and there's something else. It's just, well, Lily's keen to host a patisserie, puds and fizz evening, and we've a favour to ask . . .'

'Ah yes, of course I can. That'd be lovely. And that sounds a great idea for a supper club night. Right up my street. So, what's the favour?'

'Ah hah, all will be explained when we see you.' Nikki was being all mysterious.

'Okay.' She'd have to wait to find out, apparently.

'Perfect, I'll confirm with Lily, and give you a text shortly.'

*

There was a riot of noise at Nikki's house. Her three boys, aged between eight and thirteen, seemed to be arguing about sofa space and the TV controls.

'Right, you lot, garden, now!' Nikki roared.

'But Mu-um, I was just playing on my PlayStation. It's those two who are messing about.'

'I don't care, Hamish. We need a bit of quiet time to think in here. We have an important meeting and things to discuss.' Nikki gave a surreptitious wink at Lily and Cath. 'So, get out the back, get some fresh air and play some football . . . and be nice to each other, okay?'

They trooped off somewhat reluctantly, but Lily's offer of taking a stash of her freshly baked choc-chip cookies out with them – that she'd brought for the coffee and chat – softened the blow.

'Thank heavens for that,' Nikki sighed as the decibels dropped dramatically. 'Welcome to my world.'

Cath smiled empathetically. She'd only had the one child, but it was always super noisy and full-on when Adam ever had friends around. Hah, thinking of him living at her cottage recently, even on his own and at twenty-two, he was able to raise the decibels.

'So,' Nikki continued, after handing out mugs of coffee, 'here lies a clue to our request. Lily's doing pastry as one of her modules next term in her Food Diploma... Science and Nutrition. Very fancy pants, hey Lils, no more good old Home Ec. like we did, anymore. Anyway, she's hoping to test out her new skills and recipes.'

'Sounds a good idea.' Cath was nodding.

'But one, my house is far too full and noisy for the next Supper Club. And, I've used up all my brownie points on the Seventies night with Kev and his mother, so there's no way I'd be able to get him and the kids cleared out for another evening. And, two . . .'

Lily took up from here. 'And I'm sorry, but my parents aren't up for hosting a houseful. To be honest, it's a bit of a sore point with me trying to push forward my cheffing plans. I'm still working on that, so I really don't want to go upsetting things at home.'

'So,' added Nikki, 'and I know you've already hosted twice – but well, could we use your place to do some prep, and ideally have the super-snazzy garden shed as a venue? We'll clear up and take care of everything foodwise?'

Lily was looking nervous but hopeful. Nikki grinned expectantly.

'Is that all? Well, that's no problem. I'd love to have you all round again. I think it's a great idea,' responded Cath with a wide smile. 'Oh, this is exciting. What are you thinking of making? And did you say fizz, I'm happy to donate a Prosecco to the cause. We could ask the lads . . . and perhaps Will . . . to bring a bottle along, too. Spread the costs.'

Oh, shit, *Will*. Hmm, bloody hell, she wondered how that would go down. But a meet-up was bound to happen at some point. And hey, there was no way she'd put a halt to these Supper Club plans because of their recent falling-out. However awkward it might prove to be personally.

'Ah, thank you so much, that'd be great.' Lily was animated, her kohl-lined eyes beaming. 'And the menu, well . . .' She listed her ideas, as Nikki and Cath's mouths watered. She'd obviously been thinking about this a lot. The planned sweet treats and pastries sounded delightful.

The three of them chatted some more over coffee and cookies, until a half hour later when the young lads blasted back in from the garden, muddied and with clothes skew-whiff, saying they were starving and what time was tea? Normal family life chez Nikki had resumed, and it was the cue for Cath to get going.

*

Despite Cath's ongoing misgivings about her and Will coming face to face, Supper Club was here again, with Nikki and Lily taking over Cath's kitchen. Whilst Cath busied herself setting up the summerhouse shed, her mind drifted to how things might pan out.

Soon after the date was set with Nikki and Lily, she'd texted 'all' on the WhatsApp group inviting them to 'Puddings and

Patisserie Night', care of Lily, at Cheviot Cottage. Whilst the boys answered immediately with a big 'Whoop, we're in!' and a thumbs-up emoji, it took a further twenty-four hours to hear back from Will, with his muted 'Yes, thanks.' Had he been busy, or in fact mulling over whether or not he wanted to go? It was certainly going to be tricky for the two of them. And, having kept their heads down recently, it was the first time they'd be face to face since their childhood sweetheart revelation.

And, if he and Cath couldn't get past their youthful hurts, then how did that bode for the friendship group? All those wonderful suppers she'd hoped were yet to come for them all. She didn't want a black cloud cast over this evening for everyone else's sake, so whatever had happened between them she vowed to be polite, but not to crowd Will either. To be fair, in her current guilt-tinged state of mind, she was more than happy to give him some space. They both needed time to get their heads around this blast-from-the-past revelation.

Lily had gone to a huge and impressive effort. She was going to take a load of photos to help support her Food Science coursework, and of course for her social media – you never knew who might be looking, she said animatedly. It was all a big dream, but she was very much hoping for some local chefs to spot her talents, just a comment or a 'like' would be a boost.

To add to the fun this evening, she was going to let the supper clubbers vote for their favourite puddings; she would then use them for the dessert course of her A Level three-course menu. Cath loved her enthusiasm, and the support that Nikki, her aunt, was giving her. She wanted Lily to feel the whole group were behind her too, sort of pastry-chef cheerleaders.

Yet, they needed to be honest and fair with their judgements. After all, nobody learned by being told they were perfect all the time. The schoolteacher in her was coming to the fore. It was core to who she was.

The guests (well, the three lads) were due to arrive at 6:30 p.m. for a glass of fizz in the garden, eek. She was so damned nervous about seeing Will again. Whilst fluttering queasily inside, Cath tried to put those feelings to one side. She needed to make this evening right for the girls; Lily had gone to so much effort. With a batch of tuition fees coming in, she'd splashed out on a nice French sparkling crémant, not quite champagne but as near as. Wonderful aromas of baking filled the cottage kitchen and were drifting up to the shed – a mouthwatering promise of what was to come – where she was laying out forks and spoons, a small white tea plate and napkin for each person, as well as her pretty glass jars for the tea-light candles.

The sun was shining for now, phew, though the forecast showed the chance of showers later. At 6:29 p.m. sharp, Andreas and Dan arrived with three tied posies of roses in various colours, one each for Lily, Nikki and Cath. Oh, how sweet of them. They also presented two chilled bottles of fizz, and an elderflower pressé – especially for the young chef. After all, Lily wasn't quite the legal age to drink.

'Hello, hello! We are so excited about this evening. Puddings and Patisserie, Lily, you're a little gem,' exclaimed Dan.

'Hi, lovelies! So looking forward to this one. A bit of time out and some R&R is much needed, so bless you,' Andreas added.

With that, the doorbell went again, and Cath felt her heart

seize. She walked to the door filled with trepidation, taking a slow breath before opening it. Will was stood there, reticent, and looking anxious himself. Oh crikey, did they kiss on the cheek, give a friendly hug?

The awkwardness was so apparent, like an electric field. Cath remained a step or two away, and merely said, 'Hi, come on in. We're all here.' As if to send him on his way to chat with the others . . . and give him a chance to escape her. Her heart was pounding inside, and felt all amiss. Oh, *Matty*.

Cath chatted with the lads, asking after Maria, who Andreas was concerned about again, saying she didn't seem quite herself. Though her wrist was healing as well as could be expected, she'd mentioned having dizzy spells.

'Oh, that's such a worry for you, Andreas. I really did enjoy my visit with her, when you were away. She had so many wonderful stories to tell.'

'I bet she was full of London life in the Swinging Sixties, was she?'

'Yes, and it sounded so interesting . . . oh, and I heard about how you were a plump little angel.' Cath grinned cheekily.

'Oh no, not the tales of my puppy fat again?'

They both snorted with laughter.

Cath snuck away, busying herself helping Lily in the kitchen. She knew she couldn't avoid the group for long though, as a rather anxious Lily was ready to serve her delicious savoury pastry nibbles. There were mini cheese and nduja sausage whirls, and Northumberland Nettle Cheese straws. Now outside in the garden – avoiding the far too cosy constraints of the summerhouse shed for the moment – with a glass of fizz to hand, Cath made sure to stick near Nikki, to avoid being stranded beside Will, who seemed as keen to keep his distance too.

Food and friendship filled the balmy summer air, along with some fun, with the lads telling tales from the Greek Cypriot wedding and their trip to London, but Cath couldn't help but feel the tension between her and Will all the while. This was harder than she'd imagined. There was a huge and uncomfortable divide between them. She just hoped the others didn't see it.

An hour into the evening, and Nikki went looking for Cath, catching up on the landing outside the cottage's bathroom.

'Hey, Cath, what's up between you and Will? You've hardly shared a word all night. And there's some really odd looks going on? Talk about frosty, it's like bloody icicles between you.'

'Ah, don't worry. It's nothing, honestly . . .' Cath said, unable to stop the heat rising in her cheeks.

'Which tells me it really is something,' was her friend's response.

Damn, Nikki wasn't going to be fobbed off that easily.

'It's a bit complicated, but we're fine, honestly.' She did not want to be talking about this now. And, she realised, if anyone needed to know their youthful story, and her side of things, then firstly it was Will. Then perhaps this horrid stand-off might get resolved.

'He's not still holding a grudge about that bloody car park thing, is he?' Nikki hazarded a guess. 'But you two seemed to have sorted that a while back.'

'Hah, no, that was ages ago.' Cath wished it were something

that simple. Mind you, it might be a good hook to rest this on. 'Well, at least I had thought so. But hey, who knows . . .' She tried to sound light-hearted.

'And nothing's happened between you? Ooh, you haven't gone and told him you fancy him or something?'

She flushed bright pink. 'Of course not, Miss Bloody Marple. Enough said, okay.'

'All right, all right. Keep your hair on.'

'Anyway, please, just leave it . . . He might just be feeling a bit off or something.'

'Sure.' Nikki pulled a 'been told-off' kind of face, as she disappeared into the loo.

*

Lily walked carefully up the garden steps and into the fairy-lit shed, where the five other supper club members were waiting in mouth-watering anticipation. She came bearing the first of her Puddings and Patisserie platters.

'Firstly, we have a selection of pastries – there are peaches-and-cream horns, passionfruit-and-lime choux parcels, and summer berry tartlets. I've made them all bite-sized, so you can test lots of different things throughout the evening.' Lily sounded proud and nervous, all at once. 'And I want your honest opinion on which ones you think work the best and are the tastiest. You're the judges, and I'm going to use your favourite trio to replicate in my A Level practical.'

'Oh, the pressure's on, folks,' said Dan.

The food looked delicious and the presentation was beautiful too; the platter of precisely placed patisserie was scattered delicately with tiny edible viola flowers, and lightly sprinkled over the profiteroles were tiny flakes of gold.

'Wow, Lily, these look so professional.' Cath beamed supportively with genuine delight.

'Oh, *MasterChef*, here we come,' added Dan.

'No, it has to be *Bake Off*. You can be Prue, Dan. I'll be Paul. Honestly, you'd blast them out of the park with these, Lily,' responded Andreas.

'No soggy bottoms around here, obviously,' Dan came back with a grin.

'They look amazing, Lily. Well done, you.' Will at last was smiling.

Thank heavens for that, Cath mused, a chink in his new-found solid-steel armour had finally been discovered.

'Well, enough of the looking, can we dive in yet, Lils?' Nikki was eager to taste. 'Plates and forks at the ready!'

Lily had made sure there was one of everything for all of them.

Cath placed the choux bun to her lips firstly, tasting the meltingly zingy fruit cream and delicious puff of light pastry. 'Yum, this is soo good.'

Will had a fruit tartlet to hand. 'Ooh, fresh **strawberries**, raspberries and blackcurrant, and then . . . mmm, **that** delicate creamy middle. What's on the base, some kind of custard?'

'Crème anglaise to be precise,' answered Lily. 'But yeah, it's a French-style custard.'

'Well, I think this has won me over **already**,' said Will.

Cath wished she had a chance left to win him over too, but sadly she felt all her chances were now gone.

'Don't jump in too soon,' warned Andreas. 'This peach

horn is a dream. And, we have a whole evening of goodies to get through.'

'Oh yes, I'm going to start making notes on my phone,' said Dan, 'lest I forget.'

After the delectable pastries came mini cheesecakes . . . served with another glass of fizz. Then just as Lily headed back down the garden to plate up her last 'smorgasbord' of puddings, as Dan described them, darn it, the plinky sound of raindrops started, which soon turned into a drumming on the shed roof.

'Oh, we might well be stranded up here,' observed Dan wryly.

'No worries, there are worse places to be, we have a full bottle of fizz in the ice bucket,' responded Nikki. 'And I don't know about you, but my tummy needs a little break. I think I'm nearly pudding'd out.'

'Ooh, they've been bloody lovely though, haven't they?' sighed a contented Andreas.

'Absolutely,' agreed a proud Nikki.

'Your niece is super talented,' added Will.

'Yep, the hard bit will be choosing a favourite,' Dan said.

'Okay, so why don't we each jot down our best three. I could get a notepad,' suggested Cath, then looking out at the inky-clouds and pelting rain added, 'Or even better, let's send them on the WhatsApp group. And then Lily can look at them in her own time, and see if any firm favourites stand out.'

'Oh, I'd love to know the overall winner, though.' Andreas was childlike in his eager tone.

'Well, I'm sure we can suss that out ourselves by the end

of the evening,' Dan answered. 'Just do the maths. There's only five of us, after all.'

'Okay . . . smarty pants.'

'Fizz anyone? Looks like we might be stranded up here for a while . . .' Cath intervened. They were used to the lads' jokey sparring by now. No harm was ever meant by it.

As the rain started to blow inside, they part-closed the doors and shifted their seats a little further back into the shed. Though it was rather snug in there, it also now felt a tad chilly. Luckily (well, strategically), Cath had positioned herself two seats away from Will, so they weren't sitting side by side. There had still been no real conversation directly between the two of them. Cath hoped that other than eagle-eyed Nikki, the others hadn't twigged. The last thing she wanted was to spoil the evening for them.

'I'll go and see if I can help Lily.' Will got to his feet, slipping out of the small space and into the rain.

'Oh, you'll get soaked!' shouted Dan.

'No worries, I get soaked on my bike all the time . . .' And he was off.

A short while later, the two of them came up the garden path, the rain still pouring. Will was being gentlemanly, holding one of Cath's umbrellas – sourced from the coat stand by the front door – over both Lily and yet another tray of her delicious-looking desserts. Lily stepped inside the shed, mostly dry, and the puds still perfect, whilst Will shook the wet brolly off outside. His clothes were pretty much drenched, but he didn't make a fuss.

'Ah, you're soaking, mate, come on in and dry out next to us.' Dan patted the empty seat.

'It's fine, it's nothing worse than I get out on the bike at times.'

'Yes, but you're usually in Lycra. Quick drying, and tight.' Andreas quirked an eyebrow cheekily.

Will shook his head at that, but had to smile. 'True, but I'll be fine. And most importantly the puddings are saved.'

The group gave a rowdy 'hurrah'.

'Well then, you'll be the only thing with a soggy bottom,' quipped Dan.

They all had to chuckle.

The latest display of desserts were all in little pots. 'These are dark chocolate and chilli mousse, and these are lemon possets,' Lily announced. 'And that's it, that's your lot.'

'Oh, thank heavens for that,' said Dan. 'I mean they're all downright delicious, but I don't think my tummy could take any more.'

Andreas gave Dan's slight paunch a little pat. 'I wouldn't be so sure about that.'

And laughter filled the little hut once again.

*

The evening rolled on, and so did the thunder, which added some drama to the proceedings. There was no point in going anywhere, so they stayed right there, enjoying the last of the puds and the bubbles, and apart from Will and Cath's frostiness, the company.

The overall dessert winner was voted to be the passionfruit profiteroles – 'A mouthful of bliss' – closely followed by the lemon posset – 'Creamy, zesty and totally delicious'. For third place, Lily was going to have to re-check the top three and tally them up to see if there was a runner-up, as everyone seemed to have their own special favourites.

A short while afterwards, as the weather began to ease, Will stood up to go. It was only just past nine-thirty. 'Sorry folks, got a big cycle ride tomorrow. Need to get my kip in, and I've probably had far too much of this stuff already.' He pointed to his now empty fizz flute. 'It's been great though. Thanks so much, Lily, Nikki . . . Cath.'

He aimed a polite nod at Cath, who stood up as the hostess, ready to show him out.

'Ah, no need to see me out. You stay up here and enjoy yourselves.'

It would save an awkward goodbye, at least. Will then gave a polite, 'Thank you' to Cath as he passed. But it felt to Cath like he'd turned back into Mr Grumpy all over again. But hey, in the circumstances, she couldn't really blame him, could she.

The others stayed, chatting, and enjoying the rest of the soiree. Despite the rain, and huddling in the shed, it had turned out to be a lovely evening of friendship, food and fizz. Cath hadn't been able to relax as much as usual, of course, what with the stand-off with Will. It really had taken the shine off her evening, which was such a shame. Would other supper clubs in the future be this difficult for the pair of them? Had it totally altered the dynamics of the group? Would Will even want to keep coming? Or should it be her to duck out politely? These concerns weighed upon her.

But it was still about tonight, she reminded herself, and ambitious Lily had done an amazing job. Cath felt proud of her, managing to achieve all that at such a young age. She wished her all the best for her baking future, and despite the chasm between her and Will, she really hoped that Lily and the others had had a wonderful time this evening.

It was almost midnight when they took the plunge, ducking out into the renewed showers, to head back inside the cottage. The supper clubbers gathered up coats and belongings in the hallway, getting ready to head home.

Nikki whispered in her ear, as she gave Cath a peck on the cheek. 'Hey, you need to tell me what's going on with you two. No getting out of it... next time I see you.' It wasn't going to be brushed under the carpet that easily, dammit. 'And thank you so much for hosting. You've made Lily's night,' Nikki then said louder.

'I think she's actually made ours,' Cath countered. 'Thank you for such fantastic food. Well done, Lily, that was a huge effort, and you must have put so much time into the menu. I'm sure any of it would go down well as part of your course, but the profiteroles and lemon posset were to die for.'

'Hey, when your bakery or bistro opens, Lily, let us know,' said Andreas. 'We'll be there!'

'Aw, thanks guys.' She looked so proud, bless her. Her confidence was growing.

They gathered at the door. A selection of brollies and rain macs having been borrowed for the short, but inevitably soggy, walk home.

'Umbrellas at the ready . . . and we're off,' Nikki declared at the doorstep.

'Never fear, nothing can dampen our spirits. That was a cracker of a night, Lily,' said Dan.

Cath stood waving and watching them go. And then her

heart sank. Though she'd tried her best to stay chirpy, keeping up the 'hostess with the mostess' act, her spirits had been well and truly dampened by Will's continuing coldness towards her. Dammit, could things ever be right between her and Will from now on? Had she and her naïve and thoughtless antics from years ago ruined the future of the Supper Club group?

Another voice rang out in her mind and tremored in her heart too. Had she totally scuppered any chance of getting to know the real Will anymore? The man that Matty had become? And if so, why did that hurt so much?

Chapter 42

Cath sat nursing a cuppa. It was slightly chilly there in the potting shed, so she was huddled with a fleecy rug wrapped around her. She'd just finished clearing the last things from yesterday's pudding night, and though that had been lovely and was a big success for Lily, she couldn't help but feel tired, and a touch lonely. This was the place, after all, that only a few weeks ago, she and Will had talked, watched the stars, and held hands. She had this sinking feeling that life was going amiss again. That she was somehow sliding away down the wrong path.

Sitting there, thinking about her and Will, the past and the future, Cath decided she was going to have to grab the proverbial bull by the horns. She held her mobile in her palm, intending to message, but then stalled over the best wording. She had a couple of false starts, deleted them, and then, before she had chance to change her mind, fired over a text:

Will, I know this is difficult, but would you mind calling by my cottage for a chat? Or I can come to you. I think I need to explain why I did what I did, back then. I feel I owe you that much.

She also owed it to herself, she realised. What she had done back then had been a regret of hers, for so many years now. And, as well as explaining that to Will, perhaps giving them both a second chance, she felt she very much owed it to their wonderful Supper Club group to try and put things right between them . . . or as right as she could. She'd work at building a bridge for the two of them; it might never now lead to romance, but it might make living in this same small village that little bit easier over time.

She took a slow breath. She could only try. And, after that, it was over to Will to see if he could forgive, if not yet forget.

*

Cath had an anxious wait for a reply, trying her best to get on with everyday life in the meanwhile. And finally, twelve hours later, there it came. A sinking feeling lodging in Cath's gut as she began to read his response:

I don't think that's a good idea, Cath. Best just to leave things be, okay. It was a very long time ago, after all.

The hurt was there in the tone of his text. Cath sighed, thinking that the damage must have been done all those years ago. She knew he'd gone through so much else recently, too. He must still be hurting from the trauma of losing his wife . . . the woman who'd rebuilt his trust. No point adding to his turmoil, stirring up the past once more.

Well, there was her answer and she had to abide by his decision. The past was staying firmly in the past, and only she and Susie would ever know the truth about it. Even though it would be hard, she'd cover up the coolness between her and Will from the others somehow, and come up with some white lie to tell Nikki. But beyond that, oh, who knew how it would affect her life in the village from now on? She felt like she was missing Will already. Her heart felt leaden.

But it was what it was. The impasse was evidently to continue.

She was walking the next day, getting a blast of fresh air and a nature hit to try and bolster her mood, when she saw him passing by in his car. She felt winded as she gave a polite half-wave. He nodded, an acknowledgement but no smile. And her world felt all wobbly . . . but she'd just have to learn to live with that, wouldn't she?

*

Instead of wallowing in self-pity, which was never a good thing, Cath decided to go and do some good with a visit to Maria. A short drive through the leafy hawthorn-hedged country lanes with sunny rays blasting through the windscreen, brought her to Kirkton and the care home.

She was told Maria was out in the garden, making the most of the sunny day, and found her with a wide-brimmed hat on and a cup of tea, sat in the shade of an old oak tree. The birds were singing all around, and a sparrow was hopping near the elderly lady's feet, no doubt on the lookout for biscuit crumbs.

'Hello, Maria.'

'Oh, hello. It's Andreas's friend, isn't it . . . Cath, yes. Isn't it beautiful out here. I get fed up being cooped up inside all the time.'

'Yes, it's a gorgeous garden,' Cath agreed. The hydrangeas were in full bloom, bold bushes with deep-purple and red bursts of ball-shaped blossom. 'Are you warm enough? Can I fetch you anything?' She'd noticed a slight breeze.

'Oh, I'm fine, thank you. It's quite balmy today.' The old lady was wearing a navy cardigan over a polyester blue-floral dress and thick tights. 'How kind of you to visit again.'

'I really enjoyed it last time. It's no bother at all.'

'Well, pull up a seat. And if you ask Linda, that's the one in the green top, just over there, I'm sure one of the ladies will fetch you a cup of tea. I quite fancy a top-up, too.'

Cath was soon settled on a white plastic garden chair beside the elderly lady, with a cup of tea to hand. 'And how are you doing?'

'Pretty good. I get the cast off next week, thank heavens. So, no more being treated like a baby.' She puffed out a sigh. 'Anyway, how are you, young lady?'

'I'm good thanks.' Cath appreciated that she was very lucky with her health and her new home – all the other Will stuff could be put aside for now. 'Oh, and can you tell me more about the wedding?' she added. 'Andreas said the family had sent some photos to you.'

'Oh yes, I had some marvellous prints in the post, and they sent a piece of wedding cake all boxed up. Delicious it was, proper iced fruit cake, plenty of brandy in it too.'

'Ah, lovely.'

'It was a big fancy do in some posh hotel, by the looks of it. Andreas said how wonderful all the food was. Shame I missed all that.' Maria gave a small tut, but then smiled. 'And Eleni, her dark hair all piled up like a princess . . . and oh, her dress looked so magical. Many, many layers of tulle in a beautiful ivory, with a fitted bodice that sparkled with little jewels. Reminded me of photos we had of her when she was little and off to ballet class, such a pretty girl.'

Cath smiled too, picturing the little girl now all grown up and at her own fairytale wedding.

Maria was on a roll, evidently proud of her family. 'Oh, and five bridesmaids, she had. All looking lovely, in shades of lilac.'

'It all sounds wonderful.' Maria's gold wedding band then glinted in the sun, catching Cath's eye. 'How long were you married, Maria? What was your husband like? Was he anything like Andreas to look at?'

'Well then, it would have been . . .' Maria paused to think '1966 when we were married . . . so yes, fifty-eight years ago.' Her mind was still sharp. 'But sadly, Theo passed, ten years back.' She paused, taking a sip of tea, her left hand slightly wobbly. 'And no, he wasn't particularly like Andreas. He was tall, yes, but very lean, with sparkling blue eyes. Quite unusual for a Greek-Cypriot. I always thought he had a touch of Prince Philip about him.' She smiled, remembering. 'I think Andreas looks more like my side of the family – has the thicker set of our men, and darker eyes.'

'Yes, I can see he looks like you.'

'My Theo was a kind man, he always had time for others . . . and he was hardworking. He worked in a shipping office. Taught himself accounts and everything once we got here to London, wanted to make his way in the world.' Her dark eyes lit up with the memories. 'And we used to laugh a lot. About all kinds of things. We'd go dancing too, if we could find someone to take care of the children. Mind you, he could drive me mad at times . . . stubborn as an ox. But we rubbed together well. Lasted a lot of storms. It was a good marriage.'

Cath nodded. It must be lovely to get to that age, and know

you'd had that solid base behind you, though you then had the pain of losing your rock.

'And what about you, Cath? You have a son, yes?' Cath had mentioned Adam at the last visit.

'Yes, Adam. He's twenty-two now. All grown up. And well, the reason I'm living up here now is for a fresh start . . . I think Andreas mentioned to you that my husband had left me.' The fuckwit-of-a-husband phrase still played in her head. Cath had pulled it out several times since her last visit, to make herself smile, and remind herself she really was better off without him. 'We'd been married for thirty years. Breaking up was difficult . . . messy.'

'Oh, I'm sorry to hear that. How are you finding everything?'

'Pretty good now. I love the village, and Northumberland. The coast and the countryside are so beautiful here. And I've been made very welcome, especially by your Andreas and Dan, so I've a lot to be thankful for . . .'

'That's an awful lot of change to cope with on your own. I've seen friends and family go through similar over the years. It was never an easy time for them.'

Maria had a thoughtful way with her words, and a lovely calming voice. More than eighty years of experience were on her side. Cath still felt troubled by the recent developments in the village, and the way things felt so unresolved with Will, *Matty*. She'd even dreamt about him last night; oh, and he'd looked so young in her dream. She was transported back to when he was really just a boy, and she a young girl, all that time ago. When the world had felt exciting and full of opportunities, and when their young love seemed to be the start of something.

'Maria, you've seen a lot of life, can I ask you about something?'

'Yes, of course. Go ahead, my child. There's nothing much can take me by surprise, not anymore.'

'It's just that I need a bit of advice. In confidence.'

'Of course. And well, if I did tell anyone around here . . .' she nodded at her fellow guests, glimpsed through the day room window, with a wry smile '. . . they'll have forgotten in five minutes. Not that I would tell, of course. Your secrets are safe with me. Fire away.'

Cath felt instinctively that Maria was someone she could trust. 'All right, so there's someone I've met recently . . . someone from my past.' Cath took a slow breath. 'When we were young, we had a brief relationship. It was lovely . . . a holiday romance, I was only sixteen, and well, the truth of it is . . . I feared I was pregnant.

'A few weeks later, I learned it was a false alarm. I'd totally panicked at the time, I really had meant to keep in touch with him, but didn't.' She paused to take a sip of tea, her throat dry with emotion. 'We lived a long way away from each other, so I couldn't see him to explain. I'd sent one note at the beginning saying what a lovely week it had been, but then with all the worry, I didn't answer any of his other letters . . .'

Maria was listening calmly. 'And how is this troubling you now?'

'Well, it's been so strange, but we met by chance when I moved up here, and I didn't realise it was the same man. And at first, he didn't recognise me either, and a lovely friendship was growing between us. But now he's worked out who I am, it's all gone wrong. He can barely face me.' Cath watched a honey bee hover over an ornamental daisy. 'He's told me how much it hurt him at the time . . . me just dropping him like that. And I know he's had a really bad time lately with his wife dying just two years ago. I feel like I'm stirring up too many bad memories for him . . . but deep down inside, I can't seem to shake off this feeling that we might still have something special between us, something to look forward to.'

'Hmm, have you talked with him properly, told him the truth?'

'Not all of it. Not about the pregnancy scare. I did ask to see him this week, but he's cut me off. Can't really blame him . . . it's exactly what I did.' Cath sighed. 'Maria, is it kinder to let things be, or do I listen to my heart and try to speak with him again?'

'Will you rest until you do?' She quirked an eyebrow.

'No.'

'Well, I think there's your answer. Life's far too short not to try.' The old lady gave a kind smile, then added sagely, 'No need to go in like a bull in a china shop, though. Slowly, slowly, if needs be. If he's been hurt, like any of us, it might take time. And then, if the answer's still "no", at least you can be proud that you were brave enough to ask the question.'

They seemed like very wise words indeed.

'Thank you, Maria.' Cath took another soothing sip of tea, and then changed the focus of the conversation. 'So, how's life here in the home?'

'I'm looked after very well, I have to say, if a little too restricted. I'd love to break out one day, go off up to the high street or something. I used to have little trips out with Andreas sometimes . . . before this darned falling lark.'

'Perhaps we could ask to get you a day pass or something? If we're allowed, I can drive you back to the village, and you could have lunch at my cottage with Andreas and Dan? Would you like that? I'll check with Andreas, of course, and if the home is agreeable . . . Well, I can only ask . . .'

'Oh, that'd be wonderful. It'd be like *The Great Escape*.'

'Hah, I'll not be charging over the wall with you on a motorbike.' Cath laughed. 'But as long as you can fit in my Mini.'

The pair of them chuckled. The conversation rolled on over another cup of tea served with custard creams. The wind then changed direction, and Cath helped Maria slip a blanket over her knees. After chatting some more, they then decided to take a slow stroll around the garden together looking at the colourful summer plants – as well as the hydrangeas there were tall blue delphiniums, giant yellow daisies, and peachy-pink scented roses in the border. Then, as the air began to cool, they headed back into the warmth of the home.

'It's card game time, Maria, are you joining us?' one of the carers called over.

'Oh yes, I enjoy a game of Rummy.'

'Well, I'll take my leave then. It's been lovely visiting today, Maria.'

'It's been wonderful to see you too, child. Take care.'

'And you. Oh, and thank you so much for listening.'

'You're most welcome.' Maria gave a sage nod. 'And do come and see me again . . . and yes, let's have that lunch trip. *The Great Escape* it is! There's only so much Rummy, tea and cottage pie I can take.' She gave a beautiful cheeky grin, which lit up her lined and lovely face.

Chapter 43

A few days later, and Cath had been in to Kirkton to pick up some groceries. Realising she had an hour or so to spare before her next tuition, she thought she may as well pop in to the care home and catch up with Maria. It felt good to give something back in life, to give some of her time. And she had quickly grown fond of the interesting and at times feisty old lady. Maria's body may have been failing with age, but her mind was still as sharp as a pin. Age was no barrier to friendship.

Cath strolled into the airy reception area of the home after being buzzed in. 'Hi, Linda.' She recognised the blonde bob of the friendly middle-aged lady who was sat behind the counter. 'I'm just here to visit Maria. Is she in the day room?' She'd already started to head for the corridor.

Linda stood up. 'Oh, it's Cath, isn't it . . . Can you just wait here a minute, please? Take a seat if you'd like.' Her smile looked rather tight.

'Oh, all right.' This was unusual, but Cath wondered if Maria was perhaps using the bathroom, or felt tired and was still in her room.

She settled down on the maroon seat-pad of a functional armchair, taking in the smells, sights and sounds of the care home around her. Bright flowers in a vase; a large bunch of carnations in reds, yellows and white. Books, and a couple of magazines – a copy of *Living North* and a *Woman's Own* – laid out on the coffee table before her. Voices drifting from the day room area . . . kindly questions and frailer-voiced answers. The aromas left from lunch, slightly meaty with mashed potato overtones, and beyond that the bleach-infused scent of cleaning materials.

A buzzer was going off repeatedly further down the corridor, along with anxious, slightly raised voices. The bustling of swishy-soled shoes. Cath felt suddenly more alert and looked up, in the direction of the noise, listening more intently now. There was a sense of quietly managed commotion. The hairs on the back of her neck began to prickle, an instinct rising that this had something to do with Maria . . .

Julie, the home manager, then dashed by and into her office, giving Cath a polite nod as she passed. The office door closed, and then a phone call, the words a muffle from here. The receptionist caught Cath's eye and gave a gentle smile.

A few minutes later, Julie came back out. She approached Cath. 'I'm sorry, but Maria can't take any visitors just now . . . She's taken a fall.'

'Oh, no! Is it bad? Is she hurt?'

'I've had to call an ambulance. And her son is coming in, too.'

'Andreas . . . oh.' The poor thing. He'd be so worried. 'Is it okay to wait? In case I can help in any way? I'm a friend of Andreas,' she explained.

'Yes, that should be fine. Please wait here for now, though.'

'Of course.'

'There are things I need to do. Excuse me, I have to go.'
And with that Julie was off down the corridor.

*

It wasn't long before Cath heard the scrunch of gravel outside.
She saw the lads' car with Dan at the wheel. Given the short
time it had been, he'd surely been driving over like some kind
of stunt man. Andreas stood out, looking shocked and pale,
as an ambulance pulled in behind them.

Andreas dashed from the parking area and into reception.
He saw, but hardly registered, that Cath was oddly already
there. 'My mother . . . Maria . . . ?'

Dan rushed in, hot on his heels.

Manager Julie came out to meet them, her tone full of
measured calm. 'Come on through. We've made her comfortable.'

'Oh . . .' Andreas's voice was full of anguish. Cath's heart
went out to him.

With that, the paramedic team were ushered by. The corridor bustling, on alert, for a few moments, and then a hushed
stillness swallowed them all.

Cath sat waiting patiently for news. She picked up the local
magazine and flicked absent-mindedly through the pages.
Time slowed, the tick of the wall clock felt very like a toll.

Voices once more, the striding of shoes, and a stretcher
trolley came into view, carrying a very frail and pale elderly
lady. Bless her, Maria. Cath stood up instinctively, it felt like
a salute, her heart in her mouth as she watched them go by.
Stay safe. Good luck.

346

Andreas was close behind the medical team, uttering, 'I'm her son . . . I want to stay with her.' His face was ashen.

Dan followed him, as close as a shadow.

'Just give us a second here, lads.' The ambulance staff addressed the duo calmly as they reached the exit doors. A carer from the home was also close by, handing over a bag of personal essentials to the paramedic team. Manager Julie keeping pace a few steps behind.

Cath waited a short while, then followed them all out, keeping a respectful distance. She watched as they began to load the stretcher into the emergency vehicle.

Andreas calling, 'Mama . . . I'm right here. Can I go in with her, please?' He was pacing like a caged animal at the rear of the ambulance.

'Yes, you will be able to,' the paramedic's answer came kindly. 'Just give us a little space here for now.'

The wheels rolled up the ramp, then came a metallic clunking noise of the stretcher being secured. The paramedic speaking loudly, calmly, 'We're just making you comfortable here, Maria.' Seconds ticked away and yet it was like time was on hold.

'Okay, come on up now, son,' Cath heard, as the paramedic popped his head out of the rear doors. 'There's room for one. Strap yourself in here, just beside her.'

Andreas stepped forward. '*Mama mou*, I'm here.'

'I'll follow in the car,' Dan called after him, and also to Maria. 'Take care, my loves.' He then re-grouped briefly with Cath – who explained she'd been about to visit – and the cluster of care staff on the steps, thanking them all for their help, his car key ready to hand.

The blue lights went on, and they watched as the ambulance pulled away with its precious cargos.

*

Dan phoned Cath from A&E, late on the afternoon of the fall, asking if she'd mind calling at the flat to take Shirley back home with her for the night. They didn't know how long they might be. He hadn't then shared the sorrowful news, protecting Andreas's feelings until his partner had had a little more time to try and absorb it himself. There were things the doctor had needed to confirm, despite a no-resuscitation order being in place, and arrangements to be made, so Maria still had to be admitted.

*

Cath hadn't intended being there in the flat when they finally arrived home the next morning, but had gone over to find a couple of toys and a chew to keep Shirley entertained, which she hadn't thought to bring with her last night.

It had been a good thing having the little dog as company. After an evening spent together on the sofa, Cath put the terrier's fleece-lined bed down on the floor of her bedroom, beside her bed. The pair of them were restless through the night, wondering what was happening with the two men they cared so much about. It felt reassuring to have each other close by, at least.

So, there they were in the flat as Andreas and Dan came back. Andreas looked shattered, as he found the words,

348

through his tears, to tell the end of Maria's story. 'Oh, Cath, I held her hand all the way to the hospital. She knew I was there, at the very last . . . calling me *Yie mou*, my son. Thank God, I'd made it in time. But oh . . .' His voice cracked, the harsh reality of it all hitting home. He took a slow breath before adding, 'She'd already passed by the time we reached the hospital.'

'Oh, my love.' Dan took his partner into his arms.

Cath moved close to lay a hand gently on Andreas's back. 'I'm sorry, Andreas. I'm so sorry.'

Shirley gave a whimper, nestled at their feet.

Within their arms, in that shield of support, Andreas whispered, '*Adio, Mama*', closing his eyes.

And the room felt filled with the heaviness of love and loss.

Chapter 44

The news of Maria's passing tore a chunk right out of Cath's heart. She hadn't known her long, but she had already grown very fond of the elderly lady. She'd hoped their friendship might have had a chance to flourish, that they'd have the opportunity to give a little light to each other's lives.

Bless her, Cath mused, she'd never got her chance to make it to *The Great Escape* lunch.

The doctors had diagnosed a stroke, with her earlier falls likely to be linked with that, Dan had explained. Poor Andreas must be totally devastated. Cath had popped back with the rest of Shirley's things soon afterwards, offering to help with anything at all, and then left the boys in peace. Naturally, they were rather shell-shocked, and she sensed they might need some space.

She spotted the 'Closed due to unforeseen circumstances' sign up in the shop's window that next morning, as she had gone for a short walk trying to clear her own head. Bless them, the lads were most likely holed up in their flat, trying to come to terms with the awful reality of it all.

*

Back at the cottage, Cath was left wondering how best she might help Andreas and Dan, remembering how floored she'd been when her own mother had died. A part of you knew that your parents couldn't possibly live forever, but however old they were, it was never enough. Your mum was such a huge part of your life from the get-go – if you were one of the lucky ones. And her loss had been one of the hardest things that Cath had ever had to deal with. The flip side of love is loss, and she knew that Andreas would be struggling with gut-wrenching grief.

She made a group chat with Nikki, Lily and (taking a breath) Will, letting them know of Maria's passing, and suggesting they club together and leave some food and gift parcels to help the boys out, and to hopefully cheer them somewhat. After all, a little kindness went a long way. Cath offered to cook a main course that the boys could easily reheat, pondering on what might be the nicest comfort food in the circumstances . . . and then waited to hear back from the others.

Within seconds, her phone was buzzing, offers of sympathy and help bouncing in, pronto. Lily was more than happy to make a cake or some tray bakes for them, Nikki had already heard the awful news and responded with an 'Oh, it's so sad. I spoke with Dan earlier. Bless them all.' Adding that she'd have a little think how best to help them foodwise. A minute later, and Will came on with 'That's such sad news. I'll take some nice coffee and some beers around.' He was there too, to help support the lads when it counted, the pair of them putting aside their own personal issues, and that lifted Cath.

She settled on making a cottage pie. Always a comfort, and if they didn't fancy it straight away, it would easily freeze. She quickly set off to the butcher and grocer in Kirkton for her ingredients. The sky was a bold azure-blue today, the sun bright and brash. The birds still singing. Life, as always, was going on.

It dawned on her that she was heading the same route as just those few days before. The last visit had been a shock, but Cath felt so glad she'd popped by and had that earlier time in the care home garden with Maria – the memory precious. Was it now time to take the old lady's advice and knock on Will's door, try to explain her youthful actions, well inactions really, once and for all? She was so pleased that Will had at least answered the chat message. It was good to know that he was still there for the group.

*

An hour or so later, the cottage pie was in the oven baking through, aromas of rich beef, leeks and herby gravy filling her kitchen. She'd take it around, once it had cooled a little, having decided to give a polite knock on the lads' door and leave the dish without any fuss, being as unobtrusive as possible.

Her own doorbell then went. Nikki was stood there with a gentle smile, and a holdall of goodies. She and Lily had pooled their offerings, apparently, and there was a freshly baked strawberry and cream Victoria sponge in a large Tupperware carry box, chocolate brownies, a bottle of Prosecco with a handwritten note tied around its neck: **Some fizz in memory of your wonderful mother, Maria xx** – Nikki had thought they might want to celebrate Maria's life. And, various crisps, nibbles and olives, along with a large bar of Cadbury's caramel (Andreas's naughty indulgence), in case snacks were the only things they fancied. Nikki suggested taking the whole lot over together in person, as a kind of foodie hug-in-a-box, and Cath had the perfect wicker basket to pop it all in.

While the cottage pie was finishing off, Cath popped the kettle on and they had a quick brew.

Nikki got down to business swiftly. 'So hun, what really is going on between you and Will?'

Darn it, there was nowhere to hide. 'Oh, Nikki. It's complicated. We'll work it out between us somehow, I'm sure.' Her words were more hopeful than she actually believed.

'Hmm . . . and you're sure you can't tell me anything? Just a snippet?'

'No, sorry, Niks, it doesn't seem right to, not yet. And please, don't mention anything to anyone else in the group.'

'Of course not, I'm not that daft . . . I'm no meddler. But if you ever want to chat, you know where I am.' She placed a sympathetic hand on her shoulder.

'I know, and thank you.'

Cath didn't know where any of this with Will was going herself. She was still trying to process it. Clinging on to the hope that somehow there was a way they might sort things out, at least to continue as friends.

*

Cath and Nikki walked across the village to deliver the food parcel, intending to be discreet and leave the basket on the step, after politely ringing the bell. But just as they pressed the buzzer and were about to step away, Will arrived with his freshly ground coffee, and a six-pack of local ales.

'Hey.' He gave a cautious smile, but then there was an awkward pause, with Nikki looking from Cath to Will and back again, her expression bemused.

'Do I need to bang your heads together now or later?' Nikki couldn't help herself.

'Ah,' Will floundered. He then popped his offering down beside their laden food basket.

In the meantime, the back door to the shop opened, and the two lads were standing there.

'Oh, what's all this, then?' Dan asked, looking bemused.

'Hello, my loves. What's going on here?' A pale and drawn-looking Andreas was there too.

'We are so sorry for your loss, boys,' said Nikki.

'Umm, we were just going to leave this here for you. We don't want to intrude,' explained Cath. 'A little Red Cross parcel.'

'Just some foodie bits,' Nikki added. 'From Lily too.'

'And a few beers,' Will finished. 'Sorry to hear the news, lads.'

'You're beginning to sound like the three bloody Musketeers!' Dan managed to smile. 'But, it's nice to see you.'

'Aw, you lot . . . Come here.' Andreas opened his arms wide.

Cath couldn't help but smile, a happy-sad smile. And as they finally pulled away from a warm group hug, the lads peered into the basket, delighted with their gifts. 'Oh, that's so very kind and thoughtful.' There were tears and even more hugs all round.

'You can come in, you know . . .' Andreas said, once they'd all stepped apart, opening the door wider for them. Yet, he stood there looking wracked with grief.

'No . . . thanks, lads, but not right now. It's very lovely of you, but I think you might just need a bit of time out.' Cath was firm, her tone caring.

'We'll catch up very soon though, guys,' Nikki added. 'You take care of yourselves.'

'And if there's anything at all we can do, let us know,' Cath said.

'Absolutely,' Will chipped in. 'D'Artagnan at your service.'

The lads couldn't help smiling at that.

*

Maria's funeral took place eight days later at the old stone church in Kirkton, where just a few years before, she used to help with the flowers. She'd initially had a small bungalow in the town, after moving up from London to be nearer to Andreas, before becoming frail and having to move into the care home. A city girl who'd quickly grown to love her Northumberland countryside home – much like Cath.

It was sunshine and showers on the day of the service, and inside the church were colourful displays of carnations and scented freesias, roses, gerberas and lilies – all of Maria's favourites. The supper club gathered in one of the wooden pews to show their respects and to give their support – Will, then Nikki and Lily, and Cath in a line.

Will looked pale and was particularly quiet. He was standing there, oh so handsome in his smart black suit, but seemed lost. Cath wondered if being at a funeral was bringing it all back to him. Could this be the church where he had lain his wife to rest? Her heart went out to him.

They'd been asked to wear black but with a splash of colour. Ties and scarves, blouses and shirts in all kinds of bold shades lifted the sombre attire, and the flowers on the wooden coffin were an array of summer blooms, in oranges and purples, yellows and reds.

There were readings, one especially heartfelt by Andreas – who just managed to make it through, with the supper group willing him on. Songs that filled the ancient space, the congregation being in good voice, and a poignant poem read by her daughter, Andreas's older sister, Alexandria, with not a dry eye left in the church. A real celebration of her life. From the family stories and tributes, and the many friends and relatives gathered, she'd been a well-loved lady, who'd had a good and full life.

There were tears and laughter at the wake, held at The Star Inn in the village. And, of course, lots of gorgeous food – a buffet prepared and served by the pub, but with personal touches, no doubt initiated by Andreas, to give a Greek-Cypriot twist to the proceedings. Lots of family had come up to stay overnight; the village and pub suddenly filled with London accents, and Greek expressions, with stories of Maria's various antics, and touching memories.

Eleni and her new husband were there, having taken the trip up from London by train, and Cath found herself chatting with them later. Cath told them how delighted Maria had been with all the wedding photos they'd recently sent. She smiled as she then heard how Auntie Maria was known as the fun but feisty one, back in the day. She could be strict too, but always fair, and sociable and kind with it. Her family suppers were legendary, apparently.

'Hey, Andreas, do you remember when you didn't come home that night?' Eleni started. 'Mum told me all about it. Been clubbing too hard at The Roxy, slept on some mate's floor . . . but you didn't think to tell your Ma . . . Maria had been so worried, and then went totally crazy with you. You were grounded for weeks! And banned from baklava . . .'

'Yeah, that was the worst of it, she made me forgo my favourite food. Anyhow, stop spilling my secrets, Eleni. I was only seventeen . . .'

They both grinned.

Andreas's sister came over to see Cath too, talking about how much Andreas loved his new life up here. How Maria had settled in well, and been made so welcome by the local community too. A world away from her small flat, her last London home, in the borough of Enfield. Andreas's family seemed lovely, so warm and friendly, much like Andreas, and of course Maria. The characterful matriarch no doubt having nurtured and influenced them all.

Will had called in at the wake, and had a word with the lads, but didn't linger. Cath never had the chance to talk with him, other than a brief, polite 'Hello' and 'How are you?' earlier, as they'd met at the church. The pair of them merely sharing a guarded smile across the room at the pub. The awkwardness was still there, and she had to admit it hurt. But hey, one day at a time, she reminded herself. And today really wasn't about the two of them, it was about celebrating the life of a wonderful lady.

Chapter 45

With family staying over, lots on, and still immersed in grief, before leaving the wake, Cath offered to help the lads by walking Shirley. It was the least she could do at such a busy and emotional time for them, and she'd grown fond of the little terrier. Dan happily took her up on her offer, asking if she'd call round the next day to take the Westie out for a stroll.

It was a sunny Sunday afternoon, and the early-September countryside was looking glorious, a patchwork of pale gold and green. Cath and the terrier were enjoying their wander in the open grassy fields that bordered the river. There were no sheep grazing here just now, and they were away from any roads. At times with the lads, she'd seen Shirley trotting about off lead, so thought it might be an ideal place to give her a little freedom to sniff about a bit, and perhaps do her business. They had gotten used to each other by now, after all.

All started well, with Shirley keeping just a few paces away from Cath, happily mooching about, as they skirted the edge of the field. That was until they came upon a small copse of trees, to one side of the field, which had a low wooden fence around it. It was Shirley who spotted it first, dashing over, barking animatedly, and then with laser-like concentration she sat staring fixedly at one of the trees. Cath was looking to see what the commotion was about when a grey squirrel zipped down the trunk to land teasingly just in front of the dog. Then the creature whizzed off through the copse and away . . . and so did Shirley, like a bolt of lightning.

'Shirley, no! Wait! Leave it!' Cath called frantically. *Oh shit*.

But Shirley very much had other ideas, and was already on the hunt. Cath lost sight of the dashing duo within seconds. As panic began to rise within her, the next thing she spotted racing out away from the copse wasn't a squirrel, oh no, but a rabbit bolting across to the far end of the field, with . . . oh yes, Shirley in hot pursuit. Cath tried her best – and failed miserably – to catch up. Jeez, could that little dog run! The rabbit went off through the parallel wires of the field's fence . . . and so did Shirley. Bloody hell, Cath cursed herself, feeling panic rise within, she should never have let her off that lead.

But it was too late, the dog was on the loose, and Cath wasn't quite sure where. Heading for the spot where she last saw the dashing duo, she stood calling as loudly as she could, 'Shirley, come on. Here. Good girl!'

This became a regular chorus, as she ploughed on over the next field, with still no sign of a white terrier's furry back. *Shit, and double shit*.

What was she meant to do now? Keep going forward? But she wasn't sure quite which way. Retrace her steps? Stay still? She stuck with the latter option for the next fifteen minutes, calling frantically, adding 'biscuit' and 'dinner' to her repertoire to try and entice the errant Shirley, but nothing was bringing the little dog back. Cath started to feel sick. What if anything happened to her? Could she be stuck down some rabbit hole? Might she have dashed onto the nearby lane into traffic and be injured? Tried to swim the river . . . and couldn't? Her head was filled with tragic and awful scenarios.

She needed help, but she really didn't want to alert Andreas and Dan to her reckless move in unleashing the dog, and then losing her . . . not just yet. The last thing they needed right now was extra worry. Nikki, Lily . . . and Will, they might help. They could have a quick look around the village? Perhaps even pop and subtly check if Shirley was in fact back on her own doorstep by now; it wouldn't be out of the question. Then she could stay here by the river, carry on calling and keep a watchful eye out for the canine absconder. She puffed out a heavy sigh, as she fired over a short message to the three of them.

Help needed! Lost Shirley in the Tillside Park Farm fields near river. I'm still here looking. Can you check village area for me? And perhaps by the shop in case she's bolted home. Thanks x

A call came through within seconds from Nikki, despite the fact that she'd only just finished serving out her Sunday roast for the family, bless her.

'Hell-oo, I'm out in the street now.' Nikki was stood there in her slippers. They all knew how much that little dog meant to the lads. 'So, where are you now, and what's happened exactly?'

Cath relayed the tale of the squirrel and subsequent rabbit chase, feeling the panic mounting the longer Shirley stayed missing.

'Right, I'll work my way down the street. I'll get Lily on the case too, I'll get her to do the start of that walk by the river, yeah?'

'Yeah, we started on the path from the village by the bridge.'

'Okay, yep, no worries. And we'll keep in touch.'

'Okay, thank you. I'll stay here, where I last saw her. She might come back this way. I'm near that little copse down by the river, Blakelaw way, about half a mile from the village. I'll keep calling for her.'

'Ah . . . Will . . . over here,' Nikki shouted out, still on the phone.

Oh, he'd come out, too. There was some muffled offline discussion and then, 'Right, Will's off to the shop to have a hunt around there – I told him to be subtle. I figure the lads don't know yet.'

'No, I mean we'll have to tell them soon, if she's still lost . . . but let's try and find her first. They're having a stressful enough time of it, as it is. Shit, I've been so stupid.'

'It could happen to anyone.' Nikki tried to keep Cath's spirits up.

'Not if they didn't let the dog off the lead,' Cath cursed herself.

'Ah . . . don't worry, we'll find her.'

'Thanks.' Cath finished the call and let out a heavy sigh.

Back to the task in hand, she scoured the landscape, trying hard to keep a cool head. But still no little white Westie. Oh no, she'd never forgive herself if anything bad happened to her.

*

A full thirty minutes had passed, which felt like three flipping hours in all honesty. Cath was frozen between leaving and looking elsewhere, feeling that the Westie might just appear back on the trail where she'd disappeared, having retraced her scent and her steps.

Just as Cath felt like sinking into an emotional heap, ready to have to drag herself back to the village empty-handed, she spotted a figure coming towards her over the field. A male figure . . . God, she hoped they hadn't had to call Dan out from the family afternoon, or something. As he neared, from the dark hair, familiar trim profile, and the way he walked purposefully, she realised it was Will. That was a better scenario, but still made her feel emotionally unsteady.

'Any luck?' she asked as he approached.

'No, sorry . . . you?'

Her heart sank a little further. 'No.'

'Where did you last see her?'

'Over there, heading into the next field and away. I didn't know a Westie could run that bloody fast. I got to the fence there.' She pointed to the far end of the field. 'But there was nothing.'

'Okay, I'll go have another check further that way . . .'

'And I'll keep calling, and searching this way.'

After ten more minutes, they decided it was time to head back. If they'd had no luck between them so far – and Lily and Nikki had confirmed no sightings in the village as yet – then they'd now need to involve Andreas and Dan. Whilst reluctant to further spoil their difficult weekend, Cath understood that Shirley's owners might have more idea of where she might be, and a better chance of getting her back.

Cath felt dreadful turning up at the family gathering. Dan was full of cheery 'hellos', but then when she and Will took him aside to explain, and with Andreas soon joining him, the atmosphere plummeted.

'Oh no, not Shirley,' Dan exclaimed.

'What, what's up now?' Andreas was over.

'She's gone missing . . . off in the fields by the river. I'm so sorry.' Cath was apologetic and honest.

'But how?'

'Cath let her off the lead,' Dan explained.

'Oh, for Christ's sake, that's all we need.' Andreas turned to Cath, his tone sharp, eyes stone-cold. 'How could you have been so bloody stupid? She's a terrier, she goes hunting.'

The roomful of family guests were now looking at them. Cath felt like shrinking.

'I'm sorry. I'm so sorry, lads. I didn't think.'

'Too bloody right.' Andreas's anger spilled over.

'Well, let's get a search party together . . .' Dan started thinking practically.

'We've already been looking . . .' Will explained further. 'It's been over forty minutes now,' he confessed on Cath's mortified behalf.

Andreas and Dan paled.

A village search ensued for the wayward white Westie. Dan also thought to post a message on the shop's Facebook page: 'Missing dog, white West Highland Terrier, Shirley . . .'

Cath felt absolutely terrible. And after Andreas's outburst, even Will was looking at her as though she'd got it all wrong again. Lily and Nikki had arrived back from their hunting mission too, and were standing in the family-and-friends fallout zone, which had gathered outside the shop. Swiftly, they all turned their energies back to the search, with the focus off Cath for now at least.

She felt at such a low point. The lads were rightfully annoyed with her, her supper club friends disappointed in her, the dog was still missing and at peril, and she was damned angry with herself at being such a crap dog walker . . . and a stupid selfish teen . . . and, oh, there were such heavy layers of sadness within her at Maria's recent passing.

*

An hour later, and re-grouped back outside the shop once more, still no Shirley. Cath couldn't hold back the tears any longer. Will told her to go on home, and get herself a cup of tea, saying they'd still keep a core of the search party going. Dan nodded in agreement that she should go, and Andreas still couldn't find it in himself to speak with her. They all thought they'd be better off without her, and she couldn't blame them.

Chapter 46

Back at home, the cup of tea tasted like dishwater, and she felt dreadful, blaming herself for being inept, and along with seemingly everybody else, bloody annoyed with herself. How could she have been so stupid as to imagine it was okay to let the little dog off the lead? Okay, so she'd seen the lads do that occasionally in the past, but they were Shirley's owners.

The message she'd been longing for came in a half hour later . . . finally. She was almost too afraid to open the WhatsApp from Dan. But there they were, the best words ever . . .

She's back at last. Search over. Phew. **She's muddy, knackered, but fine.**

Ah, thank God.

She later learned from Nikki that after an hour-and-three-quarters, and much doggie-type fun, Shirley had come home all of her own accord. Dan had discovered her sitting in the shop's doorway, tongue lolling, covered in mud, totally shattered, but unharmed. There were big licks all round for Andreas and Dan, who hadn't minded their clothes and faces getting muddied at all.

Everyone was so relieved, but Cath couldn't forget the lads' earlier words, and the feeling that she'd let everyone down.

In bed that night, she lay restless, unable to stop blaming herself. She was so relieved the dog was safe and sound in the end. But it was no thanks to her; she'd only wanted to give the dog a bit of freedom, but she dreaded to think how things might have ended differently. What would happen with her lovely supper group now? Will was hardly speaking to her anyhow even before all this today. Oh, and Dan and Andreas would never trust her with Shirley again – and rightfully so. And she'd loved spending time with that little dog. A few hot tears ran down her cheeks and into her pillows, before she finally drifted off. She buried herself under the duvet, the emotions of the day all too much.

*

The next morning, Cath turned up at the village stores, with a homemade lemon drizzle cake, made in the early hours of the morning when she couldn't sleep, so sorry for all the bother she'd caused. In fact, with a 'tail between her legs', very much like Shirley must have done the day before. After her restless night, Cath was determined to face things head on. The lads might not feel very much like trusting her again, and fair enough, but she needed to apologise properly.

She also held a hand-tied bunch of flowers; a beautiful circle of white lilies, white carnations, purple agapanthus and blue Scottish thistles, which she'd just collected from the florist in Kirkton. She paused for a second or two, waited for a customer to leave the village stores, then took a deep breath and went on in.

Thankfully, the shop was now empty. It was a careworn-looking Andreas who was at the counter, and he looked up with an 'Oh.'

Cath took a breath. 'I'm here to say how truly sorry I am. I should never have let Shirley off the lead, and I'm so gutted to have caused you both all that worry.' There was a lump catching in her throat, as she re-lived the dreadful emotions of yesterday afternoon. 'For you and Dan.' She passed over the bouquet.

'Oh, they are beautiful.' Andreas's tone was cool but gentle. 'Dan, it's Cath . . .'

'Oh, Cath . . .' Dan appeared, having come down the stairs from the flat.

'By way of an apology . . .' Cath said, as Andreas lifted the flowers for Dan to see.

'Thank you, lovely.'

'Well, it's me who should be saying sorry, too . . .' Andreas looked a little sheepish.

'You . . . how?' Cath couldn't work out what he was trying to say.

'Yesterday . . . I reacted in the heat of the moment. I was tired and emotional – it had been a long and tough weekend – and well, I overreacted. I shouldn't have growled at you like I did.'

'Well, I deserved it. And it was at such a difficult time for you both, that's why I feel even worse. It was me who was stupid enough to decide to let the dog off. I-I just never expected her to do that . . . She's always been so calm and steady in my back garden.'

'We should have thought to warn you,' Dan added softly. They'd obviously been chatting together about the incident.

'It wasn't the first time,' Andreas confessed. 'She can be a little madam. Saves it for once in a blue moon, so just when you think she's calmed down, then ... bumph ... spots a squirrel ... and she's offski.'

'Or a hare ...' added Dan. 'But she can't really keep up with them. And she is most partial to a rabbit hunt.'

'Oh, don't I know it.' Cath let this news sink in.

'Did it as a teenage pup the first time ... that was a rabbit ... We lost her for a whole hour. We were having heart failure by the time she came back, I can tell you.'

'Yes, swanned back to us, casual as you like, to exactly the place we'd lost her. But we couldn't be cross with her, as it was such a relief.'

'So, she's been kept on the leash in open countryside for years now,' Dan added. 'She's fine around the village streets and in the garden ... but in a field ... uh oh.' He shook his head knowingly.

'I bet she thought she'd won the lottery when you let her off,' continued Andreas. The lads managed a wry smile at that. 'Hey, why don't you come on up to the flat,' added Andreas kindly, 'I'll put some coffee on. Dan, would you be okay minding the shop a short while?'

'My pleasure.'

It was an olive branch back to their friendship, and Cath began to relax a little. Little sparks of hope for a happier future here in the village began to flicker within her as the two of them mounted the stairs.

'Here she is, the little minx.'

Shirley looked so innocent, stood there on the landing, all fluffy and white, wagging her tail and giving an excited bark to welcome Cath.

'Well, no more country escapes for you, little lady.' Cath patted her soft white head. The dog's behaviour all began to make sense, and though she'd made the daft decision to let Shirley off, Cath had truly learnt her dog-walking lesson.

'She's a right madam, and a natural hunter, however cuddly she looks, so it isn't all your fault, petal. So, let's move on, hey. The antics of a critter-chasing Westie shouldn't spoil a lovely friendship.' Andreas's hand was on her shoulder, and Cath suddenly felt like she might cry, relieved and thankful all at once. She'd been dreading how life in the village might pan out, believing she'd fallen out with her new companions.

The coffee was rich, warm and soothing, as was the conversation, the two of them chatting about how lovely the funeral had been despite it being such a sad occasion.

Andreas then mooted another Supper Club evening, much to Cath's ongoing relief. 'Oh yes, we absolutely need to have another supper get-together, now that Mama's funeral is over. Bless her, she always said that cooking was caring. Yes, a little bit of time to chill out with some foodie fun and friends would be lovely again.'

'I'd really like that,' said Cath, a glint of happiness lighting within.

'Okay, I'll put something out on the group chat, see what we fancy doing. Oh, and isn't it Will's turn to host?' commented Andreas.

Cath felt her heart flip. How the heck would that go down?

'Or perhaps we could . . .' Andreas continued. 'We never really hosted as such at the beach. It was more a communal effort.'

'Ah, but you've had so much to deal with lately,' Cath

countered. 'Let us look after you both again, for this time at least. And if it's a no-go for Will,' she mooted, her thoughts flailing wildly, wondering if he'd be prepared to invite her to his place ever again, 'I'm always on standby at the cottage.'

'Well, let's put it out there, and see what the others think, first.' Andreas was already reaching for his phone, ready to message.

Her heart gave a little lift. Phew, one hurdle was over, it looked like the supper club would continue, but there was yet a bigger hill to climb: the massive mountain between her and Will. The next supper meet-up might well be a test. Could Will cope with the thought of having her there at his house for a supper? Should she even go or should she politely duck out this time to give them all some space and save his feelings?

She wasn't at all sure what to do for the best. She remembered the way he'd so coolly sent her away, whilst they continued looking for the terrier. That had felt like another brick in their own personal wall. It was a brick that weighed on her heart. After everything, he might not even want to host or stay a part of their supper club group any more, not when it involved seeing her.

Despite all her best intentions of steering clear of any new relationships, her heart had led her that way anyhow . . . and yet again, it was hurting. Yes, she'd made a positive step forward with Andreas and Dan for sure, and that was great, but another challenge awaited her . . .

Chapter 47

The next challenge wasn't the one she'd imagined.

That very evening, as she was getting out of a warm, soothing bath and beginning to feel a little more like herself, she heard her mobile ringing from downstairs. She had left it in the kitchen. There was no way she could get there in time without risking an injury on the narrow cottage stairs, and hah, she was in fact naked. She decided to check the caller and ring them back, once she'd had chance to dry properly and get her PJs on. It'd be nice to sit down and have a natter with whoever it was; unless it was a junk call, of course.

A few minutes later, she reached her phone. Oh, it was Adam. Well, that was nice. She'd go and make a cup of camomile tea, ready to settle down in the front room and call him back for a chat.

She dialled. It took several rings before he answered.

'Ah . . . he-ey, Mum.' His voice sounded groggy, somehow off.

She struggled to put her finger on what was odd about it. Had he been drinking perhaps? It was almost ten o'clock at night, perhaps he'd been out with friends or something? Oh, but why wasn't he working? Wasn't this in fact one of his shift nights in the bar he'd told her about?

'Adam, are you okay?'

The question lingered between them for a few seconds.

'Ah . . .' His subsequent 'yeah' came out flat.

'Adam, something's up. You don't sound at all yourself . . .'

'Argh, sorry, Ma. I shouldn't be b-bothering you with this...
It's all right. I'm fine . . . honest.'

She wasn't going to be fobbed off that easily. 'Well, something's troubling you,' she persevered. 'Talk to me . . . Is it
money?' she prompted. He wasn't in a well-paid job doing bar
work after all, and a flat and expenses, even if shared, soon
added up. Cath didn't have an awful lot of spare cash herself;
but she could certainly help him with finances by dipping into
her small savings account if necessary.

'Well, partly . . . it's just . . . I've only gone and lost my job
in the pub. They said they wanted me for the s-summer,' his
voice was slightly slurry, 'but now we're in September, there's
a queue of eager students turning up again, happy to take
minimum wage.'

'Oh, Adam. That's such a shame . . .' Cath sighed.

'And well, yesterday, I got a last-minute interview. Something
I'd really love to do . . . a zoology research project linked to the
uni, so I texted . . . let the pub know, and took the afternoon
off. Hah, let's just say it didn't go down well . . . I-I was fired.'
His tone sounded so dull, weary.

'Ah, sorry, son. But hey, it's good news about the interview,
at least.' Cath tried her best to be upbeat, trying to boost her
son's battered confidence. She knew all too well the stream of
'no thanks', of second interviews that had led to blind alleys,
and rejections that he'd already had to deal with.

'Well . . . I'll just hang out and wait for the email saying

"Thanks, but no thanks". There're literally hundreds of us trying to get one job . . . I keep hitting my head against a brick wall with it all. S-so fucking frustrating.'

She'd normally admonish him for swearing like that, but she could hear the pain and frustration in his voice. She let it go. Silence ensued, with both lost in their own thoughts and emotions for a few seconds. Concern was mounting in Cath's already troubled mind. Her son sounded so low.

'Adam, is James there?' That was his flatmate.

'Nah, he's off with the new girlfriend, Kim.'

Oh, he was there on his own, bless him.

'Just little ol' me . . . and my mate, Jack Daniels.' He gave an ironic chuckle.

No wonder he sounded odd. He was down and he was drinking, not a good combination. Jesus, might he be thinking of doing something stupid? Or not really thinking at all? Anxiety thrummed like an alarm bell in her mind.

She'd never dreamt until this moment that he might feel totally depressed, might consider hurting himself . . . not even with all the shit going on between her and Trevor, but tonight he sounded different. With all that had happened as a family, that destruction still very raw for all of them, and now this, coming back to a jobless Leeds, it was no wonder if he might feel like he wasn't getting anywhere.

And he sounded so bloody low.

Her maternal instinct fired up. 'Right, that's it. I'm coming down. It'll take a couple of hours in the car. I need to see you, Adam. I need to be there for you.' Cath was resolute.

'Mum, there's no need . . . I-I'll be fine.'

'No, you're not fine.' She was certain of that.

373

'Ah shit, I knew I shouldn't have rung. My bad. I've got you all worried now.'

'Well, I'm glad you did.' That he'd at least reached out to her; surely that was a good sign. 'And I'm coming, whether you like it or not.'

She heard him groan.

She was actually already on her way up the stairs, ready to remove her cosy PJs as quick as she could, pop on some clothes and chuck a few things in an overnight bag. She'd seen the 'Three Dads Walking' recently on the BBC news, dealing with the aftermath of their daughters' suicides. So dreadfully sad. She wasn't going to risk anything. She had to go and see him . . . she had to be there with him. See the emotions in his eyes, feel the warmth of his hand. Share a hug.

'I'll just grab a few essentials,' she explained, still on the line for now. 'And I'll call you back shortly from the car. Adam, are you sure you'll be all right? I can keep talking if you like . . .'

'Mu-um, I'm o-kay,' he slowed the words, for emphasis. 'I think . . . you might be o-ver dramatising this . . .' He drawled, then gave a hiccup.

'I'm on my way . . .' Her mind was buzzing into action . . . She could get a late-night Travelodge down there or something. Even better, the flat's sofa would do, where she could keep an eye on him. If he'd drunk that much, he might be sick or anything.

In less than three minutes, she was locking the door and dashing for her Mini. Her mind flashing up scenarios, as she revved up the winding hill to the moorland that led to the A1. The road that led to her son. She prayed he would be all right in the meanwhile.

She was doing the only thing she could . . . go to him.

Though it had turned into a midnight dash, this was no Cinderella moment. They'd been chatting on the phone as Cath made her way down, and Adam still seemed okay, though he'd sounded a bit pissed off with her the third time she called, saying he just wanted to be left alone and sleep.

She navigated the city streets, and found a parking space on the roadside in Kirkstall – satnav telling her she'd got to the right spot – reverse parking in a rush at a slightly odd angle, but she left it anyhow. She'd sort it out in the morning. A parking fine was the least of her worries.

There it was, Carlton Towers. A bland beige-brick five-storey tenement. She found the main door, and beside it a grid of numbered steel button buzzers. Which flat . . . ? Shit, she didn't even know. Why the hell hadn't she been here, yet? Yes, they'd chatted regularly, but it was almost six weeks since he'd moved into the flat, after all. Guilt bit at her. She'd been too damned wrapped up in her new country life, that's why. And yes, another voice added, she was afraid of having to face Trevor and the new girlfriend . . . of coming face to face with the wreck of her old life. She hadn't felt ready for that. But . . . at the expense of Adam, she now realised.

Right, the flat, which one? Something A, came to mind. Well, that was useful . . . she scolded herself. Six, seven? She pulled out her mobile, and called him. No answer this time. Crap. He was probably asleep now, dammit. Hopefully, asleep . . . *Don't even go there.* She swiftly scrolled back through a plethora of chit-chat messages to find the one with his new address. There, finally . . . Seven A, phew . . . She was just about to try the buzzer when an Asian guy headed towards the glass door, coming out of the building. She took her chance, smiled sweetly, faking an air of confidence, and he held the door open for her. Yes!

She bounded up the drab concrete stairs that felt more like they belonged in a multistorey car park than a residence, now passing four, five, six, six A . . . damn, another floor to climb then, up to Seven A . . . and there it was. The silver figures stuck onto a depressing black-paint-chipped door that had seen better days. She pressed the doorbell – a plastic rectangular square with a button, that had been re-stuck to the door with thick blue electrical tape – and hoped the bloody thing worked.

Come on, come on . . . It was taking far too long. *Come on, Adam, open the door.*

She pressed again, hearing the faint buzz from the other side and then rapped out a knock. Cath was so damned relieved to hear the disgruntled, 'O-kay, okay . . . I'm coming.' Adam's voice. Ooh, thank phew, thank fucking phew.

The door cracked open, Adam standing bleary-eyed. 'Jeez, you'll wake up the whole building at this rate.'

Cath really wouldn't have cared if she had. He was there. He was fine, if looking frail. Her gorgeous son. Her heart pulsed with relief. 'Oh, Adam.'

She gave him a massive hug. He emitted a half-protesting groan, but then melted into her arms, smelling of baked biscuits, a little musky of sweat and the smoky whisky sharp on his breath. Yes, he was grown up, an adult in the eyes of the world. But that tie remained between them, no matter what . . . he would always be her little boy. *Oh, Adam.* Tears were misting her eyes.

In the lounge now, shabby grey curtains half-heartedly drawn, a dim table lamp only serving to highlight the half-empty bottle of Jack Daniels with a used tumbler beside it. Adam slid himself down wearily onto the worn maroon velour sofa.

Cath sighed. 'This isn't the way to make things better, Adam . . .' But she wasn't angry, just so very sad. Guilt was sitting heavy within her. How didn't she know? How hadn't she realised things were this bad for him? Had they, she and Trevor, and the whole shit-show between them, had it a lot to do with messing him up? No doubt. Oh yes, their family was well and truly broken. Cath bit down on her lip.

'Maybe . . . maybe not. It felt pretty good at the time . . .' Adam was still evidently very drunk at this point, giving a wonky smile, which slid into a grimace. 'Ugh . . . don't feel so good now . . .'

'Are you going to be ill?'

'Just need a mo.' He sat still, then closed his eyes, as if trying to anchor himself.

Cath stayed with him, a hand gently rubbing his back, monitoring him. Oh, but if he was going to be sick then she might need a bucket . . . or yes, in absence of that, a washing-up bowl. She found it in the tiny kitchen, removed a couple of used mugs, swilled it out and returned with that and a pint glass of water, which she placed in front of Adam.

Now was not the time for a lecture, or more reasonably, a talk about what was underlying all this. That could wait until tomorrow and the chance for him to clear his head.

After checking he didn't need to be sick, making him drink the water, and then waiting ten minutes more, while she chatted generally, she suggested getting him to bed. The pair of them trundled in a little zig-zag to his student-style bedroom. She sat him on the bed and got him undressed down to a T-shirt and boxers.

'I'm okay,' he managed to slur, 'I can do this.' Evidently trying to hold on to some modicum of decency, but nearly sliding off the bed.

'I'm sure you can . . . but just get under the covers, Adam,' her stern mum-voice muscled in, and did the trick, as he rolled in under the duvet. Hmm, she hadn't had to use that for a while.

After waiting up a while, sat there perched on the end of his bed with a cup of tea for herself, and then looking in on him a couple of times more, finding him snoring softly, she realised she felt totally shattered. Cath slept in her underwear and T-shirt on the sofa, under a navy fleece blanket that she'd remembered sending Adam off with to uni several years ago. Back when they were all full of the hopes and dreams of a bright future. So much had changed. Life felt so damned precarious at times. And just when you thought you were getting it back on track, a big bloody truck slammed into you.

Chapter 48

Waking up with a dead arm and a cricked neck, Cath pulled on her dressing gown – one of the few things she'd packed – and crept into Adam's room, moving towards his bed to check his breathing, which was rhythmic and steady. His eyes gently closed. That was good. The room smelt sour, stale; she'd give it a good spruce up once he'd got up.

Actually, she thought, as she quietly retreated, leaving him to rest a while longer, she'd give the flat a damned good clean, right through. Yes, she'd draw open the curtains, crack open windows, and go and buy some rubber gloves and a load of cleaning products. She had a strong idea there wouldn't be much useful – other than washing-up liquid (and perhaps even that was hopeful) – under that kitchen sink.

*

Adam finally woke to a thumping headache, a scrubbed kitchen, and a plateful of buttered toast served with strong coffee and orange juice. Cath had gone for a stroll and found the local corner shop with its basic metal shelving, harsh electric strip lights, mounds of crisps, fizzy pop, chocolate bars, several rows of cigarettes and vapes in lurid colours behind the counter, and a few store cupboard basics, including yes, some cleaning products. A world away, Cath had mused, from Tilldale's characterful village stores and the friendly faces of Dan and Andreas.

'How are you feeling now, son?' Her tone was calm, understanding.

'Pretty shit . . . there's a marching band in my head right now, my own fault, I know.' He looked up at her. 'Sorry, Mum . . .'

'Hey, I'm sorry I hadn't realised you were feeling this bad, sooner.' They shared a hug.

They chatted about how things had been since Adam had got back from his travels, talked about the split between her and Trevor, and the heart-wrenching break-up of their family, being open and franker than ever before. And Cath got him to promise that he'd at least go and see a doctor, talk things over with a professional, how the feelings of depression had developed. Get help if he needed, even though he assured her it was a one-off, just a crazy low point.

*

Cath decided to stay another night here with Adam in the flat, despite his protestations that he'd be all right now. While he had another snooze mid-afternoon, she found an alternative mini-market and bought enough basics to make a large pan of chicken curry, a cottage pie, and a pasta bake, along with some Klip It–style containers to conveniently batch up the meals. Her nurturing instinct strong; feeling the least she could do was leave him with some good homecooked food. It served to keep her busy too, shift her mindset from the dark places she'd found it lurking ominously last night.

Adam offered her his bed, now covered in freshly washed and ironed linen, for the following night, but she said she was fine – her back protesting as she spoke the words. She wanted him to have another good night's sleep, be it at her own discomfort, lying easily about how it had been quite comfy on the sofa really.

That evening, with his flatmate still away, they'd talked some more. Adam was made up with all the homemade suppers, but Cath also warned, 'You've got to start looking after yourself too, Adam, I can't be down here . . .'

Or could she? Is that what he needed, to know he had that support nearby? Someone to pop in and chat with. She wouldn't be wiping his nose for him, or too interfering, of course, just there for him. Could she up sticks and come back . . . back to her old life in the city . . . for his sake? She was sure her old school, or another locally, would have some kind of role – maths teachers were always in demand, or supply teaching, something at the uni . . . her mind was on a roll.

'Adam, would you rather I came back down this way? Be honest with me . . . I could sell the cottage and look to get a flat or something down here?' But even as she was saying the words, trying her best to sound upbeat about the idea, in case this was what he really needed right now, she felt all wobbly. What was she promising? Despite all the recent blips, she'd really started to feel that Tilldale was her home. And her friendships with Andreas, Dan, Nikki, Lily . . . and gorgeous Will, her Matty. Her heart was taking the knock already, just at the thought of it. There'd be no way of finding a way forward for her and Will if she upped and left.

But she'd do it. If Adam's answer was 'yes'. She'd give it all up for her son's wellbeing, to keep Adam happy and safe.

'You'd do that? Really?'

She nodded, feeling the tears well just at the thought of it, and fighting them back down. 'Look, you don't have to answer right now, you've had a difficult enough time. Just think on it, Adam. Then we can chat again soon.'

*

The next morning, with flatmate James now back in the apartment, and the space already cramped, Adam insisted that it was fine for his mum to go. She sensed he needed some personal space to start processing what had happened, too. Though it was hard, she knew she couldn't wrap him up in cotton wool, that she'd have to trust him to move on with his life. With a few careful moves in place – the doctor's appointment made, an open conversation on the phone with Trevor advising him of recent events and for his joint support to be there for their son, plus Cath having a quiet word with flatmate James about Adam's recent drinking binge, making sure he also had her mobile number if need be – she felt happier to head on home. He seemed a nice lad to be fair, one of Adam's old uni friends, and someone she could trust.

The offer was still on the table of her moving back down, which she reminded Adam about just before she left. The thought of him being able to drop in for a Sunday dinner was a nice one . . . though there were lots of other implications that she was uneasy with, but she'd said it now, and she was adamant she wouldn't let Adam down again.

On his threshold, which didn't seem quite so gloomy now, they shared a heartfelt hug. Adam finally pulled away. 'Thanks, Mum, for everything.'

She smiled warmly. 'It's never any bother, Adam. Call me any time you need. You take care now, yeah . . . Let me know how you get on with the GP. Oh, and there's a cottage pie left in the fridge for you and James.'

'Ah, brill . . . cheers. You're a star.'

And with that, she thought of the stars and the clear night sky of Tilldale . . . and Will. And took a slow steadying breath.

'I'll ring when I get back.'

'Okay.'

'Love you, son.'

'Love you too, Mum.'

It was a tricky goodbye. She felt all wrong, and yet she knew it was right that she had to leave. He had to learn to find his feet again, too. She had a feeling there'd be lots of calls over the coming days, just to check in.

*

Cath set off in her Mini – which yes, had a bloody parking ticket – negotiating the busy streets, the buses, traffic lights. Strangely, it all felt chaotic, noisy . . . and yet she'd lived here for almost thirty years. Something then drew her to head not straight for the motorway, but to go back to their old street, the family home, where they had raised Adam.

It hadn't all been bad, after all. She might even call in on

Helen, she mused . . . but that might be a step too far for this visit. And, she really didn't want to have to explain Adam's recent blip, or have to tell any white lies.

There it was: the road sign for Limestone Lane. Her insides squeezed a little. And there was Jan and Mark's place, next door to Helen and Geoff, their blue Tesla still parked in the drive. It really hadn't changed much, but she hadn't been away for long, after all. And there, a smart semi-detached red brick house. She slowed. Oh, at least they were keeping the garden tidy. Some other family's place now. She felt an odd pang for the what-might-have-beens, and for the good times they'd once had. But looking at the house, well, it was just a house. A well-presented decent-sized semi on a nice suburban street . . . but it truly didn't feel like hers anymore.

Nothing much had changed here on the street where she used to live, and yet everything had changed . . . inside her.

Her heart had moved to Northumberland. This city, this road, the house, already felt alien. And though she had promised to move back, to find a new place to stay, a base for herself here in Leeds if that's what Adam really wanted, she knew if she had to do that, a huge part of her would be left in Tilldale and Cheviot Cottage. It made her feel a little sick to be honest.

With that, she pressed on the accelerator with the merest of glances in the rear-view mirror – just to check if the road was clear. She couldn't wait to get home.

Chapter 49

The rolling green of the hills, studded with black sturdy cattle and woolly-beige sheep here, crops ripening to gold there, and in a nearby field the hum of a tractor as it turned the rich brown earth, followed by a swathe of silver-tipped swirling white seagulls. Cath's Mini wound its way down the steep bank, the last leg of the journey, back home to her Tilldale valley.

Back in the cottage, weariness overcame her, all the emotions of the last few days playing out in her body. Keep going, overnight bag unpacked, a cuppa on the go, and then, a moment to pause in her sunny-yellow kitchen. Wow, what an unexpected couple of days it had been. And, until she heard back from Adam – and there was no way she was going to pressure him on a decision for a while – she resolved that it was time to get on with her life in this village. The next thing she thought of was Will. The situation between them was such a tricky one, and she still wasn't sure what might happen next, but however much that hurt, she had to keep putting one step in front of the other and keep building a future for herself. But hey, no one had said upping sticks and starting a brand-new life for herself was going to be easy. There were bound to be hiccups along the way, she told herself.

After a quick, reassuring chat with Adam, Cath spent the next couple of hours at her desk in the spare room catching up with her online students. She'd had to reschedule a couple of tutoring sessions. It was still so satisfying knowing she was doing her best to give those youngsters the extra help they needed to pass their exams, and to get on and achieve their life goals. Though she'd given up her secondary school teaching role, thanks to Trevor and their no-go pipe dreams of early retirement, the passionate teacher in her was still very much present, and she was able to carry on doing what she'd always loved. Finding ways to get her students to click with an equation, understand a logical pattern, and yes, it would then all fall into place. She just wished life was that simple.

Life often felt to her like a game of snakes and ladders; you'd just be climbing up, thinking you were getting somewhere, and then, oops, there you were sliding back down again. The highs and the lows. The journeys we are all on, sometimes meandering pleasantly, and sometimes a scary rollercoaster ride. But despite how rocky the journey might be, Cath was determined to keep pushing forward.

Later that afternoon, she poured herself a small glass of Pinot Grigio, took her current read – *Lessons in Chemistry* by Bonnie Garmus, a fabulous story of female feistiness and determination – and sat in her garden soaking in her country life; sparrows and chaffinches were busy in the shrub borders tweeting away, cumulus clouds meandered high above, with blue sky prevailing for the moment. This was the life she'd chosen for herself. Her cottage in the country, her own second chances space, silver-lined with a sense of freedom, of time for herself.

And perhaps, she was about to lose it all . . . if Adam wanted her support. If he needed her to be there nearer to him. However enchanting it seemed here, had she in fact been selfish setting off for this new rural life alone? Was she about to come sliding back down and land in the confines of Leeds city once again. What was the right thing to do? For Adam? For her? But she knew that whatever he wanted, she would do . . . she wouldn't let him down, not this time.

*

Oh. Her heart gave a little kick. She'd just settled down in the front room to watch some easy-going TV. And here was Will posting on the group chat:

Hi all, must be my turn to host by now. So, if anyone fancies taking their chances with my 'limited' cooking skills, can you make the evening of either Fri 20th or Sat 21st September. Let me know. 😊

Crikey, so, he'd taken the plunge and offered to host. That was really quite brave of him in the circumstances, Cath thought, knowing he'd be feeling awkward, for sure. The big question now was . . . *should she go?*

*

An hour later, and after ruminating her way through her ironing pile – she was never going to settle watching the telly now! – the answer was loud and clear in her head.

Bugger it! Life was too short, and she loved that bloody Supper Club. That friendship group had made her smile again when life had been so very tough, and they'd all helped her to

387

find her feet in the village. If she ducked out now, it would be even harder to go back and join in the future.

She'd have to face Will at some point. They'd managed to get through the funeral, and the terrier search, but this was going to be super close quarters at his home. They needed to clear the air before this next Supper Club . . . and, once they'd faced each other honestly, then she'd decide if it was right to go for Will's sake. And, if they could at least manage to stay as friends, she'd settle for that. To see him again, to get to know him more. To have their wonderful Supper Club continue. It wouldn't be easy, especially at first, but she would learn to cope with it, if that's what it took to keep the Supper Club going. The main thing was not to spoil it for all the others. She so wanted to keep seeing them all. The Supper Club was their hub, their hope.

Before she could change her mind, she threw on her trainers and marched up the village street.

*

It was time for the truth.

If the two of them were going to be able to move on with their friendship . . . if the Supper Club had any hope of a future, all hurts and misunderstandings needed to be cleared up. Better now, before they were gathered again next week at Will's house.

After speaking with Maria in the garden of the care home that day, that's what Cath had intended doing, after all. But time and circumstances since had made it feel like the moment had passed, or perhaps she'd been subconsciously trying to duck out again. But it was never too late. Whatever the implications might be thereafter.

Though their weeklong holiday romance was fledgling, it had felt so intense at the time. Though she knew that it was nothing like what Will had evidently had in his marriage, it was only the start of a relationship really, at least she could be honest and finally tell him what had really gone on. And then, maybe, they could start patching up their friendship at least, and over time learn to not feel so awkward in each other's company.

This was a conversation to be had in private. She didn't like to just turn up out of the blue, but she had a feeling if she asked to call in on her own, the answer might be a resolute no.

No foodie gifts this time, just her. *Go on, go now* – a voice spoke inside, *go while this feels imperative*. And she did. Rushing up the street, passing a friendly neighbour with the briefest of hellos. Then knocking on his door, with a heart full of anxiety and also hope. It was time for them both to move on, to shake off the misunderstandings of their past.

The door opened. Will didn't exactly look pleased to see her, his frown giving that much away. 'Oh . . . hi.'

'Hi, Will, is it all right to come in? Umm, I need to explain something . . .'

He paused, then merely nodded, as he let her follow him through his kitchen. He didn't offer her a coffee or anything. This was no cosy chat.

'Sorry to just turn up like this, but knowing we'd have to meet again soon . . . with the Supper Club evening coming up, well . . .'

He was listening, dark eyes intent, but with a coolness. Would that coolness always be there from now on?

They stood staring at each other. Less than a metre between them, and yet a world apart.

Cath plucked up the courage, she was here now, and this was it. 'Will, l really need to try to explain . . . I know I did wrong all those years ago, not answering your letters, ducking out. But I was scared and young, and inexperienced. I know that's no bloody excuse. Looking back, it was only decent to have let you know what was going on . . . but at the time, I didn't know how.' Cath paused; this was harder than she'd thought, here, face to face with Matty as a man.

'Okay, here goes . . .' She took a slow breath. 'A couple of weeks after I got home, after I'd answered your first letter, I realised my period was late. Really late. And it scared me to death.'

He said nothing, but kept his eyes fixed on her as she explained.

'I totally panicked . . . It would have changed everything . . . having a baby so young. I don't think I could have gone through with an abortion, but then I was about to start my A Levels, and I was fixed on training to be a teacher. That's what I'd wanted to do for years.' It all began to spill out. 'All my dreams seemed to be in the balance. Being a mum was never in the equation back then . . . not at sixteen.'

She paused, noticing his family photos all around. His wife, his daughters. The real loves of his life, of course they were. Will was staring at her. His emotions were so hard to read. Was this confession the right thing? Was it just stirring up old wounds? Was she still the same daft young girl? A blip in his past.

Will hadn't yet said a word.

But she'd started, so she may as well finish her story, their youthful story. 'It was just a scare,' she continued. 'I finally got a test, and it was negative, but by then a few more weeks had passed . . . and I hadn't been in touch . . . and I knew I needed to get my head down and study, concentrate on my school work, get my uni place. A relationship, long distance, however much I felt for you . . . and I did feel so much for you then, Matty, but it wasn't going to work. And time had gone on and I didn't know how to explain all that . . . so I didn't. I just left it. I'm sorry, Will.'

Cath gave a small relieved sigh that the truth and her apology were out, that the lad she'd hurt all those years ago at least knew why, and that she had very much cared for him. That he had finally heard the explanation she should have told him thirty-six years ago, back in 1988.

Will looked a bit shell-shocked. 'Right . . . well . . . at least I know now.' He stood quiet for a few seconds before adding, 'But I would have been there for you then, whatever, Cath.'

And she hadn't been there for him.

Was there a way to move forward from this? Had this revelation helped, or just widened the divide? Cath was desperate to fix things, but from his reaction the chasm seemed to still be there between them. But she had to try, to keep trying. 'If it's okay . . . if we can find some way . . . can we at least be friends again, Will. Hey?'

She so wanted to keep in touch with this lovely man, and she so wanted the Supper Club to continue in its wonderful all-embracing friendly way.

Will looked at her, the hurt still there in his gorgeous eyes. 'Oh, Cath, I'm not sure if I can . . .'

Cath took a big gulp, trying to stem the tears that she knew were swelling in her eyes. There was nothing else to say. Would she even be able to come along to his Supper Club now? She thanked him for his time, and turned to leave. Her bye sounded so lonely as she left.

At least she'd tried. *I've been brave, Maria*, she thought on her way back down the street. But sadly, it hadn't seemed to be enough.

Chapter 50

'Hey, Mum.'

'Ah, hi, love.' Aw, that was nice, Adam was calling her. She'd been trying hard not to hound him; trying to get the balance between regularly checking he was all right, but giving him the space he needed to get back on his feet for himself. 'Everything okay?'

'Yep, pretty good. Feeling more myself, thanks. And I got to see the doc.'

'Great . . .' She held off from saying, *And?* Giving him chance to frame his response.

'Yeah, that went fine . . . good, really. We had a bit of a chat. Gave me a load of helpline numbers, information, some of it looks useful. I could have gone on anti-depressants, but you know, I just want to see how I go for now. The doc was okay with that, saying that the option's there should I need. He was pretty cool, actually. Oh, and . . .' Adam's voice suddenly sounded more serious. Cath found herself holding her breath. 'I have been advised that, as lovely as it is that you've offered . . . well, I've been warned against you moving down here.'

What? 'You have?' That sounded rather odd from a doctor,

who didn't know a damned thing about their family circumstances. She felt the heat rising through her.

'Yeah, he said it might drive me to despair, having you lurking on my doorstep.' He said it deadpan.

She finally caught on. 'Adam . . . that's so not funny.' But she had to concede a small smile. It was nice to hear him jesting again, more like his old self.

'Honestly though, Mum, I've had a chance to think, these past few days . . . about a lot of stuff. And you selling up, coming back down here, it just doesn't make sense. You love it up there in your cottage, that little village, I can tell. You've had all that shit with Dad to deal with . . . it's your time, you need this. Your new chance of happiness.' He paused. 'Really, don't let it be about me, making you sell up . . . unless there're other reasons I don't know about. You can come down here, make me that Sunday dinner you were promising, and I can come up and visit sometimes too. I'll be fine, really. We'll work it out.'

Could she take him at his word? Or was he just braving things out for her?

He seemed to twig her misgivings. 'I do need my own space here, Mum. And I've got Dad not so far away, if I need. He came to see me last night. Brought us a Chinese takeaway, actually. Seems to be okay. Back on with Steph. So that's cheering him up.'

'Ah, I'm glad he's been over.' The two of them had spoken, and Trev had promised to look in on Adam. He had also mentioned being back with his girlfriend now too, and that hadn't hurt anywhere near as much as it might have done a few months back. They could still work as a team where it mattered, she mused.

Adam then asked about the latest village antics. She wasn't going to delve into that particular can of worms, instead merely mentioning there was to be another Supper Club soon. Hah, it was no way near as sleepy here as he might imagine. But yes, this village was her lifeline, her meant-to-be place. He was right about that. Her relief that she seemingly no longer needed to up sticks and move again was already flowing like soothing Northumbrian honey in her veins.

The conversation ended soon after, with virtual hugs and kisses, and a warm feeling that Adam was going to be all right. A little of her mother-guilt about the break-up with Trevor and the sale of the family home, the upset it had caused to all their lives, peeling away.

It was one step at a time for her son, and for her, trying to navigate their adult relationship with honesty, humour and respect, but at last she felt it was all going in the right direction.

*

There was another relationship that she really needed to keep steering in the right direction, too. Despite the frosty reception to her side of their youthful story from Will, Cath was determined not to duck out anymore. This was the new Cath, taking life, love and friendship by the horns.

She decided to private message Will, saying that though she'd love to come along to the next supper event, she was offering him an easy way out if he felt uncomfortable about it. Cath was determined to keep trying hard for them to remain friends . . . to give it time, but she didn't want him to feel awkward. She was waiting for his response.

An hour after sending the message, there was a rap at her door.

Oh, Will was there, looking so damned attractive in dark jeans and a plain khaki T.

'Hi.' His expression and tone were gentle.

'Hey.' She found she couldn't be cool with him, a hopeful smile already playing on her lips.

'I'm sorry if I didn't take it well . . . your explanation the other day . . .' he started, looking distinctly awkward.

'Hey, come on in.' This was evidently not a conversation for the doorstep.

Both stood in her hallway now. 'It was all just a bit of a shock . . . well . . . hearing that you might have been pregnant back then. I'm sorry if I wasn't very understanding.' He looked right at her.

'It's okay . . .' She felt a calmness come over her. He was here now, they were talking again, and that meant so much.

'And I've seen the lads, they've actually been giving me some cooking lessons in advance of Friday . . . I certainly need it. They told me about your Adam. I'm sorry you've had all that worry. How is he?'

'Ah, he's doing okay. Thank you. I think he's through the worst of it. Just hit a real low. It's hard for them, isn't it, youngsters today. All those hopes and dreams after uni . . . and then the reality, with good jobs so few and far between.' She drew a breath. 'And it really hasn't helped him, all this stuff going on between me and Trevor these past couple of years. It's been a total mess and he's been in the middle of it. We hadn't always noticed . . . Your children are still so vulnerable, even if they are grown-up adults.'

Will was nodding understandingly. 'There's no magic shield when you hit eighteen is there? Life still sends in those knocks.'

And didn't the pair of them know it.

'The Supper Club at mine,' he continued, sounding slightly uncertain of himself, 'I'd like you to come along, Cath. Shall we give this friends thing a try?'

'You sure?'

They both knew it wasn't going to be easy for him – for either of them.

'Sure.'

'O-kay. Well, thank you.'

So, Supper Club at Will's was a yes.

He gave a cautious smile, then added, 'Sorry, but I've got to go, get back to the shop. Got a delivery due at six.' He was preparing his exit, there was of course no hug or kiss on the cheek, but at least something had shifted positively between them. Cath still felt a whole heap of emotions when she looked at him, having once hoped for so much more. She'd have to settle for friendship, and they'd still need to work at making that feel comfortable again, but hey, this was way better than the stalemate they'd had for weeks now.

Chapter 51

Tonight was the night, Supper Club at Will's, and as Cath got changed into her floaty-floral summer dress, she couldn't help but feel nervous. If they could get through this one, take those steps to re-build their friendship, then there might be hope for the future, fingers crossed.

On the group chat, it was agreed that everyone would take something to help out, with Will making the main supper dish. Andreas and Dan had given him a couple of cooking lessons to boost his skills and confidence, bless them. Lily and Nikki were on puddings, and Cath said she'd do the starter – a baked goat's cheese salad, served with homemade red-onion chutney. The ingredients were all ready to take over in her basket. All she had to do was give the rounds of cheese a light toast under the grill, and assemble them with some salad leaves and the relish – easy-peasy. The cooking was the simple part, it was trying to maintain a natural approach with Will that would be tricky.

She set off, with an anxious whir inside, as she made the short walk up the village. Her plan was to arrive a few minutes late, hoping that someone else in the group would be there first to take the pressure off the pair of them. At 7:08 p.m.

she knocked on Will's door, her head a bit of a mush and her heart feeling sore. All the while, she told herself it'd be fine, she just had to be polite. All she had to do was to make chit-chat with Will where needed, then steer herself towards the others.

Will opened the door, looking smart – and oh, she had to admit, handsome – in a pale-pink linen shirt, the sleeves rolled up revealing his lightly tanned forearms, and black jeans. A waft of gorgeous aftershave hit her. She felt a little unsteady.

'Hi, Cath.' His tone was calm, if a touch cool. Was he trying too hard to sound normal?

'Hello.' She tried to smile, but everything was feeling pretty difficult already. And, damn, why was there was no sound of chat or laughter coming through from the rest of the house? In fact, it sounded ominously quiet in there.

'You're the first,' he acknowledged. 'Oh, and Andreas and Dan have had to pull out. Something about Dan having a terrible migraine, and Andreas not wanting to leave him as Dan was feeling a bit sick with it, too.'

'Ah no, that's such a shame.'

'Andreas did pop in with some homemade olive bread and a salad dish earlier though, so that was good of him.'

'Ah, that's nice. They are always so kind, the lads. And of course, you've been having some cooking lessons, too.' Cath chivvied the conversation on, as she hovered on the step.

'Yeah, the lads have been great. We had a bit of fun when they came and showed me how to make a couple of dishes. And hey, it actually wasn't as difficult as I'd feared. Oh, sorry . . . come on in.' It suddenly dawned on him that he was keeping her waiting.

She followed him to the kitchen which was filled with

aromas of chicken . . . and peppers, she thought. 'Well, some-thing's smelling good, anyhow.'

'My secret supper.' Will managed a small smile at that. 'So, can I get you a drink? A glass of wine, or a gin and tonic?'

'Ooh yes, I'll have a G&T, thanks.' She bloody well needed a stiff drink to help keep this conversation up. *Come on, Nikki and Lily, hurry up, girls.*

With that, Will's mobile rang. 'Hel-lo,' he answered. There was a pause, and then, 'Oh . . . oh, I see, well that's a shame. And what about Lily?'

Another pause, as she watched Will's face drop further. 'Oh . . . right.'

He ended the call looking a little pale, then he gave an anxious cough. 'Well . . . uhm, I'm sorry, it looks like it's just you and me.'

Oh shit. 'What on earth's happened?' Cath was suddenly fearing the worst for her special gang.

'Well, it seems that Kev's dropped Nikki right in it. He's had to dash off on some emergency electrical job, and she doesn't have a sitter anymore. Too last minute to get anyone else, either.'

'Oh.'

'And Lily's calling in with something for our pudding course,' he continued, 'but then she has to go and visit her grandma this evening. She'd forgotten all about that appar-ently, and her parents have gone off it with her. She sent her apologies with Nikki.'

'So, it's only us two . . . hmm, well that's a bit awkward, isn't it,' Cath admitted openly. 'I've got six starters all ready to make here, too.' She took a large gulp of the gin he'd just handed her, then swiftly added, 'Look, I can head back home if you like. We can reschedule when the others can make it . . . I know this must be difficult for you.' It wasn't at all easy for her either in the circumstances.

'Oh . . . umm.' Will looked a bit lost. 'I'm not sure. It feels a bit rude kicking you out.' He paused, giving himself a moment to think.

'Honestly, it's okay. I can leave.' It would be easier to just gather her things and go. It was going to be bloody tricky otherwise, a dinner for two.

Will's shoulders seemed to sag, then lifted a little, his brow slightly creased as if he was struggling to know what to do for the best. 'Look, the supper's already in the oven. It seems a shame to waste it. Umm, I suppose you could stay for that, at least . . . if you want to, that is. And Lily is meant to be calling in.'

Should I stay or should I go now? started playing in her head. Weirdly, she suddenly wondered if Matty . . . Will, might remember that track by The Clash from years ago. And, flipping heck, she definitely felt like trouble. But a big part of her did want to stay – to try and put things right between them. And well, he hadn't shown her the door at least.

'Okay, but only if you're sure,' she said.

He nodded.

This was going to be so uncomfortable; supper for the two of them, but hey, maybe they'd get chance to talk some more. It might even help move the friendship back on to more stable ground. One small step at a time.

'Thank you.'

Sat in the lounge five minutes later, gin to hand, and a bowl of cheesy nibbles that she was diving into far too often – she was putting it down to nerves – they chatted about Adam being a lot better, and the latest from the bicycle shop, there being nothing of particular note, mostly services and broken chains . . . and broken hearts, thought Cath. Wishing things might have turned out differently for the two of them, back then and now. They were trying their best, but it all felt slightly laboured between them. Was this really such a good idea, her staying?

She glanced out of the window for a few seconds, catching a glimpse of a blonde-haired lady with a pink baseball cap on, who happened to be walking by. Suddenly the woman ducked down, tying a shoelace or something perhaps. Oddly, she'd had the look of Nikki, just for that split second. Must be someone who looked a bit like her – there were always people staying in the village on holiday, especially at this time of the year.

Thankfully, it wasn't long before Lily called in. That helped break the tension, at least.

'Hi, guys! I'm so sorry to have to let you down. But here it is, pudding for you.' She passed over a delicious-looking meringue and cream dish. 'Passionfruit pavlova.'

Was that a little smirk Cath saw drifting across Lily's lips?

'Oh, that looks amazing, Lily. Thank you,' said Will. 'Are you staying for a drink, or perhaps some food?'

Please, thought Cath. Anything to help ease the atmosphere in here.

'Ah, sorry, guys, I'm gonna have to dash. Mum and Dad are

ready to go to Grandma's . . .' She made a show of checking her watch. 'In around five minutes, so I'm going to have to head back right away. Soz. But have a lovely evening.' She gave them both a big smile, and was already turning on her heels and heading off for the doorway, Will following to see her out.

Wow, how could the two of them keep this up? The conversation had been stalling for the past ten minutes, as it was. Cath took another large sip of her gin and was up on her feet. She needed to keep busy. And, despite the fact her hunger had disappeared entirely, she told Will she was going to the kitchen to prep the starter. Her head was beginning to thrum, and she was already wondering at what point it might be okay to leave. A swift exit straight after the main seemed like the best option.

*

Cath was head down purposefully prepping food in the kitchen. She'd popped salad leaves onto two plates, taken from the original stack of six left ready on the side.

Now to cook the goat's cheese. She'd brought baking parchment and laid it out on the grill pan, placing two rounds of the cheese on it. Grill on, warming up . . . Will was now stood at her shoulder, watching – close, a little too close.

'Ah, so that's how you stop it melting away into the grill pan,' he commented.

'Yep, simple when you know how.'

'I'm picking up tips all the time.' He smiled then.

'We'll make a chef of you, yet,' Cath responded.

The act of cooking was thankfully thawing the atmosphere between them. It gave them something else to focus on at least. She was keeping a close eye on the grill, as the cheese could cook very quickly. And then, she could feel his breath somewhere near her shoulder. Was he watching that closely, too. Oh. A charge of electric raced between them . . . well, in her imagination, of course. She couldn't like him anymore, not in that way. And if she bloody well did, she could never show it now. It was only friendship on offer. Suddenly she felt way too hot. It was the grill, must be the grill. To keep the Supper Club intact and ongoing, the two of them merely needed to muddle through politely. But, here, having to pretend she felt nothing, this was just excruciating.

A delicate bubbling sound and gorgeous cheesy aromas were filling the kitchen. Thank heavens, it was ready. The cheese rounds toasted and lightly golden. It was a miracle she hadn't burnt it, to be honest. Time to serve them with the chutney and salad leaves, and to sit down and eat . . . if she could manage to. She gave herself the smallest of the two pieces, and took a deep breath, before she turned around to face Will.

'Ready.' The food might well be, but she didn't feel ready for any of this at all.

*

'Thanks, that was delicious.' Will sat back on the kitchen bar stool.

They'd decided to give the dining room – which had been set up with glasses and cutlery for six – a miss. It would have felt very odd, the two of them sat there formally at the table, looking across at each other. Will had suggested they stay in the kitchen and sit at the breakfast bar, which felt far more casual, propped side by side, and was a bit of a relief to Cath, to be honest.

'And it didn't take long to cook either,' he observed.

'Yeah, it's really easy to be fair. You just grill the goat's cheese, arrange salad on a plate, add a dollop of chutney, and you're there.'

'Hah, I think even I could manage that. And hey, fingers crossed for the main . . .' He raised his eyebrows along with a smile. 'So, what else has been on for you today?' he asked.

'Oh, had a short stroll down by the river. Dog free,' she added with a roll of her eyes, remembering all too well that fateful day.

'Ah.'

'And hey, thanks again for all your help that day.' She understood that it wouldn't have been easy for him to come to her aid.

'No worries. I did it for the lads.'

Ooh, that sounded a bit prickly.

She soldiered on with the conversation. 'And I took a trip to the Kirkton deli for the cheese, and then later this afternoon I had a couple of online tutoring sessions.'

Will looked up at her with those dark expressive eyes. 'You always did want to be a teacher, didn't you.' His voice was soft.

'Yes, and I was, well, still am in a way, with the tutoring . . . a bloody good one too.' She was proud of her job, her achievements over the years, not just the titles but the fact that she was able to help those kids.

'It's a part of who you are, isn't it, teaching,' he added thoughtfully.

'Yeah . . .' Oh my, he got it, her, more than Trevor ever had.

She went quiet, the past tense of his previous words sinking in. 'You remembered that, didn't you . . . even before our chat the other day.'

'I remembered it all, Cathy.' He slipped back to his old name for her. 'There was something about that week . . . about you . . . that stayed with me.'

His tone shifted everything between them. She let her gaze settle on him. He then seemed to shake himself out of it, leaping up off his seat. He took a dish of salad out of the fridge, and proceeded to cut the olive loaf. 'Yeah, Andreas made the bread himself, it's so nice of them. Let's hope Dan's okay, that migraine sounded awful.'

'Yes, let's hope so.'

He took the bake, which he'd prepared earlier, out of the oven, and began to dish out his meal. Smells of herby chicken, roasted peppers, olives and warmed bread, filled the room. He carried two plates over. 'Well, here goes, Will's Easy Greek-Style Chicken Bake. Good luck to me . . . and to you for eating it.' He gave a warm smile, which was lovely to see.

Could they in fact move on from all this? Could she help him learn to cook, to enjoy life again . . . one step, one day at a time. Her heart seemed way too full.

Dinner was really tasty, though with her stomach still fluttering anxiously, she couldn't manage to eat as much as she'd have liked to. The cooking lessons with Dan and Andreas had certainly paid off, and the all-in-one chicken bake with new potatoes, peppers, feta and olives went down well, despite Cath's appetite not being up to scratch. She declined pudding, though it looked delicious, deciding that would be a step too far for her rollercoaster tummy. Was it time to go?

They'd survived the meal at least, Cath thought with a sense of relief. And they seemed to have made a bridge towards a new, slightly faltering sense of friendship, well she hoped so. They could work on things from here.

Will was making coffee for them both in his Nespresso machine. It smelt rich and aromatic. Oh, she couldn't just up and go quite yet. But then, in just a few sips' time, she'd be heading home.

Coffee to hand, they sat a while longer on the stools, side by side. The tension felt palpable between them.

'Jeez, I am still finding this difficult, Cath,' confessed Will, staring down into his cup. 'Everything you told me the other day . . . it's been hard to take in.'

'It's okay, I understand. And I'm sorry . . . about everything that happened, that I wasn't brave enough to explain it all to you back then. I should have done. But I'm hoping, somehow, we can find a way forward now. I'd love to keep the Supper Club group going . . . for all of us.' She didn't dare tell him how much she felt for him now, too.

'Me too.' He nodded, looking serious. 'But it won't be easy . . .'

'No,' she conceded.

A few seconds of stillness followed, with just the beating sound of the kitchen clock ticking, like a heart.

Will shifted in his seat, turning to look at her. 'It hurt so much . . . back then . . . because I cared for you, Cathy. I really thought there might be more for us. And, I really thought you felt it too . . . whatever was going on with you back home shouldn't have changed that. Ah, I guess I was just a daft young idiot.'

'Oh, Matty, no, you weren't an idiot . . . I did care for you . . . I felt it all too. I'm so sorry.' She took a long, slow breath.

His brow was creased. 'Hey, it was all years ago, Cath. I moved on . . . it took a while, admittedly. I developed a thick skin; you have to in life. I learnt to stay detached . . .'

Cath felt awful that her youthful actions had made him feel that way, that it had been her who'd taught him how to hold back on life. The closeness between them was breaching once more. But it was only fair that he had the chance to say how he'd felt about everything back then, too. There were always two sides, sometimes more, to every story told.

'That was until I met Jane,' he admitted, and he held Cath's gaze, his expression happy-sad all at once. 'And slowly, bit by bit, she broke down my defences . . .' He gave one of his gorgeous smiles, with the creases around his eyes deepening, as he remembered.

Cath hadn't seen that smile in a while. 'Will, I'm so glad that you had a lovely relationship with your wife . . . a good marriage. And I'm really sad for you that it had to end the way it did . . . for you and Jane. Life can be shit sometimes.'

Will nodded, tears brimming but not quite spilling. 'It's why all this, meeting you again . . . feels so hard. And that night at yours, under the stars, it was all too much. There's such a feeling of guilt too,' he admitted shakily. 'Just thinking about someone else . . . it feels like a betrayal to Jane, to our marriage.'

'Oh, Will.' Life was such a tangled web, of hurt, of grief, of betrayal, but ultimately of love. Instinctively, Cath reached for his hand. He flinched momentarily, but then let her take it.

Of course, their holiday romance was just fledgling, even if it had felt extraordinary at the time. It was nothing like what Will had experienced with his wife. But she was glad she'd finally had the courage to explain what had really gone on all those years ago. And now was the time to try and patch up their friendship and find some way to move forward.

She so wanted to stay in touch with this lovely man, to see him sometimes, and she so wanted the Supper Club to continue in its wonderfully supportive way. 'Will, is there a way we can be friends again?'

Will looked down. 'Oh crikey, Cath, I'm really not sure if I can . . .'

Oh no, she felt a huge lump in her throat. After everything, he probably didn't feel he could ever trust her again. What a bloody shame. But what more could she do? She'd have to accept it . . . even if it did make her feel raw, bruised. A crushing 'Oh' escaped her lips.

Will lifted his head, held her gaze. 'I don't think that's enough for me, Cath . . . Cathy.'

What was he saying?

He stopped talking, stood up and moved closer, taking her face gently in his hands . . .

What's happening here? Cath was struggling to make sense of it. She felt him guide her to standing. They were face to face, and so very tinglingly close.

'I've been wanting . . . and scared to do this for a long time.' He brushed a tender fingertip slowly down her cheek, moving it towards her lips.

Every nerve ending in her body was on high alert. Was this real . . . ?

Without realising it, they were stood directly in line with the kitchen window. His lips then followed his fingertip, and he was kissing her right on the lips, softly at first, then more deeply, passionately. Cath responded . . . It was wonderful, and sensual, and not like friends at all. And as he finally pulled away, it was there in his eyes. All the affection, all those emotions, he'd kept back for all this time.

'Oh, wow,' was all Cath could utter. *Their first kiss . . .*

Well, it wasn't really, was it, she suddenly realised! But after all these years, it felt very beautiful, and very much like it.

Will then stepped back just a little, with an understandable edge of caution, they'd both been through so much, after all. 'Can we take things slowly? One step at a time, hey.'

They'd been through thirty-six years' worth of life, in fact, since that very first kiss, and if all of that had taught Cath anything, it was not to hold back on living any more. Yes, of course, if they needed to take things steady for Will's sake, step by step, then naturally, Cath was more than okay with that. Going slowly was very different to holding back.

'Of course.' She gave a huge grin, feeling her heart soar. 'And well, I really liked that first step . . . very much.'

They smiled at each other, the love there plain to see in their eyes, a love that would now get a chance to grow.

'Hey, maybe we can start with a few cooking lessons?' Cath grinned.

'Sure, sounds great . . . up close and personal in the kitchen.' Will quirked a very sexy eyebrow.

'Hmm . . . absolutely.' Just thinking about the heat around tonight's grilled cheese episode made her temperature shoot up again.

Cath was sure she heard – oddly – a round of applause coming from over the front garden wall. And, oh blimey, yes, a Nikki-sounding 'Whoop!'

The penny then dropped. Cath and Will gave each other a bemused, yet happy look. The little – *lovely* – bloody Supper Club sneaks must be out there watching.

Then, a row of oh-so-familiar heads popped up to peek over the low stone wall, grinning wildly, with hands clapping and waving. Andreas gave a loud wolf-whistle.

'Way to go, guys!' shouted Dan, with absolutely no sign of a migraine.

'Can we come in for dessert?' called out Lily cheekily.

'Don't want to be interrupting anything, mind.' Andreas was laughing warmly.

'Well, someone needed to get you two together!' Nikki stood up, baseball cap in hand, shouting triumphantly.

'Well, you lot have spoilt the moment now, anyhow.' Will chuckled, as he leaned out through his now open window to speak with them all.

But the moment wasn't spoilt, not at all. With Will's arm wrapped firmly around Cath, the two of them had time on their side and everything to look forward to.

And a few minutes later, sharing Lily's gorgeous dessert with the rest of their wonderful friendship group, it felt like the icing *and* the cherry on the cake. Life was absolutely looking up.

This really was the Supper Club of Second Chances.

The Recipes

Supper Club 1: Cath's King Prawn and Lemon Tagliatelle

Supper Club 2: Andreas's Honey, Fig and Feta Bake

Supper Club 3: Nikki's Seventies Bloody Mary Prawn Cocktail

Supper Club 4: Andreas's Northumberland-Greek Honey Cake

Supper Club 5: Cath's Comforting Cheesy Leek Cottage Pie

Supper Club 6: Lily's Luscious Lemon Posset

Supper Club 7: Will's Easy Chicken, Pepper, Feta and Olive Bake

Cath's King Prawn and Lemon Tagliatelle (Serves 4)

40g butter
6 spring onions, chopped
1 heaped tbsp plain flour
300ml milk
Salt and pepper
1 tbsp lemon juice
1 tsp lemon zest
250g tagliatelle (dried)
250g cooked king prawns
140ml double cream
Grated parmesan, and 1 tbsp finely chopped parsley,
   to garnish

Melt the butter in a deep frying pan, and gently fry the spring onions until tender.

Stir in the flour, and cook for one minute. Gradually stir in the milk to form a smooth, thick sauce.

Season to taste, and add the lemon juice and zest. Set aside.

Cook the tagliatelle as per the instructions, and drain.

Put the sauce back on to a medium heat and stir in the prawns and cream to heat through, then mix with the cooked tagliatelle. Serve garnished with grated parmesan and a sprinkling of parsley.

Olive bread (or any freshly baked bread) and a crisp green salad would be wonderful with this! Bon appétit!

Andreas's Honey, Fig and Feta Bake (Serves 4 as a starter)

200g feta cheese
4 figs, quartered
2 sprigs rosemary, 1 with leaves picked and chopped,
    the other left whole
A drizzle of olive oil
Salt and black pepper
2 tbsp honey (The heather honey from Chain Bridge
    Honey Farm, Northumberland, is delicious, but
    feel free to use your local honey.)

Preheat the oven to 200°C/180°C fan. Line a baking dish with non-stick parchment, then add the whole feta, fig segments, chopped rosemary leaves, a drizzle of olive oil and some salt and black pepper.

Bake for 15 minutes, then take out and drizzle the honey over and lay the whole sprig of rosemary across the cheese. Bake for a further 10 minutes, until the feta is golden.

Serve with crusty bread and/or salad leaves.

Nikki's Seventies Bloody Mary Prawn Cocktail (Serves 4 as a starter)

Sauce
100g mayonnaise
Juice of ½ lemon
1 tbsp tomato puree
1 tbsp Worcestershire sauce
4 drops Tabasco sauce

25ml shot of vodka

250g cooked, peeled king prawns
2 baby gem lettuces, shredded
Sprinkling of crushed chillies and lemon wedges, to
    serve

Mix all the sauce ingredients together until smooth.

Add the prawns and coat well. Serve in glass dishes, on a bed of crispy shredded lettuce, with a light sprinkling of crushed chillies to decorate and a wedge of lemon.

Andreas's Northumberland-Greek Honey Cake

150g plain flour
1½ tsp baking powder
1 heaped tsp grated orange zest
½ tsp ground cinnamon
Pinch of salt
150g caster sugar
170g unsalted butter, softened
3 eggs

Syrup
150g Northumberland (or your local) honey
100g caster sugar
100ml water
1 tsp lemon juice

Preheat oven to 180°C/170°C fan. Grease and flour an 8-inch circular cake tin (I use a non-stick springform tin).

In a bowl, combine the flour, baking powder, orange zest, cinnamon and salt. Set aside.

Beat the caster sugar and butter together until light and fluffy, then beat in the eggs, one at a time. Stir in the flour mixture, and beat until smooth. Pour mix into the prepared tin.

Bake for around 30 to 35 minutes and test with a skewer to see if it comes out clean. Leave for a few minutes then remove from the tin and cool on a rack whilst making the honey syrup.

Combine the honey, sugar and water in a saucepan. Bring to a simmer and then stir in the lemon juice. Pour into a small jug. Transfer the sponge to a plate. Make a few skewer holes in the top of the sponge and slowly pour two thirds of the syrup over the cake.

Serve cold or warmed, with a drizzle of the remaining syrup and some thick cream or vanilla ice cream. Delicious!

Cath's Comforting Cheesy Leek Cottage Pie (Serves 4)

1 tbsp olive oil
1 large (or 2 small) onion, chopped
500g lean minced beef
Salt and black pepper
1 tsp dried thyme
300ml beef stock
1 tsp Worcestershire sauce (optional)
1 level tbsp tomato puree
1 heaped tsp cornflour, mixed with a little cold water

Topping

900g Maris Piper/King Edward potatoes, peeled and
   cut into large even-sized chunks
50g butter
2 tbsp fresh milk
Salt and black pepper to taste
2 medium leeks, sliced
50g mature cheddar cheese, grated

Heat the oil to medium in a deep frying pan, add the onions and fry until golden brown. Add the mince and toss to mix and brown well, breaking up any lumps that may form. Add salt and pepper, thyme, then the stock and Worcestershire sauce if using, and stir in the tomato puree. Simmer for 20 minutes. Add and stir through the cornflour mix to thicken. Simmer on low for a further 5 minutes. Remove from the heat and keep covered whilst you make the topping.

Preheat the oven to 200°C/180°C fan.

Boil the potatoes in salted water for 20–25 minutes until cooked right through (test centre with a knife). Drain well, add 40g of the butter, milk and seasoning, and mash (using a hand masher) to a smooth puree.

Fry the leeks in a large knob of butter until just tender Fork through the mash.

Tip the meat mixture into a medium baking dish, and then use the leeky-mash to top your pie. I use two dessert spoons to gently scoop the mix on top and a fork to level out, leaving a bit of texture. Sprinkle over the cheese, and a touch of black pepper.

Bake for 25 to 30 minutes, until the top is golden and crispy. Serve with a seasonal green veg.

Lily's Luscious Lemon Posset (Serves 6–10 in mini pots)

570ml double cream
155g caster sugar
Juice of 2½ lemons
10 blueberries, and a grating of lemon zest/dusting of
    icing sugar, to decorate

Bring the cream and sugar to the boil in a large pan, stirring occasionally with a wooden spoon. (Be careful, it boils up surprisingly high!)

Continue to boil rapidly for 2 to 3 minutes.

Remove from the heat, whisk in the lemon juice, and pour into small glasses or cups/ramekins. Allow to cool, then refrigerate for at least four hours, or overnight, until set.

Decorate with a blueberry in the centre and a sprinkling of grated lemon zest/dusting of icing sugar. Serve with a shortbread round or thin caramelised biscuit. Scrumptious!

Will's Easy Chicken, Pepper, Feta and Olive Bake (Serves 4)

750g Charlotte or new potatoes, cut in half if large
600g boneless chicken thighs, cut into large bite-size
    chunks
2 tsp smoked paprika
1 large onion, sliced into 8 wedges
1 red pepper, de-seeded and cut into chunks
3 cloves garlic, crushed
Salt and black pepper to taste

2 tbsp olive oil

200g feta cheese, crumbled into chunks

16 pitted black olives

2 tbsp flat leaf parsley, roughly chopped

Preheat the oven to 200°C/180°C fan.

Parboil the potatoes for 5 to 6 minutes.

Toss the chicken in the smoked paprika to coat. Place in an ovenproof dish. Add onion, red pepper and garlic. Drain the potatoes and add to the dish, season and toss together with the olive oil.

Cook for 15 minutes, take the dish out of the oven and toss, then return it to the oven again for a further 15 minutes, until the chicken is cooked through and golden. Add the olives and feta to the top and bake for 3 to 4 more minutes. Remove from the oven and sprinkle over the parsley. Serve with a green salad and fresh crusty bread.

A Letter from Caroline Roberts

Thank you so much for choosing to read *The Second Chance Supper Club*. I hope you enjoyed it! If you did and would like to be the first to know about my new releases, click below to sign up to my mailing list.

The Second Chance Supper Club is inspired by my beautiful Northumberland village, my love of food and the way it brings people together, and also by the twists and emotional turns that life can take us through. I think we all deserve a second chance and some good friends to buoy us up when times are tough.

I hope you loved *The Second Chance Supper Club*, and if you did, I would be so grateful if you would leave a review. I always love to hear what readers thought, and it helps new readers discover my books too.

Thanks,

Caroline x

Acknowledgements

A book is nothing without a reader, so heartfelt thanks to all my readers and the book blogging community for your wonderful support over the years. I do love hearing from you on my Facebook and Instagram, so please continue to keep in touch.

The Second Chance Supper Club is very much inspired by Northumberland village life and my local community, who welcomed me into their fold over twenty years ago. I have to thank Chatton Village Stores, and especially Pat and Sarah, who let me interview and observe them as they served, chatted and baked.

Thanks to Maths teacher advisor, Rebecca Moss, for her helpful insights, whose dreams of becoming a teacher came at the same point as I was trying hard to get my books published – we both very much achieved our goals.

Thank you to Yianna and her Greek-Cypriot dad for their help with Andreas's family's phrases and Greek-inspired recipe ideas. Also, thanks to Yianna's husband 'Doctor Dan' for his medical advice in the illness and care of Maria.

Any mistakes you may find are wholly my own. I endeavour

to try my best but sometimes a typo or a piece of information slips the net! Writers are only human, too.

My writing community friends are so appreciated. Thanks to my Romantic Novelists' Association friends for their support, kindness and inspiration over afternoon teas, kitchen parties at conferences, and pooled lunches! Thanks also to the hard-working librarians, and bookshop staff and owners, for promoting our books, supporting so many writers on the way.

My publishing director, Georgina Green, and the editing, marketing and creative team at HQ, thank you for giving me an exciting new chapter with your publishing house. I'm very much looking forward to working with you ongoing, and getting to know you all more.

Big thanks to my agent Hannah Ferguson for believing in and guiding me with this new book, plus the team at my Hardman & Swainson.

Last but never least, my family and friends, for their patience and support. I spend many, many hours on a laptop upstairs in the spare room in a world of my own with make-believe people. Thanks for giving me the time and space to create these characters and stories.

All best wishes,

Caroline x

Dear Reader,

We hope you enjoyed reading this book. If you did, we'd be so appreciative if you left a review. It really helps us and the author to bring more books like this to you.

Here at HQ Digital we are dedicated to publishing fiction that will keep you turning the pages into the early hours. Don't want to miss a thing? To find out more about our books, promotions, discover exclusive content and enter competitions you can keep in touch in the following ways:

JOIN OUR COMMUNITY:

Sign up to our new email newsletter: http://smarturl.it/SignUpHQ

Read our new blog www.hqstories.co.uk

𝕏 https://twitter.com/HQStories

www.facebook.com/HQStories

BUDDING WRITER?

We're also looking for authors to join the HQ Digital family! Find out more here: https://www.hqstories.co.uk/want-to-write-for-us/

Thanks for reading, from the HQ Digital team

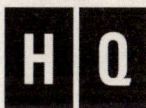